I0760510

THE RECKONING

RUBY JEAN JENSEN

Gayle J. Foster

THE NIGHT THE CHILDREN CAME HOME

The children began dancing, laughing, going in circles around Cory and Matt. The nightbirds, the frogs and insects, grew silent as suddenly as the children had begun to giggle and sing.

Cory heard their words, but couldn't make them out. It was as if they spoke and sang in a foreign language. The fear he had felt did not lessen. His body was cold and taut, and even though he was aware that Matt was trying now to rise, Cory felt as if he had been plunged into a world different from the one he had always known, a world worse than the worst of nightmares, a world he could not see with his real eyes, or hear with his real ears. He was so scared he froze, hunching inward as if to protect himself from attack.

Car lights moved on the street, turning and playing through the leaves of the trees that lined the driveway.

The tallest boy and oldest girl bent suddenly over Matt's hand and the trap. Cory saw their fingers, strong and swift, opening the trap. For a heartbeat they were there, silent, working with the trap, and then they were darting away. Cory whirled, his gaze searching the area, the moonlit field, the vacant lot, the trees with the black shadows. The kids were gone . . .

First printing: September, 1992 Printed in the United States of America

Published by: Gayle J. Foster, Carrollton, Texas

Library of Congress Control Number: 2021905564

Cover Art by: SelfPubBookCovers.com/ Shardel

❀ Created with Vellum

CHAPTER ONE

"WE'RE NOT HERE FOR YOUR MONEY, WE'RE HERE FOR YOUR SOULS!" evangelist Dalton Walsh shouted, the muscles in his neck pushing like ropes against his skin with the power of his voice. When Walsh gained his full voice, he had no need of the microphone that stood on his portable pulpit.

He raised his arms. Ahead of him the faces swam together, all lifted toward him. As usual, the tent was packed. Three thousand square feet of people, who had come to an old-fashioned revival. Not one of the metal folding chairs squeaked. No one moved. Walsh's voice thundered in his own ears.

"Have you said no to Jesus Christ? Do you want salvation and forgiveness? Then say YES to Jesus Christ, YES to salvation. Stop living under the power of evil! Let the good rise and combat the evil that is here in your small, outwardly peaceful town, just as evil lurks in every village, every city. Let the good that God has created rise, now, and destroy the evil! For the *power of God doth raise the dead, casteth out the devils!"*

Suddenly the platform on which he stood jerked sideways, rocked back, and then began a steady listing roll. He stumbled toward the tilting pulpit, reaching for support. The earth jerked and rocked. His voice choked off. The tent rippled and swayed to one side and back to the other. The ground beneath his feet rose and fell as if a mighty beast moved beneath it. The faces before him blurred, then, as they steadied, looked shocked, eyes widening, mouths opening. Walsh grabbed the pulpit to steady himself. The congregation lifted slightly, unevenly, and a murmur buzzed beneath the tent top.

He held tightly to the pulpit as the world abruptly grew still and breathlessly silent. It had come and gone, all in a few heartbeats. He felt drained of blood, and his heart pounded and raced. His skin was cold, as if overlaid with a thin layer of ice.

Walsh saw with an added sense of shock that a tall, dark-haired youth was standing in the open doorway of the tent, at the other end of the long aisle. Electric lanterns hung on each side of the doorway, and their light fell upon the narrow face, the handsome features. The youth had come with the quaking of the earth, as if born of it. The look on his face as he stared at Walsh added a deeper layer of coldness to Walsh's cheeks, as if the hand of death had brushed past.

In the brief moment Walsh's eyes met the youth's, he tried to read the expression in the boy's eyes. A silent cry, a pleading cry, as if he looked at Walsh for the answer? Walsh started down the aisle toward him.

As of one, the congregation turned, their eyes following Walsh's. The silence was profound for just a moment, and then a voice cried out.

"Patrick!"

It was a woman far back in the congregation, near the door, a soft, private cry of recognition that Walsh heard as if the name had been whispered in his ear, and at that moment someone moaned and fell.

Walsh heard the metal chair collapse and saw the rising of the crowd near the door of the tent. Sounds of murmurs grew louder.

In the blink of an eye the boy was gone.

MATT REED STUMBLED on the dark path beneath the trees. For a moment it seemed the earth turned liquid and rippled like small waves across a pond. With an arm thrust out against the rough bark of a tree, he steadied himself, then he went on.

He knew the wooded hills, the paths the animals took to their dens. He had destroyed more animal dens in his seventy-two years than he could count. Moonlight through the forest spotted the ground along the edge of the bluff that rose on his right, plunging the ground beneath the trees into an unusual darkness as black as the interior of a cave. He pushed the button on his flashlight briefly, regularly, just enough to reveal his location.

He knew where all the caves were, the bluffs with their little animal dens, the holes leading to beds of stone. He knew the springs and branches where the animals drank. He knew where to place his traps.

In his left hand he carried the tow sack that sagged heavily with the bodies that three of his traps had produced. One red fox, two opossums. In his right hand he carried the flashlight. His rifle jostled against him as he walked, hanging by its leather strap on his shoulder. When he crossed a path of moonlight, his shadow fell ahead of him, long, broad, dark, like a giant leading the way.

He stopped to listen. Something was in the third trap. A couple of times he had seen a large wolf, or dog, in the trees on the hillside behind his house. He had shot at it, but it ran. The first time he thought he had hit it enough to slow it down so he could catch it, but it ran limping ahead of him, always managing somehow to keep a tree between it and the bullets that sang nearby. "I'm going to catch that son-of-a-bitch," he said to himself that second time as the wolf-dog successfully eluded him again. It was probably one of those curs from that Nina person's so-called animal shelter. To his mind they should all be shot.

Whatever it was—dog, coyote, wolf—he had it now.

He pushed the flashlight button and heard the frantic jerking and leaping at the trap as the animal tried to escape. Let the bastard jump. The trap had him. Its eyes flashed their reflection toward him, then blinked to darkness. He heard a whine of terror. Music of the wild. Yes, he had the wolf-dog, finally. Got him. Got the stinking cur.

Matt stopped, laid the sack of dead animals on the ground, and slipped his rifle off his shoulder. One or two clubs on the head with the barrel of the gun, and the critter in the trap would stop trying to get away. He blinked his flashlight on and caught again the reflection of the eyes. Wide-set, they obviously belonged to a large animal, though it jerked around so much he couldn't see anything but its glowing eyes.

He approached cautiously, the gun gripped in his right hand, the flashlight transferred to his left. Its beam wavered, touching the trunks of trees, so numerous in this area, becoming lost among the undergrowth of fern and brush. Last winter's leaves crunched under his heavy boots. Something skittered away, running like a deer. Matt jerked the light up to catch it, but saw nothing beyond the tree trunks and the endless darkness beneath the trees. His light beam swung back and searched the ground for the trap and the animal that had grown still. They sometimes did. After thrashing around and almost tearing off the foot in the trap as they heard him coming, they often settled down, crouching lower and lower, growing still, only their eyes moving. As if they knew.

Matt's flashlight caught the glint of metal, and he swung it back and pinpointed the spot. The trap yawned, its teeth open and waiting, long metal points as sharp as slivers of glass, longer than any fang, strong enough to hold a bear.

It hadn't been sprung.

What the hell . . .?

He steadied the light beam and stared at the trap. Slowly he approached until he stood over it, the light disappearing into the jaws of the trap. The damned thing hadn't even been sprung.

Then what had he heard? What had he seen?

He swung the light up and around. No animal's eyes reflected from the darkness.

Suddenly he was heaved off balance. As if something beneath the ground had shoved upward he felt the earth tip, tremble, then shake violently, like a large animal rising up from its sleep and shaking its body. The trunks of the trees swayed, rushing toward him and away. He flung his arms out, but found no support. He felt himself tipped forward, and though he struggled to stay on his feet, he was falling. Falling, on his hands, his face, collapsing to the ground as it rolled crazily beneath him.

He came down heavily on his knees and left hand. His right hand clutched for control, and he heard the trap before he felt it. With a soft hissing sound, like a snake striking, it closed, snapping shut, going through the soft tissue of his right hand, crunching easily through the bones of his wrist. The pain shot up his arm like a runaway forest fire into his head—harsh, ripping. He screamed and tried to jerk free. As if he didn't know that once the trap closed its victim was caught, forever, or until freed by someone who knew how to open the trap. He, caught like a wild animal, tried like an animal to escape from it.

He jerked upward, his left arm reaching out, his hand closing over the slender trunk of a bush. The earth had grown still. Or his head had stopped spinning. Whatever it was that had happened was over, except the trap was cutting fire into the flesh and bones of his hand and wrist.

He turned, half-crouched, blood dripping in the leaves. It had the sound of a slow rain, dripping onto the forest floor. His left hand held the flashlight, and his thumb pressed the button as if glued to it, his reflexes frozen. The light beam swung. It touched upon black figures, moving toward him, their eyes lighted as if from within. They gleamed with that flat, metallic look of a reflected animal eye. Matt's light swung erratically, catching the eyes, losing whatever bodies they had in the darkness.

The light beam jerked as he pivoted. He was surrounded. Whatever it was, hordes of them, animals, something whose eyes reflected the light, eyes slanted like the eyes of cats, green lights, small angles in the darkness, edged closer and closer. Something mad, like the earth itself. Like his head now with the pain consuming his arm. Or maybe there were no eyes at all, just the reflection of the fire in his own brain.

He dropped the flashlight and felt frantically along the ground for his rifle. Above his harsh breathing, his fumbling in the leaves, he heard sounds. Soft, padding steps. Twigs snapped. They were there. Bodies attached to eyes that reflected light, after all, not the fire in his own brain. He could hear them as they drew near. Their feet pushed through the leaves, step by step, their breathing was like a distant wind growing stronger and closer.

The round rod beneath his fingers at first felt like the body of a snake, cool, smooth, alive. He jerked his hand away, then recognized the feel of the gun barrel. *The rifle.* He grabbed it, wresting it out of the dead winter leaves, the cool, green summer fern. With his left hand he grabbed it up, turned it toward the sound of the creeping horde and fired, his finger holding the trigger down as he swung the rifle in a low arc.

He gained his balance and ran, the rifle clutched under his arm, his left hand gripping it tightly. On his right hand the trap dangled, the chain that had secured it jerked free and dragging behind him like something following. He could hear them behind him, dark forms gliding swiftly through the trees.

He ran, stumbling with exhaustion, driven as much by fear as by pain. His breath caught in his lungs, his heart thudded, ripping his blood through his veins and into his hand. The trap was a dead weight now. His hand felt heavy and club-like. His right arm felt as if it had died and was dragging behind him with the trap and the chain. The pain throbbed steadily in his shoulder, neck and head.

Howls lifted strongly and musically in the still night air as he ran, his body bent forward, as if the next step would pitch him onto his face.

As the howls thinned it seemed he could hear the voices of children. He ran faster, but no matter how hard he ran, their voices came closer, taunting, run, run . . .

WALSH STARED at the doorway of the tent. He hadn't seen the boy move, yet he was gone, replaced by the moonlight beyond the door. Not even a shadow remained.

Walsh moved quickly along the aisle, reassuringly touching the shoulders of nervous people as he passed by. The youth had appeared, and disappeared, leaving behind something Walsh did not understand. Voices left disjointed phrases in his mind.

" What happened?"

"—not earthquake country—"

"—Patrick, Patrick—"

"Patrick Moore . . ."

"Who fainted?"

"Halley Reed—Halley—"

Murmurs moved through the congregation like the ripples under their feet moments ago. They seemed more disturbed by the woman who had fainted and the youth who had stood momentarily in the doorway than they did of an earthquake in country that had never had an earthquake in its history.

Walsh motioned at his assistants to start the singing of hymns as he rushed down the aisle. He had to see that the person who fainted was all right, then he had to stop the boy from leaving. It was crucial that Walsh speak with the youth.

He lifted his arms as he passed down the aisle. People were standing now, turning, looking toward the back, toward the front, beginning to act confused. Walsh felt they were lucky the congregation had not rushed all at once for the exit. It could have been very serious.

"It's all right, folks! Just be seated, please! Everything is all right!"

Behind him, rising in soft comfort, the singers began with the most popular gospel song.

Amazing grace, how sweet the sound,
That saved a wretch like me!
I once was lost, but now am found—

The music blended with the murmurs of concern rising in the back of the tent, and the frantic cries of a child.

"What's wrong with Gram? *Gram!* What's wrong, Gramma?"

"She just fainted, she'll be okay, Cory."

Walsh pushed through. "Excuse me, please, just be seated."

The woman who had fainted looked to Walsh like an old-fashioned country woman, the kind one saw in the old countries of Europe. She looked to be in her sixties, with greying hair pulled back tightly into a bun at the back of her head, as if she had never been to a beauty parlor in her life. She was slightly overweight, dressed unbecomingly in slacks and jersey pullover blouse. Two younger women and a couple of men were helping her up from the ground.

Walsh set the chair back on its legs and reached out in an effort to help the woman. She looked up, face pale, no makeup. The skin of her cheeks quivered, and fear saturated everything about her.

At her side, on his knees, a towheaded boy about nine years old watched her with worried eyes.

Walsh saw her look over her shoulder toward the tent door.

"Halley?" one of the women asked, "Are you all right?"

"Gram?" the boy pleaded.

"Yes, yes," the woman said. She slid into her chair, trembling. "I'm fine. Fine. It's all right, Cory. Just give me a minute to get myself together."

Walsh patted the shoulder of the woman who trembled in the chair, then made his way past the disturbed row of guests and into the open doorway. He had to catch the youth before he was gone.

Behind him the hymn grew louder as people in the congregation began to sing.

Walsh left the tent and hurried around to the left side. Moonlight, brighter than he remembered seeing it ever before, spilled a soft, still glow on the field surrounding the tent. Cars of the congregation were parked haphazardly in front of the tent, while to the back were the RVs, trucks and cars of his entourage. There were no trees in the ten-acre field, and no one walked in the moonlight in any direction. Below, buried in the trees in the small valley town, a few street lights peeked out, winking like the fireflies that were now nearly invisible in the light of the moon. All around, circling the field where the tent stood and the town in the valley, hills rose, their solid cover of trees black in the moonlight.

To the west a single highway led through an opening in the hills to the freeway two miles away. Beyond that a city of half a million lived, scarcely twenty miles down the road. Two worlds, so close, yet so far apart.

Walsh hurried back around to the front of the tent and to the right where most of the cars had parked. Then he saw the group of young people.

They were as they always were in every gathering in every state, city, village, rural area. They always stood in a little group, leaning against a car. They came to the meetings out of that curiosity that drew all the congregation, but to show their disdain they remained outside, talking, laughing, telling jokes about preachers and middle-aged followers and young girls, about nationalities and homosexuals, about angels. Sometimes about Jesus Christ. And occasionally, in their desperation perhaps, about God. In their disdain they were showing their need, without realizing it. People needed God. The youth who had stood in the doorway needed God. It was an intrinsic need of every human. Walsh believed that with all his heart.

The group of teenage boys and girls grew quiet as Walsh approached. One of them, a tall handsome boy but not the one who had stood in the doorway, straightened, threw down his cigarette and put his foot on it as if expecting to have to defend himself.

Walsh stopped near enough to see their faces. Their features softened by moonlight, all were beautiful, the best of God's work. A girl, about sixteen, stood with three boys a bit older. Inside the car another girl leaned against a young man who had his arm around her shoulders. None of them was the youth who had stood in the doorway of the tent. None of the faces had that strange, intense expression that had been on the face of the boy in the doorway.

"I'm looking for the boy who came to the tent just a few minutes ago. He stood for a while, then left."

No one spoke. They stared intently at Walsh.

Walsh added, "During the earthquake. At that moment, he appeared in the doorway. Have you seen him?"

One of the boys leaning against the car asked, "What earthquake?" while at the same time two others shook their heads, looked at each other, grinned and shrugged. The old guy was nuts, their actions suggested.

"He was tall, about your height," he motioned toward the tallest of the youths. "Someone called him Patrick. He—during the earth tremor. . ."

Walsh stopped. The looks on their faces suggested they not only had not seen anyone, they had felt no earthquake. He tried once more. "Have you seen anyone come out of the tent?"

"No sir," the girl said. "I've been facing the door the whole time. I would have gone in, but all the chairs were taken. But no one has come out but you." Walsh looked from face to face. The curiosity was there, the wondering. He could see truth on their faces. They had seen no one. He turned. The doorway was clearly visible. Coming out of it now was a small group of people, while behind them the singing of hymns swelled.

The young woman was holding onto the left arm of the woman who had fainted. Halley Reed, someone had called her. The other lady, a woman in her forties who was wearing a neat polka dot dress, was helping on the other side. The little boy rushed ahead and opened a car door. Walsh hurried over.

The younger women released Halley, and she moved awkwardly into the car. Walsh made a token effort to help her, though she was steady now. His hand patted her arm.

"Are you going to be all right, Miss Halley?"

"Yes, thank you, Reverend. I just think I'd like to go home now. Nina will take us. I hate to take her away from the service. But she said she'd take us home."

"Perhaps you can come back tomorrow night? We'll be here a couple of nights longer."

She nodded. The little boy, a slim little sun-bleached blond who reminded Walsh of himself at that age, got into the backseat of the small car. The lady in the polka dot dress backed away from the car and stood beside Walsh.

The young woman driving waved good-bye and started the engine. The car backed slowly around and eased away toward the gate onto the paved road across the field. On the other side of the road a hill rose, as black and silent as an unearthly wall. The whole area had a strange, unearthly look now, even the bright moonlight. Nor had Walsh ever known such stillness, with no sign of a breeze whispering in the grass of the field, no birdcall from the woods, no insects buzzing as they were earlier.

Walsh held out his hand to the lady with the worried look left standing by him. "I'm Dalton Walsh. And you're . . . ?

"Lois. Lois Trahem."

Her handshake was firm and forceful, stronger than handshakes from many men. She was a capable lady, this Lois Trahem. But even in the softening light of the moon he could see the worried crinkles at the corners of her eyes.

Walsh slipped his hand under the lady's elbow, and guided her back toward the tent. "We're sorry to be losing part of our good congregation. I hope you will be staying longer, Miss Lois?"

"Yes, a few minutes. Halley will be fine, I'm sure. Nina will see her safely home. They're neighbors, you know. No, you wouldn't know that, would you?"

"The young man, Patrick, I think someone said his name is. Do you know him?"

"Yes, Patrick Moore."

"He's a local boy, I gather."

"Patrick," she said, and her sigh was deep and audible, "Patrick's home is actually between Halley Reed's and Nina's, down on the edge of town." She motioned ahead, where the bench-land sloped off to a line of trees along a street, and to hills beyond. "He disappeared a year ago. This is the first time any of us have seen him since then."

"Disappeared?"

"Yes. Went into hiding, some people say."

They were nearing the tent door. Walsh stopped her with his hand touching her arm briefly. He saw a round face with a sweet expression, lips curving naturally upward at the corners, cheeks creased as if she were accustomed to smiling often, though now the look on her face was serious. Her eyes, blue or green, gazed past him. She wore glasses. Her hair was short and curly, brushed to one side. Although she had worn lipstick, it was bitten mostly away, so that only a dark edge showed the outlines of her lips. She pushed her glasses up with the back of her hand. Her eyes looked at the hills beyond him. He waited. There was something she wanted to say.

"Patrick," she finally said, "is wanted for murder, Reverend Walsh. Last year he—they said he was the one—killed his mother, dad, and younger sister. It was awful. I work for Dr. Tyler, and I went with him to the Moore house, and it was the worst thing I've ever seen. Blood everywhere. They had been shot, with a shotgun. Patrick was gone. So was the gun. The police have been looking for him ever since, I suppose."

Moonlight glinted on the woman's glasses. Walsh saw the hand movement again as she pushed them higher on her nose. He was aware of the tentative call of a whippoorwill back in the hills, and an answering call farther away. A loud bird voice, softened by distance, traveled through air that was still and waiting. The night had awakened again.

Not far away the teenagers stood beside the car, silent, watching, listening. Beyond, the field lifted gradually toward the dark trees of the hillside. But no one walked there. No one walked anywhere in the moonlight surrounding the revival tent. Walsh felt the icy brush against his cheeks again, on the back of his neck and down his spine.

It was as if a ghost had materialized for a few moments in the doorway of his tent, and caused the ground beneath to tremble. It was as if God himself had placed a weight upon the ground beneath the tent.

Some might say the devil.

But he didn't believe in the existence of a devil, or evil, as a separate entity, as something capable of causing the anticipatory sense in the air, of a happening that would burst upon them suddenly, as the earth tremor had.

Nor did he believe in ghosts.

CHAPTER TWO

RUDY GRABBED THE BALL AND RAN, HIS HIGH-PITCHED LAUGHTER VERGING ON a squeal as his older brother, Dennis, cut across the black shadows beneath the big tree in the corner of the yard. Rudy headed for the street, feeling as if Dennis would tackle him at any step.

Behind, running out of the yard from the other side, cutting into the street, came Jenny. He wasn't afraid of her grabbing the ball. She was no bigger than he. He'd been playing football with Jenny since they both were in the first grade, two years now, and knew her strategies. But it was a lot more fun when Dennis played with them. And more fun still when Cory was here to play. But Cory's house was dark tonight. Cory's dad and stepmom, David and Rachel, had gone on a vacation today and Cory was staying with his grandma and grandpa across town. The game was uneven without Cory.

"Get 'im, Dennis!" Jenny shouted, running out beneath the streetlight and down the street toward Rudy.

Hey, whose side are you on? Rudy didn't have the breath to ask. Giggles rolled out of his throat. He ran fast, his bare feet slapping the pavement. Ahead of him more large shade trees threw black shadows into the street. Since Cory was gone, there were only three of them playing tonight. He and Jenny against Dennis. At least he thought that was how they had called it at the start. In the house their parents, his and Dennis's mom and dad, and Jenny's mom and dad, who lived just next door on the other side from Cory, were playing cards. Most of the other people in the neighborhood had gone to something called the revival. Even Eddie and Carla, who usually played ball with them.

"What's a revival?" Rudy had asked Cory this morning when he was getting ready to leave. Rudy watched as Cory packed enough clothes for two weeks, jeans, T-shirts, socks, underwear. Then, when Rachel reminded him, pajamas. A whole pile grabbed out of the drawer and shoved down into the side of the suitcase.

Cory stopped and hooked his thumbs in his back pockets the way he did when he was thinking. Cory was in Rudy's class, but since Cory was going to this revival thing, he must know what it was.

"I think," Cory said, "it's like when you bring something back again."

"You mean—" Naw, he couldn't mean that. Dead people can't really be made alive again. Movies were only movies, they weren't real. The dead who came back from the grave were just actors made up to look weird. But, he had to ask. "Like, bring back the dead?"

They looked at each other. Rudy watched Cory's eyes bug. "Let's go ask my mom," Cory said.

They went to Cory's stepmom, Rachel.

"What's a revival?" Cory asked, while Rudy stood at his shoulder.

Rudy had never heard Cory call Rachel "Mom," in front of her. But he didn't call her Rachel either. She'd been his mom only two years, and Rudy thought Cory wasn't sure if she wanted to be called Mom.

"A revival? You mean like the one in the big tent tonight?"

They nodded.

"It's a meeting. Like church."

"Church?" Their voices yelled together, as if they were twins. Rachel smiled.

She was ready to go. David came in to get suitcases and Rudy had to say good-bye. He ran next door and stood in his yard and waved. Cory was only going across town. Maybe he could come over and play, sometime. Two weeks seemed like a long time not to see his best friend.

Now, in the dark and the moonlight, they played ball, while Cory was at revival, which was nothing but church. Rudy felt sorry for him.

Jiggers, barking all the time, the way he always did when he and Rudy were running, took a short cut beneath black shadows and came out into the street. He ran right in front of Rudy, tripping him, and both of them tumbled together. The ball rolled out of Rudy's arms and down the middle of the street. Jiggers untangled himself from Rudy and went after the ball, growling and biting at it. He was a black streak in the dark shadows, only the white around his neck and along his belly showing.

"Hey," Jenny yelled with delight, "Jiggers tackled him!"

Rudy pushed himself up with his hands. Jiggers rushed back, leaving the ball rolling. The black fur of Jiggers brushed against Rudy's arm. Rudy felt him stop, and stiffen.

Jiggers stared into the shadows of the street where the tall trees came together above like an umbrella. The dog growled. Jiggers had never growled like that before.

In the fenced backyard of Jenny's house, her family's two little dogs stopped barking. They began an eerie howling.

Suddenly, everything changed.

The air, the night, the fun.

Rudy squinted through the darkness.

A group of strange kids stood in the shadows. There were five or six of them, indistinct, shadowy figures. It was as if they had suddenly risen there, where they had never stood before. A rush of fear held Rudy.

A boy, shorter, younger than Dennis, stepped closer and picked up the football. He tucked it into the crook of his left arm as if he intended to keep it. Rudy, on his hands and knees, aware of a burning sensation in his hands where he had slid on the pavement when he fell, stared at the group of kids.

A girl, with long blond hair, who looked Dennis's age, thirteen or fourteen, stood deeper in the shadows behind the boy. Rudy saw another boy, closer to his own size, and a girl, like Jenny, only this girl was wearing a dress and carrying something . . . a small child . . . no, a large doll. Her hair hung long, part of it forward over her shoulders. In the deep shadows it looked like ghost hair, it was so pale.

Behind Rudy came Dennis's voice, curious, light, friendly. Surprised. "Hi."

There was no answer from the kids. They moved slowly closer. They moved in a way that made Rudy want to run. He edged back, and got to his feet. At his side Jiggers was now growling fiercely, the hair on his back standing stiff. Rudy's hand touched the dog's shoulder and his fingers gripped the stiffened hair. The dog's body pushed against Rudy protectively.

"Hey," Dennis said, closing in behind Rudy. "That's our ball. Do you mind tossing it back?" His voice wasn't so friendly now, as if he, like Rudy, sensed something bad and scary about the strange kids.

The guy with the ball said nothing, but there came a low chattering from deeper in the shadows as the other kids sidled closer. It was as if they spoke in a language Rudy couldn't understand.

"I'm Dennis Niles," Dennis tried again, "and this is my little brother Rudy. And that's Jenny." He motioned back with his thumb. "She lives in that house. What's your name? Where're you from?"

They were closer, though Rudy hadn't actually seen them move. It seemed suddenly that they had fanned out and were forming a circle around him. Dennis, and even Jenny, who stood somewhere back down the street. They were closing Rudy and his brother and Jenny off from their houses, edging them toward the darker shadows. Fear raced through Rudy, straight down to his bladder. He felt it open up. He grabbed his pants and squeezed it off. Then he quickly released it before anyone saw and guessed how scared he was.

But he had a feeling the strange kids had seen, all of them, even though Rudy stood in the shadows. He had a feeling they knew how scared he was. They wanted him to be scared. That's why they were acting like they were, moving one step at a time, not answering any of Dennis's questions. Not speaking at all. Not being friendly. The more scared he was, the more scared all of them were, the more power they had over them.

He stood his ground, shaking, glad that Dennis had come out to play. What if it had been only him, Cory, and Jenny? Cory wasn't even as big as himself or Jenny.

Who were these kids? What did they want?

Moonlight shone in streaks on the pavement between trees. The street light on the corner was mostly hidden beyond the leaves. Jenny's dogs were quiet. For a moment Jiggers, too, was quiet. It was as if they were all holding their breaths—him, Dennis, Jenny, the dogs.

The shadowy figures erupted into movement. They rushed inward and Jiggers leaped to meet them, snarling, snapping. Dennis ran forward. He brushed by Rudy and gave him a hard shove backward with his arm. Rudy stumbled and almost fell again.

"Get Dad!" Dennis shouted.

Rudy wavered between not leaving Dennis alone with only Jiggers to help, and going after their dad. He saw the boy and the older blond girl collide with Dennis. He saw Dennis fighting, kicking, his fists and arms flashing, blending with the fists and arms of the other kids. He saw another boy rushing into the center of the fight.

The young blond girl carefully placed her doll on the edge of the pavement, then with her hands lifted and her fingers shaped into claws, she rushed forward. Moonlight streaked briefly across her face. Rudy stared, unable for a moment to move. A face that had a moment ago seemed like the face of a pretty little girl, changed. Rudy had a nightmarish feeling she wasn't a little girl at all, but something else, *something* . . . a *thing* terrible and evil.

"Get Dad!"

Dennis's cry blended with Jiggers's snarling growls and the sounds of fighting. Both of them were lost somewhere in the tumbling shadows.

Rudy ran. Hot rushes of air pulled from his lungs. At the front walk he ran head-on into Jenny. They grabbed each other, steadied, then ran together up the walk to the house. Doors banged back against the wall as they rushed together into the house, and from the family room came the sound of Rudy's mother's voice. "Shut the door! Bugs will get in!" Rudy didn't have time to answer, or go back and shut the door.

Still together, still clamoring for space, he and Jenny fell into the family room. Rudy's lungs felt like they held sizzling acid, and the sound that came out of his mouth was little more than a rasp.

Jenny squealed, "There's some kids out there fighting Dennis!" Then she went on talking, talking, as if she couldn't stop. "Jiggers tackled Rudy and Rudy fell and the ball rolled and that strange boy picked it up and our dogs howled and Jiggers started growling and they're fighting Dennis and Jiggers—"

Rudy's dad immediately shoved his chair back and stood up. He was a pipe layer, and his shoulders and arms were strong and thick. They bulged against his summer T-shirt.

Rudy's mother stared at Jenny, then at Rudy, her eyes almost as round with surprise as were those of Alice, Jenny's mother.

"What kids?" she asked.

But Jenny had stopped talking and couldn't seem to start again. Rudy couldn't speak either.

All of them got up, leaving their chairs shoved back from the card table. Jenny's dad followed Rudy's dad. Rudy whirled, pushing ahead of his mother. He hurried down the hall behind the men. Before he reached the door he heard his dad's footsteps pounding down the driveway, and heard him shout, "Hey, What's going on here?"

Rudy ran. He pushed out of the door behind Jenny's father, Mitch. In the street, through the weird, dark spaces beneath the tree, the strange kids ran, fanning away, disappearing into the deeper shadows away from the streetlights, avoiding the bright moonlight. Rudy's father, Sandford, paused, then was running too, his footsteps loud on the pavement of the street. The little dogs in the yard behind Jenny's house barked frantically, the high-pitched sound of Chihuahuas. Jiggers was silent.

Rudy cut across the grass of the adjoining lawn and out into the street.

Sandford had reached Dennis and was lifting him up. Rudy heard the voices of his dad, of Mitch, of Dennis. Dennis wasn't dead, he wasn't killed, they hadn't killed him.

Rudy almost collapsed, his legs became so weak. He hadn't known until now that he had been afraid those strange kids would kill Dennis.

"I'm okay," Dennis said in answer to the questions the parents were throwing at him, but he was crying. Rudy hadn't heard Dennis cry in so long it made a strange pain in his heart. Their mothers had reached the street now and joined the moving shadows. Rudy's mother put her arm around Dennis's shoulders.

Sandford and Mitch ran a few yards down the street looking for the kids.

"Jiggers," Dennis cried, his voice high and quivering. "Mom—Jiggers. Look for Jiggers, Mom. They hurt him."

"Go get a flashlight," Sandford ordered. He came back and stood looking into the grass at the edge of the pavement.

Rudy ran back to the house and into the utility room. He grabbed the electric flashlight out of its holder on the wall and ran back out. He paused as he passed Dennis, who was being brought back into the house by their mother, Alice, and Jenny. His face looked scratched and bloody, and one eye was already puffing. He was still sobbing, and asking about Jiggers.

With the flashlight clutched in his fist, Rudy ran, forgetting to turn it on. He crossed through the darkened lawn of Jenny's house next door and came out into the shadows of the street. His dad and Mitch were bending over something.

Rudy dropped to his knees beside the dog. The black body blended with the grass, as if the grass too were black. But something lighter gleamed all along his body. Lying so still, on his side, bowed backwards, he looked so very long, as if he had become a large dog, not a medium-sized one just right for a nine year old boy to have as a playmate. He looked as if he had been pulled apart. Sandford pushed Rudy back.

"Don't look, Rudy. Go on to the house."

"Jiggers! Jiggers! Dad, what's wrong with Jiggers?"

But he knew, in the coldness of his bones, where he suddenly knew things without being told. Jiggers was dead. They had killed him.

As if his vision cleared suddenly, Rudy could see that Jiggers had been torn down the length of his stomach, and the stuff that gleamed lighter in the darkness was his insides.

They had been pulled out of him, as if the kids had been trying to take his skin away.

CHAPTER THREE

THE SOUND OF GUNSHOTS BACK IN THE HILLS EAST OF TOWN CAME CLEARLY through the still night and into the open window of the patrol car. The engine hummed softly as Thomas put his foot on the brake and sat still, listening. It sounded like an assault rifle, its shots a staccato ripping into the night. Or a round of large firecrackers.

The silence that followed the shots lasted only a moment, then the air filled with the rising howls of dogs from the shelter and the answering howls of dogs spotted here and there in their yards across town. Down at the corner widow Betsy Smith's toy Manchester let out a high-pitched yelping, and he heard her call to them. They hushed as they went into the house. He clearly heard the door close, a half block away.

He listened and heard no more gunshots. He removed his foot from the brake and let the car ease forward. A hunter back in the hills somewhere. Illegal, but what the hell. It was too far away for him to do anything about, and it wasn't his business anyway. He was chief of police of Spring Valley, and his duty was to see that everything was quiet and peaceful in town at bedtime on a Sunday night. Tomorrow, though, he might notify the game warden. Close the barn door after the horse was stolen.

Chief of Police Thomas Abbot let the car drift slowly. All was well in the little town. He took a street to the right that had only one house in an eighth of a mile. On the bench-land to the west he could see the big revival tent in the field, and the cars parked in front and back. The moonlight was so bright it was almost like day.

It was a good night for an old-fashioned revival.

Earlier in the evening he had driven slowly around the tent in the field. Through his open window he could hear the voice of the preacher inside. For weeks before the evangelist and his entourage came to Spring Valley, flyers fluttered around town, announcing an old-fashioned revival. The printed word offered "A return to old-time morality." The two solid, long-standing churches in town sat calmly on, their ministers questioning only what the evangelist wanted in a place as small as Spring Valley. There were scarcely a thousand souls available and most of them belonged to either the firmly established Baptist or the Christian church.

Behind the big circus-like tent were the trucks that carried the power generators and other equipment, and the RVs and trailers that belonged to the traveling revival. The moonlight left few shadows in the ten acre field. A long trail, marked through the green pasture grass by the tires that had passed over it, sloped downward toward the road into town.

Parked in front of the tent were the dozens of cars of people who had been drawn to the revival. Beside one car was a small group of teenagers, their cigarettes like fireflies, glowing, then resting. Thomas had resisted an urge to tell them to go inside and listen to the sermon or go home. The kids weren't hurting anything, they were just hanging out, their favorite pastime.

Thomas drove on, glad to see that the revival hadn't attracted rowdier kids from other areas. Spring Valley, isolated by the surrounding hills, had only one paved road out, and was pretty much ignored by the city kids twenty miles away.

He had come full circle around the town, and now eased the patrol car out onto the highway leading out of town.

There was no traffic in either direction. Ahead, on his left, its back against a dark tree-covered hill, was Lane Yardley's honkytonk. Called "Lane's place" around town, it advertised itself as simply having beer and a dance floor, no name. This being Sunday night, it was closed, but the neon lights rippled on and on, miniature colored rivers in tubes of glass. It looked weird in the moonlight, and lonely, the gravel parking lot empty, the white pebbles as pale as a skift of new fallen snow.

Lane Yardley was a slender, swarthy man, who was friendly enough on the surface, but seemed to be a loner. For the past four years he had lived alone in the apartment in the back. He had built the club about ten years ago, and at that time had a young wife and small son. Then four and a half years ago his wife, Sheila, ran off, leaving Lane and their ten-year-old son, Willy. The next summer, four years ago this month, Willy disappeared.

Lonely for his mother, he went to find her, so it was figured. Sheila had wound up in Chicago, but Willy was never heard from again. There were people in town who did not believe Willy had run away.

So much trash going on there at Lane's place, the older people who used the park benches down on the square said. Who knew what kind of pervert might have picked up that boy? And what about the other kids? Same thing.

Thomas didn't know. He had searched for Willy, and found nothing. The sheriff's department had joined in the search, and the county rescue people, as well as volunteers from town.

There had been a couple of other runaways, before and after, and, as if culminating those, the murder of a family last year.

Since then Thomas took better care in patrolling town. Although he had always taken care to wear a neatly pressed uniform, he had kept his holster and gun locked in the trunk of the car, along with a rifle and a shotgun. After the murder of the Moore family, Thomas started wearing his .38. Just in case. So far he hadn't had it out of its holster except to clean it, but it was there, a reminder that one day he had walked into a house that was ruined by the blood of its owners and one of their children. A reminder that the killer was still out there, somewhere, and the sheriff and state police all believed it was Patrick, the seventeen year old son.

It was true all evidence pointed to Patrick. But no one had ever questioned him, because he had disappeared that day as if he had slipped off the earth.

Thomas couldn't really bring himself to believe Pat was guilty. He had known the boy as a good worker, dependable, decent as they get. He had worked at Nina's animal shelter since shortly after it opened when he was about twelve. Does a boy like that murder his family?

Thomas wanted to find Patrick and talk to him before the sheriff's department and state police stepped in again.

In this past year Thomas spent most of his time patrolling the town, looking not only for Patrick but for anything out of the ordinary. Several times during the day and night he drove the streets, checking the homes and the few businesses. He carefully checked Lane's place, which some of the townspeople thought should be burned down.

As he drove tonight through the wide, quiet streets, the town looked normal, the way it had four years ago after Willy Yardley didn't come home from Nina's animal shelter. The streets remained peaceful and quiet, the way they were the night Karen Davis disappeared a year before Willy, and after Cliff Patison disappeared, a year after Willy Yardley. On the way home from Nina's animal shelter, all of them. One child a year for three years. Then a peaceful, but wary year passed with nothing happening. Then the next year all hell broke loose in the Moore home.

But still, the town had that quiet, tranquil quality, the streets wide and clean and shaded, the houses surrounded by wide lawns, privacy fences, shrubs, trees. Even following the murder of the Moore family the town looked like something one would find on a picture postcard.

Thomas turned around in the gravel parking lot of Lane's place and headed back into town. There was a feeling in the air that he didn't like. All this peace and quiet, and beneath it, what?

Maybe it was just having the revival meeting in town. Nothing had happened in the past year. There was no reason to feel on edge on this particular night.

He drove slowly back through town toward the animal shelter. On the outskirts of town the yard of the houses were no longer one acre plots, but contained five, ten, or more acres. The street passed Matt Reed's property, one of the largest and oldest houses in town, set on about five acres of valley land and a few more of wooded hillside. The house, big to start with, had sprawled too as Matt, big old grey-bearded Matt who was still strong as a bull, built a somewhat decrepit addition on the rear. It looked like a windowless shed, not substantial enough to withstand a hard wind. But Thomas had never examined it, so he couldn't really judge. It was, Matt Reed had told Thomas, his taxidermy shop. He at times stuffed and mounted animals for museums, and he had wanted his shop close to the house, rather than down in the barn where there was no water or electricity. Cheaper to build the shop onto the house.

Thomas wondered how Halley liked having her house messed up that way. But what little he knew about Halley Reed told him she was probably too meek to object.

Moonlight left deep shadows under the trees in the yards of the homes. The street lights were left behind.

Thomas drove on, up the slope and into the trees of the foothills where Nina's house had lights on the porch, in the yard, and out by the kennel and runs.

A dozen or two dogs barked at him as he turned around in the gravel driveway near the shelter. Thomas figured Nina, like many in town, had gone to the revival too. Her car was gone from the carport.

He would have liked to stop in for a cup of coffee for just a few minutes. So far, his contacts with her were mostly about the occasional stray cats and dogs he picked up around town. Since the town was too small for a dogcatcher, the chief of police and Glen Galaway, the only officer, were also the dogcatchers. Usually it posed no problem. Open the back door of the patrol car, call to the homeless pooch, and it jumped right in, happy and eager to find a home at last even if it was just the backseat of a patrol car.

Nina had impressed him first with her compassion. When he was a senior in the local high school she was probably just starting second grade. He hadn't even spoken to her until she was twenty-two and opening the animal shelter on the rise of the hill.

In the seven years since then, and especially in the last few months, he had made every excuse he could to go up and check on her. She was living alone, isolated from close neighbors.

After the second child, Willy Yardley, disappeared after having worked at the shelter one afternoon, even though it had nothing to do with Nina, she had refused to allow kids to come to work alone. But the rules lagged and were broken, and kids rode up and back on their bicycles with no problems. Thomas assured her it was just a coincidence the missing children had been at her shelter, but he couldn't erase her sense of responsibility.

The first child, Karen Davis, was a mature thirteen year old, tall for her age. She looked sixteen, at least. Her mother, Megan, worked at Lane's place, and Karen often hung out there in the afternoons. Everyone thought she'd run away with some guy.

Willy Yardley had gone after his mother. He had mentioned to friends that he was going to someday. He had even told Nina he was going to live with his mother. As soon as he knew where she was. As soon as she wrote to him and sent him money to come.

Then, a year later a third child disappeared on his way home from Nina's. Like the others his bicycle was gone with him. But with Cliff, there was a little dog, too.

Nina absolutely refused for children to bicycle up to her place. For months she cut down on volunteer work. Then this summer, she had said if three kids came together, okay.

The kids enjoyed the shelter work. Thomas had been there and seen them. They actually did do some work, mostly putting down fresh straw for beds. But more than anything else they petted, brushed, groomed, ran and played.

Those things, Nina said, were the most important.

He drove back around and out the driveway. There was no road going on past Nina's house into the hills. At the foot of the slope a paved city street made a corner, going on to edge the town on the west and the north. A private lane, cutting into the field at the left, dead-ended at a house that was now dark and silent, the scene of the Moore family murder, the only murder Thomas had investigated during his ten years as chief of police.

As he looked at the low ranch-style house with its few shade trees, back down the long, narrow lane, all that happened a year ago was so vividly clear it was as if Thomas were only now going into the blood-spattered house.

In the kitchen he had found Diane, the wife and mother, her head blown half away. The living room held the little girl, Shelley, killed with a shotgun blast through the chest, and her father, Clyde. Clyde had been running for the telephone. He had fallen face down, his hand reaching out, inches from the table. There was very little left of his head and back.

The seventeen-year-old son, Patrick, was gone. No murder weapon was found. The gun rack above the door still held a rifle and two old shotguns, none of which had been fired in years.

The family had died only the night before Nina found them. Patrick had been helping her at the animal shelter three days a week for five years, and he hadn't called or shown up that day. It was the first day he had missed, and because of the other children Nina was worried and drove down to see if Patrick was all right. Through the kitchen door she had seen the blood.

The sheriff's department had felt it was clear that Patrick was the killer. Then, like too many of the town's children before him, he had simply disappeared. Run away.

"It's not possible!" Nina had cried, and Thomas remembered the sound of her voice well. "I know Patrick! I knew all the kids! I don't believe it."

Thomas wasn't sure he believed it, but the sheriff's department, the crime squad from the state police, all eventually believed it. Teenagers do strange things, the police psychologist said, sometimes terrible things, and the people who knew them never understood. Or believed it was possible.

Thomas drove on past the long driveway that led back to the Moore house. Moonlight touched the top of green grass that hadn't been mown this season.

He entered tree shaded streets where the houses, though still widely separated, were closer together. Yards were bordered by fences or hedges or lines of trees. But his thoughts, as he let the car move quietly, its lights marking a path between the street lamps, remained with Patrick Moore. The same questions disturbed him now as then, the same puzzles remained. If Patrick had killed his parents and sister and then run away, so completely without trace, how had he managed it? The family car was still in the garage. The pickup in the driveway. Patrick, the sheriff's department claimed, had melded into the city, barely twenty miles away. Getting to the city was no problem. A kid on the interstate just over the hill, a motorist willing to pick him up, someone traveling through who wouldn't be reading a local newspaper, and getting away was easy.

Thomas's attention was suddenly snapped to the present as he realized a kid was standing in the middle of the street less than twenty feet away. Thomas slammed the brake to the floor. The boy was about eleven years old, tall and thin, wearing skinny-legged blue jeans and a pullover knit shirt. The car lights outlined him clearly: a good looking face, dark hair falling down onto his forehead. The boy stared past the glare of headlights as if he could see the driver of the car. He stood without moving in the middle of the street, his feet widely spaced, his fingers hooked into his back pockets like an old-time gunfighter in a belligerent stance.

As Thomas put the car in park and opened the door, he noticed the boy was not alone. Behind him stood several shadowy figures. An older girl, larger, probably thirteen or fourteen, with long blond hair and wearing a loose shirt over jeans, stood a few feet behind and to the left of the boy. On the other side was another boy, a bit younger and smaller. Behind them, in the edge of the shadows where the car lights began to fade, stood a younger girl. About ten years old, she was dressed differently than the others. Instead of jeans she wore a frilly blue dress with a full skirt that reached just above her knees. In her arms she carried a large doll. Behind her, on both sides of the street, shadows shifted, and from them three or four more children took form.

"What the hell . . . ? Thomas muttered to himself. What were a bunch of kids doing out on the street in the dark? Didn't they know it was dangerous to stand in the middle of a street with a car coming toward them? They had fanned out in front of him as if they were deliberately blocking his path. Who were they, and what the hell did they want? Only a couple of heartbeats of time had passed, with dozens of questions going through Thomas's mind.

"Hey!" he said, his car door opened, one foot out on the pavement.

They ran. Suddenly and without a word they turned and ran into the deep shadows of trees that divided two yards, between two darkened houses.

"Stop!" he yelled and ran after them, leaving his car door open, the engine idling.

In the grass between the houses he stopped. His car was still in view, sitting with a door open, the engine running, the key in the ignition. The kids had disappeared as completely as if the night had swallowed them.

He walked back to the car, looking in all directions. The neighborhood was quiet except for a dog that had started barking a block over. But it was in the direction opposite where the kids had run.

Thomas drove the car into the driveway of the nearest house and turned the engine off. There was a light in a back room. The O'Briens lived here in one of the earlier houses of the area. It was a one story white frame with screened porches front and back. The yard was large and neat. Most of the people left in town were on the upper side of fifty. Those kids didn't belong anywhere around here, yet as he thought of them he began to feel he had seen them before. Visitors? Grandkids come home?

He went to the back door of the O'Brien house and knocked, and knocked again. The porch light came on.

Jess O'Brien opened the kitchen door and peered curiously out. He was barefoot, his shirt half buttoned.

"Howdy Jess," Thomas said. "Sorry to bother you. Did I get you out of bed?"

"Naw, naw." He came across the porch and unhooked the screen door. "What's up, Tom?"

"I'm checking on a bunch of young kids, ages maybe nine or ten to, well, the oldest girl, maybe thirteen or fourteen. They were just now out in the street in front of your house. They ran like hell when I got out to talk to them. Would you know who they are?"

Even before Thomas finished his question he could see the answer on Jess O'Brien's face. It was as blank as a child's face whose teacher had asked a math question.

"Kids?"

"Any visitors in the neighborhood that you know of?"

Jess's eyes searched the darkness beyond Thomas. Thomas turned. Beyond the shadows beneath the trees, beyond the yard behind the alley and bordering the next little street a street lamp glowed. Moonlight filled empty spaces between heavy shadows. Nothing moved. The dog across the way had stopped barking. The night was as still now as the shadows beneath the trees.

"No," Jess said. "Nothing, no visitors that I know of. Just the revival up at the edge of town. My wife went, with a couple of the neighbor women. They ought to be home pretty soon. But when I was a boy revivals weren't as unusual as they are now, and it was nothing for them to last till midnight or later, so there's no telling."

Thomas thanked Jess O'Brien and walked away. The porch light went off, the door closed.

Thomas walked through the darkness turning, looking. It had a haunted quality now, dark and mysterious.

By the time he reached the car he knew he had seen the three children before who had stood so clearly outlined in his headlights. But he couldn't remember where. As he drove around the block, searching, their faces remained before him. Those faces, he thought with irritation, had been completely void of expression. Like nineteenth-century photographs. Too bad they couldn't be treated like kids from another century, spanked soundly and put to bed.

Thomas eased the car to the left, and then suddenly his assistant's voice spoke to him over the police radio. Glen, on duty at night at the station, hardly ever had reason to contact Thomas. Most of the time Glen spent his nights on duty reading and sleeping.

"Thomas, come in, Thomas."

Thomas picked up the radio receiver. "Yeah, Glen?"

"Have a report of trouble over on Spring Street, at the Sandford Niles house. Can you take it?"

"Yes. What's wrong?"

"Some kids ganged up on Dennis. He's not very seriously hurt, but they killed the dog."

"I'll be damned. I'm on my way."

He speeded. Spring Street was three blocks away. For a moment it seemed he drove through areas that were familiar only from the memory of a nightmare. Beneath every tree, in every shadow, he could imagine he saw darting figures. As he drove through the quiet streets, his tires screeching around the corner as he turned onto Spring, it seemed the town was filled with strange children, darting just out of sight, like flaws at the edge of his vision.

CHAPTER FOUR

"I DIDN'T WANT TO TAKE YOU AWAY FROM THE REVIVAL MEETING, NINA," Halley said. "Cory and I could have walked home. We could have cut across the field and been home in half an hour. The moon's so bright tonight we wouldn't have minded at all."

"Of course I wouldn't let you walk. I brought you, I'll take you home. That metal chair was beginning to feel like a growth anyway."

Nina attempted a laugh, though she felt anything but humorous. She glanced sideways at Halley and over her shoulder where Cory hung forward over the front seat, his skinny elbows aimed outward, his hands small and pale clasped together between Nina and Halley. Cory grinned, but Halley didn't appear to notice Nina's attempt at humor. She stared ahead, her eyes on the road.

"Are you feeling okay, Halley?"

Halley nodded. "Yes, fine. I just need to get home and lie down, I reckon. I don't know what's—what's ailing me."

"Hey Gram," Cory asked. "Do you know who that was? That guy in the doorway? Did you see him?"

Halley nodded. "I saw him."

Yes, Nina thought. He had stood within reach of Halley. Cory, seated between her and Halley had turned his head toward the figure in the doorway, just as the others had. All of them had looked at the doorway and the tall boy who stood there, all eyes following the eyes of the preacher. The silence was profound. Nina remembered it as she remembered a particularly vivid dream. So much had happened in so short a time.

Cory cried, "It was Patrick! Wasn't it, Nina?"

"Yes, Cory," she said. "It was Patrick."

"What're they going to do with him now that he's come back, Nina?" Cory asked, his excited voice growing louder in Nina's ear. "Will they put him in jail?"

"He's . . ." Nina couldn't accept Patrick's guilt in the violent death of his family. "Thomas will probably only want to talk to him, Cory. It hasn't been proved he's the killer."

"Lots of people," Cory continued shrilly, "thought that Patrick was really dead too, only with his body buried somewhere."

Halley cringed. Nina observed the shrinking of her body as her shoulders hunched.

Nina said, "Well now we know better, don't we? Thank God. Patrick was—is a good kid."

"I worked with him at your shelter," Cory said.

"I know you did. You're all good kids." She patted his hand.

Nina turned the corner onto the street where Halley's house sat back in a large yard. A tall elm tree, one of the last in the area to survive, still shaded the walk at the front, and part of the driveway. A row of Lombardy poplars lined the outer edge of the driveway and divided the Reed land from the Moore land. The Moore house, where the murders had occurred, had been built halfway back across the field between the street and the dark green rise of the hills. Moonlight placed both houses in a strange, filtered glow like that of a day dimmed by a partial eclipse. Both houses were dark.

Nina pulled into the graveled driveway.

"Isn't your husband home, Halley? I don't see a light."

"I don't know. It'll be all right. I have Cory."

The moment Nina shut off the engine the sounds of howling became audible. Nina listened, holding her breath for a moment. There were few sounds more beautiful than the howls of wolves, and few things more unsettling than the howls of dogs. She looked toward the hillside where her house and animal shelter were hidden among trees. A couple of yard lights blinked through the leaves like lighted lanterns carried by unknown wanderers.

Cory said, "The dogs are howling. What's wrong with them, Nina?"

"I don't know." She had an uneasy feeling. It had started when she saw Patrick, and was growing stronger with the sounds of the dogs' howls.

"Do you think a bear or something is bothering them?"

"No. They'd be barking then. Howling is usually caused in response to . . . another dog howling. It's just a form of communication. Usually long distance."

But Nina felt disturbed by the sounds. She felt disturbed by everything that had occurred tonight. The strange tremor of the ground, Patrick in the doorway after all this time—and then in that particular doorway at that time—and Halley fainting at the sight of him. And now, the darkness of the big house, the shadows it created in the bright moonlight, and the very atmosphere of the area surrounding the house. The howling of the dogs seemed like a dirge. She felt a need to hurry home and see if they were all right. She had known of dogs howling when another dog died. It had happened at least twice in her experience. But mostly the howls were an answering call to something, another dog howling somewhere, music that pierced their sensitive hearing, a shrill train whistle in the distance. Or a call for help. A dog in a trap would howl. She had followed such a howl once into the hills east of her house, and found the dog with his foot in a metal trap, and the dog's paw half torn away. It had taken long, feverish minutes and all her strength to open the terrible jaws of the trap.

She felt a sudden urgency to get home.

Nina helped Halley from the car. Halley seemed a bit unsteady yet, and Nina was torn between leaving her and going on to check the dogs at the shelter.

Halley walked unsteadily up the brick path to the front door. The porch was dark, which seemed another strange occurrence in this strange night. The porch light had been left on, though it was still daylight, when Nina stopped to pick up Halley and Cory earlier in the evening. Matt obviously had turned it out. Big, bearlike Matt, whom Nina had never known very well and didn't want to know very well, had left Halley and Cory to get in on their own in the dark. Nina tightened her lips but said nothing about the light. The front door was unlocked.

"Halley," Nina said as she hesitated on the porch. "Do you think we should notify Rachel that you're not feeling well?"

Halley snapped the light on and turned at the same time to Nina.

"Oh no, oh no. Rachel and David just started their vacation, and I don't want to ruin it. I'm fine, really I am. Thanks for bothering with us, Nina."

Cory said, "We don't even know where they are, do we, Gram?"

"No, not tonight. They said they'd call when they get wherever it is they're going. Nina, don't you worry. I hope I didn't keep you from the meeting."

"Lord no. I only went because it was an oddity. I could remember my grandmother telling me about revivals that used to come through, and I'd never seen one."

Halley nodded, and for a moment nostalgia softened her eyes and mouth. "Brush arbor meetings. When I was young, younger than Cory, I'd go with my family to this place where there was a brush arbor. Do you know what that is? It's a wood frame, with brush over the top to keep out, or help keep out, the rain. There'd be lanterns hanging on the posts. Not electric, but kerosene. I can remember the bugs flying around those lanterns. But that was when I was a little girl. Younger than Cory. Almost sixty years ago. A long time."

Halley turned on the light in the entry hall, a cavernous room almost as large as Nina's whole house, it seemed from the porch. On the few occasions Nina had been in Halley's house, she'd gone to the back, to the kitchen and family room. Halley's daughter Rachel was four years older than Nina, and Nina had known her only because they attended the local school. They'd never been friends. Nor were they neighbors. During school years Nina had lived on the other side of town. When her grandparents died they had left her the twenty acres on the hillside, because they knew her dream was to have a safe place for the stray animals she was always finding. She was the only grandchild. They had also left money enough to build a home and shelter and to modestly maintain it. The land had made her a neighbor, though somewhat remote, to Halley and her husband, Matt. By that time Rachel was living out of town, going to college, working, marrying.

When Rachel moved back to town two years ago she had a husband and a stepson, Cory, a blond little boy with a perfect face, wide dark eyes, small nose and mouth, tapered chin, and a high, wide, straight forehead. He was a skinny little kid two years ago when Nina first saw him. But though he was still a skinny little kid he was growing fast and had come to put in his half day at the shelter one day a week the way his friends did.

Beyond Halley in the lighted entry room Nina saw a stairway rising against the left wall and going out of sight into darkness above.

Nina was secretly relieved Halley hadn't wanted her to come in. The old Reed house had always depressed Nina. She wasn't sure why, unless it was because she didn't approve of Matt Reed's so-called hobby. She, an animal sympathizer and protector, had no meeting of the mind or anything else with a man whose hobby was trapping animals. Nina had been working to have metal traps abolished. Of all cruel ways mankind had devised to capture animals, the steel trap was the most cruel. She donated to organizations that worked to get laws passed. It was about all she could do now to maintain her own animal shelter, and it demanded most of her time. When she was in college she was right in the middle of the activists, carrying her own sign, shouting her anger. It hadn't done much good, so she had come home and decided that she could help a few, at least. Now she donated her spare money to a small organization that offered free neutering of pets. It was the only way to stop the homelessness. Her acquaintances didn't dare get her started on the subject.

Nina said goodnight to Halley and Cory and hurried to her car. The dogs were still howling. The town dogs barked in answer and occasionally one or two howled. Nina backed out of the driveway and turned her car toward home.

The street slowly tapered away past a turn to the left and became a driveway up the hill to Nina's house. It curved right beneath the trees and ended in a circle between her house and the shelter built a hundred yards away. She drove into the carport, and without going into the house walked hurriedly along the path to the shelter. Whines replaced howls. Dogs reared up on their wire enclosures as she approached.

She entered the building. Wire and partial board walls separated the area into small rooms on each side of the hallway that ran the length of the building. Beds of fresh straw had been placed in each room, and doggie doors opened out into the divided wire runs. Light bulbs along the ceiling of the hallway left few shadows.

"Hey, guys, what's all the fuss about?" She stopped to pet the first dog, whose adopted puppies were stirring restlessly in the straw bed in the corner.

Mutter, as the big German shepherd was called, in respect for her native language in which Mutter meant the obvious, had been at the shelter since she was a young dog five years ago. Within days Nina had discovered that Mutter took over every young creature, not only puppies but kittens, orphaned raccoons, and once a baby bobcat. Mutter nursed them, nurtured them, groomed them, responded to their cries and whines and tried to make them comfortable. She was needed. She had been nursing orphans for five years that Nina knew of, all ages that needed that kind of care, none of them her own. Her milk supply had never dried up. She was, Nina felt, the essence of what God intended when he created the maternal instinct.

Right now Mutter had in her bed one kitten and two little hound pups that had been found in a nest where the other eight had died. The kitten sat up close to her puppy littermates and blinked round, innocent blue eyes at the bright lights Nina had turned on. The puppies stirred, their eyes just beginning to peek open at the corners.

Nina walked on through the corridor of the shelter, stopping to pet every dog and cat. There were twenty three animals in residence now. When the time came that she had to have one destroyed, she called in her favorite veterinarian and sat with the dog, or cat, while it received its injection. She hated seeing it happen, except when the animal was in severe pain and nothing could be done.

As the dogs grew quiet Nina left the shelter, turned out the lights within and closed and latched the outer door. She walked around the shelter, the light from the pole in the driveway revealing the gravel path. Dogs came out into the runs, and one of them, a big Doberman, stared into the darkness of the trees and growled. Its eerie sound, the uniqueness of the action, made Nina feel threatened by something she couldn't see. She tried to quiet the dog, all the time looking where she stared, sensing more than darkness to be the disturbance.

She couldn't forget the earth tremor. It was a strange feeling, the first she'd ever felt. She had never realized how dependent she was on the steadiness of the earth beneath her feet. But that, surely, would not still be upsetting the dogs. Perhaps they sensed another tremor, not yet rippling to the crust of the earth.

The night was quiet now, and into the quietness came the low, moaning call of an owl. The Doberman growled again, and Nina put her fingers through the wire to her muzzle.

"Oh go to bed, Sally," she said. "It's only an owl."

The dog wagged her tail, and when Nina looked back at her from the end of the path, she had sat down. A beautiful dog, left behind by some people who had moved to the city, she had been in the shelter now for nine months, and it looked as if she were going to stay. Sometimes Nina turned her out and let her do as she pleased. After sniffing around she always came to the step outside her office door and lay down.

She circled the shelter. On the south side the moonlight blotched the path, and below her in the valley she saw the Moore house, still dark, beneath its big shade trees. Beyond that was the monstrous house of Matt and Halley Reed. From the front the house looked like an ordinary though large farmhouse. But the addition on the back, with no special architectural design, created a monster.

She went on to her small house and out onto the screened porch, looking again at the Moore house.

She had gone to the revival out of curiosity, and for another reason less definable. It was as though she were pulled, as if she sensed something important was going to happen. On the light side she had laughed at herself as she dressed in a summer cotton dress with a flared skirt and a red sash at the waist, as if she were going to meet the man of her dreams, finally, after all these years. "Good Lord, girl," she said to herself as she brushed her hair and checked her makeup, "You're pushing thirty. You'd better get yourself a man if you ever want—what you want." She knew what she wanted. She wanted a baby. She wanted a husband, a family. All her furry companions couldn't take the place of that.

But, her real reason for going was something she couldn't put her finger on. She was not religious. She had no tolerance for a bible that said, "and the dogs shall be cast into hell with the whores." Only if the hell referred to was life itself, could she accept that. The dogs couldn't help being dogs. The whores didn't become whores alone. The Christian Bible was mostly history, mostly sermons preached in a time gone by, mostly desperate men trying to find a reason for their existence. She could understand that, but it didn't draw her to organized religion. It had nothing to offer her. Yet she found herself getting ready to go.

She had called Halley and asked if she'd like to go along.

"Well," Halley said, in that hour before dark, "I was thinking me and Cory might walk up. We could cut across the field. Rachel and David left today on their vacation, and Cory is staying with me."

"Why don't I just stop and get you?"

Halley had agreed that would be fine, if it didn't put her to any trouble.

Nina had not once dreamed that a boy she had feared was dead would appear alive and well in the doorway of the revival tent. He had stood within ten feet of her, at the end of the last row where she, Halley, and Cory sat. She had seen the light on Patrick's face. She had seen the direction of his gaze. She had seen the intensity of that gaze as he stared at the preacher.

She went outside again and stood in the graveled parking area between the house and shelter. The dogs had settled down. The vapor lights sizzled quietly and steadily. From her open door her cat, Pixie, came and rubbed against her ankle. Nina stooped, picked her up and carried her back into the house.

"Want a snack?" she asked Pixie, and sat down to divide a chocolate chip cookie with her. Every week she promised herself she'd stop buying such tempting bedtime treats and try to get an inch worked down on her rear. But every week her hand just automatically reached out and picked up that bag of Keebler's chocolate chip cookies.

She wiped up the crumbs, put fresh water in Pixie's bowl, and turned out the kitchen light. The nights were cool, but not cool enough to close windows. She looked at the screen of the windows over the sink and over the kitchen table at the end of the room and decided, as she had decided many times before, that if someone wanted in the house he'd come in, even if the window were lowered and locked. So, just leave it open and let the breeze circulate.

Sometimes she felt a little nervous, living alone up in the woods. The wild animals didn't bother her. It was that most familiar animal, the most brutal animal that made her uneasy at times. Sometimes she had a feeling someone was looking through the windows at her, not in a lustful way, but with a hatred that ran deep. When her shelter and small house were first built she hadn't felt that way at all. She had felt safe, secure, and happy, knowing she was doing all she could.

She was twenty-two then, and fresh out of college. Her ambition to be a veterinarian had fallen by the wayside because she couldn't bear to experiment on animals. So she had studied related subjects and come home as soon as she could.

But seven years had passed, and even though she wasn't aware of having made any enemies, she had suddenly, a few years ago, begun to have that feeling of someone standing in the woods looking at her. When the dogs in the kennel started barking in the middle of the night, it worried her.

Thomas had told her once, shortly after the murder of the Moore family, "Nina, keep your doors locked. Keep my number right by your phone. In fact, I have an errand. I'll be back in an hour or so," and he had returned in less than an hour with a new memory telephone, which he gave her. He had stored on it both his home number and the number of the office.

"All you have to do is reach over and push a button," he said, "and I'll be here as soon as I can get here."

She didn't tell him that sometimes at night she felt as if someone who hated her was watching.

In her bedroom she pulled all the blinds. She sat down in her reading chair, which was in the corner by windows that opened out into cool woods.

She thought of Patrick, wondering where he'd been this past year. Did he know he could come to her?

Suddenly she was seeing him again as he stood in the doorway of the tent. Light had shown on the sparse little mustache that Patrick was trying to grow. The ends of the whiskers had a reddish cast in the light.

Just exactly the way it had looked a year ago, the last time she had seen him.

CHAPTER FIVE

THE SANDFORD NILES HOME WAS ON A SHORT STREET OF NEWER HOUSES ON the east side of town. Thomas knew the family as he knew every family in town. Sandford, who was usually called Sandy, especially at Lane's place where he stopped now and then for a beer, was a husky guy who looked as if he had been a football player. He lived with his moderately plump, good-looking wife, Enid, and their two sons, Dennis, who was in junior high, and Rudy, still a sprout.

On one side of Sandford's lived their friends, Alice and Mitch Collins and their daughter Jenny. On the other side lived David and Rachel Thane, and David's son from a former marriage, Cory. The hills rose a block away, with miles of thick forest for hiding. Anyone could have run into those trees and been immediately hidden from view. Only with a tracking dog would they be in danger of being found.

Lights were on at the front of both the Niles's house and the Collins's, but deep darknesses hovered under trees between the houses, and reached out into the street.

Thomas saw a small group of people standing in the Niles's driveway, drawn closely together. Thomas parked in the street and the small group in the lighted driveway met him halfway. Their faces carried that look of surprise, indignation, fear, and excitement that was common to groups of people who had seen something alien to their experiences.

Dennis's face looked blotched with red streaks and white spots. His eyes were red and tomorrow would probably turn purple. He was pretty well scratched up, on his arms, face and neck, but none of the scratches appeared to be seriously deep. Smears of something white indicated that his mother might have been doctoring him.

His shirt had been ripped almost off. One sleeve was gone, and there was a rip down the back. He looked as if he had been rolled underneath a moving truck, then dragged through a blackberry patch.

"Better take him to the doctor?" Thomas said, half a question, half a command.

"I don't need to see a doctor," Dennis said, as if such a thing would further undermine his dignity.

Speaking at the same time his mother and Alice Collins said something about trying to get him to Doc Tyler, but Thomas's attention was on Dennis. The boy was trembling, his lower lip quivering. There might be some fear there, but most of it was anger. Rage. His eyes kept searching the darkness, but not toward the hills. He was looking down the street toward the center of town.

"Tell me what happened, who they were, where they went."

Dennis motioned northwest, toward the closed houses of other families, down the wide, uncluttered, shaded streets. "They ran, I don't know where. When my dad and Mitch came out of the house, they took off. I don't know who they were. Except—"

Sandford said, "They came from the direction of town and just suddenly ganged up on our kids."

"Our kids were out playing ball," Mitch said.

Rudy pushed forward, "Jiggers attacked them. And they—"

Dennis interrupted impatiently, "He didn't attack them! He—they—they—had no reason to hurt him."

"He was trying to protect us! And they—and they—and they killed him!"

Rudy began to cry, his fists going to his eyes to hold back the tears. Thomas put his hand on the little boy's bead briefly and gave him a comforting rub. Rudy leaned against his mother. She put her arms around him, enfolding him against her.

But Dennis had said something earlier that had caught Thomas's attention.

"You said you didn't know them, except. . . except for what?"

A look of concentration came onto Dennis's thin, young face. His dark eyes narrowed. "Well," he said, and paused, and glanced at his father.

"I just don't think it could be," Sandford said.

"Who?" asked Thomas.

Dennis said, "It's been a long time since I saw him, four years, and I was only ten then, but the leader of the gang looked like Willy Yardley."

"Willy Yardley," Thomas said, something in the back of his mind digging, but relenting before it became a solid realization. "Lane Yardley's boy?"

"Yes sir. He looked exactly like Willy, except Willy was never mean. That kid tonight was a bastard." A nerve jerked visibly in his jaw.

Sandford shifted his feet, pushed his hands down into the back pockets of his jeans. "I told Dennis it couldn't have been Yardley. He said the boy was smaller than he is, about eleven years old. The age Willy was back then. The Yardley boy was a year older than Dennis, so he'd be fifteen now. A lot bigger than this kid."

Enid said, "Willy used to come here to play with the neighborhood kids. He and Dennis were good friends."

"He looked just like Willy," Dennis said.

Sandford said, "Anyway, this kid tonight, one of these boys that was fighting—there were a couple of girls, too, the boys said—but the boys who were fighting were all small kids. Eleven, twelve years old. Larger than Rudy, but smaller than Dennis."

"Except for the big girl," Dennis said. "She was as tall as I am. She had long blond hair. The little girl, I didn't know her at all. But a couple of the other kids, they looked familiar, too."

"They all ganged up on you?" Thomas asked.

"They started—they were going after Rudy, I thought. And that figures. Rudy's pretty little. Then Jiggers went after them. I mean, he didn't back off. He stood there in the street, barking, growling. And they just kept coming. I sent Rudy and Jenny to get our dads. Then I saw they were ganging up to fight. Yeah, even though they were all smaller kids except for the blond girl, the older girl, they jumped me. All at once. One at a time I could have . . ." Dennis paused again, and something like cold, primitive fear washed across his face, leaching color away.

Sanford said, "They were vicious."

"Well anyway," Dennis said, "This one guy looked like Willy Yardley used to. Except, this guy was mean. They all were. The little girl with the doll—"

Rudy pulled his face away from his mother's arms and cried, "Had a face like a monster! It just changed, like that, and she looked like a monster!"

Thomas scratched his cheek. The encounter had been so traumatic to the two boys that only half of what they claimed could be taken literally.

But, in the gang of kids there had been a little girl with a doll. He had seen her himself. It was the same group of kids who had fanned out across the street in front of his car, and the attack must have just happened. They'd probably been running away when he met them in the street. If so, they were going northwest, toward the revival tent in the field. Or Nina's animal shelter, or one of the homes over in that area. But he knew that most of the home owners there were all past middle age, and none of them had children at home, and rarely had grandchildren around.

"Let's go take a look at Jiggers."

The two men walked with him, Sandford leading the way. With the strong beam of the flashlight like a guiding path, it brought them to the dog.

"My God," Thomas muttered.

"Yeah," Sandford said. "It's like Jiggers met up with a horde of . . . I don't know. Animals don't kill this way."

The dog, which once had been a medium sized, longhaired dog of mixed breed and friendly disposition, was now opened down the belly from his chest to his hind legs, an oddly clean rip.

"Were they carrying knives?" Thomas asked. Although Thomas didn't think it looked like a knife had been used. He saw no stab wound. His flashlight revealed a ripped belly, which answered his question even as Dennis attempted an answer.

"Maybe, I don't know. I felt sharp things, but I thought it was fingernails."

Thomas squatted by the dead dog, his flashlight aimed hard along the tear. The point of entry was in the chest, and more like a puncture than a stab wound. The outer body, the skin, fur, feet and head were in good shape, as if deliberately kept that way. Like a pelt. The dog's entrails and organs had been pulled out and were strewn in a long line across the pavement and down the street, probably as they were running away.

This was more than a killing. It was sadistic savagery. Those kids had enjoyed ripping this poor animal to pieces. What would have happened to Dennis if help hadn't come?

"How long were you fighting?"

"Not long. Dad and Mitch came out right away."

Although the dog's flesh had been torn, the object used was a mystery. Kids' hands, no matter how vicious they were, couldn't have done this.

But it wouldn't do any good to take the pelt to a vet. He couldn't take the time. He needed to find the kids and get them off the streets, out of town.

He stood up. "I guess you might as well go ahead and bury him," Thomas said.

He cut off the flashlight. The dark, for the moment, was welcome. The sight of the blood, the mutilation, the senselessness of the killing of a family pet, was sad.

"We'll get those kids," he promised.

Something dark and sad entered Thomas's heart. He had never known kids like that. Now, here they were in this quiet little town.

Who were they, and where were they from? Thomas thought of Walsh's Christian Alliance and the revival tent parked in the field west of town. There was a connection, if only in timing. The kids might belong there.

CORY LISTENED, trying to hear Gram's footsteps somewhere in the second story, so he would not feel so alone. But he had lost even the feel of them, the soft echoes of sound as they faded away. She had left him in a bedroom at the back of the long upstairs hall, and the moment she was out of hearing he panicked. He had wanted to run after her, but was afraid to leave his room in this strange house.

The black hole of fear had lightened only slightly as he tried in his mind to find her. Where was her bedroom? Where would he find her if he needed her? If he . . . needed . . . a drink . . .

He edged stiffly against the bed. He wasn't five years old anymore. He was nine now. He could get his own drink. She had shown him the bathroom, just up the hall from his room.

She had turned on the bedside lamp, and the shade made a cone of the light right down over the small table and part of the bed. There was a Bible on the table, and a small clock that wasn't running. The rest of the room looked like a world in outer space with its weird half-light, its shadows and darknesses. It looked like the night outside with its moonlight, and the black shadows where in the daytime it would only be shaded.

Gram had told him to go to bed. She had seemed different since coming home from the revival, as if the part of her he loved was in some way left there. Was it because she had seen Patrick? Didn't Gram like Patrick? She hadn't seemed glad to see him.

Cory unzipped his jeans and pushed them down, then remembered he had to take off his shoes. "Take off your shoes first, son," Dad would say. "You can't pull off your jeans over your shoes."

Well, he could, but sometimes they got caught on the shoes and then he'd have to have help getting the shoes off and out of the skinny legs. He whistled under his breath as he worked at getting undressed. If he could have gone with Dad and Rachel he wouldn't be here tonight in this strange, scary room. But they hadn't asked him. It was their honeymoon trip, delayed, they had said.

It helped to remember Dad and Rachel. Sometimes he thought of his own mother, but he couldn't remember her very well. Mostly he remembered her gravestone and going to the cemetery with his dad and grandparents before Dad married Rachel and moved here.

It helped to think of his house, of Rudy and Jenny and Dennis and the other kids he played with. Of Rachel and Dad.

They had asked him if he wanted to fly back to L.A., where his grandparents lived, and spend a week with them, but he didn't want to. They had other grandkids; they didn't need him. Gram didn't have anyone but him, and she was willing for him to stay with her and Matt.

That was great today, after the big Sunday dinner, just after Dad and Rachel left. He had even begun to feel a little closer to Matt as they watched sports together. At supper it had begun to seem a little strange, being in the big house with only Gram and Matt. As the sun got lower in the west he had begun to want to go home.

But then Nina came and they went with her to the big tent where the preacher yelled and shouted. Then came the earthquake. Cory had been in earthquakes before, and this was a little one. It had surprised him, but it hadn't scared him the way it did the others. Then he'd looked up to see Patrick standing in the doorway.

When Gram fell out of her chair she made a funny sound, almost like a moan. He was afraid she'd died. For a moment he hadn't been able to move. He didn't trust God not to take away people he loved. "Your mother is in heaven," people had told him, when he was three years old and his mother was out of his reach in her fresh grave. "She's with God." He was scared to death that God had taken Gram too.

Then Gram was trying to rise, with people all around helping her, and Cory had trouble keeping from crying, he was so glad.

What happened to Patrick? Where had he gone? Where had he been since a year ago? Gram hadn't asked, even though there was something about seeing Patrick that made her ill. All the way home in the car, Gram hadn't said much of anything.

Now she'd left him in a room alone and she'd gone away, he didn't know where.

He whistled a bit louder. He had learned a way to whistle between his teeth that was almost silent. Only Jiggers could tell when he was whistling.

Sometimes, the teacher could hear it, but she never knew where it was coming from.

He wished he knew where his dad and Rachel were. He wished now he'd asked to go with them. If he had wanted to go, he'd bet his special silver dollar Rachel would have made Dad take him along. But he'd thought at the time that staying with Gram and Matt in their big, interesting house would be like having an adventure all his own.

Only now that he was here, he'd give anything to be in his own room in the small house across town. He'd give anything to be able to look forward in the morning to getting up and riding his bike wherever he wanted to go in town. In the afternoon he and Rudy and Dennis would ride up to Nina's and help her with the dogs. They'd open the gates on the wire runs and turn the dogs out, the way Nina did on nice afternoons, and they'd all run through the paths in the woods, the dogs having so much fun, barking at squirrels that chattered from treetops and hung off limbs to scold them. And Cory having fun with them.

That reminded him again of Patrick. Cory lay in bed with his arms under his head and stared at the ceiling. Where had Patrick been since last summer?

Tonight, after leaving the revival tent, had he gone back to his house in the field between here and Nina's? Now after the bodies of his mom, dad and sister had been removed? Where, it was said, the blood on the floor and walls had turned dark brown, but was still there, never cleaned. Would Patrick have gone there, was he there right now, just across the field?

Cory slipped out of bed again and went to the window. But Patrick's house wasn't visible.

The view out his window took in the field behind the house, and the hillside rising like a black cloud. Cory pushed the window up and put his face against the screen. He could see down into the backyard. He could see part of the roof on the addition behind the house. Black areas covered part of the backyard, where moonlight couldn't sift through the thick leaves on the trees.

Then Cory's gaze fell upon something weird, something that didn't look as if it belonged. It lay in the grass. It had no discernable shape, just something long and dark, as if part of the shadows beneath the tree had broken away and fallen into the moonlight.

Hair on Cory's arms raised. The back of his neck tingled. He pulled the window down. It lowered easily to within a few inches of the bottom, and then it stuck. He tugged on it until his muscles bulged, but it wouldn't move. He heard a moan, an eerie, awful sound. It came like a ghost, lost and searching.

Cory left the window in a run and leaped into bed. He pulled the covers over his head and then remembered he hadn't turned his light out. Here he was, outlined beneath his light, his window open with only the screen between him and the shadows reaching like arms into the moonlight, and the thing that had moaned.

He wanted Dad and Rachel and his safe little room at home.

If he called Gram, would she hear him in this big house? He didn't even know where her room was. She had brought him silently into the upstairs after Nina left them, and as silently had brought him down the hall to the room. She hadn't spoken except to point out the bathroom, then to tell him good night. It was as if she had become a stranger after she fainted and fell to the ground at the preacher's tent.

Lying in bed, holding his breath, Cory heard the moan again. He listened, and pushed the covers back. A sudden thought had made him forget how scary the sound was. *Nina's dogs.* Maybe one of her dogs was hurt and lying there needing help.

Cory slipped out of bed again and then turned out the light. This way whatever it was in the backyard couldn't see him in the bedroom. He crept to the window and looked out again.

He stared, and the form took on a shape. It was oblong, somewhat like a mummy wrapped in black. It was a person, not a dog.

Now that his light was out he could see better. He made out a half-turned face in the moonlight, and a beard . . . Matt! It was Matt. He had fallen in the yard, and the eerie moan that even now rose into the stillness of the night came from him.

A heart attack! Cory's neighbor last year had fallen with a heart attack. Wasn't that what happened to men when they started to get old?

Cory ran out and down the hall. A ceiling light burned at the far end, and Cory thundered down the passageway yelling, "Gram! Gram! I think Matt's had a heart attack!"

He reached the place where the hall branched. To his left was the open banistered area above the foyer, to his right another short hall and a closed door. As he stopped, wondering where to go to find Gram, the closed door opened.

She was still wearing the slacks and blouse she had worn to the meeting. Her grey hair was loose and hanging over her shoulders like a shawl. Her eyes were rounded, looking pale blue and watery, as if she'd been crying.

"Matt," Cory told her, calmed a bit by her presence. "Somebody's out in the backyard, Gram. Lying on the grass. Moaning. I think it might be Matt."

At first Gram only stared at him, as if she hadn't understood, then as Cory started to tell her again, she asked, "Where?"

"Outside. In the backyard. I heard something make this weird noise and I looked out and I saw him, on the ground. Just like our neighbor last year, the one that died of a heart attack."

Gram turned and started down the front stairs, and Cory followed her.

Cory had never been invited to call Matt "Grandpa." He could count on one hand the number of times he had seen Matt in the two years since Rachel had been his stepmother at Christmas, and at Thanksgiving, and again at Easter. Gram came to their house sometimes, but Matt had been there only once.

Cory had wanted Matt to be his grandpa, but Matt had never been very friendly. Cory, in the same room with Matt, had always been half scared of the man. He was almost like a giant, with his big shoulders and his strange beard. It was a beard with three colors. It had both red and dark streaks scattered among the grey. It was strange in other ways too. It was like an upside down cap, worn from ear to ear around his chin. There was no mustache, just a few spriggles of hair. At first Cory almost laughed, but then he saw he could never laugh at Matt. He was timid around Matt. It was easy for him to sit quietly and say nothing, as he had this afternoon when sports were on television.

When Gram had offered to let him stay with her while his dad and Rachel took their vacation-honeymoon, Cory had thought it would be great to stay in Matt's big house. He could explore, maybe. Something he'd never done. This was the first time he'd even climbed the stairs into the upper story. Before this he had been in the living room at the front, and the family room at the back near the kitchen, the dining room and kitchen, and that was all. Oh yes, the washroom, that big room between the kitchen and the addition on the back of the house. In the washroom the windows had been changed into a wall, and the door in the short, dark hallway off the washroom was locked. Cory had found that out last Easter when after washing his hands for dinner his curiosity had gotten the better of him and he'd slipped into the short, dark hall and tried to open the door. It was locked.

Once he asked Rachel what was in the addition that had no windows.

"I was never in those rooms, Cory. And if Dad ever takes you in there you'll have known a privilege I never had. But he's got a taxidermy hobby, and—well—" She didn't seem to want to talk about it. Maybe because it was as much a mystery to her as it was to Cory. Taxidermy? What was that?

"Well," she said, "It's when you stuff animals to make them seem real."

Cory stared at her open mouthed. Then he realized his mouth was open and snapped it shut. "Stuff animals! Why would he want to do that? What does he do with them?"

Rachel had a strange look on her face. She didn't look happy anymore.

"I know once when the University was making a wildlife scene in its museum, Dad donated some animals. He gave them some raccoons, squirrels, even some birds. I don't think he works with them anymore though, Cory. I don't know. I do know that he does not like little boys, or girls, going into his workrooms. And don't ever ask him about it, okay?"

Cory followed Gram across the kitchen, across the porch and down the three steps to the backyard. Moonlight made the figure on the ground look long and wide and dark, and Cory began to feel scared again. What if it wasn't Matt after all?

"Oh my God," Gram cried and ran to the body on the ground. "Oh my God."

Cory saw her lift something heavy and black that made a metallic sound. It was fastened to Matt's right hand.

Matt lay as if dead, his face turned with his cheek against the grass. He was lying on his stomach, his arms stretched out, the right one held now by Halley.

Cory saw it was a large trap. Though he had never seen a trap before in his life, he recognized it for what it was. Blood dripping slowly from the hand had made black spots on the grass.

Matt groaned.

As if the dogs had heard, howls rose again from the shelter. To Cory they sounded lonely and sad.

CHAPTER SIX

"Oh Lord, oh my Lord. What has he done to himself?"

Cory watched Gram fumble with the trap on Matt's hand. In the light of the moon the trap looked like a jaw, a huge mouth of teeth that had no head, no body. Streaks of blood, black as the trap, had made narrow trails through the curly grey hair on Matt's arm.

The howls of the dogs rose again, mournfully, died and rose again. Matt groaned.

Cory wanted to help, but didn't know how. His fingers touched the metal of the trap and jerked back. It was cold, which seemed strange on a warm summer night. His fingers had touched something wet, and he thought it might be blood. He wiped them on his leg, and realized he hadn't put his jeans back on. He was out here in his undershorts.

Gram moved nervously, as if she didn't know whether to stay or run. She cried in a trembling voice, "Cory, you stay with Matt. I have to go call for help."

He watched her half-running, half-stumbling toward the house, up the steps and into the light on the back porch. He looked around, feeling as if weird *things* with red eyes and forked tails and razor horns were watching him from the shadows. He saw nothing move. But he saw an eye blink and blink again. He stared. No, it was only a light somewhere on the hillside, among the trees. He stared harder, and then realized it was Nina's shelter, where there were yard lights on poles and yard lights on each corner of the shelter. He didn't feel so alone.

The dogs had grown silent, and now the insects and frogs began their noises again, as if for awhile they had stopped to listen.

Matt didn't move. Cory kneeled beside him. Blades of grass made ridges in his knees. Moonlight glinted strangely on the dark metal of the trap. Great, sharp, teeth had closed together on Matt's hand as if there were no flesh or bones that could stop it from snapping shut. Like a monster's teeth they had bitten down on Matt.

Where had Matt found the trap? Cory remembered then something he hadn't thought about at the time. Rachel had once asked where Dad was, and Gram had said, "I think he's gone to check his traps." That was all. Just an isolated remark overheard a long time ago when Cory had first come to live here.

Footsteps pounded across the porch and Gram came down into the yard and halfway over to where Cory waited with Matt.

"The phone is dead, Cory," Gram cried. "I have to go get Nina. You stay with Matt. I'll be back in a few minutes."

She hurried away again, in her peculiar half-run, that almost jog that looked awkward and painful as if it had been a long time since she had tried to run. She went out of sight around the house toward the driveway, and Cory slowly rose to his feet to stand looking at the spot where he had last seen Gram.

SHE PAUSED JUST a moment near the garage. Matt's blue pickup truck was parked in the driveway, and within the garage was the Chrysler sedan. But she had forgotten how to drive. It had been too long. Even if she dared try, where were the keys?

She hurried on, down the driveway to the street. She turned right. Moonlight made the familiar area look strange, the light faded and filtered as if she were going blind. Her shoes slapped against the pavement as she tried to run.

Across the field to her right was the Moore house. Like something haunted it mocked her. The long driveway that led to it had been closed off by wire. A "No Trespassing" sign swayed, squeaking faintly with each movement back and forth. She didn't know who owned the property now that the family was dead, but no one had moved in. She wasn't even sure if the house had been cleaned up. She had heard there was a lot of blood. It caused her nightmares, as so many things did. She'd been unable to go to sleep this year without the blinds pulled.

That wasn't Patrick she had seen tonight, it couldn't have been. It couldn't have been real. It must have been the beginning of this nightmare she was in now, this nightmare from which she sought an escape and found none existed. She would go on forever, caught in this dim world.

Cory had mentioned Patrick, and so had Nina, and others. As if they had seen him too. But that too must have been part of her nightmare. When had her nightmare started? When had she slipped over the edge into this netherworld between life and death? It had come upon her like the threat of old age, so slowly she hadn't known when it started.

She had almost reached the rise of the driveway into the trees near Nina's place when it occurred to her that other neighbors were much closer. Why hadn't she just gone across the street to the Burdocks? Because . . . because it seemed as if she lived alone in the world much of the time. As if there were no neighbors. She knew the Burdocks by sight, and when she met Mrs. Burdock in the grocery store they spoke, that was all.

Nina was the only one she had thought of when she had run for help.

Her throat burned, her heart raced as she climbed the driveway toward Nina's house. Dogs in the kennels began to bark.

How could Matt have had such an accident? Matt, always in control. Matt, whom she had always thought of as being *King*. Matt was not getting old and weak and careless. Matt was still strong. King of the hills. Matt was dominant in every way, over everything. How could he have had such an accident?

She was sixteen again, slender, with a waistline that Matt liked to span with his hands, fingertips touching. He was twenty-two when she met him, so much taller than she, so massive and strong. He lifted her easily, charmed and controlled her.

"I'm going to marry you," he said, whispering in her ear the first time she saw him.

She had gone to the river to swim. The group she'd gone with, a girlfriend and a couple of boys, had dropped out of her life soon after and she barely remembered their names now. Matt had taken over. He had married her, moved her into his ancestral home, one of the largest houses in Spring Valley, and had been her king ever since. At seventy-two he wasn't weak, not Matt. He couldn't be lying there on the ground, his blood dripping slowly from his wounds. She would go home to find him up, strong, the dominant force in her world, looking at her as if she'd lost her mind. Who, him? Caught in one of his traps? Ridiculous. What a stupid woman to think such a thing. Stop trying to think, woman, just do your job.

• • •

Cory heard Matt breathing. His breath sucked in, whistling faintly between his teeth, then it eased out softly. Then in again. And then the strange little whistle again.

He heard Nina's dogs begin to bark, more and more. It was the bark that said company was coming. Was Gram only now reaching Nina's? It seemed so long.

Hours, it seemed, since she had disappeared down the driveway beside the house.

No car passed on the street. The houses he could see seemed a long way off, the only light coming from the moon.

Cory twisted, grass pressing into his knees. Across the fence and the field Cory saw Patrick's house, dark beneath its shade trees. He stared at it, visualizing a light, a very dim light in one of the rooms. Patrick was somewhere close tonight. Had he gone back to that house? Cory would have, if it had been him. Where was Patrick? Had he been living in the trees, maybe in the caves?

He had looked just like he had the last time Cory saw him. Funny, Cory would have expected him to look different, after this last year when no one knew where he was. But now that he was back, Patrick could tell the police that it wasn't him who had killed his mom, dad and sister.

Then who? In this small town, who? Cory hadn't thought of it before.

Voices reached him, as if they'd been there within his hearing, but only now heard. Cory jerked around. Ladies' voices. Nina's and Gram's? Chattering excitedly. Coming close now. They sounded funny, not quite right, somehow, as Patrick, looking so exactly the way he had last year, was not quite right.

Cory stared at the driveway where it disappeared beneath the blackness of the trees and waited for them to appear. He could hear them, but he couldn't see them. Where were they?

He knew all at once what was different about the voices. They were not ladies' voices, and not two, but more. Finer. Higher. More shrill. Children.

A group of kids, chattering to one another, giggling, high-pitched voices, excited, sounding so very close.

Cory turned, looking. Moonlight, untouched, lay between the back fence and the dark wall of the trees on the hillside. Moonlight lay on the empty lot between him and the first house back toward town. A lone tree threw its black shadow westward as the great, round moon rose higher above the hills in the east. The preacher's tent was somewhere out of sight there in the field west of town.

Suddenly the kids' voices hushed, and Cory turned again, looking toward the black shadows of the trees on his left. The boy stepped forward out of the darkness.

Cory's heart leaped. Patrick! But as soon as Patrick's name entered his mind Cory saw it wasn't Patrick. He was not as tall as Patrick. He was younger. He was outlined with moonlight, and seemed featureless, his face a dark blank. Cory stared at him. His features became gradually visible. A stranger. Cory didn't care. It was someone. Someone to be with him while he waited for Gram to bring Nina.

"Hi," he said.

The strange boy didn't answer.

From the corner of his eye Cory glimpsed movement, and he turned his head. A girl, taller than the boy, older, stood in the bright moonlight facing Cory. She had long blond hair, and was wearing blue jeans and a shirt that hung down on the outside. Her face was pretty. Her eyelashes looked long and black. She stared at Cory with a look on her face that made Cory's skin turn cold and tight. He could feel the tightness across his cheeks and into the back of his neck and hair. She stared at him as if she were threatening him, as if she were asking in her silence what he was doing here.

Then Cory saw there were other kids. He turned slowly. He and Matt were surrounded by kids, standing far apart. Another boy, shorter than the first, his hair short and spiky and glowing pale blond in the moonlight, stepped closer. He stopped, and stood in silence.

Farther back stood a little girl wearing a ruffly dress that ended just above her knees. In her arms she hugged a big doll. If she stood the doll down it would be more than half as tall as she was. Her arms held it tightly against her.

Farther back in the shadows he made out the figures of a couple more kids. Boys, it seemed, or girls with short hair and blue jeans.

Cory tried again. "Hi." His voice trembled with uncertainty.

The tall girl's stare changed from Cory to Matt.

Cory crouched closer to Matt's side. He could feel the warmth from Matt's body, but it didn't comfort him. "That's my grandpa," he said. "He got hurt."

They didn't answer. Cory saw they were all staring at Matt. It was as if they didn't see Cory at all, or hear him speak.

They had moved closer. Those back in the shadows of the trees had come forward to the edge of the shadows. Cory could see their eyes. The moonlight seemed to reflect in them the way light reflected from a mirror. Or from the eyes of wild animals in car light at the side of the road. There was something unfriendly and threatening in the way the kids didn't talk to him, and kept creeping closer when he wasn't looking.

He and Matt were surrounded now, as they formed a circle.

Sometimes he looked at a kid to find he was the one being stared at rather than Matt. Then the strange, light-reflecting eyes would switch to staring at Matt again.

Cory's lower lip jerked when he tried again to explain. "My—my—my gram has gone to get Nina . . . they're coming now."

He wished the kids would leave. Go on where ever they had been going.

Maybe they had been walking down the street when they saw him and Matt in the backyard. And had come to see what was wrong. But why didn't they say something?

"You—you can go now," he stammered. "Gram and Nina are coming. They'll take care of—of—"

They said nothing. Their feet on the grass made no sound as they slowly edged closer. Cory watched, twisting, trying to see them all at once. Only the kids in the shadows remained still, not coming into the moonlight.

Suddenly Matt moved. He groaned and turned, pushing himself up to droop half-reclining on his elbow, his head hanging forward as if he were sick, or drunk.

The children began dancing, laughing, going in circles around them. The nightbirds, the frogs, and insects grew silent as suddenly as the children had begun to giggle and sing. Cory heard their words, but couldn't make them out. It was as if they spoke and sang in a foreign language, or as if one word spoken at the same time as another cancelled out both in Cory's understanding. The fear he had felt did not lessen. His body was cold and taut, and even though Matt was trying now to rise, and the kids were dancing a circle around them, Cory felt as if he had been plunged into a world different from the one he had always known, a world worse than the worst of nightmares, a world he could not see with his real eyes, or hear with his real ears. He was so scared he froze, hunching inward as if to protect himself from attack.

Car lights moved on the street, turned and played through the leaves of the trees lining the driveway.

The tallest boy and oldest girl bent suddenly over Matt's hand, and the trap. Cory saw their fingers, strong and swift, opening the trap. For a heartbeat they were there, silent, working with the trap, and then they were darting away.

As the car lights swept closer Cory heard the metallic rattle of the trap as it was dropped at Matt's side.

The children, laughing, chattering, ran. Cory whirled and searched the area, the moonlit field, the vacant lot, the trees with the black shadows. The kids were gone.

It was like Patrick, back at the meeting. The kids were there, and just as suddenly not there. And Cory had not seen, could not see, where they went.

As the car drew nearer along the driveway Cory kept searching the dark areas for the kids. He had a feeling that although he couldn't see them, they were watching.

A moan rose softly from Matt as he swayed.

Softly too, came the voice of one of the children. Cory twisted, looking for the speaker, listening as the child talked. It was one of the boys. He sounded scared. The words at first seemed garbled. Then they cleared.

". . . it's getting dark and I have to go home. Please let me go home." He began to cry.

Cory jerked back, looking at Matt as the bearded man fell backwards to the ground. Cory stared, incredulous.

The child's voice had come from Matt.

CHAPTER SEVEN

Cars pulled past Lois as she walked away from the revival tent in the moon-bright field. Drivers, calling through open windows, asked, "Want a ride, Lois?"

She'd smile, shake her head, say, "No thanks. It's only a mile. I thought a walk in the moonlight would be fun."

Five times she had to explain, while to the others who knew her, as almost all of them did, she waved a good night. She had been Dr. Tyler's office nurse since his wife-nurse died seventeen years ago, and there were few people at the revival tonight that had not come to Dr. Tyler for help sometime in those seventeen years. A lot of them were regulars, coming in at least once a year for their physicals.

Dr. Tyler still occasionally made a house call, if the patient were too ill to come to the office, and most of the time Lois went along. She knew where everyone lived, and if they had a problem she knew that too. Most of them got along with their lives without too much happening.

She loved Dr. Tyler with the kind of warmth that made her happy just to see him. He was a no-nonsense kind of guy who said pretty much what he thought, but most of his thoughts were of the gentle variety, and so Lois loved him, loved her job. When she started working for him she'd been thirty-one, childless, unhappy, married to an alcoholic who was unable to keep a job. Without experience to back her up, Dr. Tyler gave her the chance to become his nurse.

"You'll do all right," he said, handing her an orange and a hypodermic needle. "Try giving this orange shots that won't make it flinch and bite and kick, and you'll have had enough experience to begin. As long as you're alert and sympathetic to the needs of the patients, you'll make it all right."

She had learned to give the shots. She had kept the orange in her refrigerator until it collapsed. An odd attachment had formed, and she talked to it, half-humorously and half-seriously, as if it could hear. For two months it was a willing patient, then it shriveled. She wrapped it and put it into the freezer and it was still there. Sometimes she and the doc laughed about the poor old orange.

Her husband had died of cirrhosis of the liver five years later. Nobody was able to stop him from slowly killing himself. So many people said at the funeral, trying to comfort her, "It's good you never had children." She didn't feel that way. She wanted children, and hadn't been so fortunate. But after Carl was gone, she never found anyone else she wanted to marry, and her maternal instincts were partly fulfilled by a variety of pets. And then totally fulfilled by her nephew, Cliff.

Lois cut across the field to avoid having to explain to any more people that she had just wanted to walk tonight. When she had started to the revival meeting, it was still light, that time of a summer evening just moving into twilight. When she was a kid she'd done a lot of walking to and from activities in town. She and her friends had walked over to the ball games, they'd walked to the various places that sold ice cream and soft drinks. They had ridden too, a dozen of them piling onto whatever car was available. But tonight she'd had an urge to get out into the clean, soft air of the summer night and walk.

At the corner of the field she came to a couple of strands of barbed wire, drooping from leaning posts, and climbed through, holding her skirts carefully away from the barbs. Once through, she crossed the ditch, crossed the road and entered the graveled lot of Lane's place. It was dark tonight except for the neon sign that advertised beer. At the back of the club she saw, when she had passed by and found the path through the trees, a light shining out onto the hillside from an open window. She knew the owner of the club only because he had come to see the doctor a few times, and because she had something in common with him. Both of them had a missing child.

She walked on down the path toward town. The narrow, shaded path was used by many people who preferred to walk to Lane's place for their beer and a little companionship. Cliff used to walk it, to see playmates whose backyards joined the path.

As she walked into the shadows beneath the trees her feelings turned sad. Depression had not been a very constant companion in her life. She had felt guilty and depressed for a couple of years after Carl's death, because she kept telling herself that if she had handled things differently maybe she could have helped him stop drinking, if she hadn't been so forgiving all the time. Maybe she should have threatened him with divorce. Maybe she should have stood up against his behavior more. But one day Dr. Tyler said to her, "Haven't you flayed yourself enough, Lois? Each of us is responsible for our own actions, once we reach the age of that ability. Your husband was an adult. He was fifteen years older than you, wasn't he? Then his habits were already deeply entrenched when you met him, whether it showed or not. Get on with your life."

Living alone, she had gladly taken in her nephew, Cliff. He came to her four years ago, a little skinny kid ten years old with hair so blond it was almost colorless, and eyelashes to match. But his eyelashes were long and thick and tipped with brown, so that he had a Kewpie doll look. She had seen Cliff at her mother's, his grandma's, off and on since he was two years old, and she adored him. She had taken care of him when she could, when her mother was feeling unwell. With his parents off doing whatever parents do when they're searching for themselves, Cliff needed love. Lois gave it. When Grandma grew too ill to give him good care, Cliff came to live with Lois. He had been with her only a few weeks when her mother died. Cliff and Lois were alone. Her brother, Cliff's absentee dad, came to the funeral like a stranger. Then was gone again. He didn't write or call.

"Maybe you're lucky," Dr. Tyler said.

Maybe, she thought. Maybe she could stop waking up in the night, cold with dread that Max would come and take Cliff away. She didn't worry so much about Cliff's mother, Dallas. She had deserted Cliff when he was a baby.

Cliff seemed happy with her. He had a home, a bicycle, a dog, friends, and a school he felt at home in. He laughed, talked, and ate anything Lois cooked. She loved cooking for him. She loved seeing him on the floor in front of the TV when it became too dark to play outside, with his arm around his dog. She loved seeing him asleep in his bed, the dog beside him.

One year later he was suddenly gone. One warm summer day he got on his bicycle, called good-bye to her, and he rode out of sight toward Nina's, the dog at his side. He was going to help at the shelter, just as most kids in town did at one time or another. It was becoming a town custom. Almost every boy or girl who wanted to spent an afternoon occasionally working at the shelter. They cleaned, fed, watered, petted. Mostly, Lois thought, they petted. But it was good for them and she was fully in favor of it. Nina, who had started the shelter only a few years earlier, taught the children that animals had feelings. They felt pain and they felt sorrow. Cliff's own dog, a little beagle he had brought home from the shelter one day, ran alongside the bicycle.

The picture had remained with Lois all during the long three years since. Cliff, his white-blond hair in a crew cut, riding his bike, his narrow little rear only occasionally touching the seat as he pumped wildly, and the little dog running alongside with that happy grin on his face. The two of them, happy, safe. They lived in a town where nothing would hurt them. Kids roamed freely through the wide, tree-lined streets. There was no danger in Cliff and his dog going the half-mile or so over to Nina's to work for an afternoon.

Why hadn't she remembered that one year earlier Lane Yardley's son had disappeared? And one year before that the daughter of Megan Davis also disappeared? Both children had gone to spend an afternoon helping Nina at the shelter.

She hadn't thought of them because those two kids were runaways. Karen Davis, who lived alone with her mother, had reached a rebellious thirteen. She was mature for her age, and looked fifteen. She had run away. Probably with some guy who had stopped in at Lane's place.

Willy Yardley, a boy tall for eleven, had run away. To find his mother, it was rumored around town. His mother had run off too, with a liquor salesman who came to Lane's place regularly. She had gotten tired of being a barmaid, the rumors claimed, and one day she was ready, with her suitcase packed, and she'd left. Left Lane Yardley and their son Willy. A few months later she sent them a postcard from Chicago.

One month later, after school was out for the summer, Willy had followed her, the rumors claimed. Only Willy was never heard from again. The police contacted his mother, and she had not seen him nor heard from him.

If Willy ever found her, Lois had not heard of it.

But on that day she watched Cliff ride off with his dog happily running along, she had no premonition that she would never see the child again.

When Cliff wasn't home by dark, Lois called Nina.

"He left two hours ago, Lois," Nina said. "He and his dog."

Lois waited a while longer, standing in the front yard, looking for Cliff. Maybe he had stopped to play.

The moon was full that night too, just as it was tonight. She had watched it rise above the trees east, a big round ball of red that looked like an enormous drop of blood. It gave her a terrible feeling. As it peeled away from the trees it grew lighter and smaller and, sailing free, its light shone almost as brightly as the street lights.

She called the police that night shortly after she called Nina. Her feelings of worry increased with each passing minute. She heard the tick of the clock as she waited on the porch. It was the same clock that had sat on her grandmother's mantel seventy years ago, and always before now it had been a comfort. But that night, with the moonlight on the porch, the ticking of the clock counted away moments of life, bringing death nearer, nearer.

The anguish stayed with her, dimming only slightly in the three years since. The anguish, the wondering, the hoping. The police said he had run away. There were no indications of anything else. The kid was gone, the bike was gone, and, most revealing, the dog was gone. If something had happened to Cliff, Thomas told Lois, then the dog would have come home.

Then why, she demanded, aren't they more easily found, since the kid had a bicycle and a dog with him? How many kids and dogs are wandering along the highways? Why would Cliff leave? He loved it here, he really did.

Thomas tried to sympathize. He came up with all kinds of possibilities. Maybe one of Cliff's parents came and got him. Saw him on the street, took him, his bicycle and dog into the car, and left. Or maybe kid and dog went out to the interstate and got a ride with a trucker, and set off to find his parents.

Lois didn't think Thomas believed it himself, but he had to put something on the police report, and so Cliff had been listed as missing. A runaway.

Seeing Patrick tonight had brought it all back, so painfully. She didn't want to be with anyone, she only wanted to walk and think.

Patrick hadn't killed his family. She knew that if she knew anything at all. She had said so last year, when it all happened. When she expressed her opinion Thomas told her, "I agree, Lois. But you know, that's what people always say, if they know the suspect, if he's a friend or part of their family, they always say, hey, he's a good guy. He may have a temper, but he would never kill. I don't think Patrick is guilty either, but all the investigators from the sheriff's department and the state police do, and they've got an outsider's viewpoint. They're looking at evidence and facts. Me, I just want to talk to him, and get his story."

She tried to see Patrick as a killer. What did she know about him? He'd been coming to Dr. Tyler all his life, for whatever shot was needed, whatever vaccination. At six months old he was one of her first patients. She still remembered the feel of his soft little thigh and her reluctance to use her orange piercing expertise on that tender flesh. But she had. He needed his shots. Nervously she inserted the hypodermic needle, and he flinched, jerked back and cried, and she cried with him, trying hard to hide her tears. He had stopped crying as in her arms she had dabbed the injured spot with an alcohol swab and put him back into his mother's arms. "You'll be fine," she told him soothingly, and he was.

The next time she gave him a shot he cried also, but by then she'd learned they all cry, sometimes before the needle is inserted, so it wasn't necessarily her lack of skill. They yelled louder when Dr. Tyler came at them with a needle, so the doctor usually handed it over to Lois.

She knew Patrick, and yet she didn't know him. She had never been around him except at the office, or at a game where she watched him as she watched the other players. He had grown up tall and handsome, young and slim and lithe, and his hormones kicked in and he had started dating. Then one day he killed his mother, father, sister, so they said. Then he disappeared.

Tonight, precisely one year later, he had come home.

Did Thomas know yet?

The path came to a narrow little dirt road that ran between the backyards of houses and the rising hillside. It was used as an alley by the home owners, traveled once a week by the trash truck. Most of the fenced backyards were homes for at least one dog, usually more, but Lois immediately noticed something odd. None of the dogs rushed to the fence to greet her. None barked from a doghouse or a back porch. The night had grown as silent as if the houses and yards had no occupants.

At the end of the block the dirt road turned left and became a driveway. Lois followed it to a street. She saw a few lights on behind drawn blinds or draperies. Moonlight touched the pavement in spots and sprinkles between trees. Street lights on the corners helped little more than the moonlight. The town had a closed look, all occupants either asleep or withdrawn into their own private places. Her footsteps seemed to ring on the sidewalk, and she began to walk on the grass.

Her own house was old but solid and in good repair, built back in the twenties by a family her grandmother might have known. It was a white, cottage style with a porch crossing the entire front and wide wooden steps rising in the middle. As she did every year, she had brought out most of her houseplants, so the porch was like an outdoor living room, with stands containing plants placed between welcoming wood rocking chairs. At one end of the porch, now in darkness, hung a porch swing.

It was squeaking erratically, that one small link she had failed to oil, as if the wind were blowing hard, moving the swing just enough to make it squeak. Only there was no wind. Someone was waiting for her, sitting in the dark on her porch swing.

Lois started up the walk toward the steps, then stopped. Goosebumps rose all along her arms.

"Hello," she said.

There was no answer. The porch swing grew silent, as if whoever was there had paused to watch her closely.

She had left the kitchen light on, and the porch light at the back of the house. Inside the house her small dogs were quiet.

Lois tried to see into the darkness of the porch without moving nearer. Perhaps no one was there. Maybe the swing had swayed from some other momentum. Yet nothing could have caused it to swing on its own.

Then she heard someone walking.

The footsteps were rapid and soft, as if a barefoot child ran across the porch. The footsteps came down, crossing the step that squeaked. He became visible in the shadows beneath the trees in her front yard. She stared.

Spiky blond hair, in a short crew cut, like Cliff's, looked ghostly pale in the darkness. As Lois's eyes adjusted the child moved, and a thin streak of moonlight touched him briefly.

Cliff. It was really him. He had come home. My God, Cliff had come home.

She saw him clearly as he came toward her. She saw the faded blue jeans he was wearing, with the horizontal tears in the knees, so much in style three years ago. She saw the green and yellow striped T-shirt, the very same shirt he was wearing the day he disappeared.

He stopped, still several feet away from her, just at the edge of the moonlight that had revealed him so clearly.

"Cliff," she cried, her heart in her throat, pounding, suddenly making her so weak with joy she didn't know if she would be able to reach him without collapsing. "Oh my God, Cliffy, where have you been?"

With her arms outstretched she took a couple of steps toward him.

Then she stopped, a puzzled coldness washing away her delight. Cliff. Exactly as he was three years ago. Cliff, still rather small for his age. Still the size of an eleven year old boy who was short enough she could hold him in her arms and rest her chin on his head.

Still wearing the same clothes. His hair the same.

She didn't move.

Like a stranger the boy stood a few feet away, waiting.

Waiting?

Three years ago he would have run toward her. He would have thrown his arms around her waist and hugged her, and then they would have walked toward the house with him talking so fast and so excitedly she could hardly keep up with his words. Now, the child stood. The child that was Cliff, and yet was not Cliff.

She stared into the shadows where he stood half in, half out, moonlight skimming his hair. He didn't move. She had a sensation of others, farther back in the shadows. Of movements, creeping, sneaking.

Suddenly she was on the verge of panic. Fear, as primitive as the instinct to run, almost paralyzed her.

She began to edge sideways, toward the driveway and the pathways of light that reached from the street light on the corner and the porch light at the back of the house. Step by step she moved sideways without taking her eyes from the figure on the front walk. Behind him she picked up subtle movements in the depths of the shadows beneath the trees, but she couldn't move her eyes from the boy that looked so much like Cliff.

If he moved, she couldn't see it.

She reached the driveway, and then she was running. She passed through the shadowy darkness of the carport, her leg striking the car bumper. She reached the light, her breath short and gasping. She ran up the steps to the little porch at the back and jerked open the screen door. As she fumbled with the lock she threw a quick glance toward the driveway. He hadn't followed her.

She unlocked the door, stumbled through, locked it. The kitchen light was still on, which somehow surprised her. Her two little dogs, a Chihuahua and a pug, came out to meet her, the Chihuahua barking, the pug twisting her little tightly curled tail. Behind them Tom came stretching languidly to rub against her ankles. He was larger than either dog. The three of them slept together in a large basket at the side of her bed. Nothing had disturbed them.

She shushed the barking Chi-chi, then went through the house to the living room where she turned on the lights of the front porch and the one yard light. Located halfway down the walk, it was an imitation of a nineteenth century lantern, on a six foot metal post, and it lighted the walk from the porch to the street. It, and the porch lights, lighted the entire front lawn and part of the yard at the end of the house. Shadows beneath the trees were absorbed by the lights.

No one was there.

It was as if she had imagined the whole incident.

CHAPTER EIGHT

The car pulled up close to Cory and Matt, the lights so bright they hurt Cory's eyes. Nina and Gram got out of the car and came running. Nina dropped to her knees at Matt's side. Cory scooted back out of the way and stood up.

"The trap is off," Gram cried. "How on earth did you get that trap off, Cory? Has Matt been up?"

Cory started to answer. He pointed toward the deep shadows beneath the trees. He wanted to tell them about the kids. But they were too busy to pay him any attention.

Nina tried to lift Matt. Matt groaned again and moved. Slowly, he sat up, Nina's arm behind his back. His head hung forward, beard touching his chest. His left hand went to his forehead, then dropped again.

Nina stooped over him, Matt's wounded arm supported carefully in her hands. The wounds were dark brownish-red with drying blood. Drops of liquid blood oozed out, like red tears. The hair on his arm had matted.

Cory turned his face away. He hadn't been able to see the wounds so well in the dark. The trap's long teeth had been embedded. Now the wounds looked like bloody tracks that disappeared down Matt's arm into his fingers. The trap lay in the grass on the other side of Matt, closed, its teeth snapped together like the teeth of a crocodile. It still was such a black menace Cory couldn't bear to look at it.

With her foot Nina nudged the trap away.

"Matt, can you hear me?" She spoke loudly in his ear, as if he were deaf. "These wounds are terrible, Matt. We need to get you to a hospital."

He shook his head. "No. No."

He tried to rise, but fell back weakly. With his left arm he pushed against Nina, as if trying to shove her away.

Halley said, "No, no hospital. He'll never allow that."

"I'm all right," Matt mumbled, as if his mouth were filled with blood, too. "Just get away and leave me alone."

"You need help," Nina persisted. "You caught your arm and hand in one of your own traps, Matt. You could get an infection."

"I'm all right! Just go away and leave me alone. I'm going upstairs . . ."

"He needs the doctor, at least," Nina said aside to Gram.

"No! Goddamnit! No . . . doctor . . ."

"He's already been called."

"Get the hell away from me," Matt mumbled thickly, and shoved Nina. She fell away, but caught and steadied herself with her hand on the grass.

Matt struggled to rise, then he drew a long sigh and sunk again to the ground. His eyes closed, and he looked as though he had gone to sleep.

"He's lost consciousness," Nina said. "He must have lost quite a lot of blood."

She took off her belt and drew it tightly around Matt's arm just above his elbow.

"It doesn't look as if he's bleeding a lot, though." She looked down, at the dark drips of blood on the grass, at the trap, and back up at Cory. "How on earth did you get the trap off all by yourself, Cory?"

"I didn't," he said. "Some kids did."

"Kids?" Gram asked. "What kids?"

They stared at him. Before he could answer another car pulled into the driveway and stopped behind Nina's car. A door slammed. Dr. Tyler came toward them carrying a black satchel. He was not very tall, as Cory's dad and Matt were, and he always looked as if he were walking fast.

Gram and Nina both moved back.

Dr. Tyler patted Cory's cheek.

"Been standing guard, eh, Cory? Good."

Dr. Tyler bent over with his stethoscope and began listening to Matt's chest.

"He was up just a minute ago," Gram said. "He doesn't want to go to the hospital. He'd never consent to that."

"Got caught in his own trap, huh? How on earth did he ever allow that to happen? He sounds fine. Heart strong. Let's see about his blood pressure."

Cory was aching to tell them more about the kids, but he stood back, silent, rocking from one bare foot to the other. Waiting. Waiting for someone to ask him about the kids.

THOMAS HAD COVERED the town from Spring Street to Clover, the outer streets on the south, east, and north side. He hadn't seen a sign of activity. No one was walking across a yard or sitting on a porch. He aimed the spotlight between houses, and deep into the shadows of trees in empty lots. No one. No movement, except that once a cat lifted its head and its eyes reflected the spotlight for a moment before it disappeared into the grass again. It was as if the children had evaporated.

As the cars began to arrive home from the revival meeting he swung away from them to Reed Road, from which Nina's private driveway branched. As he drove closer to the Reed house he saw the cars parked in the driveway and the one with both front doors open and the lights on.

In the full glare of the headlights a small group of people seemed to hover over and around something on the ground. Then he spotted Doc Tyler's car. And the other, a small sedan, was Nina's. Something was wrong here.

Thomas swung the patrol car into the driveway behind Doc Tyler's car and stopped.

Nina and a little boy about Rudy Niles's age rushed to meet Thomas.

"I'm so glad you're here, Tom," Nina said.

"Just doing a little bedtime patrol. What's going on?" he asked.

Nina started telling him something about needing help with Matt when Doc Tyler signaled with an arm wave for him to come nearer. Tyler said as Thomas approached, "Whoever said the police are never there when you need them?"

"Matt got caught in one of his own traps," Nina said.

Cory breathlessly said, "Some kids took it off."

It was the remark about kids that settled foremost in Thomas's mind. He took a better look at the boy, and saw he was the Reed's step-grandson, Cory. He lived with his dad, David Thane, and his stepmother, Rachel, right next door to the Niles's house. In a dark little corner of Thomas's mind something which never believed in coincidences attempted to make a connection. Kids there, and kids here? And once, in front of his car, halfway between? Coincidences bothered him. He could never accept them as just accidentally happening. If the kids had been on the street, at the house, where Cory lived, and then here where Cory actually was, there must be some kind of connection. There must be a pattern emerging, but he just couldn't see it. The connection might not be Cory, but something else. Of course the kids Cory mentioned might simply be some local kids. No, it couldn't be. None lived in the area, now that Patrick Moore was gone, and his sister dead.

Thomas wanted to ask Cory about the kids, but didn't have time at the moment. Later, he promised himself.

With long steps he approached Matt. Dr. Tyler stepped back. He folded a blood pressure sleeve and tucked it back in his black bag, all the while talking.

"Doesn't want to go to any hospital. Doesn't want any help. Just wants to be left alone. Matt's always thought he could live in this world without help. Never needed it, doesn't need it now. How'd you ever stand him so long, Halley?"

It was the kind of lighthearted question that required a joking answer. Halley said nothing. Thomas saw her face in the glaring car lights, and she appeared fixated on Matt, as if nothing else were alive for her. She stared at him intently, but she looked frightened.

Matt, dressed in black denim, wearing a black shirt, probably to make himself less visible at night, was struggling to sit up. He wobbled and almost fell. Halley became more alert and put her arms behind his back to help him.

"His vital signs are all right," Dr. Tyler said. "He doesn't appear to have any broken bones, by some wild chance. If we could just get him into the house, where I could cleanse and bandage his wounds, he'll be all right."

"I don't need help," Matt muttered, hardly able to hold his head up. He held his right arm at an awkward angle from his body, and Thomas could see that it was bloody and pierced in several places from his elbow to his hand.

"What happened to you, Matt?" Thomas asked as he put his hands under Matt's arms and lifted. At about five-six or seven Doc Tyler was too small, and at fifty-five or sixty too old, to handle Matt. But Thomas was close to Matt's six feet two or three, though not as muscled. Grunting and heaving, he got Matt to his feet. He felt like dead weight. Folks were talking again, too many at once. There was something said about getting caught in a trap. Something more about being stubborn.

Most of the conversation came from Dr. Tyler, who had a point of view different from Nina or Halley.

It must have been a shock for Halley to find her husband with one of his own traps on his arm. Thomas himself was wondering how it could happen to someone so experienced handling traps. It was like an experienced hunter shooting his own foot.

Cory pranced around, a little kid filled with energy and excitement. He wanted to help and didn't know how. Thomas caught a glimpse of the trap on the ground. A black hazard.

Half-carrying, half-dragging Matt toward the door, Thomas grunted, "Those things are against the law, Matt, you damn well know that. Illegal. Times have changed. People don't own the wild animals the way they used to." Matt wouldn't give a good goddamn that it was against the law to use those high-powered steel traps. So he caught himself in his own trap, huh? Justice had a way of its own sometimes.

He paused for a better hold on Matt, pulled Matt's good arm around his neck, and hoisted Matt's almost totally limp body up and started carrying him toward the house. It was no doubt the first time Matt had been carried since he was a baby.

"What's the easiest way to a bed, Halley?"

"There's a daybed downstairs—" Halley started to say, and Matt interrupted, demanding in a mutter, "My own room. I want my own bed. I'll be all right. I can get there."

"Sure. Sure you can," Thomas said, with a touch of sarcasm. He'd go to his own bed and die there, probably, his arm a mass of infection. "What you oughta do, Matt, is let Doc call an ambulance and send you to the hospital."

He felt Matt stiffen against him. "No. No!"

Matt began trying to walk, to support himself. Thomas felt the trembling weakness of the man's body. The sudden lack of healthy mobility. Last week he had seen Matt Reed at the local sport shop, and he'd looked as strong and as well as he ever had.

"You out hunting tonight, Matt?"

Matt breathed heavily. He tried to answer, but his voice failed, ending in a faint moan.

"Checking your traps?"

They reached the steps. Thomas got a better grip on Matt and lifted, his right arm around Matt's body. Half-carrying the man, he concentrated on getting him upstairs.

Halley led him across the back porch and into a large kitchen. It was the first time Thomas had been in the Reed house. From there Halley led the way into an inner hall and to an enclosed stairway in the back of the house. The stairway looked too narrow and too steep. Thomas paused, looking up. Matt's head had drooped, his chin resting against his chest. He was dead weight again. It was as if Matt were going in and out of consciousness.

"Just let him down here, Thomas," Doc Tyler said, "And we'll get an ambulance. We need a stretcher and couple of men."

Matt roused again, half-lifting his head. Without answering Doc's command, he lifted a foot and placed it on the bottom step. He pulled up to the second step. Thomas moved with him. The man was determined that no ambulance attendant would get close to him, and if he were that determined, Thomas would help him to his room. With Tyler trying to help on the other side, they started climbing.

They reached the top of the stairs, with Matt still struggling to lift one foot after the other. At the top, with Thomas's own breath too short and fast for questions, Halley pushed in front. The hall was twice as wide as the stairwell. It was long and opened at the other end onto the balcony and stairway down to the front of the house. Doors were closed along the way, except for two on the left. The first opened into a bedroom where the bed had been used, the covers thrown back. Thomas saw a small pair of blue jeans over the foot of the bed. Cory's room. It was the first time Thomas noticed Cory was dressed only in a T-shirt and undershorts. The second room was a bathroom. Halley motioned them on, toward the front.

Matt groaned faintly, his head drooping, his feet beginning to drag. Thomas felt a sudden concern. Wounds on a man's hand and arm, even deep wounds, should not have caused the problems that Matt seemed to be having. Yet Doc said his vital signs were good. What was wrong?

Matt's room was the last room on the right, just before the back hall divided into the wide balcony over the entry below.

"This is his room," Halley said, and the way she said it, and the way the room looked, with no sign of a feminine presence, Thomas knew Halley did not share the room with him.

It was a large room, with a black leather recliner in the corner of the inner wall, a reading lamp beside it. Against another wall stood a desk, a large dresser and even larger chest of drawers. Two doors opened in the wall opposite the foot of the bed. One led into a private bathroom, the other into a closet. Both doors stood open.

Halley rushed to the bed and turned back a bedspread and light blanket. The sheets were white and fresh.

Matt sank back onto the bed with a long sigh, his eyes closed.

Thomas's arm and neck ached, and he stood quietly a moment regaining his strength. Matt looked now as if he had gone suddenly and without reservations to sleep.

"Better cleanse that wound," Doc said in a low voice, as if talking to himself, or to Lois, his nurse. "Get some antiseptic on it. Give him a shot of antibiotics. Think we can get him undressed and into pajamas, Halley?'

Halley looked at Doc with something in her eyes that made Thomas feel sorry for her. He understood. Matt would be furious if his wife undressed him like a child, and in front of everyone.

Halley quickly moved to Matt and began removing his shoes and socks. She stuffed the socks carefully into the shoes and pushed them under the bed. Then she looked at Tyler.

"He wouldn't want his clothes taken off. Can't he just lie here on the bed with his clothes on? Until he wakes up and can do it himself?"

Dr. Tyler shrugged round, chubby shoulders. "I don't suppose it'll hurt him to sleep in his clothes. I'll get his wounds cleaned and bandaged."

Thomas looked at Matt's hand and arm. The metal teeth of the trap had gone through the palm in several places, and through the wrist and lower arm as if there were no bones. Dr. Tyler picked up the arm, manipulated the fingers and wrist. By some oddity, it seemed the bones were unbroken. The wounds were closed, caked with dried blood.

"Doc," Thomas asked, his voice low, hoping Halley, who had moved away from the bed, wouldn't hear "would those wounds cause this debilitation?"

"I'm sure he must be in mild shock, although there are no physical symptoms. We'll get him comfortable, cover him up, and check on him frequently through the night," Dr. Tyler answered. "Outside of that, who knows? Different people, different reactions. I can tell you this. He ought to be in an emergency room somewhere, getting his hand x-rayed. But I felt his wrist and arm, and I think the teeth missed the main bones. I don't think anything's broken. And if the man doesn't want to go tonight, I guess it's his hand, right? He'll be better tomorrow."

Thomas looked about at the room. He'd hate to wake up here, with this massive furniture, in this gloomy atmosphere. A table lamp beside the bed and the ceiling light were on. But the ceiling light, encased in a dark glass globe and hanging from a twelve foot ceiling, didn't help much. The lamp was dimmed by a Tiffany shade that must be the real thing, probably purchased in the nineteenth century. It was beautiful but didn't emit much light.

"Tomorrow," Dr. Tyler said, "he may wake up with his mind changed. If he doesn't want to go to the hospital, he can come down to my office. I'll x-ray his hand and see if there's any bone damage. If he won't come to the office, then I don't suppose this is any life-threatening situation. Many creatures in the past, human and animal, have survived pierced flesh and broken bones without help."

Tyler pulled up the blanket to cover Matt to the chest. He placed the wounded arm on a towel Halley handed him, and began to cleanse away the blood.

"His heart is sound and his blood pressure normal. If I thought he was in danger, I'd call for an ambulance without permission. Meantime, let's just let him sleep, he'll be all right. Has he been doing anything lately to make him exceptionally tired, Halley?"

Halley stepped closer. "No," she said. "He watched sports on television this afternoon. He stayed around the house all morning. Rachel and David ate Sunday dinner with us at noon, then they left on their trip. After supper Matt went to his room and Cory and I went to the revival meeting. I didn't even know that Matt was going out to check his traps."

That was the longest speech Thomas had ever heard from Halley Reed. Of course he wasn't around her much, either. But to him she had seemed a very quiet woman who stayed at home, had few friends. She wasn't in any of the ladies' groups that he'd heard of, but she and Matt did attend church every Sunday. Thomas mostly saw her working in her yard. She had some nice flower beds she seemed to enjoy spending her time in.

Halley left the room, edging toward the door at first by degrees, as if she didn't know whether to stay or leave. Then she murmured, "I'd better get Cory back to bed," and with that excuse, went on out to join Cory and Nina in the hall. All three went out of sight toward Cory's room.

Thomas stood by the side of the bed while Doc cleansed Matt's hand and wrist and smeared on some white stuff out of a tube. He stayed while the bandage went on snugly, enclosing the hand and arm from fingertips to elbow. Then he watched as Doc pushed the sleeve higher and gave Matt a shot.

Thomas flinched, but Matt did not. The man's head lay with cheek against the pillow. His eyes were closed, his mouth slightly open. His chest rose and fell rhythmically. In the silences of the room his breathing was clearly audible.

When Thomas and Doc Tyler left the room Nina and Halley waited alone in the hall.

"I've done all I can do," Dr. Tyler said. "Maybe you should check on him every hour or so, Halley, and if he's having any kind of trouble, give me a call."

"I couldn't get the phone to work—"

Nina said, "It's all right. I'll stay here with Halley and Matt, Dr. Tyler. I'll call you if Matt needs you."

"Fine."

Thomas felt a surge of uneasiness. He'd rather not have Nina here, in this house, on this night. Yet he said nothing, because he had no tangible reason. Nothing he could pinpoint. Maybe, he told himself, it had more to do with those damned kids. Just a general anxiety that would pass with the night.

He had to get back out there and take another look for the kids. The only thing that had come to his mind was they must be part of the traveling evangelist bunch. While the preacher preached hellfire and damnation, kids of his entourage were out terrorizing town kids and killing their dogs.

That reminded him. Cory had said something about kids removing the trap from Matt's arm. He had to question the little boy before he left.

"I need to ask Cory a couple of questions, Halley. If he's still awake. About those kids he said removed the trap. And I'll be looking around your place here for a while."

Halley nodded, and Thomas went down the hall, while Nina, Dr. Tyler and Halley went toward the front stairs.

Thomas found Cory still awake, a healthy, alert child whose big eyes didn't look as if they ever got sleepy. Thomas rubbed the boy's head in a friendly gesture.

"How you doing, Cory?"

Cory grinned. "Okay."

"You said something about kids, Cory."

Cory's eyes grew even rounder. Excitement, or a bit of fear, sparkled in their hazel depths. "Some kids came, and they took the trap off Matt's arm, and—and—" Could they be the same kids? No. Taking the trap off Matt's arm was totally out of character of the kids he was looking for. They had viciously killed a dog and fought other children. Why would they turn around and help a man?

"What'd they look like, Cory? Who were they?"

"I don't know who they were," Cory cried breathlessly, as if he'd been waiting almost to bursting with his news, "There was a teenage girl, with long blond hair. Straight hair. And there was a boy, younger, with dark hair. And another one with real short blond hair. Others stayed back away and kind of danced and sang. There was another girl who came close. She had long blond hair too, but it was curly. Long curls, down to here." He measured on his chest. "She carried a big doll."

The same kids.

"You never saw them before?"

Cory shook his head, his eyes round and filled with their innocence and honesty. "No sir, I never saw them before."

"They took the trap off?"

"Yes sir. The big girl and the big boy. The others danced and sang. They went around us, singing."

"How did they act with you, Cory? Were they friendly?"

Cory's gaze darted thoughtfully past Thomas and back again. "I don't know. They didn't speak. It was kind of scary. They hung around a minute, then those two ran in, bent down, and when they ran away again the trap was off Matt's arm. Nina was driving in right then."

"Where did the kids go?"

"Under the trees. In the backyard."

Had they been watching from the dark all the time?

"Thanks, Cory, for the information. Now, you'd better go to sleep. It's getting late."

"Yes sir."

Thomas turned out the bedroom light and closed the door. Then he ran down the back stairs and out into the yard.

At some point Nina had turned off her car lights, and the moon made sharp contrasts between the open areas and those beneath trees. The blackness of the shadows seemed oddly exaggerated.

Thomas went to his car and got his flashlight, but even before he began looking into the shaded areas of the yard he knew he would not find the kids. They had a way of moving fast, of changing places within moments. And they'd had at least thirty minutes to move on. They could have crossed town again.

Their altruistic behavior with Matt didn't fit the profile he'd already made of them in his own mind. Kids who will gang up on other kids and so deliberately mangle a dog do not turn around and suddenly become gentle helpers. Yet he had no doubt Cory had seen the same kids he had, and their description fit the one given to him by Dennis, Rudy, and Jenny.

Something about the gang of kids seemed even more unnatural now than it had before. Thomas couldn't help the eerie dread that accompanied him into the shadows. Wherever he turned, he felt the strange children were grouped silently behind him.

CHAPTER NINE

The yard fence was built of sturdy boards, a stockade fence. It ran down both sides of the enormous yard to the street, and across the back. The front yard was unfenced. Outside the backyard fence, moonlight shining fiercely on faded red paint, was a small barn.

Thomas climbed the fence, his flashlight pointed toward the ground. The night seemed as silent and peaceful as any night, yet there was a waiting quality, a tenseness in him. He still felt as if he were being watched, yet it must be his own feelings of vulnerability, because the eyes he had felt were in the black shadows beneath the trees near the house, now seemed to be in the barn windows, little black squares set evenly in the wings of the structure.

The barnyard hadn't been used in years. Grass grew tall, as high as his waist in places. He waded through, found a small door on one of the wings, and entered.

At first glance it looked as if the interior barn walls were lined with a dark furry carpet. Moonlight cast dim squares on dark, dirt floors. Something small scurried beneath a manger. Thomas directed the flashlight beam at the wall. Animal skins, stretched, nailed on the boards of the walls. Most of them were small, the skin of raccoons and opossum. There were some even smaller. Squirrels, chipmunks. It was as if some madman had delighted in the killing and skinning and then preserved the skins for his private collection.

The corners were littered with piles of junk, boards, old rusted sheet metal where new had replaced a holey roof. Against the manger and leading up into the loft was a perpendicular ladder. He climbed it and shined his flashlight rapidly around the expanse. Bits of old, blackened hay here and there indicated that once this barn had been used to store hay and house horses and cows, perhaps goats and sheep. The family animals. But Thomas lived in Spring Valley all his life except for ten years away at school and work on the city's police force, and even then coming home regularly to see his parents, and he had never known of an animal in the pasture behind the Reed house. The barn had been used for animals before his time. Probably Matt's father or grandfather had kept a small farm.

Thomas climbed down and quickly searched the rest of the barn. Old harnesses hung on inner walls. An old buggy was parked in the wing opposite to the one with the animal skins. It was just an old barn, long deserted. There were no signs that anyone had entered in a long time.

While he was searching the area around the barn, he heard a car leave. Probably Dr. Tyler. He took a hurried last look toward the hill and its cover of trees, out over the long grass that had not been mown in years. The kids could easily have hidden in the grass, but he sensed they weren't there. Whoever they were, they were gone.

He hurried to the fence and along it to a gate that was standing open. His light showed a pathway in the grass leading toward the hills. It had been worn by frequent passage. By Matt, no doubt. It came directly from the hill, across the acre or so of grass, and to the open gate.

Thomas went through the gate and into the short, neat grass of the backyard, walking fast.

As he came up the driveway he saw that Dr. Tyler's car was now gone. Nina approached him from the front of the house.

"Dr. Tyler left," she told him. "He'd done as much as he could. He said to call him if he was needed. Halley thought her phone wasn't working, but it's okay now."

They leaned together against the patrol car. Thomas watched the shadows and the bright areas of moonlight. The night was still quiet, except for the insects that whistled and sawed, and an occasional mocking-bird song from the big red cedar in the backyard.

"I've been looking for some strange kids that showed up in town tonight," Thomas told Nina. "First, they fanned out across the street right in front of me, not long after dark. When I got out they ran off. Then I got a call from Glen that there was trouble over on Spring Street, and I went over there and found the Niles family pretty shook up. The gang of kids had attacked their kids, and the neighbor girl, Jenny, and pretty well scratched up Dennis. But the worst thing was they killed the dog. And I don't mean just killed. It was a vicious act. I was looking for them when I drove in over here."

Nina had turned and was watching him closely. "How many were there?" she said.

"Hard to say. Half a dozen, maybe more."

"And Cory said . . ."

"Yes. They evidently came here, while I was looking for them over in the southeast section of town. But here they took the trap off Matt's arm. It doesn't compute, Nina."

"Do you think they're with the traveling evangelist?"

"That's what I'm going to find out in just a minute. What strikes me as rather odd is that a couple of young kids would even know how to release a trap like that."

"Halley couldn't take it off. She didn't know how. It's an especially vicious kind of trap, the kind that injures, as Matt found out. There's a difficult release system."

"You'd have to have some experience, I would think. And how many eleven and thirteen year old kids have that kind of experience? Yet Cory said they got it off right away, with no problem."

"We drove home early from the revival meeting, and I didn't see any kids roaming the streets. You saw them. What did they look like? I think I know every kid in the area."

"Two kept back in the shadows and I didn't see them very well. But there's a girl about thirteen, with long, straight blond hair. A pretty girl. And a dark haired boy, about eleven. Narrow face, good looking kid. Then another boy about his age, but smaller, with blond hair in a crew cut. And a younger girl, maybe Cory's age, with long blond hair in ringlets, you know the kind of curls." He made a motion with his hands. "Hung down halfway to her waist. She was carrying a large doll every time she was seen. Rudy mentioned her, and so did Cory."

Nina was looking at him with parted lips. Moonlight made her face even more lovely and pale, her eyes large and dark.

"Thomas," she said in a harsh whisper, "Do you know who you've just described?"

He paused, searching his mind for what she evidently saw. He came up with nothing beyond that distant feeling of familiarity.

"Those three," she said, "the girl about thirteen with long straight hair, and tire two boys. They sound like Karen, Willy and Cliff."

Karen Davis. Willy Yardley. Cliff Patison. The faces of the boys were before him again, as clearly as they were in the headlights of the car. Of course. Willy and Cliff. Dennis had sworn the boy who led the gang was Willy, but even then Thomas had not really believed it. Yet now, with the two other names added, their faces returned to him clearly. How could he have not noticed the resemblance? Karen Davis was not so familiar to him, yet the girl he saw in the street resembled her mother, Megan, enough for him to know Nina was right. Cliff, Willy, and Karen. Disappeared from their homes three, four, and five years ago. He had helped in the searches for them. He had finally and reluctantly listed them as missing, files still open.

"It can't be," he said.

"But you described them precisely."

"Yes, maybe, and I know now that those three missing kids resembled the kids I saw. But it's got to be a coincidence. They would be several years older now. They'd look different now. And those other kids, the little girl with the ringlets was a total stranger, and the others were so in shadow I don't even know how many there were. Strangers in town. I'm sure. They . . ." He paused, "Strange thing. Dennis swore the boy who led the group looked just like Willy. They used to be friends. Dennis is a year younger than Willy."

"There's something else, Thomas," she said quietly.

"Yeah?"

"Patrick. Patrick Moore. He showed up tonight."

"What? Patrick? Where?"

"Up at the revival meeting. Suddenly he was just there, standing in the doorway as if he wanted to be seen. There was a complete uproar. The earthquake, first, then Patrick, and Halley fainted. It almost became a disaster. Everything seemed to happen at once."

"The earthquake!" What kind of madness was Nina describing? Patrick in the doorway, an earthquake, Halley fainting . . .

"You didn't feel the earthquake?" she asked incredulously.

"No."

Nina shook her head. "Well, that's what it felt like. The ground shook, and the preacher grabbed his pulpit and stopped preaching and then he stared at the door, and I looked, Halley looked, everyone looked. Patrick was standing there. Then Halley fainted, and the next time I looked for Patrick he was gone."

"I think I'd better go up to the traveling evangelist and have a talk. Did Patrick say anything to anybody?"

"No. He was there, and then he was gone."

Like the kids, Thomas thought.

Thomas opened the car door. Light from the dome looked yellow and sick in comparison to the moonlight. "You're staying here?" he asked Nina.

"Yes. At least for awhile."

"Then I'll check back later, after I see if I can find Pat and talk to Reverend whatsisname."

"Walsh. Dalton Walsh."

RACHEL TURNED OVER AGAIN, trying to find a comfortable position. The motel mattress seemed to swell in the center and droop toward each side. She had examined it before going to bed, just enough to see that it was new. New mattresses always tended to make you feel as if you were lying on a slope, it seemed to her. She wished she were back on her own mattress with the soft, flat pillow top. The trip had looked so good from the angle of her own house, but she hadn't been able to get Cory out of her mind, and the farther away from him she got the lonelier she became.

"We should have brought Cory along," she said aloud.

"Ummm," David mumbled sleepily, reaching over to pat her. "He's okay."

David turned his back to her and twisted into his favorite sleeping position. Rachel turned to her right side, put her hands together under her cheek, and stared at the motel window. The short draperies served also as blinds, and they lacked about half an inch meeting in the center. A streak of light brightened and dimmed as cars drove by and parked somewhere. She heard car doors slamming, people talking, footsteps on the walk outside the one-story motel She wanted to go home, get Cory, and start out again. But, as David said, Cory was okay. He was with Mom, and Dad. They'd take care of him. Was she becoming one of those mothers who couldn't stand to have her kid out of sight? But he was so young. Hardly more than a baby. He'd never been away from home before, not in the two years since she had married David.

The day she met David she had no premonition she had just met half of her future family. She was in her third year as an airline stewardess for Continental, and she noticed the handsome, friendly guy just as she noticed all handsome, friendly guys. She saw them, forgot them. Sometimes she had drinks and dinner with them, and they talked, and eventually parted ways. At that time she had an apartment in Los Angeles.

As it turned out, so did the handsome, friendly guy. He had been on a business trip for his company, and he followed her. Everywhere she turned, it seemed, he was there, grinning.

Finally, she became wary of him. She stopped smiling, and was getting ready to tell him to buzz off.

He spoke before she could.

"You're wondering why I keep turning up, right?" he said. "Well, I promise you I'm no weirdo. Although I suppose a weirdo would promise the same thing, wouldn't he?"

She laughed. "Probably."

He put out his hand. "I'm David Thane. I've seen you before, because I have to do a lot of traveling. But you don't remember me, do you?"

She shook her head. A lot of handsome guys traveled on her runs. As soon as they were out of sight she forgot them. She didn't tell that to David Thane. She waited.

"I didn't think so. I'm thinking of leaving my job and taking a job in some small town back in the middle of nowhere so I can see my son every day. I've been following you because you're so beautiful. I just wanted to meet you. If you want me to get lost now, I'll go away and never see you again."

"I'm Rachel Reed," she answered, something about the big mutt already niggling into her heart. A little boy? She loved children, and wanted a bunch of her own. "I'm from a little town back in nowhere, and I'm about ready to go home and settle down and perhaps get myself a son, or two, or three," she laughed as she told him, as if she weren't serious.

Within hours it seemed they had known each other forever. His parents had divorced and remarried, and his little boy, Cory, stayed with his grandmother when David was out of town. His own wife, Cory's mother, had died of cancer when Cory was only three. He was now seven.

David took her to meet dozens of family members, so many she couldn't sort them out. But the one that mattered was Cory. He seemed even younger than seven. He came to her right away, trusting and needing a mother. He was still cuddly and babyish, yet getting firm around the edges from playing ball and general rowdiness.

They flew back once to visit her parents, and look over Spring Valley. A few months later they were married in Las Vegas, at a chapel, with many of David's family there. Rachel's parents had declined to come, but sent their blessings. She hadn't really thought they would fly out, even to her wedding. Her mother had even stopped driving a car. She rarely left Spring Valley even to go shopping. Only once could Rachel remember getting her mother to go shopping in the city.

It was to buy her senior prom formal. The year of her junior prom they had made her dress, but Rachel had gone into the city with a friend a few weeks earlier and seen the most gorgeous dress in a shop. She had pleaded with her mom to let her go buy it. So finally, together, with Rachel trying out her new driver's license, they had driven the twenty miles to the city.

That day stood out in Rachel's memory as one of the best.

She and her mother shopped, ate lunch, went to a museum and finally drove home in the dark. She treasured that day because she knew it would never happen again.

It hadn't really hurt that her parents hadn't come West to her wedding, because she knew she'd be living the rest of her life barely a half mile away from them. For their wedding present her mom and dad had bought them a new little ranch house on the other side of town. It was brown brick with white railings. It had three bedrooms, two baths, a big yard newly landscaped but with one big old shade tree the builder had left. In Spring Valley trees were saved whenever possible.

There was a lot of room for Cory to play. Room for others they might have. The house could be made larger if they wanted. And no house payment.

David, Cory and she went home right after the wedding, greeted her mom and dad, and then slept that first night in their own house. Dad had even ordered the furniture store to deliver the things they would need to start: beds, chairs, a table, with the stipulation that she could exchange anything she didn't like.

Dad, who'd always seemed to exist in his own private world, who had never been close to her as Mama had, turned out to be very generous. It was his way, she guessed, of welcoming them home. Of saying, hey, it's okay, you're okay. After all, you're okay.

She had never felt loved by her dad. But then, she'd never needed anyone's love beyond her mother's. Her mother's love was so complete, so total.

But she had memories.

Dad had loved, he had worshipped, Coleen. Rachel felt now the same little pull on her heartstrings that she used to feel when Daddy paid all his attention to Coleen, with the long, golden ringlets. "You're my pretty girl," he said to her, while Rachel stood back, totally ignored by him. She felt he didn't like her because she wasn't as pretty as Coleen. She felt maybe he didn't like her because he hadn't wanted another girl. Or maybe it was because she was little, and Coleen was bigger. She was seven years younger than Coleen, and maybe there was something magic about being older.

The lack of attention from her daddy was made up by her mother. Wherever Halley went, she took Rachel with her. In those days, before Coleen disappeared, Halley drove a car. Rachel remembered little shopping trips down to the grocery store. She remembered stopping at the Dairy Queen for ice cream cones. Perhaps those memories came from only one trip, or few trips, because it was on one of those days they came home to find Coleen gone. Gone too was the boy who had come to live with them just a short time before. What was his name? She had not tried to remember his name. In some way he was connected with Coleen being out of their lives, from then on.

In some way he was connected with the silence that came down over their house. That awful, chilling silence that seemed so much a part of her early years.

She had not wanted to go off and leave her mother in the silence of that house. But her mother had insisted she leave, at age eighteen. Halley had seemed actually delighted for her. Go and start your life, she'd said. Go to college. Meet people.

She had gone, but for a while she had worried about Halley being left behind, in that house. There was something about that house . . . *something.*

Now, suddenly, in this strange motel, she felt an urgent need to go back and get Cory out of that house.

CHAPTER TEN

THOMAS STOPPED IN THE STREET AT THE END OF THE DRIVEWAY TO THE MOORE home, his foot on the brake, the engine idling. Moonlight highlighted the roof of the barn in the weedy pasture behind the house, and made a dull star in the picture window at the front of the ranch house. He didn't think Patrick had come home. There was a feeling here, even at the end of the driveway, of the desolation, the emptiness of that place of death. He had felt the same thing the day he'd driven in there in answer to Nina's frantic call one year ago. 'Thomas . . . Thomas, I went to see if Patrick was all right, and I saw blood on the cabinets in the kitchen. It's splattered all over those cabinets, Thomas!"

He had never heard Nina so near to hysterics.

He'd have to return and search the place, tonight. Now that Patrick had been seen, he'd have to take down the 'No Trespassing' sign, go in, look through the house and barn. But for now there was another place Patrick might have gone before he'd come here. If he came here at all.

Thomas drove on. He turned left onto a short street that made a cul-de-sac for two houses. Clyde Moore's uncle and nephew lived there, surrounded by an acre of trees. One of the houses was dark, but the other had a porch light burning.

Thomas parked behind an old Chevy that he recognized as belonging to Donny Moore, an older cousin of Patrick's. The neighborhood was quiet. Not even a television interrupted the silence.

As he approached the lighted porch a deep-voiced dog beyond the door woofed once. Thomas rang the doorbell and waited, looking at the big, brown, furry dog through the screen door. A Saint Bernard, he was wagging his tail and smiling the best he could.

"Howdy, Buster," Thomas said.

HE HAD an urge to reach in and rub the big furry head. The dog reminded him of his own. Buster and he had lived alone these past five years, since his divorce from his wife, Angie.

He felt the same tug of something fine and sensitive within himself, that thing he privately called his heartstring. Angie was a city girl. He had married her there, and then thought he could move her to a small town. She wasn't happy. When he offered to leave with her, she gently but firmly told him no. They had nothing in common, she said.

That was true. They didn't even have a child. She'd been married before, and had one child. But her mother had kept the baby since he was two years old, and even though Thomas wanted Angie to bring the little boy to live with them she wouldn't.

"He's been with Mama too long," she said. "Three years now. I don't want to separate them."

Angie's interest was education. She wanted to go back to school. The last he heard of her she had received her doctorate in something or other. By that time he had to look at the truth. Angie wasn't for him. She had no interest in having a family, and that was his main goal. He wasn't ambitious enough for her. Angie settle down with a chief of police of a town of one thousand people? Angie raise a couple of kids?

He could almost see the funny side. How had they managed to get together in the first place? Those old hormones at work again. A physical attraction that slowly eroded.

SUDDENLY THE DOOR was opening and both dog and Donny Moore stepped out onto the porch.

"Tom," Donny said, putting out his hand. "Haven't seen you in a while."

Donny was perhaps ten years older than Patrick. He was married and had three small children. He worked in an accounting firm in the city. His father, next door, was Clyde Moore's brother. The family had been close.

"Donny, I got the message that Patrick's back in town—" Donny's quick frown brought a pause to Thomas. He could see in the man's face that it was news to him. But Thomas went on, "I figured he would probably come here."

Donny had begun shaking his head before Thomas stopped speaking. "Patrick isn't here. We haven't heard from him since before the murders."

"Could he be at your dad's? Is there anywhere you know of that he might have gone instead of coming here?"

Donny shook his head and led the way off the porch and into the yard between the two houses. Earl Moore, a widower, came from somewhere in the shadows to meet them.

In the moonlight Earl's lined face showed the same expression as Donny's. The head shaking, the questioning look in the eyes. Except with Earl it was stronger.

"That boy," said Earl with fervor, "Is not even alive. Like I told you last year, Tom, you find that killer, and you'll find that he killed four, not three. Patrick wouldn't have done what was done to his family. They got along. Pat wasn't crazy. He was a good boy. Whoever went in there and shot that family, killed Patrick too. I don't know where his body is, but there's plenty of room back in the hills to hide it, you know, and I know."

Last year Thomas explained to Earl that the sheriff's department had used tracking dogs, and had found nothing. Now, Thomas quietly dropped his little bomb.

"Patrick was seen up at the revival tent just tonight. He stood in the doorway, right in sight of half the town."

After a loaded moment of silence Earl burst out, "I don't believe it!"

Donny said nothing. He shoved his hands down into his pockets and stared hard at Thomas.

Then in a soft voice he demanded, "Says who?"

"Nina."

There was no need to mention any other names. In fact, Thomas wasn't sure how many others had seen and recognized Patrick. It was enough for him that Nina had. It was enough for the Moore men, too.

"Nina!" Earl Moore said. "Nina saw him?"

"She saw him."

Earl shook his head, but he said nothing.

Thomas stayed a couple of minutes longer, then he left. He didn't have to search their homes. When they said they hadn't seen Patrick, he believed them.

Megan Davis turned off the television, got up and stretched. This was one of those nights when nothing was interesting. She hadn't been able to get comfortable in her TV-viewing chair. She couldn't get interested in either the TV shows or the new novel she was trying to read. The paper hadn't been at all entertaining, except for "Calvin and Hobbes."

Her head hurt a little, her neck was aching. She hated Sunday nights. The other nights of the week she was fine. The people who came to Lane's place kept her entertained. Bringing them drinks and sandwiches, pausing to talk, the business, the activity of her job kept her alive. But Sunday nights nearly killed her, it seemed.

She went to the kitchen, got an aspirin from the cabinet and a glass of water. She stood looking out the kitchen window at the hillside beyond.

If the moon had ever been so bright before, she'd forgotten when. Except . . . the night Karen disappeared.

The moon was very bright that night. But there had been a few clouds in the sky, and the light of the moon contrasted sharply with the darkness that came when a cloud stood for a moment between her and the moon.

She had walked the streets that night, for a couple of hours, before she'd started driving the streets. Covering the areas Karen might have gone.

Karen had ridden her bicycle that afternoon over to Nina's as she did once every week or two, and Nina said she'd left at four o'clock, just as she always did. Nina had volunteered to drive to meet Megan at the convenience store over on Maple, where Karen usually stopped for something to drink. So Megan had taken the route from her small house two blocks from Lane's place, and met Nina just as twilight was starting. Neither of them had seen anything of Karen, and the girl who was working at the store then said she hadn't seen Karen in several days.

Megan stood with Nina outside the store. Nina looked as worried as Megan felt. Her arms were folded across her diaphragm and she looked at the empty street beyond with a frown between her eyebrows.

A couple of the boys Karen had wanted to date drove in and stopped, driving too fast, acting a little too wild to suit Megan. They were Dale Thom and Roger West, ages about sixteen. Too old for Karen. At thirteen Karen was looking grown up. Like Megan, she had developed early. At eleven she'd worn her first bra. But Megan didn't want Karen to make the same mistakes she had, and wouldn't let her date.

She spoke to the boys as they came near. "Have you seen Karen this evening?"

Both boys at least gave her the courtesy of looking serious.

"No." They looked at each other, and there was nothing secretive there. "No we haven't, Miz Davis," added Roger.

They hesitated, then went on into the store.

"Megan," Nina said, "Let's call Thomas."

Without waiting for an answer, Nina went to the pay phone on the corner of the store and made the call.

"He'll be here in a few minutes," she told Megan.

Trees had been left at the edge of the parking lot on both sides of the corner lot. Maple Street ran north-south past the store, and Pine ran east-west. Pine Street led in a couple more blocks, past two large houses that had been among the first built in Spring Valley, to the square in the center of town. The town's few stores mostly took up only one block across from the square. The rest of the area was filled with houses and large yards. Would Karen have gone to the square, where sometimes kids collected on some of the benches where during the day the older, retired generation sat?

Megan didn't know. Karen had never been late before, except when there was a ball game, or something where there were a lot of kids. Then, Megan couldn't really trust her to remember the time. Even after she got a new watch for Christmas.

"I forgot!" Karen would say. "I forgot to look at the time! So, is that a capital crime?"

Oh Lord. Never in the years of rearing Karen by herself had she thought of a time when Karen would begin to act as if she hated her mother. They had been so close. So close, and so alone.

This was too personal to discuss with Nina. Or anyone.

The streetlights on the corners blinked on. But rising in the east, half-hidden behind fully leafed trees, was the largest, reddest moon Megan had ever seen. The sight of it scared Megan.

"Maybe I should go home," Megan said. "Maybe she's home by now. Maybe she just took a different route. Maybe she went by the square to see who was there. Maybe she got her drink at the grocery store or the Dairy Queen."

"If you think you should go home, I can talk to Thomas."

At that moment Thomas drove into the parking lot. The city patrol car was two-tone brown, with an emblem in white on the side designating it as belonging to police. On top the beacons were blue. But he came quietly. Megan had seen the village patrol car daily since she had moved to Spring Valley eight years ago, and had never seen the beacons revolving. The town was exactly what she had been looking for. The worst crime so far, that she'd heard of, was a fight in the parking lot of Lane's place, one night. Two guys fighting over one woman. They weren't even local people.

Thomas got out of the patrol car. He was not in uniform. There had been a time when Megan felt something might develop between her and Thomas. But tonight it seemed a frivolous wish that had blown away on the wind, suddenly unimportant.

Nina said, "Karen left the shelter around four o'clock, Thomas, and didn't come home. We have driven around and looked. It's getting dark, and we're worried. Megan needs help."

"I'm going home," Megan said. "She might be there by now."

Thomas said, "I'll check in with you later, Megan."

As she left she heard him asking if there had been other kids at the shelter today, or if Karen had been alone.

"She was alone. She came about two o'clock and stayed until four. She rode away on her bicycle."

Megan drove home anxiously and found her house quickly darkening. Even as she went around turning on lights, calling out, she had a terrible premonition the silence in the house would last forever.

She paced the floor. The night darkened quickly.

Thomas came by, and she went out to the yard to talk to him. He hadn't found Karen.

"I'm going to call the sheriff's department, Megan. I'm going back to open up the office—we usually close around seven because there's just so little need to keep it open. I'll get Glen to come in and take calls, and I'll keep looking. It would probably be better if you stay home, just in case we need to get in touch with you."

The phone rang as Thomas backed out of the driveway. She ran, her heart pounding. Was Karen calling her from a friend's house?

"Megan?" Nina's voice said. "I wonder if you need someone to stay with you while you're waiting. Shall I come over?"

She didn't know Nina well. She had met her a few times, and when she'd heard that Nina offered little part-time jobs to students, helping her clean the kennels and groom the dogs and cats, she had driven up to talk to her. Karen was interested in working there occasionally, because she knew other kids who did. It was something Nina had started last summer. "Good for the dogs, good for the kids," Nina had told her that day. Then, laughing, "And good for me too. They really help."

But she didn't want to be with anyone tonight, she wanted to do her waiting alone. She thanked Nina, but told her no.

They had nothing in common. Megan needed Karen's daddy, but she hadn't even heard from him in five or six years.

At midnight, after a deputy from the sheriff's department had come and asked a bunch of questions, after Thomas had been back for more information about Karen's clothes, Megan left the house and started driving again.

She had driven the quiet streets slowly, looking, looking. Had Karen fallen at the roadside? Even as she searched, she knew it wasn't so. It was as if she knew the future.

Karen was gone.

Information about her thirteen-year-old daughter had never arrived. It was as if both she and her blue-and-white bicycle had dropped into a huge hole that closed again.

In the five years since, Megan could hardly bear to stay in the house. But she was afraid to leave, because this was the home Karen would return to. If she ever came back.

It had been a long and lonely five years. She hadn't had ten minutes of easy rest since then. She used to wonder how people lived after a child was kidnapped, or otherwise disappeared. Now she knew. It was hell.

Megan looked at the old black telephone. Karen had hated it. Megan had planned to get Karen a little blue princess phone for her fourteenth birthday, and have it installed in her room, on her own private line. Even though Karen was gone, Megan had bought the telephone. It was still in its box on Karen's bed, still tied with a ribbon, waiting.

Megan picked up the black kitchen phone, and then looked at the clock. It was too late to call Lane. He'd told her more than once that he slept on his night off, starting about 6:00 P.M.

She replaced the phone.

What she needed, she decided, was a drink. Wine almost always put her to sleep within minutes.

She went to the cabinet, stretched tall, and pulled down the only liquor she kept in the house. The wine was years old, and only a small amount was left in the bottom. But it was enough. As she'd always told herself, one reason that she could be successful as a cocktail waitress for so many years was that she wasn't a drinker.

She would marry Lane, if he would ask her. It seemed to her they had a lot in common. First her Karen ran away, the sheriff said, and even Thomas finally agreed. And then Willy, a year later. She could believe it about Willy. He had missed his mother so much.

Lane had missed her too.

Megan couldn't help feeling a little jealous. Even now, now that Sheila was gone and would never be back. Although it was four and a half years since Sheila left, Lane wasn't ready to look seriously at another woman. When he was, he was the kind of man Megan wanted. A one-woman man. The trouble was, would he ever want any woman other than his ex-wife?

She stood at the sink to sip the wine. The taste of it made her wrinkle her nose. How could her customers at Lane's drink alcohol with such relish? She had tasted beer twice and almost gagged on it both times. She had tasted whiskey, especially the nights that followed Karen's disappearance. Sheila and Lane had almost poured it down her. She'd never forget the horrible taste, the burning sensation that followed it all the way down her gullet and into her stomach. She had tried vodka. There was nothing worse on God's green earth. Except, perhaps, kerosene.

Megan set her half-cup of wine down on the counter and went out the back door, leaving it open. She stood on the step a moment, then walked out into the backyard. Trees cut off her view of neighboring houses. That was one of the reasons she had brought her little girl, when Karen was barely five years old, and moved to this quiet town. It seemed cozily isolated from the real world. Her settlement from her divorce left her enough money to buy the white two bedroom house, just big enough for her and Karen. It was surrounded by a big yard, and there were lots of trees and shrubbery on the property lines. And a path past her backyard shrubbery led straight to Lane's place, so she could walk back and forth to work.

She had tried to get work at a few other places around town, before she went to Lane. She put in applications at the bank, the grocery store, and the little restaurant. But a couple of weeks passed, and she was beginning to get scared. There were fifty dollars left in the bank, and nowhere to turn. They had a home, with insurance paid for one year, but nothing else. A moving van had brought the furniture she needed, so they had beds and chairs and a couple of TVs. They didn't have food.

She didn't miss her marriage. It had been one of those romances built on high-rolling dice. She, a cocktail waitress in Las Vegas, was overwhelmed by the attentions of this mature man who had already been married three times, and had five children among his wives. Miles Davis. Successful businessman with a car dealership, and a love of nightlife. He liked her because she was young and cute and didn't drink. He made up for that on his own. After Karen was born he lost interest, and when Megan decided she'd rather live alone than with Miles, he let her go. But he fought her for the money, and all she got was enough for the house.

With Karen in the car, she started cross country. It was a lovely summer, and she ended up in Spring Valley, on a road that petered out in a little town with wide, shady streets, quiet homes, one supermarket, one little bank. One of each thing that was necessary, and nothing else except lots of privacy.

Never in the world would she have guessed that it was here that she would lose her child.

On lonely nights as she waited for Karen to come home she longed for Miles, of all people. She wanted comfort from him, because surely he would care too. But she never contacted him. The police had. Thomas told Megan a few weeks after Karen disappeared that her father knew nothing about her. She hadn't gone to Las Vegas.

Miles sent no message to her.

She hated the way her thoughts wandered back, every time she had to spend an evening alone. Or even as she cleaned up her house each morning, her thoughts wandered. Always going back.

SHE WALKED toward the back of the yard, but stopped, listening.

An eerie sound rose from somewhere far away. At first it seemed a human cry, and then with chills coursing down her arms Megan recognized the howls of dogs.

Nearby a dog barked a couple of times and then attempted his own howl.

Silence fell. Insects, which seemed to fill each night with sound, frogs, whippoorwills, mockingbirds, all hushed.

Megan turned back toward her kitchen door, suddenly uncomfortable being outside. She felt watched, vulnerable, unprotected.

Something leaped from shrubbery nearby and ran across the backyard, and Megan froze. She relaxed as she glimpsed its long body close to the ground. It was only the neighbor's cat, a big fat tom that patrolled her own yard as much as his own. He probably made kittens all over town.

What had frightened him? The howling of dogs? They were quiet now, their chilling cries settling back to silence with that odd moan with which they had started.

Megan had taken only a couple of steps when she noticed someone was standing at the corner of the house. The figure stood still, no more than a dark shadow within shadows. But Megan saw the definite outlines of shoulders, head, and the lighter color of a blouse or shirt. Whoever it was stood without moving. He or she had a clear view of Megan, who stood full in the moonlight.

She started to speak, then paused. She was no longer sure it was a person. Was there a shrub at the rear corner of the house which she had forgotten? If it were a person standing there, wouldn't he say something, at least move? In the years she had lived here she had never been bothered with prowlers. She had never been afraid, until now.

She decided she would go casually back to her door and go inside, as if she hadn't seen whoever, or whatever it was at the corner of her house. It was a form of self-protection. If the person thought he hadn't been seen, he might go on and leave her alone. If it weren't a person, but a shrub she had forgotten, she could laugh about it tomorrow.

But as she reached the step she had to force herself not to run. It wasn't a bush at the corner of the house. She was now sure of that. The drain came down there. She had cut the grass around the metal pipe many times. A flat rock lay in the hole washed out by the rainwater as it rushed through the pipe, and small stones had been uncovered in the soil. There was nothing else at that corner of the house.

She closed and locked the kitchen door, then turned out the light.

Quietly she went to the kitchen sink where she had left the cup of wine on the counter, and looked through the window above the sink.

A girl stood in the moonlight in almost precisely the place where Megan had stood. Moonlight turned her long blond hair silver. Her face was turned up toward the kitchen window as if she could see Megan. There was no smile on her face, but a concentrated frown, as if she were squinting against a bright light.

Megan's heart nearly exploded.

"Karen!" she cried. "Oh, my God, Karen!"

Until now, she realized, deep in her heart she had thought Karen dead. She had never expressed it aloud or even admitted it to herself, but in the deepest privacy of her feelings, she had known Karen was dead. Karen would not have run away. True, she was getting interested in boys, but she was only thirteen, she wasn't dating. She hadn't run away with some out of town boy as the Sheriff suggested.

"Karen!" she called. "Sweetheart, just a minute, I'll open the door."

She fumbled with the lock. The damned lock that had a little tumbler that turned. Why wouldn't her fingers work? Through the glass on the door she saw Karen walk closer to the step, and pause, still standing in the grass. The frown had left her face and a faint smile turned up the corners of her mouth. But her eyes were shadowed and dark, so very dark, as if they had sunk into her skull. Still, she was beautiful. The most beautiful thing Megan had ever seen in her life.

"Karen! Just a minute, sweetheart, I can't open this damned door."

Slowly the chills came. Up her arms, onto her neck, onto her scalp. As if her body saw things her brain refused to see. Slowly she began to realize that something was wrong.

Her fumbling hands finally felt the tumbler turn. She heard the lock click open. But she was staring out the door at the girl waiting for the door to be opened.

It was Karen, her child. But she was still wearing the loose, blue-and-white-checked oversized shirt. It hung over her jeans, the way she liked it. The same shirt. Her hair was exactly the way it looked that last day Megan had seen her, five years ago. Her face was still dimpled and roundish, just beginning to dip in at the cheeks. Her lips were pink and without lipstick. Karen had only begun to experiment, and that day she went to Nina's to help at the shelter, she had worn no makeup.

Karen, come home, was no older than the day she left.

CHAPTER ELEVEN

Walsh said goodnight to each of the people who traveled in his entourage, as he always did. The two maintenance men, Jim Tobias and Larry Ford, traveled without their families. They managed trips home during the month when the Alliance planned on a week's stay in a particular place. They spent winters at home, as they all did. Away from home they both slept in a trailer pulled behind one of the two trucks. It had two separate sleeping quarters, one bath in which the entire cubbyhole turned into a shower with a turn of a knob, one tiny kitchenette, and a place for two comfortable chairs and a small television. Most of their leisure time they sat outside, as did almost everyone. Enjoying the night air.

Jim was a smoker, and was outside having a last smoke. Once, in the beginning of their association, he had apologized to Walsh for his smoking.

Hiding his personal feelings about any habit, Walsh had quoted a bit of scripture, "'Not that which goeth into the mouth defileth a man; but that which cometh out of the mouth, this defileth a man.'"

Of course Jesus was speaking of those who ate with dirty hands, and if Jim ever read his Bible, he knew that. But Walsh's opinion that Jim was taking a form of poison into his body was not going to make Jim stop smoking. He bit his tongue against quoting more scripture. Why make Jim feel guilty? Jim was a strong young man in his early twenties. As time went on and he grew older he'd make better decisions.

This evening the babies were crying. One of his assistants, a young minister named Josh Avery, traveled with his wife, Carla. They had two babies: Tommy, two years old and Greta, six months. Josh was walking outside their RV, bouncing Greta in his arms.

"Why don't you let me carry her for a while?" Walsh offered. He could see the frustration on Josh's face. Since the congregation had broken up and begun to leave Walsh had heard the crying of the children in the RV several yards behind the tent.

Josh turned the baby over to Walsh. Even with only the moon as a light, Josh's face clearly registered his relief.

In another RV, occupied by the secretary, Susan Putman, and her husband, Vance, who was a writer, their little dog, Chipper, yipped in tune with the baby's cry. They also traveled with their cat, who carried the name of Charlie. Charlie was a lady, as Walsh understood. At least she was silent.

Walsh didn't bounce Greta. Instead he started singing softly an old lullaby his mother used to sing to him. Greta hushed immediately.

The baby in Walsh's arms warmed his heart. It helped push away the memory of the evening and allow memories of the past to return. His own daughter was twenty-seven now and had three children of her own. He was delighted that her life was running smoothly, with healthy children, a good home, and a good husband. But at times, he remembered her early years with nostalgia, and the loneliness that had come when all his family was gone and he was alone in the big house where he and Grace had reared them, had been in such contrast to earlier times that he had wondered why God didn't make the human heart more resilient.

He'd closed the house, made an arrangement for the yard to be taken care of, hired the people he needed to help him, and began his evangelistic travels.

He discovered God had put resiliency into the human heart after all. It only took time. Many nights of sleeping. Each night helped to dull the death of a much loved wife. Of parents gone within months of each other. Of the death of one son, and the unsettled life of the other.

His older son, Ruben, had died in the crash of the small airplane he was flying. He'd been an experienced flyer, and nothing was ever determined about what caused the death. He was young, twenty-three, and had no family.

The other son, Drew, had always had problems. It was Drew who broke the window when the ball slipped the wrong way out of this hand, so he said. It was Drew who got the traffic tickets. It was Drew who married a lovely girl, Ann, then lost her and their two children. Drew was into drugs. Ann tired of it and told him she was through. Walsh put him into rehabilitation centers twice. At the present he had a job, and, Walsh prayed, wasn't using anymore.

Eating with dirty hands might not defile a man, but now there were many drugs that did. They changed a good though maybe clumsy and careless boy into a bum.

But it wasn't his place to judge.

"Judge not, that ye be not judged. For with what judgement ye judge, ye shall be judged."

He liked the poetical writing of the King James version.

Walsh walked with the baby around to the back of the RVs. Moonlight softened the landscape. Somewhere in the trees of the hills, not far away, came the mournful howls of dogs. Not one or two, but many.

Hadn't someone mentioned that the young woman named Nina ran a shelter?

As the cries of the children drifted to silence, and the yipping of Chipper hushed, so too the howls drifted away. The night seemed inordinately quiet by contrast.

Walsh was glad when crickets in the grass began to chirp. Katydids in the trees started their buzzing accompaniment. From some of the RVs Walsh could hear the murmur of voices. Television. But those who enjoyed watching shows after the night service kept their sets turned low. Walsh would not have heard them if he hadn't been walking close by.

The baby had drooped across his shoulder. Her breath touched his neck, sweet and warm. He carried her back to the front of the Avery RV. Josh was sitting on the step, his chin supported by his hands. He stood up when Walsh appeared.

Walsh put the baby into his arms.

"She's sleeping like an angel," Walsh said.

"Thank you, Dalton."

Walsh walked away as Josh took the baby indoors. It hadn't been easy for the young people to call Walsh by his first name rather than Reverend, but he had reminded them over and over he preferred it that way and finally they had complied with his wishes.

Back home he accepted Pastor as a title. He still worked at the church during the winter, as an assistant pastor, but he was thinking about keeping his revival on the road year round. They weren't rich, but the Lord provided just enough for them to keep going. They never asked for money, but donations were accepted. Unfortunately, they had to be, in order to move about in this day and age. And donations had been generous lately. He also used money from his own investments. The people with whom he traveled had become his family, and he shared all he had with them.

Everyone had gone inside. Walsh walked in the silence, around the trucks that hauled the equipment, around the trailers and RVs, and around the tent.

He stood at the front of the dark tent. All the lights had been turned out, but enough moonlight filtered into the tent for him to see the dim rows of chairs, carefully arranged for the service tomorrow night.

Walsh turned away and looked across the field to the road. The field sloped slightly downward, and the fence broke to allow for the gate. Beyond, the moon shone brightly on the pavement of the highway. There was no traffic. It was, Walsh had discovered, a dead-end road. It led to the little village of Spring Valley, a sparsely populated town of large lots, acreages, and small farms within the city limits. There was a square in the center of town with benches and a statue of a Civil War general, as so often was found in small Southern towns. Most of the houses had porches, chimneys, and neatly stacked ricks of firewood in the big backyards.

His secretary, Susan, made all the arrangements in advance, working with a secretary from his church back home. Susan told him the field was owned by a widow in town, Maryann White. It had once been part of a farm, but had not been used, except for arts and crafts fairs, in the past twenty years.

Twice a year, in the spring and again in the fall, a large crafts fair was held. Crafts people brought their wares from almost every state in the Union to Spring Valley Arts and Crafts. That was how Susan had found out about it, and decided it might be a good place for the revival.

Walsh seldom paid attention to where they were going next. That was Susan's job. This evening though, out of curiosity, he had asked her.

"North," she said. "Now that summer's coming. We have several places expecting us during the next month."

"How much longer are we staying here?"

"Just one more night."

One more night.

He stood alone now, looking off toward the little town, hidden among the cover of trees. Only the twinkle of an occasional light indicated a town was there.

He wanted to leave. Tomorrow night seemed a long way off.

Yet he couldn't leave. He hadn't finished his job here.

He had never felt this way before. Usually there was a feeling of leaving something or someone well-loved behind. A regret in not being able to stay. As if he left a bit of himself everywhere. As if he had become a part of the people who came to him, looking for God, for Jesus, and finding. The finding was the comforting part. People who went home with the tears of salvation in their eyes. People who had let Jesus into their lives.

But here, tonight, something else had happened.

The youth had desperately needed help, but Walsh couldn't pinpoint his feelings about it.

He felt if he stared through the moonlight long enough, that eventually the boy would reappear. He would be standing there, waiting, as he had stood in the doorway.

He would wait for Walsh to approach him, to speak to him.

Walsh heard the dogs howling again, and he turned toward the sound.

Through the trees he saw a yard light.

On a street below, beyond a line of trees at the edge of the meadow, a car moved. Slowly. So slowly that as Walsh watched it he began to feel there was something wrong. Whoever was in that car was looking for something.

The car disappeared into the cover of trees in the village.

The dogs grew quiet.

Walsh turned and walked. He walked to the hillside on the west, and stood in the cathedral silence of the tall trees, in the edge of a forest that he knew reached at least two miles before it broke for the freeway that curved north and south through the area.

Along that freeway were frequent small towns, and the beginning of a large city. It seemed a world apart from where he stood.

When he came out of the trees and looked back at the collection of cars, trucks, RVs behind the big tent, he saw that all lights had been turned out.

Out on the road a nightclub, closed for Sunday, rippled blue, green, red, and yellow lights, in neon tubes. Walsh walked toward it. He came to a barbed wire fence that sagged from disuse and walked along it. The wires cast thin shadows in the moonlight.

He reached the passage over the culvert between field and road and stood a moment looking at the nightclub. The graveled parking lot was empty, stark and gray in the moonlight.

Walsh started to walk on when he glimpsed the movement of a figure. He stopped.

Someone stood at the corner of the long, log building of the nightclub. Walsh's heart paused a couple of beats. *The youth.*

He appeared to be staring toward Walsh.

Walsh started toward him, then stopped. This person was much smaller, much shorter. It was a child, eleven or twelve years old. As Walsh stared, the figure stepped back out of sight behind the club.

Evidently, Walsh decided, there was an apartment there in which the manager, with his family, lived.

Walsh watched a moment longer, but the club once again looked as deserted as it had earlier.

Walsh turned back toward the tent. He couldn't see his watch in the moonlight well enough to read the exact time, but both hands appeared to be reaching toward eleven or twelve.

He wasn't sleepy, but he should go to bed. As always he could lean against his pillows and read his Bible. It was then, relaxed in his bed, surrounded by silence, that he made mental notes for his next sermon and marked passages in the scripture.

He walked faster, his hands in his pockets, no longer looking for the youth to appear in the moonlight.

Perhaps tomorrow night he would come.

He was wanted for questioning in the murder of his family, people had told him. Patrick Moore, age seventeen when he disappeared one year ago.

He would probably be in custody by tomorrow.

Walsh made a mental note to contact the local police tomorrow and ask about Patrick.

Walsh had reached his RV and was opening the door when he saw the lights of a car sweep past him and brightly illuminate the windows of his RV.

He turned, surprised.

He hadn't heard a car approach, yet it was now pulling alongside the tent. Walsh saw it was a patrol car, with the beacons on top unlighted.

Walsh went back to meet the tall man who stepped out of the car.

CHAPTER TWELVE

THE REVIVAL TENT LOOKED LIKE A DIFFERENT PLACE FROM THE ONE THOMAS had driven around earlier in the evening. All the cars from town and surrounding areas were gone. The tent was dark. Behind the tent no lights were on in the half dozen or so RVs and trailers that were part of the traveling evangelistic service.

Thomas drove up to the east side of the tent, near the end of the truck that hummed with the generator that supplied electricity. He parked, got out. Choosing the nearest RV, he approached the door. He was just getting ready to knock when a voice spoke behind him.

"Good evening, sir."

Thomas's heart felt as though it turned over. He wasn't sure he hadn't jumped. The man standing in the moonlight was medium sized, balding, with a pleasant face slightly on the round side. He held out his right hand.

"I'm Dalton Walsh, evangelist," he said. "What can I do for you, Officer?"

Thomas introduced himself.

"I'm looking for a group of children, Reverend. Do you have children traveling with you?"

"Children? Well yes, we have two." Reverend Walsh smiled. "We seem to travel in twos, except for the bird. A couple of cats. A couple of dogs. Two babies. One bird."

"Babies," Thomas repeated with mixed feelings. He had hoped the children were from out of town, traveling with the preachers. Or they had been drawn by the revival. Perhaps their parents had gone to the revival and left the kids outside to run wild, the way some parents did.

"Yes. One is six months old, and the other is two years."

"Were there any kids hanging around outside that you saw, Reverend? Kids who came with their folks, and then stayed out to play."

"We try to discourage that sort of thing, officer. There were a few teenagers outside. But they were quiet."

"Well, did you happen to see a group of youngsters that ranged in age from about nine or ten to a girl thirteen or fourteen?"

"No, I'm sorry. No one but the older youths. They were sixteen, seventeen. These other children you're looking for, what's the problem?"

"They've been causing some trouble around town," Thomas said cautiously.

"I thought maybe you had come to see about the young man who came to the tent doorway and left again. I was told his name is Patrick Moore. But I expect you've heard about that. About his appearance in our doorway."

He smiled again, that half-smile that seemed to hold sadness rather than friendliness. Yet there was nothing unfriendly about the man's eyes. In the moonlight they were dark. His thinning hair was light brown. The moonlight highlighted streaks of silver. Thomas didn't bother to ask Walsh where Patrick was. He had probably gone on home. Maybe he was tired of being on the run and had come home to turn himself in. Yet even as Thomas told himself that, he felt there was something wrong. It wasn't going to happen. Patrick was wanted by several police agencies in the state. But Thomas only wanted to talk to him.

"How many people are traveling in your group, Reverend?"

"Just call me Walsh, please. It's easier to say. Also, I believe that only God is Reverend. Let's see," Walsh cradled his chin thoughtfully. "How many in the group. There are two assistant pastors, young men learning. The wife of one, and their two babies. The other isn't married. There is my secretary, and her husband. There're the ones who have the little dog and the bird. There are also the two men who handle the tent, the generator and that sort of thing. And there's the choir director. She plays piano and leads the singing of hymns. She has a dog and the cats. Mrs. Sampler, the choir director, has grown children at home. And . . . well, I'm sorry I can't help you."

"If you don't mind giving me a statement about Patrick, then I think I can go away and leave you alone, Rev . . . Walsh. If you'd come over to my car, please? I have a small recorder there."

"Certainly."

The statement didn't amount to much. It seemed that Walsh had seen no more than Nina had seen. The puzzling thing was the sensation of an earthquake.

"The ground actually shook, huh?" Thomas asked again, looking out over the hood where moonlight changed the color of the patrol car's ordinary light brown to a rich golden brown.

"Yes, as God is my witness, the ground shook. Trembled. As I think back, it was a strange feeling. I've never been in a severe earthquake, but I've felt a few trembles. For a moment there I felt as if I were standing on a rolling ship."

Thomas talked longer than he had intended to. Curious about a man who spent half his time traveling the country with a tent, he quizzed the evangelist.

"It's simple," Walsh said. "When I was a boy I went one evening to a little tent where a man was preaching. And something very warm and loving laid its hand upon me. I thought of it as the hand of Jesus, a calling from God. I was saved that night. I went up to the mourning bench, and I knew my life was going to be different from then on. It hadn't been very satisfying up until then."

"However, it didn't happen all at once. I went on through school, and became a pastor in what I now think of as a regular church," he laughed softly and paused. "I married a lovely woman, and we had three children. Then a few years ago she passed away, one of our sons died, and I was too restless to stay there without her. So I sold everything but my wife's house, our home, and, as the kids say, hit the road. But only in the summer. We hang on by the skin of our teeth, surviving mostly on donations given voluntarily. I don't have the hat passed around for money, but I'm sorry to say we do keep a cup at the door."

Thomas saw, in the soft light of the dome, something in Walsh's eyes that made him think the man had not yet found what he was searching for. He had soft, kind eyes, not brown or blue after all, but a dark greenish grey; but there was a sadness there that, to Thomas, shouldn't have been. Even with the deaths in his family. Weren't most preachers pretty sure of where they stood? Didn't they believe so firmly in a heaven that he would have said his wife and son were in a better place?

He said good night to Reverend Dalton Walsh, the man who didn't want to be called Reverend. On the way out he slowed to read the sign once more. Sure enough it announced Pastor Dalton Walsh, not Reverend, as the evangelist who would be preaching sermons each night of the meetings.

Thomas drove out onto a highway that was empty, and past Lane's place, with the empty parking lot. The sign blinking *beer* looked half sick in the moonlight.

He turned left on the first street and drove beneath the shade of trees that lined the edge of the field. At the end of the quarter mile, the street turned right. Along its treeless strip the driveway to the Moore place turned into the field on the left. Farther on, among tall shade trees, was the Reed house. Thomas turned into the drive to the Moore house.

He stopped, got out and unwired the barbed wire that he had strung across the driveway. The 'No Trespassing' sign was still hanging on the improvised gate, although weather had taken its toll and the letters were not as bright as they were last year.

He drove slowly down the long lane, his tires almost silent on the sandy ground, and parked at the side of the house. He turned the car lights off and sat still, looking and listening. There was a barn a hundred yards behind the house. In the backyard was a shed for gardening tools and lawn mowers. He had searched that shed, as well as the other buildings, many times last year, after the discovery of the terrible murders. Tonight, as then, there were no movements. Not even a bird flew. It was a place deserted, a place still haunted by death.

With the flashlight in hand he got out of the car, easing the door closed without latching it. He stood looking at the windows of the house. Moonlight was reflected off the glass. Curtains inside hung still. No hand pushed them aside, or let them fall back into place. Thomas went to the back door.

He would have been surprised had Patrick answered his knock. If the boy had deliberately stayed away one year, what had brought him back? Thomas had the keys to the house back at the office, but he also knew where an extra was hidden. He had put it there himself, under a loose brick at the edge of the brick steps. It was the key that had been in Clyde's pocket.

He opened the back door, and stepped onto the utility porch. It was a corner room, with windows on two sides. Outdoor jackets still hung on a hook on an inner wall—jackets that had been worn by Clyde, Diane, Shelley, and even Patrick. Back at the office was an inventory of every item in the house. Nothing had been touched after the murder. Thomas himself had locked the house, wired the driveway, left the automobiles sitting exactly as they had been.

In the beginning, he had come regularly to check out the house, to look for signs of Patrick having returned. He only wanted to talk to the boy. The state police and the county sheriff's department had Patrick down as the only suspect in the killing, but Thomas wasn't ready to go that far. Someone had brutally killed the Moore family, and Patrick was gone. But Patrick didn't seem the kind of kid to do such a thing. However, he knew that murder was committed daily by people who didn't look as if they'd ever do such a thing.

There had been three pets left behind, one dog and two cats. Nina had taken them. There had also been a pony, a couple of saddle horses, and a couple of calves. They were sold, and the money used to pay the taxes for the place. Thomas wasn't ready to turn it over to the state. Patrick owned it. And someday, Thomas and many others felt, Patrick would turn up.

"Hey, Pat," Thomas called, and his voice rang with gross intrusion on the silence.

The house had a musty smell, and a feeling of emptiness, like a cave. His voice seemed to come back at him from rooms long unoccupied.

He didn't speak again. He went through the house, using the flashlight. The utilities had been turned off the month following the murder.

Blood had stained the white cabinets in the kitchen where Diane had been killed. Blood was a dark brown stain on the rug in front of the TV where Shelley had lain. Clyde had run to the phone, and blood crusted the walls, soaked the carpet and the phone table. White chalk outlines were still visible where the bodies had lain.

Thomas carefully checked Patrick's room. Nothing had been moved. Every item in the room had taken a permanent place in Thomas's memory. The wrinkles in the bedspread, the baseball glove tossed carelessly onto the bed, were still there.

Thomas checked the closet. Nothing was missing. The same number of shirts that had hung there a year ago were still there.

Thomas didn't bother with anything else. T-shirts in a drawer, socks, underwear. If Patrick had slipped back in for clothes at various times during the year, there was no sign of it.

Thomas left the house and stood in the bright moonlight of the backyard. The barn, in its fenced lot behind the yard, looked big and dark and silent. No animals, no people.

He returned to his car.

Across the field the Reed house had lights on in a couple of second floor rooms and in both front and back on the first floor. He thought he could see that Nina's car was still there, in the shadows of the trees along the driveway.

CORY HUDDLED IN HIS BED, the summer blanket pulled up around his chin. Nina had come and turned out his light, and the only light in the room came through the open door to the hallway. It wasn't enough light, but he didn't get up to turn on the bedside lamp again. He was supposed to go to sleep. But how could he go to sleep when his eyes kept popping open and his head kept thinking?

Also, he kept hearing things.

He heard mostly the sounds of boards creaking. Of the walls making sounds, as if the house were moving. He heard footsteps go down the stairs. He heard a door close somewhere. It sounded far away. Had Nina gone home? Had Gram gone to bed? Or had Matt gotten up and closed his door? Was Matt walking in the halls?

He wished he could see through the walls.

He got up and tiptoed to the window and looked out. Down there, where he had seen Matt, now he saw a streak of light that must be coming from the kitchen. It ended at the place where Matt might have lain. The moonlight began, and the black shadows at the sides of the barn and shed were growing longer. The trees pushed their shadows further east.

Cory went back to bed, and cringed when the bedsprings squeaked. He wanted to make no sound at all. Because if he made no sound at all, *it* wouldn't hear him. It, whatever it was, that seemed even now to be creeping along the halls.

He wished he were home, in his own bed, where he could hear the voices of Rachel and Daddy. *Mama.*

He had never called her that, except in his own thoughts. He wasn't sure she wanted him to.

The voices seemed at first to have been there for a long time, but unnoticed. It was like before, when they first appeared. Outside, in the shadows of the trees.

He began to listen.

The children were coming again. They were talking together, a little girl's voice, more than two or three boys' voices, and the softer, deeper voice of the older girl. But their voices sounded strange, as if they were deep in the walls.

They were coming closer. Their voices were so clear it seemed they were outside in the hall. He began to understand a word here and there, as if they were tossed out from a puzzle. *Hurry,* a voice said. And *where are you?* But mostly the words mingled and became chatters, laughter, and once, it seemed, the sound of crying. The sounds were so varied, and so mixed, that Cory felt as if he were listening to several radio stations at once, all carrying the voices of children.

He slipped out of bed and went to the door.

Yes, the voices were clearer now. He looked in both directions. On his right the hall ended at the door of the back stairway. On his left the hall went past the bathroom, other bedrooms, Matt's room.

It sounded as if the voices came from the front of the house, farther away than he had thought, always one step, one wall, away.

Cory slipped forward. Maybe the kids had come to the front door, and were downstairs now talking to Gram.

As he slipped on tiptoes down the hall he found they weren't downstairs, but much closer, their voices softer than it had seemed from his room. Finally, it was just one voice speaking.

He stopped, listening. A little girl was talking.

The voice of the child came from Matt's room, beyond the closed door.

CHAPTER THIRTEEN

CORY LISTENED INTENTLY, BUT COULDN'T UNDERSTAND WHAT THE GIRL WAS saying.

It occurred to him that he was eavesdropping, and that wasn't nice. He drew back from the door, turned toward his room, and then paused. He was afraid. He didn't want to go back to his room alone. What if the rest of the kids were there, waiting for him? But he wasn't afraid of *kids*. Why would he be afraid of the kids? Because they were out so late at night? Because their parents didn't make them come home and go to bed? Because . . . he didn't know why, but something about them made him a little afraid. He wanted to square his shoulders and say to himself he wasn't afraid. Who, me? No way, Jack. But . . .

Other voices reached him. Nina's. Gram's.

Cory ran to the balcony and looked over. No one was in the entry below. Gram's voice reached him faintly. She was somewhere downstairs talking to Nina.

Cory went down the stairs, drawn by the warm comfort of familiar voices.

Halley and Nina stood on the porch. The porch light spilled out onto the grass and blended with the moonlight. The long front yard was bright in the moonlight, except where the big shade trees grew. The black shadows beneath them gave Cory the same tug on the hair at the back of his neck as the sound of the children's voices.

Nina was getting ready to leave, and Cory had to stop her. He was afraid she would leave, and Gram and Matt would somehow disappear too, and he would be left alone in the big, strange house with the kids.

"Gram. Nina." He spoke through the screen door. A brown beetle crashed against the screen, then roared off toward the light in the porch ceiling.

Both women turned to him as if he'd startled them. Neither said a word for a moment as Cory stuttered to tell them about the kids. His tongue seemed to be flopping around in his mouth like a piece of wet gum. He couldn't get the words out.

"Cory!" Nina said, "It's getting so late for a little boy. Can't you sleep?"

Please listen. Cory struggled to tell them, before they should send him back to his room without listening to him. The words finally came, so fast they ran together like the words of the strange children. "Nina, Gram, there's somebody in Matt's room."

They stared at him. Against the ceiling a beetle buzzed crazily, and in the trees the katydids and jar flies grew noisier, like an orchestra revving up. Gram repeated, "Somebody in Matt's room."

"Y-yes!"

Nina asked, "Who, Cory?"

"It sounds like a little girl." He hesitated. "I heard the kids talking and stuff. I think it's the kids that took the trap off Matt's arm."

Nina asked, "Halley, who could they be?"

Gram started shaking her head, back and forth, back and forth as if she couldn't stop. Her hair was longer than Cory would ever have thought. It hung past her shoulders, thick and grey. Had it been on anyone else, the way it parted on her forehead and hid parts of her face, he would have thought it was like a witch's hair. But he could never think that of Gram.

"We don't know any children anymore, Nina, except Cory."

Nina looked puzzled and doubtful. Cory wondered if she didn't believe him, but suddenly she was coming back into the house, with Gram following.

The three of them went up the stairs, Nina leading. Cory had to hurry to keep from being left behind where the black shadows of the trees reached toward the light on the porch, as if they were slowly widening and growing and would in a few moments swallow the house, Cory and all.

"How on earth did they get into the house?" Nina asked, but Halley, coming breathlessly behind her, didn't answer.

Of course the doors probably hadn't been locked. Entry would have been easy. But she couldn't imagine a group of strange children entering an occupied house uninvited.

She paused by Matt's door.

A girl was talking, softly, steadily, in Matt's room. The voice was light and filled with laughter, but the words impossible to understand. There was no answer from Matt.

Nina looked at Halley and saw the woman had lost all color. She looked terrified. Her eyes were rounded and her cheeks and chin quivered.

"Who is it?" Halley whispered to Nina. "When did she come in?"

Cory stood back against the wall, behind Halley, opposite the door. Nina said to him, barely above a whisper, "You stay here with your Gram."

He took a couple of steps forward, reached out and put his hand in Halley's. Halley backed up and stood beside him, both of her hands gripping his tightly, curled around his small hand as if he were her lifeline back to normality.

Nina quietly turned the knob.

She was surprised to see the bedroom lights were out, the room dark except for a pale filter of moon glow that crossed the room from the curtained windows. The girl's voice came through the darkness, soft as rainwater, the words still strangely impossible to grasp.

As Nina pushed the door open, light from the hall moved softly to displace the darkness. The bed was large and dark, the carved headboard against the wall to her right. Matt was still lying on the sheets, dressed except for shoes and socks. He didn't look as if he had moved. No one stood near the bed.

Nina snapped on the overhead light.

The girl's voice ended abruptly.

No one stood in the shadows of the room, in a corner, or sat in the leather recliner. Puzzled, Nina walked forward into the room and stopped near the dark walnut footboard.

Matt's head began tossing on the pillow, back and forth, as if he were struggling to lift his body but was paralyzed from his shoulders down. He turned his head away from the light, back toward the door, and then back again. A faint groan, sonorous and rasping, came from his chest.

Then with a long sigh he grew still. He breathed deeply and evenly, as if in a sound sleep.

Nina went to the nearest inner door and opened it. It was a large walk-in closet, large enough to hide several children, but no one was hiding there. Another door opened into a bathroom that contained a commode, wash basin and shower. It too was empty.

Nina returned to the bedroom and went to the windows. Both were open, but the screens were hooked. She looked back at the open doorway to the hall, and saw Halley and Cory were where she had left them, Cory's hand still grasped closely in both of Halley's. Nina got down on her knees, beginning to feel like a fool, and looked under the bed. It was an antique bed, high enough off the floor for a man to crawl under, but there was nothing beneath it except a few dust motes.

She got up. If she had been alone when she heard the girl's voice, she would have thought she had imagined the whole thing. But Cory had heard it, so had Halley.

Nina started back toward the door.

The girl's voice started again, speaking clearly, "I told Mama I wanted to go to summer camp, and Mama said she'd—" The words grew faster, like an old record playing on increasing speed. The words ran together, no longer lucid. They poured out in a jumble, and turned from happy to mournful, and then collapse into tears.

Nina stared in horror at Matt.

His lips were only slightly parted. He didn't look as if he were speaking, yet the voice seemed to come from him.

As the voice drifted to silence, as Matt drew another deep breath and turned his head away, his right cheek resting on the pillow, Nina began to feel cold and frightened. She felt if she could only see beyond the veil of reality that covered her eyes, she would be able to see the speaker. Then, she wasn't sure she wanted to.

She looked back toward the hallway. Had Halley heard? She hoped not, she prayed not.

Nina went quickly to the door, forcing a smile to her face, hoping it wasn't as tremulous as she felt it was. As she stepped into the hall she pulled the door softly closed behind her.

"There's no one there," she said in a low voice to Cory and Halley. "It's all right. It was just Matt. He seems to be restless, and moaning and talking in his sleep."

Cory looked at her with wide, doubting eyes. She was afraid he would argue with her, and raise Halley's suspicions, but he didn't. She put her hand on his shoulder and pushed him gently toward his room.

"You go to bed. Both of you. I'll sit with Matt for awhile. If he gets worse sometime in the night, I'll call you, Halley."

"Oh, Nina. Don't you need to rest?"

"I will, later. But for now I'll stay with Matt. Tomorrow everyone will feel better. Both of you, to bed now."

She waited until she was alone in the hall before she opened Matt's bedroom door again. The dread she felt was like taking a step in the dark into unknown territory. At the last moment, she almost turned away. But she had promised Halley.

She opened the door and stepped into the room. She stood at the door, watching Matt. His face was still turned toward the far wall. His chest rose and fell in long, slow, deep breaths.

She closed the door, went to the recliner and sat down. Beside it stood a round library table and a lamp. Reading glasses lay on the local Sunday newspaper.

She didn't like Matt Reed, but she began to feel a little sorry for him. He looked so uncomfortable in the black denim shirt and trousers. She knew he hated being as helpless as he'd been tonight, in which he'd had to have help just to get to his room, and had been unable even to undress himself.

She waited. There was no sound in the room, but the summer insects increased their pace, and the trees outside Matt's windows seemed filled with a constant buzz.

Nina sat still, listening to the soft breathing from the bed. Finally she got up, went to the bed and, working as unobtrusively as she could, unbuttoned Matt's shirt and loosened his belt. She took a summer blanket from the foot of the bed and pulled the corner over him.

SHE TURNED AWAY, thinking of going to see if Halley was asleep. If she weren't, Nina would tell her good night and go on home. Matt seemed only to be sleeping. He must have been talking in his sleep in a tone that only sounded like a childish voice.

But strange children had been seen by several people tonight, so it was possible the sound could have come from somewhere near. Outside, perhaps? From the deep shadows of the trees?

Nina went to the window, but saw nothing in the darkness of the tree's leaves and branches. She had heard nothing for the several minutes she had been in Matt's room. A time that seemed like hours. Perhaps she should go home now, say good night to Halley, and come back tomorrow. Or call, at least.

She went to the door and started to open it.

A child suddenly was crying, "—please, please, don't hurt me. I won't tell anyone, I promise I won't—"

Nina whirled back. The sound came from somewhere near Matt. The voice had been that of a child again, not the same girl, the same voice as before, but a boy. It sounded distantly familiar. The crying went on and on, chilling Nina to the bone. As she drew hesitantly nearer to Matt, it seemed the voice issued directly from him.

Matt began tossing his head, back and forth, back and forth. Then his arms jerked wildly, throwing aside the sheet blanket she had pulled over him. The voice poured from him, soft, words buried in tears, the wailing of a child.

Nina stood frozen, listening, unable to tear herself away. What was going on? The crying of the child was heart wrenching. But what was it? Matt, reverted to childhood? She didn't know.

He suddenly grew still. The voice was gone, leaving a blessed silence. He sighed deeply and appeared to be soundly asleep again.

She stood in the quiet for several minutes, staring at Matt. For the first time she was facing something she did not understand.

She needed to talk to someone. She didn't know who. She turned toward the door, and again was stopped dead by the voice of a different child. A girl, it seemed. She was laughing in delight. Then she began to talk.

"Thank you, oh thank you. She's so beautiful. When did you get her, Daddy? Did you have her all the time, just waiting?" The words grew faster again, and the voice changed.

A boy said, "Yes, I've been up at the shelter. Nina's got a bunch of new puppies only about this big. Mutter is taking care of them. Like she adopted them."

There was a pause. Nina's heart pounded in disbelief. The voice was hauntingly familiar, one of the children who came to help at the shelter, but so mixed with the memory of dozens of voices that she couldn't separate it and put it with a face, a name.

Then the same child was speaking again, sounding farther away, the voice carrying a faintly reverberating sound as if spoken in a cave. "I have to go now. It's getting dark and I have to go now. Aunt Lois will be worried. I have to—"

Cliff? *Cliff Patison's voice?*

Nina stared intently at the man on the bed, seeing no movement of his lips to indicate he was speaking. His face jerked, trembled, quivered.

Where was the voice coming from? She listened and watched incredulously.

The voice of the child grew fast and the words ran together, and then a different sound of crying began, a different voice, crying, crying, in the same hopeless, heart-wrenching way.

She wanted to run away from this, whatever it was. But it was as if the voices were in some way calling out to her.

Laughter turning to tears.

A girl's voice becoming that of a boy's.

As if different children were there in the room.

Laughter. Tears.

Pleading to be allowed to go home.

CHAPTER FOURTEEN

It will never go away. Don't ever think it will go away.

Halley had never allowed those thoughts to form in her mind before. Always, she'd had some hope, skimming the surface of her mind. But the fear—the fear was always there.

Every night when Halley came into this room, this old nursery, where Coleen lived her first five years, where Rachel lived all eighteen of her years at home, and where she too had lived since Rachel was three years old, the fear came for Halley. Prayers had not returned Coleen to her arms. Prayers had not removed the loneliness or the fear. And tonight, at the revival, where she had gone in desperation, the appearance of Patrick was a mockery of her hopes, her prayers, for forgetfulness.

She would have thought he was a ghost, appearing before her eyes only. But others saw him too. Why had she been so sure Patrick was dead? Why had she mourned for him, as if he'd been part of her family? She hardly knew the boy. Riding by on his bicycle, delivering papers, he had stopped at times to speak to her. But that was years ago. Before he had started working for Nina at the shelter.

Halley turned in bed and tried to get comfortable. She hadn't wanted to undress. Like her husband, who had insisted on being left alone, left in the clothes in which he had tramped through the hills as he had done all his life, she too wanted to stay dressed as though night hadn't come. But she had changed from the slacks and blouse she'd worn to the meeting, into a short-sleeved, knee-length cotton nightgown.

She would not be able to sleep. Her mind felt as if it had been stirred with a large spoon, and memories intruded and mixed with all the happenings of the day and night. Rachel and David leaving, waving from the car as they drove away, was like a photograph behind the vision of Matt, on the ground in the moonlight, with that ugly, metal trap on his hand and blood, looking so black and unnatural in the moonlight, turning the grass black. It was as if Matt didn't have red blood, like everyone else, but a substance that was viscous and black.

Her feelings about Matt were as mixed as her thoughts. She had slowly come to feel isolated from the man she had worshipped. Alone, she had lived in the big house he had brought her to when she was a young bride. Alone, she had stayed in the room that was Rachel's, when Rachel was little more than a baby.

The old nursery.

It was at the front of the house, off the balcony, oddly isolated from the bedrooms along the hall. Once, Matt told her when she questioned the location of the nursery, it had been a sitting room. But even before that it had been used as a schoolroom, back in the days of his grandfather's family, when there had been almost a dozen children and no local school. Then, after a school was built in Spring Valley, and the schoolroom no longer needed, it had been turned into a sitting room for the aging grandmother who was disturbed by too many kids running around. For years then, it was left without a use. Then Matt's own mother had turned it into a nursery.

Matt had insisted that the old nursery be used for his daughters, even though it was large and drafty and opened onto the balcony. The balcony railing was safe, though, because the posts were too close together for a child, even a very small one, to slip through. Gradually Halley came to see that the nursery was as safe as any room in the house. Her babies learned early to go up and down the stairs. She could still see Coleen in her short little dress, her diaper sticking out beneath the hem, down on her knees backing down the steps like a crawdaddy in the branch.

Coleen.

Gone forever. Halley never knew where or why.

The foster boy, Jeremy, was also gone. He was the second foster son they'd had in the past few months who had run away. But never, never would she have thought that Coleen would go.

She had changed into her newest dress, a blue dotted Swiss with ruffles and bows, over a full underskirt that held it out, and she had carried away with her the beautiful new doll her daddy had bought her.

Memories entwined. She could still see Coleen's face, such a beautiful face, light up and become even more beautiful when she saw the new doll. It was always the same. Every time her daddy brought her a new doll, Coleen's face brightened as if it were Christmas all over again.

In contrast was the small face of Rachel, lightly freckled, a face that to Halley was also beautiful but which, when Matt first saw Rachel soon after birth, he'd said, "God, ugly little thing, isn't she? She's nothing at all like Coleen."

Was that why he had seemed never to look at her again?

Halley took Rachel everywhere she went, while Coleen was more often with her father. She took Rachel with her to the grocery store that last day. In those days she drove, and the car Matt furnished for her was a two-toned brown station wagon. Rachel stood up in the seat, in those days before seat belts, and Halley drove to the store, parked in the half-empty parking lot and with Rachel's hand in hers went into the store.

Rachel sat in the little seat on the grocery cart, and pointed at things as they went along the aisles. At age three she could speak in long, complicated sentences, just as Coleen had at her age, and it seemed she could read.

"Let's have some of that, Mama, and that. I like macaroni and cheese. And let's have some of that, Mama. I like tuna casserole. Coleen likes it too, and so does Jeremy."

"How do you know what Jeremy likes?" Halley remembered asking, smiling at Rachel's grown-up talk.

"Because I know."

Jeremy had been with them only a few days, and Halley wasn't sure he was going to settle down. He reminded her of Daniel, a boy of thirteen, thin and unhappy, an outcast from family. Daniel had stayed with them two months, and then one night he disappeared. He had run away from foster homes before, and the social worker had no doubt he had run away.

Taking in foster children had been Matt's idea. One day when Rachel was only a few months old he had surprised Halley by saying, "We have all this room, Halley. We don't need any more kids of our own, but how about the kids who don't have homes? I think I'll talk to Social Services and tell them we'll take a child."

Halley had no objections.

About a year later Gloria, a teenager, came to live with them. She stayed six months, until she was eighteen, and then, having graduated from high school in Spring Valley, she left and took a job in the city. From there she went to Florida and reunited with her mother and siblings.

Halley knew only that the children had been taken away from the mother for an undisclosed reason. But Gloria had told a few stories about her mother's problem with drugs, so Halley assumed that was why her kids were taken away. Later, they were given back.

Other children had stayed a few weeks, a few months, all of them older teenagers. Dissatisfaction seemed to settle on all the children who came to live with them. They began to run away. It was as if a plague had settled over the household. They would stay a few days, or a couple of weeks or months, and then run away. Four of them, within two years. All boys.

It was nothing they were doing wrong, the Social Services people assured them. Teenagers were restless. They remembered families, and longed to be reunited. They wanted to be free to do their own thing.

That past year Daniel came, and he seemed to be adjusting. But he stayed only two months. Then Jeremy, a freckled, thin boy the same age, had been brought to them last week by the social worker.

Halley and Rachel went home that day with bags of groceries, and Halley parked the station wagon close to the kitchen porch. In the store Halley and Rachel had eaten a treat at the snack bar. Donuts and milk. Rachel had ridden on the little merry-go-round in the corner of the store. Halley had paused to talk to a church member, Mrs. Bennings. Time had passed, and it was time to cook supper.

Rachel ran ahead of her into the house, holding the door open while Halley carried in bags.

The house was quiet. Too quiet.

"Coleen," Halley called. Then, "Jeremy!"

There was no answer. Rachel remained quietly at her side, going with her into the front hall. There was no sound upstairs. Halley climbed the stairs with Rachel following. She went first to the room the foster children used, and saw that Jeremy was not there. She looked into Coleen's room. Coleen too was gone. She had taken the large, new doll that Matt had given her.

She searched the house. All but Matt's private rooms in the addition on the ground floor, where he had his shop, his hobby. The rooms he had built for himself. The door into that private area was locked. There was a cellar beneath the rooms, and a door that opened out of that area. He always used the cellar door, going about his business without coming into the house. She didn't care that he closed her and the children out of there. She didn't want the children to see those poor dead animals, nor did she want to see them. She hated the mounted heads in his office, the deer, with the lonely brown eyes. The bear skin on the floor. Matt had told her years ago, early in their marriage, that the eyes weren't real. But to her they looked real.

The one time she had voiced her revulsion at his love of hunting, he had looked at her with such wrath she felt as if he had struck her.

Matt would never hurt her. He was a good man. A good husband, she supposed. A good father. He had adored Coleen. He had been oddly indifferent to Rachel, and once had referred to Rachel as "your girl." Yet he was generous with her.

Halley thought his indifference to Rachel was probably caused by his grief in losing Coleen. After Coleen was gone, he seemed even more distant than he had been before. Or, perhaps it was she that withdrew. Terrified of losing Rachel, she had begun sleeping on the daybed in the nursery, and she still slept there, on the narrow bed in the corner.

She had kept Rachel too close. She knew that, but couldn't seem to stop herself. As Rachel grew too large for the crib and youth bed, Halley had simply moved one of the twin beds to the nursery, and Rachel grew up there, sharing the large nursery with her mother.

Rachel had been so accepting of the situation, and Halley understood Rachel was humoring her. But she couldn't bring herself to let Rachel go, even into a room of her own, until the day she graduated from high school and Halley could finally tell her, "Go now, go to college, get a job, do whatever you want. It's your right."

She helped Rachel pack her clothes, and almost pushed her out of the house. Halley was miserable with loneliness, but so glad to see Rachel go.

With tears in her eyes she had gone back into the nursery. Rachel, she thought after her lovely young daughter had driven her small car away, suitcases piled in the back seat, Rachel, so young and pretty and happy and out to see the world, Rachel is safe. At last, Rachel is safe.

Then, shocked at her thoughts, she had gotten busy. Work. Work, work as much as she could, keep herself busy. That was the answer. Grow her flowers and vegetables. Live with them, let them nourish her soul. But at night when she went to her room to rest, the fear returned.

Halley turned over again, seeking always that elusive state of ease.

She had even gone to Dr. Tyler about it once, long after Rachel was gone and there was no reason for her to be so afraid.

"As soon as I stop working and try to relax," she told the doctor, "I start shaking. It's like—it's like I'm not supposed to rest."

"What else, Halley?"

"What else? What do you mean?"

"Thoughts, feelings, things like that. What do you think about?"

"Nothing," Halley said, and paused. She sat in his office, looking through the slats of the Venetian blind on the window behind him. She could see the trees in his backyard. His clinic was in one corner of the yard of his home.

"When you go to your bedroom to rest, you start shaking," the doctor prompted.

"Actually, it's the old nursery. Both my babies lived there. Coleen for her first five years. Then we fixed up a nice room for her near ours on the main hall. It was pink and white, with floral wallpaper. Pink and white, touches of blue."

The room was just as she had left it, the door closed. Her dolls were still there. *A child of ten does not run away.*

She had said that to her husband, to Matt. She had cried that to Matt. And he had said, "No, perhaps not, but a child of ten can be persuaded to leave by an older child. We'll never have another foster child in this house."

That was all Matt had ever said. He had never mentioned Coleen's name to Halley. Even on her birthday. And Halley stopped speaking of Coleen to him. She saw the black misery in his eyes. Or perhaps it was the reflection of her own misery she saw. The fear, too, that was with her always, even after Rachel was grown and . . . safe.

"Anxiety," Dr. Tyler said, and wrote her a prescription for some tiny white pills.

They helped. But she didn't like feeling that she was dependent on any drug, so she rarely took them. When the anxiety was severe, all they did was make her feel better. When it wasn't so severe, they put her to sleep. She still had half a bottle in the medicine chest in the nursery bathroom.

HALLEY GOT up and went to the bathroom. She looked at the bottle of little white pills. Then she decided against them.

She took a summer robe from her closet and put it on over her nightgown. She left the nursery and went to the hall.

Lights were on in the hallway, on the stairway, downstairs in the entry, along the hall leading back to the kitchen. She had not turned out any of the lights, even in the kitchen or on the back porch or front porch. Matt would be furious if he knew.

She started toward Matt's bedroom, and stopped.

Nina stood just outside the door. She stood with her head down, her forehead lightly touching the door, as if undecided about something. She jumped and whirled, startled by Halley's footstep on the bare floor so close by. She recovered immediately, color returning to her cheeks.

"Halley," Nina whispered, putting a cool hand on Halley's arm. "Are you all right?"

"I couldn't sleep," Halley said.

Nina stepped away from the door. With a slight pressure on Halley's arm she guided her a few steps away. Then she stopped, her hand still holding Halley's arm.

"Halley, do you believe in possession?"

CHAPTER FIFTEEN

Lane Yardley had dozed off in his chair. The newspaper in his hands dropped, and he jerked it up, then let it drop again. He put his head back. Sleep was his greatest blessing. He could sit down in his chair on a Sunday night, the only night of the week that he allowed himself that luxury, and go to sleep before he read his newspaper.

Half a dozen times during Sunday afternoon and evening he fell asleep. Then he'd rouse himself, read some more, and fall asleep again. The silence felt so good. Being alone felt good. He was only forty-three, but sometimes he wondered if he were burning out, getting too old to run a nightclub anymore.

He didn't know how long he'd been napping in his chair when the voice woke him.

He blinked and listened, his heart settling down from its sudden leap. On Sunday night the club was so quiet he thought he could hear the slow, stubborn drip of the beer faucet in the bar forty feet and one wall away. It was almost a haunted quiet. The door between his living quarters and the bar and dance floor remained locked most of the time, but he was always aware of the silence in the big room after the people were gone. It was as if their presence somehow lingered. Their voices remained, captured by the walls, long after they were gone.

And that, he thought as he sat listening on this Sunday night, was what had woke him. A voice from Saturday night.

He hadn't closed the door to the club last night until past three. The customers were having such a good time they didn't want to go home, and he hadn't made them. If he turned out the outside light that claimed the club was open, then Thomas, if he happened by, couldn't get him for operating on Sunday.

Thomas, though, wasn't apt to be patrolling town at three in the morning. He usually made his last tour around midnight on Saturday night, and an hour or so earlier on week nights. All the customers straightened up and took notice when that tall, rangy, easygoing guy came through the door with the gun strapped to his waist.

Lane smiled, thinking of it. Thomas looked laid back and tolerant, but he could get tough. One night he came in, several months ago, when one guy in a crowd that had come "out to the sticks" from the city was trying to pick a fight. He was the kind that couldn't take liquor. Give him a drink, and he started thinking of all the bad things that had ever been done to him, and wanting to take it out in hide, anybody's hide. In about ten seconds after the man turned to challenge Thomas, Tom had him out the door with orders to his crowd to take him home. They hadn't shown up again. So much for slumming in the sticks.

Many of his customers came from the city and surrounding areas. A few came from town. Several of his town customers came along the path at the base of the hill for an afternoon beer and some conversation, then went home before the night crowd from the city came out. There'd been a petition or two trying to close him down. One day one of the petitioners, a little lady in a neat pillbox hat, the kind worn when Lane was a kid, had even brought her paper to the club for customers to sign. They'd all signed it, even Lane, and they all had a good laugh. Even the little lady took it all in fun. Otherwise, why would she have shown up here? Some of the petitioners, though, were more serious. But none of them had succeeded in closing him down.

Thomas came out now and then to talk to him.

"Keeping everyone under control, Lane?"

The chief of police always said the same thing. Thomas was the typical Texas Ranger type, and sometimes he even wore the wide-brimmed hat. He was at least six inches taller than Lane, who at five-eight wasn't exactly a big man. But Thomas always seemed to be a gentle man. Lane had never heard differently.

Thomas came about once a week to sit at the bar in the afternoon, drink a beer, and carry on a half-serious, half-joking conversation with Megan. Megan, a slender blond who was good looking enough to draw men, but friendly enough to draw women also, and level-headed enough to handle both without problems, got along with Thomas the chief of police and Thomas the customer.

Lane stretched, got up and went to the stove to get a cup of coffee. Then he stopped, concentrating, listening. The voice again. This time for real. A voice not from the club in the front of the building, but somewhere outside his apartment door.

"Dad."

Dad. Dad. Dad.

Lane's skin tightened. Teasing fingers played along the backs of his arms and neck and into his heart. He felt as if his cheekbones protruded through the skin on his face. He almost dropped the cup. He carefully set it down, then reached over the sink and pulled aside the curtain.

Moonlight, so bright he could see the path behind the club, filled the narrow space between the building and the base of the hill.

He let the curtain drop.

He stood a moment listening for a repeat of the voice, afraid to hope. After all this time, after four long years, could it be . . . Willy was home? No. No. He had listened for that voice, he had lain awake nights, for a year or more, listening for that voice, and it hadn't come.

Now, on a moonlit Sunday night, when the club was silent, Lane was hearing things.

His mind was playing tricks on him. Willy wasn't coming home. Willy, he thought back then, four years ago, had gone to be with his mama. Lane didn't blame him. Willy had loved his mother more than anyone in the world. But she said he wasn't with her, and if that were so, then Willy hadn't run away after all.

Lane became convinced that Willy was kidnapped, on his way home from working that afternoon at Nina's shelter. Who knew what creeps drove the quiet streets looking for kids? Summer brought strangers into town, sometimes. He had to admit, his club also brought them. He had almost driven himself crazy trying to pick out somebody who had been in his club around the time of Willy's disappearance who might have taken Willy.

But there hadn't been any strangers hanging around.

Then he had driven himself even crazier trying to decide which of the men, or women, who were regular customers, might be a closet kidnapper. But he couldn't make sense of that. If a local person had taken Willy, that meant he was dead. Because he hadn't come home.

He had told Thomas, "I think my boy's dead. Look at the people in town, Tom. Who could have done this?"

Thomas told him, "I understand your frustration, Lane. But the men in town are family men. They have kids of their own, most of them. Most of the population is middle-aged or more, and have grand-kids. Which one would you choose?"

He didn't really know the town people. Only about a fourth of them ever came close to his club.

He had talked to Nina a dozen times, and she told him, "I think you're right, Lane. It's so much like the disappearance of Karen, it's like a pattern. I hope I'm wrong, and the kids ran away. But last year, you know, the same thing happened with Karen."

The three of them, Megan, Nina, and himself, drove and drove again the path Willy, and Karen before him, must have taken. Down the hill from Nina's, and along the street that bordered the arts and crafts field on one side, and widely spaced houses on the other. The street was a quarter mile long, and there were only three houses. All of them were occupied by widows in their seventies and eighties. None of the ladies had seen Willy ride by.

At last Lane had given up, hoping Willy had run away and, not finding his mother, at least found a life of some kind. Any kind.

"Dad."

There was no doubt now. It was Willy.

Lane crossed to the door in two long steps and jerked it open.

Willy stood in the moonlight. The same kid, his boy, his little boy, a little tall for his age, dark and good-looking like his mama.

"Willy! My God, boy. Where have you been?"

He almost fell down the three steps at the back of the club, his arms outstretched. He saw his boy, standing in the moonlight, not moving forward to meet him. At the bottom of the steps, when his bare feet met the cool grass of the narrow backyard, Lane stopped. His arms fell slowly. The boy stood brightly outlined in the moonlight, his dark hair falling down on one side of his forehead, his lips smiling, smiling.

No, the smile was not a smile but a grimace, a sneer, a cold stretching of the lips.

Something was wrong. With his blood rushing in his ears, Lane stood, looking at the boy in the moonlight, just yards away.

Willy was no taller than he had been four years ago. He was wearing the same clothes that Lane had described to officers of the law a dozen times, a hundred times. *Blue jeans, blue knit pullover shirt with* the picture of a lion on the front.

Lane heard a sound that was like a sob. His own, not from the boy, the illusion of his son. Thoughts sped rapidly through his mind. He was still asleep and having a nightmare, a vivid, realistic dream. He was finally losing touch with reality. He was going, gone, gone.

No, the moonlight was real, the boy who stood before him was real, somehow, in some weird, terrible way.

Lane backed up, felt the step behind him and walking backwards climbed the three steps without taking his eyes from the boy, from Willy, from the cruel grimace of the lips, the slow twisting of the face, the changes that brought the chill of death to Lane.

He backed into the house and closed the door, surprised as he did so that the boy had allowed it to happen. He pushed the lock button and raised his hand to bolt the door, and saw that his hand was shaking.

"Dad."

The voice was behind him. He whirled.

The boy stood in the shadows just beyond the open door into the club. *How had he gotten in?*

Lane whirled back to the door and with his hands shaking so hard he couldn't control his fingers tried to unbolt the door. He could feel the cold behind him, touching his neck, the back of his arms. It grew in intensity to a painful searing of his skin. Low moans of fear rolled from his lips. He felt moisture on his chin.

Then he stopped and stood for a moment with his head down. What the hell was he doing? The kid, whoever he was, had simply come in the door from the junk room, that catchall room at the end of the hall where the bathrooms were. That lock had been picked before.

The kid, whoever he was, wasn't a supernatural creature able to appear at will, moving suddenly from the moonlight to the doorway between his rooms and the club. But even if he were a ghost, what harm could a ghost do?

Lane turned. The boy hadn't moved. Light from his reading lamp beside his recliner cast a shaded glow on the boy's face. Darkness from the empty room behind outlined him in black.

Flashing dimly was the neon light, touching the kid's dark hair with suggestions of red, green, yellow.

"Who are you?" Lane asked.

The boy didn't answer.

Lane felt himself weakening, the fear coming again like a second warning. He clenched his hands to keep them from trembling.

The features of the boy were Willy's. Willy, four years ago, stood within a few feet of him.

"Willy?" he said. Could it possibly be, after all?

He started forward. It seemed he could see a change of expression in Willy's dark eyes. How could it be possible that his eleven-year-old son had returned. How could he be wearing the same clothes? How could . . .

Suddenly the doorway was empty. The boy had disappeared.

Lane stopped, fear making him cold, his skin rippling with chills. But it was a different fear. Something he could handle.

So it was true. He had seen an apparition. A ghost.

Now he knew his son was dead.

He stood still, wondering.

Then he heard a sound from the dark room beyond the door that still stood open. Footsteps on the hardwood of the dance floor came closer.

But they weren't the footsteps of a boy. They were soft and padding, a rhythmic trotting, coming from the hall to the bathroom toward the open door of his quarters.

He had to close that door.

Before whatever it was reached it, he had to close the door.

The junk room door must have been left open, letting something in. A dog? Only a dog. Why was he so afraid?

He ran to the open door and was reaching for it when he saw them.

Not a dog after all, but a group of children. He stood staring from one to the other.

Willy stood there, in front.

Willy, and fanned behind him was Karen, and Cliff Patison, and a little girl he had never seen before. She carried a large doll in her arms. Behind her, standing equally spaced distances away, there were three or four more young boys about Willy's size. Shadows obscured their features. They seemed almost to be figures made of darkness and shadows, touched only peripherally by the continuing wave of neon lighting at the bar.

Lane's mouth opened and closed. He realized they were moving, closing in, surrounding him, trying to cut him off from his living quarters.

The telephone was under the counter on the far side of the room. If he could reach it . . . if he could reach it what good would it do?

His eyes swept the children's faces again. Their beauty was like masks permanently set to their faces. Only the youngest girl smiled, as if she were an extension, a clone, of the doll in her arms, as if her face were as permanently set as the doll's face.

Their eyes were bright, sparkling, and as unalive as glass.

Lane turned, seeking escape from this, whatever it was, real or unreal.

He could see the moonlight beyond the open door to his quarters, through the window over his sink. He reached for it, as if it could help him.

He felt the tug on his back as something clutched his shirt. Then a hand encircled his ankle and jerked backward, and Lane was falling, his arms thrown out. They were on him, a giggling, chanting, tearing mass. They were all at once singing. Incredulously he heard the song, the old song.

"Here we go round the mulberry bush, the mulberry bush, the . . . "

Lane's scream mingled with the haunted remains of music.

CORY LISTENED. His door was closed now. Halley had closed it after Cory told her about the voices. She had patted him on the cheek, pulled up the sheet blanket and tucked it under his chin. Go to sleep, she'd said.

Cory had tried. With his eyes shut tight he heard every sound in the house, it seemed. There were sounds he thought of as house sounds, but nothing made by humans. There were no footsteps of Gram or Nina to make him feel safe. But now, just as he was beginning to feel sleepy, he heard the fine, lifted, children voices again.

He listened.

They were singing. Kids singing. It sounded like, "Here we go round the mulberry bush, the mulberry bush, the mulberry bush. Here we go round the mulberry bush, so gently in the morning."

They were laughing and chattering and then they were calling. A little girl called in a singsong voice, "Cory. Cory! Where are you! We went to your house, and you were gone. You're hiding from us, Cory. Hiding, hiding."

Cory began to frown as he listened. Who were these kids who knew his name, and even knew where his house was?

"*Co-rey* come out and play. We dare you, Cory. We dare you. Double dare, double dare. You're a chicken, Cory! Rachel's baby, sissy boy!"

Then again they were singing, and laughing and chattering words he couldn't understand.

It sounded as if they were outside. Playing in the moonlight. They knew him, but he didn't know them.

Cory got out of bed and slipped on tiptoes to the window. It was still partly raised, and a soft, cool breeze touched his face as he pressed his nose against the screen.

The moon had moved west, and the shadow of the addition at the back of the house, and the big tree beyond it, reached farther over into the yard.

The place where Matt had lain, where Cory had spent so long at his side, was now shaded.

He could still hear the kids playing, but they sounded farther away, as if they had gone on to something else.

He looked and looked, across the field to the hillside, and toward the grass field at the side of the house. But he didn't see them anywhere.

Their voices drifted on, soft and distant, singing, chattering, and daring him to come and play.

CHAPTER SIXTEEN

Nina stood with her hand on Halley's arm at the side of Matt's bed, hoping her presence supported Halley emotionally. They had stood there for several minutes it seemed to Nina, long minutes that dragged like hours, and Matt slept as if he were in a coma. There were no voices issuing from him now, and Nina couldn't bring herself to try to explain what she had heard. Who would believe it? Perhaps there was a logical explanation. Yet she knew there was none. She had heard, yet as time passed, she was ceasing to believe.

She whispered, "Does Matt talk in his sleep, Halley?"

Halley didn't answer. Nina felt the arm she was holding grow tense suddenly, and her eyes turned back to Matt, following Halley's stare.

His eyes were open and he was looking up at them, and Nina felt stunned at the cruelty in the dark stare. It was like looking into the eyes of the source of all evil in the world.

For a half dozen slow heartbeats he stared upward at her, directly at Nina, then with a long sigh his eyes closed.

Halley turned her face toward Nina. Her eyes were wide and questioning. She started to speak, and the voice of a child began softly from beyond them.

Halley jerked back to look down at her husband. Matt's lips were parted, but not moving. The voice seemed to emanate from somewhere in the aura around him. The jabberings of the child were indistinct, as if she were too far away to be clearly heard. Nina did not recognize the voice, but Halley's hands jerked to her mouth.

"Oh my God," she whispered.

The child's voice continued, then Nina noticed that Matt's eyes were slitted and he was looking sideways beneath his lashes at her, at Halley. But the stare was blank, as if he didn't see them. The child's voice went on. It sounded happy and cheerful, as if the little girl were telling something that delighted her to someone she cared about.

There came a pause. The world seemed soundless for a moment. It was as if even the night birds had paused, holding their breath.

Halley gasped, as if she were trying to find her own voice. But the interval of silence was brief, and then the child was speaking again, but with a change in tone. She spoke through tears. The words dissolved beneath the tears until the child was crying, sobbing forlornly on and on.

Halley wailed, "Coleen! That's Coleen's voice!"

Coleen. For a moment Nina didn't know who Halley was talking about. Then a memory returned, something she had heard about when she was very young. The Reeds had a daughter, older than Rachel, who had disappeared when she was only ten years old. Her name was Coleen.

MEGAN STOOD with her hand on the telephone. She had dialed Lane's number, but there was no answer. She had lost count of the rings.

She broke the connection.

If she called the police department, what good would it do? What could she say? I have a prowler at the house. It's a girl who looks exactly like Karen. Like Karen looked five years ago, the last time I saw her. Karen, who I've thought was dead. Because she would never have done this to me, not Karen. Even if she had run away, she would have contacted me.

She had talked to Thomas many times about Karen, about what might have happened to her. She was riding a bicycle that day, and it had disappeared with her. But no one driving the highway out of town saw a girl on a bicycle. And there was no bicycle left at the side of the road between Nina's shelter and Karen's house.

Megan had driven that road so many times she could close her eyes and see every detail of it. West a block, turn right onto the street that had a field on the left side, with walnut trees all along, and widely spaced houses on the right. The street continued on a quarter mile then swung right. Nina's driveway cut off at the corner, going left. The driveway crossed a field and lifted into the hills and trees where Nina's house and shelter were.

Karen had left Nina's at her usual time, about four-thirty, Nina said. Riding her bicycle. Megan traced the trail she had always taken. Back down the driveway to the corner of the street, then along the street by the walnut trees, then left and a block home.

If she had taken a different route for some reason, where would it have gone? What houses would she have passed? The Moore house sat back from the street, and none of the Moores had seen Karen. Not even Patrick, who was Karen's age, and whom she knew from school as well as having seen him at Nina's shelter.

She might have gone past the Reed's, if she had changed her route. And it was there Megan paused. She barely knew the Reeds when she saw them. Matt Reed reminded her of a wrestler. He was a large man, with strong, beefy shoulders. He wore a strange, shaggy beard around his chin and cheeks, but his upper lip was bare. His eyebrows were bushy and thick and his eyes looked out from under them with a dark steady intensity that chilled Megan the day she stopped at his house and asked if he, or his wife, had seen Karen.

"We wouldn't know her if we saw her," he said, and Megan had a feeling he wanted to shut the door in the face.

Later she told Thomas, "What about Matt Reed, Tom? He's weird."

"Matt Reed? He's one of the originals in town, Megan. His family was one of the founders. Matt owns half the town. He may seem a little gruff, but he can be friendly, too."

Weeks later she asked Thomas if they ever investigated Matt Reed. Thomas told her, "We have asked everyone in town, Megan, if they saw Karen that day. No one remembers seeing her. If her bicycle had been found at the side of the road, we would suspect foul play. But it's gone. All evidence points to her riding away, somewhere."

The same pattern held with the kids that disappeared later. Willy, Lane's son, and Cliff Patison. Bicycles disappeared along with children. And one dog.

She and Lane had talked about it. Kids, bicycles and dogs don't just disappear. Someone was responsible.

She started to dial Thomas, but couldn't remember his number. The telephone was only a small, simple phone. She'd never had the need for one of the phone that listed thirty numbers, and you only had to push a button.

She'd never had the money for extras. Karen's new phone, the one that had never been unwrapped, was that kind of phone. But Megan had no need of one herself.

She heard the sounds of someone outside the house. A scrape along the wall. A creak of a board on the front porch. The slide of a window.

The slide of a window.

Someone had opened the window.

Footsteps followed, crossing a room somewhere in the front of the house. But they weren't the steps of a child. They sounded like the running steps of an animal.

Megan dropped the phone. She had to get out of the house. Why hadn't she screamed for help from the neighbor?

"Mama?"

Karen's voice. How many times had she prayed to hear Karen's voice again?

Megan stood still, facing the door that opened onto the hall.

"I'm here, Karen," she said.

The questions were unanswered. Why had Karen come into the house through a window, like a thief? Why had she not changed in five years? None of it mattered. Karen had come home.

Suddenly the house seemed filled with the voices of children, yet the voices were soft and muffled, as if they were on the other side of a wall. It could have been six, seven years ago, when Karen was in her room with friends, and they were giggling and talking and at times singing, several voices at once.

"Here we go round the mulberry bush, the mulberry bush, the mulberry bush, here we go round—"

No, no. Karen had never played that game. It was an old, old game, the kind children played years ago, back in Megan's grandmother's time. She had a faint memory of playing it with her own grandmother, when she was barely large enough to sing and play. Her grandmother had held her hands and they had circled, singing the old song.

Karen and her friends never played the game.

In another part of the house the soft, dancing steps went on and on, and the song continued, in the voice of girls and boys playing an old game.

"—here we go round the mulberry bush, so early in the morning."

. . . so early in the morn-ing. Rachel jerked awake, the song dying away in her dream.

She stared through the darkness into her past. The dream had brought back memories she had forgotten. She remembered now seeing Coleen and their daddy playing, and she had wanted to play too. But he had told her she was too little. She stood back watching. "I want to play. Can I play too, Daddy?" And his answer was always, "You're too little."

Rachel watched. Daddy took Coleen's hands and swung her round and round, with Coleen laughing so hard she could barely sing the song, "Here we go round the mulberry bush, the mulberry bush . . ."

At that time Rachel thought the mulberry bush was the tuft of grass on the ground around which they swung laughing, singing, playing. Maybe when she was a big girl like Coleen, Daddy would let her play.

The scene changed.

She and Coleen were alone. Coleen was fixing her doll's bonnet, stretching the lace so that it stood out, tying the ribbon under the doll's chin, untying it and tying it again in a nicer bow. And all the while she was talking about a giant.

"A real giant?" Rachel asked. She thought about the giant in Jack and the Beanstalk. And there was another one Mama had read to her about who had only one eye right in the middle of his forehead. But she knew those weren't really real giants.

"Yes, a real one," Coleen said. "That's why you must never leave your room at night. That's why you must always stay close to Mama and Daddy."

"Does he *live* here?"

"Yes."

"In our house?"

"Yes, right here in our house. I think he sleeps during the day. But in the dark, you must be very careful."

"Have you *seen* him?"

"Yes. At night. And I hear him walking."

Great chills ran over Rachel's skin and left rough goosebumps. Coleen could see she was afraid if only she looked. But Coleen was fixing her doll's clothes. Daddy had brought her the new doll even though it wasn't even her birthday.

"Why don't you tell Mama and Daddy?"

"Oh no. Don't ever say a word to either of them. If you do I'll never tell you anything else!"

"I won't but—"

"He's a very bad giant. He eats people. Especially little kids."

"And he lives in our house?"

Rachel turned over, feeling in the strange dark of the motel bed for David. He was turned on his side with his back to her, but his body was solid and warm. She moved against him. He made a sound in his sleep, turned onto his back, and slipped his arm under her head. With her cheek cradled in the warm dip between his arm and neck she tried to get her mind away from that old conversation she had forgotten.

How strange the way memories suddenly came back, brought by a dream. But now she recalled vividly seeing Coleen and their daddy whirling in the game and singing the song. "Here we go round the mulberry bush." That was all she remembered of it. She still felt the hurt of being left out.

She remembered sitting on a step somewhere at the house with Coleen, and being told about the giant.

Once she thought she saw the giant. She was asleep in her bed in the nursery. Her mother had tucked her in and gone to take her bath. Rachel went to sleep.

She woke suddenly, and the giant was coming through a doorway. She was in a place she had never been before. She could smell cool mustiness, like the nut cellar. The doorway was strange and dark, and very high, but the giant was so tall his head was stooped forward so that he could pass into the room where Rachel was trapped in the corner.

She screamed in absolute terror. Screamed and screamed. The light came on, and she was in the nursery. The doorway wasn't huge and dark, and the giant was only her father.

Her mother was there to comfort her, and her father looked on in silence. She was ten years old, the same age Coleen had been when she disappeared.

Rachel remembered the unease of growing up in that big, silent house. After Coleen's disappearance her Dad seemed more of a background figure than an active part of her life. She and her mother were together. Halley even insisted that Rachel stay in the nursery although there were several empty bedrooms in the house. In all her eighteen years at home, Rachel had shared the nursery with her mother. She hadn't thought much about it at the time, except she knew her mother clung to her because of Coleen. She wouldn't have moved away, but it seemed that Halley wanted her to go. Even though her mother waved from the porch that last day with tears in her eyes, there was a smile on her face.

Memories struggled like mixed signals in Rachel's mind. Or perhaps it wasn't memories, only feelings. A feeling at last that something more than the disappearance of Coleen was wrong in that house.

It was ridiculous to think Coleen was telling the truth as she knew it. Giants do not exist. Giants that eat kids. It was not something that Rachel could even tell David.

But Cory was in that house. And he didn't know not to leave his bedroom at night. No one had ever told him about the giant that eats kids.

She was being silly. She was being ridiculous. But she had to go get Cory. She suddenly was filled with a sense of doom. A premonition that if she didn't hurry and get Cory out of that house she would never see him again.

She loved him, *loved him.* She hadn't realized how much. He was her little boy, her own little child. He had come to her filled with trust, and she had left him vulnerable and unsuspecting in a place that was not kind to children.

"David. David?" She sat up, throwing the cover back.

"Hmmm?"

She turned on the lamp. The sudden light caused David to squint his eyes and cover them with an arm. Then he took his arm away and looked at her.

"What? What's wrong?"

"I don't know what's wrong," she said as she got out of bed and reached for her clothes. "But we're going back after Cory."

David sat up, and laughed shortly. He watched her. "You're serious."

"Yes, I'm serious. Hurry, David, please. I'm worried about him."

David put his feet out onto the floor. He sat slumped for a moment before he straightened and began to dress.

"What on earth could hurt him, Rachel? He's with your folks. Why don't you just call?" He looked at his watch. "It'd be better to wake them at midnight than . . ."

"No. We have to go get him. Please, David."

She shook with anxiety. Inexplicably, she was afraid they would get there after it was too late.

CHAPTER SEVENTEEN

THOMAS DROVE INTO THE PARKING LOT OF LANE'S PLACE, GRAVEL SNAPPING beneath the tires. He parked horizontally to the log veneer front. It was close to midnight, and Lane was no doubt asleep, but Thomas couldn't wait until tomorrow to talk to him. The more he pictured the leader of the gang of kids the more he felt it really was Willy Yardley. What he was doing back in town, roaming the streets, was a mystery. But the whole deal with the kids was a mystery.

He got out of the car and walked around the end of the building. Long, low and rustic, made of stained logs, it was built to look as if it were part of the woods that rose on the hill behind it, and would have succeeded if it hadn't been for the neon lights. Lane lived in an apartment at the back, but Thomas had never been in those rooms.

He had heard rumors that one of the reasons his wife, Sheila, left, was because she didn't like the apartment. But that seemed a rather inadequate reason to leave your child and husband. Still, to Thomas, any excuse for leaving a child would have been inadequate. He supposed if one had to understand how other people's minds worked, the excuse of the lady falling in love with the traveling salesman was as good as any other. He just couldn't understand how any parent could go off and leave a child. He had more respect for some killers than he did for deserters.

He hadn't known Sheila well. She was usually around, a pert blond girl who seemed to be enjoying herself. She worked behind the counter helping Lane mix drinks or draw beer, while Megan took care of the tables and booths.

Lane's car was parked beneath a carport at the end of the building. There was a collection of green plastic trash cans in a small fenced enclosure. A path made through the grass led around to the back. Moonlight slanted brightly between the hill and the rear wall of the club. The path ended at a door that had three steps.

There was a light somewhere in the rooms beyond the door. He could see it shining as if muted from the small window high in the wall.

Thomas knocked on the door and called out, "Lane?"

There was no answer, but the door moved with his knock. It was unlocked.

Thomas pushed the door inward a few inches and called again. Still there was no answer. Strange, he thought, that the door was not even quite closed. Unless Lane was somewhere outside.

There seemed to be no life around the club. The moonlight was too steady and too bright, the darkness under the trees too dark. The night too still.

Thomas pushed the door open and stepped into the room.

It was a kitchen, rather long, with a sort of living room, or family room at one end. A recliner had a newspaper on the floor beside it. The muted light came from a floor lamp at the side of the chair. There was a couch against the wall, piled with cushions, magazines, clothes. A coffee table looked about as cluttered.

Nearer to Thomas was a round kitchen table with chairs pushed against it. Only one was sitting askew, as if Lane always used the same chair. The table was cluttered also, except for the spot near the chair. The kitchen part of the apartment curved around the wall in one corner. A few cabinets, a small apartment-sized stove, with the window above the sink. The refrigerator could have been as much part of the living room as the kitchen. Even the top of it was cluttered. Cereal boxes, and a couple of loaves of bread covered its flat surface.

At the end of the room a door leading to the front stood open. Neon lights, blinking silently on and off, threw a rainbow of colors dimly along the polished hardwood of the dance floor.

There was something about that open door that drew Thomas.

When he reached it he looked into a room that looked endless in the lack of light. He knew there were tables and chairs surrounding the dance floor, and at the right end would be the padded booths with the high backs, that gave people some privacy. On his left the long bar took up the entire end of the room, and reflected in the mirror there was another neon light that advertised beer.

Then he saw the dark objects on the floor. As his eyes adjusted to the lack of light, to the varying vagueness of blue, green, red, and yellow that washed in a path from the neon lights behind the bar across the floor toward the doorway in which he stood, he saw dark objects in the middle of the dance floor.

The largest object was the size of a slight man, but there was a glistening effect, as if the figure had been stripped naked and oiled. Nearby, unnoticed before, was a torn shirt. It looked as if it had been flung toward the door where he stood.

He felt back on the wall for a light switch, found a row of three and flicked them all on. A light in the apartment behind him came on. Recessed lights over the bar cast a muted glow across the tables and chairs near the bar. The dance floor was softly illuminated.

Blood was smeared across the dance floor. Thomas stared in shock at the figure in the center of the bloody floor.

It was the shape of a man, its back turned slightly toward him, positioned half on its side. At first it seemed only to be bathed in blood. Then he saw the head had no scalp, no hair.

The back of the body had no skin. The red, raw flesh glistened in the dim lights. Muscles, like ropes, lay open to the air.

Thomas was physically unable to move. Only his eyes turned, seeing the articles of clothing thrown about, trousers, shoes, socks, another shirt . . .

No, my God.

His whole being revolted. His stomach, heart, everything about him lurched. His hand reached out and grabbed the door jamb for support.

Lying within a few feet, thrown like a blanket, was the man's skin. It looked like an empty rubber suit, the scalp attached, the hair pitifully thin, the face collapsed like an old plastic mask. Blood had oozed from every pore, it seemed, and streaked the length of the torso.

Thomas turned away to compose himself, and then made himself search for the lights of the club. He found them in Lane's office.

In disbelief he looked at what had been done to Lane. It was as if they had become expert in the skinning of a body. They had been awkward and clumsy with the dog, but had succeeded with the man.

He went to the telephone and called the station. Glen sounded as if he had dozed off. He woke up when Thomas told him Lane Yardley had been murdered.

"Call Noel to take over there, and you come on over here. I'll call the sheriff's department and wait here until you arrive. Tell Noel to arm himself, and you do the same."

"Yeah. Okay."

"And Glen . . ."

"Yeah?"

"Uh—" How could he warn him, without shocking him? He would be shocked enough when he got here. He didn't know how cool Glen could be under stress. The town was usually so quiet and peaceful. Last year at the scene of the Moore murders, the only murders Glen had seen, he'd acted like a pro, so maybe he'd be all right.

"Yeah?" Glen said again. "Something really bad, huh?"

"That's right, Glen."

"I'll be there, as soon as I can call Noel to come on down."

"And Glen, keep your eyes open for that gang of kids that attacked the kids and dog over on Spring. Girls and boys, ages nine to thirteen or fourteen. If you see them, call for backup. Keep them in sight if you can. Don't approach them alone."

"Kids! You think they murdered Lane?"

"It's possible. I don't know who else. And Glen, *don't tangle with them.* Just call me. Call the Country Rescue Team, call everyone you can think of, but don't tangle with them."

"Okay."

"But just come straight on over, otherwise."

Thomas called the sheriff's department and asked for the homicide crew, and as many patrol cars as they could spare, then he began looking around.

Behind the main room was a hallway that led back to the restrooms and to a room that was used for storage. The door that led outside was also open, as the kitchen door had been.

In the apartment he found one bedroom with an unmade bed, but it didn't look as if Lane had been surprised in bed. He had been dressed, the way it looked, when he went into the club, probably to investigate a noise.

A second, small bedroom had a single, narrow bed, carefully made up. A boy's things were on the dresser and bedside table, and hanging on the walls. The closet held Willy's clothes.

Thomas heard a car and went outside. Glen had arrived in record time. He had brought the camera.

"You ready for this?" Thomas asked.

Glen nodded, his eyes questioning, but he followed Thomas without voicing those questions.

At the doorway to the club Glen's eyes swept the scene. His face lost all color. He turned away, swallowed. His Adam's apple bobbed in a way that would have been comical at another time. Then he lifted the camera, stepped past Thomas into the room and began taking pictures.

"I've looked through every room in the club, Glen, and the killers aren't here. I think it must have been the kids. They tried to do the same thing to the dog, and botched the job. I guess they didn't have time to do it right. With Lane, they must have had more time. I'll take a look outside."

He searched for outdoor lights, found them in the office, and turned them on. With the parking lot brightly lighted, he went outside to look around, although he knew with a deep down gut feeling, the kids had gone on.

He was in a hurry to get away, but he didn't want to leave Glen alone. He had to check on the other parents of the children. The youngest child was unfamiliar. He had never seen her before. The boys who had stood back in the shadows never became clear to him, even in his struggling attempt to recall their faces.

But if Nina was right, the older girl, the boy with the crewcut, were kids he knew. The more he thought of it, the more he was sure they were Karen Davis and Cliff Patison.

"Dr. Tyler, I apologize for disturbing your rest, but I didn't know what else to do. Something is wrong with Matt. Could you come over?"

Nina listened to Dr. Tyler's promise to be right there, then she hung up the phone.

She looked around. Animal heads erupted from the walls. Deer and elk mostly, but also wild boar and bear. Shadows hung beneath them, as they stared in their permanent silence toward opposite walls.

She was in Matt's office, as Halley called this large, library room. The light switch had turned on recessed lights from somewhere, and the effect was very dim. There was a lamp stand at the side of a large, modern recliner, and on the desk was an old long-necked lamp, darkened almost to black. The desk was clean. The only thing on it was the old-fashioned black dial phone. Halley had told her it was the only phone in the house, and she rarely used it. It had worked perfectly this time, and Nina suspected Halley's nervousness was the main reason it hadn't worked for Halley.

Nina had entered Matt's room alone. It was a large room, but with a closed darkness, filled with shelves of books, stacks of books, and on the walls the mounted heads of animals. Two entire walls, above the enormous fireplace on one wall, and above the large desk on the other, were crowded with the heads of deer. Although their eyes were probably glass, there was a soul look that Nina couldn't stand. She didn't blame Halley for not liking to come into this room.

She left Matt's office, with a feeling that she shouldn't have been in there at all. She suspected Matt would hate knowing his privacy had been so invaded, and that it was destined to become more invaded as the doctor returned. She went along the hall, noticing there were no wall adornments at all, not even a portrait. At the front of the house the foyer was partly furnished, with an antique sofa, a breakfront with figurines made of glass.

Against the wall the stairway rose to the small balcony above, and the old nursery. The upstairs hall was as unadorned as the downstairs.

She climbed the stairs and stopped at Halley's room. She had tried to get Halley to take something to relax and go back to bed, at least lie down, but Halley was still sitting where Nina had left her. The armchair she slumped in was once rose-colored, but had faded to a rosy grey, and Halley sat with her elbow on the chair arm and her head supported by her hand. Her eyes were dry and staring. Nina put her hand on Halley's shoulder, but Halley seemed not to notice she was there.

Nina bent solicitously. "Halley, can I get something for you? Water? Milk?"

Halley shook her head and drew a deep breath that caused her body to jerk.

Nina hesitated, then said, "Dr. Tyler is coming back."

Halley murmured, "What can he do? What can any of us do?" She lifted her head. "What's wrong with Matt, what's happening? How can the voice of my little girl be there? Possession, Nina? From what? I don't understand."

"It's just a—uh—" Nina didn't understand either, and even the thought of what they'd heard brought back that awful sense of being thrown through a reality barrier people weren't meant to pass. She tried again. "Maybe it's just that Matt, in his subconscious, is—uh—trying to bring her back?"

But what about the other voices, Nina instantly wondered. What about his strange almost catatonic physical state? She had a feeling Dr. Tyler would insist, against Matt's wishes, that he be admitted to a hospital, perhaps to a psychiatric ward, and Nina hoped he would. She wanted to be sure to meet Dr. Tyler at the door, to talk to him before he went upstairs.

She went down the hall far enough to see that Cory's door was closed. She started to leave, then with the uneasiness that had been eating at her since the moment of the earth tremor and the appearance of Patrick in the tent doorway, she softly opened Cory's door.

His room was dark, but she heard a stirring movement. The light from the hall dimly revealed his bed, covers thrown back. Cory wasn't in it.

Nina felt her stomach tighten with anxiety. Where was Cory?

A small white face seemed disembodied as he stood up in the shadows beyond the bed. Nina saw he'd been kneeling by the window.

"Why aren't you in bed, Cory?" she asked in a loud whisper.

He came around the bed, rushing, it seemed, to meet her. His hands entangled with hers. Then he was tugging her toward the window.

"Nina, come and listen. Can you hear them?"

Nina went with him to the window. The lower pane was up, and a soft, cool breeze undulated the curtains. Beyond the window a roof sloped. A really daring kid could have crawled out the window, slid down the roof, which probably was the back porch roof, jumped to the ground, and . . .

But the screen was tightly hooked. Nina checked it with her fingers. "Keep this screen closed, Cory, okay?"

"Listen, do you hear them?"

She kneeled on the floor beside him. If Dr. Tyler's car came down the driveway, she told herself, she'd be able to see its lights. Then she could run to meet the doctor. But for now, Cory was wide awake and hearing things through his window. She listened. Insects buzzed and chirped, frogs in a pasture pond sang. She heard her dogs howling and barking, though not as steadily as before she had gone out to comfort them.

"I don't know what's wrong with them tonight," she said, keeping her voice low. "The earth tremor maybe. Animals are sensitive to things like that. Their senses are far more developed than ours, in many ways."

"I don't mean the dogs, I mean the kids."

"Kids?"

"I don't hear them now, either. But a while ago, I could hear them singing some song. Like, here we go round the mulberry bush."

"Oh, that's an old game children used to play. Before television days. Sometimes even now, maybe."

"They also called me to come out and play."

Nina paused. Suddenly it seemed she hadn't really been listening to

Cory. He was telling her about children playing an old game, and calling him out to play.

In the bedroom Matt was surrounded, somehow, by the voices of children. Whether they came from him was getting more and more uncertain.

Thomas had been stopped by a group of children, all of whom sounded in description like children who, in her heart, Nina had felt were dead.

"Did you see them, Cory?"

"No. Not since they took the trap off Matt's hand. But I heard them."

The image of Patrick, standing in the tent door, a look of terrible concentration on his face, an intense stare directed at the preacher, came unexpectedly before Nina's eyes.

"Cory, was Patrick with those children?"

"Patrick? No. I never saw those kids before."

Patrick's reappearance tonight all at once seemed to have a connection, somehow, to all the rest. To the strange voices, the appearance of the other children. Yet he remained separate from them.

She put her arm around Cory's shoulders. Should she tell him what Thomas had told her about the children killing the dog? No, it might scare him. He was spending the night in a strange house. She turned him toward the bed.

"Whatever you do, Cory, don't go out to find them, all right?"

"Why?" he asked.

"Listen," she said, "I'm going to close your window and lock it. And I want you to try to go to sleep. It's very important that you go to sleep."

"They took the trap off Matt's hand," Cory said as he obediently crawled into bed.

That was another thing that made this night seem so alien, so out of sync with the real world. She felt at times that she might wake up, and all of this would have been a vivid nightmare. More and more she was feeling as if she had slipped from one world into another. She tucked his sheet blanket beneath his chin and kissed him on the forehead.

She tried to sound lighthearted. "How many times have you been to bed tonight, Cory?"

"Just a couple. I keep hearing the kids."

"Well, maybe they'll go away if you pretend you don't hear. Now go to sleep. If there are other voices, other noises, pay them no attention. Dr. Tyler is coming round to see Mr. Reed again. But you just stay tucked in bed. And when you hear the children, ignore them."

"I wonder where Rachel and Daddy are now."

"They're probably in bed asleep. Which is where you should be. Goodnight."

"Goodnight, Nina."

She turned on the bedside lamp and angled the shade away from his face. There was something about leaving him totally in the dark that she didn't like.

She hurried down the hall, and paused at Matt's door a moment. There was silence beyond. Relieved, she hurried downstairs and out onto the lighted front porch.

A car was coming down the street from town. She stood watching, hoping, hearing the occasional howling of her dogs. She wanted to go see about them, but couldn't leave Halley and Cory yet. Even in Matt's present helplessness there was a frightening quality about him.

The car turned into the driveway, the lights washing over her too brightly, throwing her too much into view. She felt herself shrink inwardly. Then the car lights swept past her and blinked away as the car stopped.

Dr. Tyler got out, pulling his black satchel from the front seat. He came through the moonlight, an almost Santa Claus type of figure, without the beard, belly and red suit.

"Troubles?" he asked.

"No fever, or anything like that, Doctor. It's not really anything I can explain."

"Well, why not, Nina?" he asked jocularly, his tone of voice softening the actual words. "He giving you a bad time?"

"No, nothing like that. He's still asleep. But, voices have been coming from him."

He didn't pause. He went ahead of her into the house and up the stairs toward the rear hall. "Voices?"

At the closed door to Matt's room, Dr. Tyler stopped and looked at Nina. He said nothing, but his eyes questioned.

Nina tried to explain. "I don't know what to tell you, except I just want you to listen, to—to—well, Doctor, I . . ."

How could she explain it? The silence was so intense it seemed to Nina she could hear the slow ticking of a clock rising from somewhere on the first floor of the house. Dr. Tyler adjusted the satchel in his hand and started to speak.

Suddenly a child burst out laughing. The doctor stood with his mouth open, his head turning slowly toward the door.

The muted sound of laughter came from beyond Matt's door.

The laughter ended and the child began to talk. It wasn't the voice that

Halley had said was Coleen's. It was a boy's voice, sweet and high, filled with excitement. But though the words seemed to be clearly spoken, they were not comprehensible.

Dr. Tyler asked, "Cory? Isn't it rather late—"

Nina as she shook her head. "It isn't Cory, Doctor." Dr. Tyler threw open the door. He stood on the threshold, looking toward the bed.

Lights created a soft illumination in the room, revealing at first glance that Matt was alone.

But the child's voice continued, soft and nearby, with isolated words becoming clear. *Home,* the child said, and *sisters. Mama.*

Then the voice changed and became tearful and the words as distinct as if the child stood by the side of the bed. "I want to go home. Please, I want to go home." The child began to cry, terrible sounds that swelled abruptly to a scream filled with terror and pain.

CHAPTER EIGHTEEN

THE CHILD'S SCREAM ENDED ABRUPTLY WITH A GURGLE THAT SOUNDED AS IF IT had to be choked off. The silence that followed seemed to be filled with the echoes of the terrible scream.

Dr. Tyler took three long, determined steps toward the bed, then stopped again, halfway between the door and the side of the bed.

"What in the living hell is going on here?" he demanded.

Nina did not answer. She entered, pulled the door closed so that Halley and Cory would not be disturbed.

Dr. Tyler approached the bed and stood looking down at Matt. He breathed evenly and deeply. Dr. Tyler went through the motions of listening to Matt's heart, checking pulses in wrist and throat, and taking his blood pressure again. He then tried to wake him.

"Matt, wake up. Matt." He tapped Matt gently on the forehead, and then pulled his eyelids open and shined a little light into first one eye then the other. He turned away shaking his head.

"Matt is in some kind of coma. I don't know what it is. He seems perfectly healthy. His heart, his blood pressure, just like they were before. Normal. But that doesn't explain what I heard. Why is he speaking and crying in the voice of a—" He cut off abruptly and whirled back to look at Matt.

Another voice, a low murmuring of a child, came eerily close in the room. Suddenly she was giggling, as if she were being tickled. Then she began to talk, words that seemed clear and distinct, yet were just beyond being understood. They went on and on, one little girl talking. She sounded as if she were in the room, and the room began to take on a haunted quality as if the child were slowly materializing.

Nina found that she was staring at a certain spot on the other side of the bed. It seemed she could almost see a little girl sitting on the grass, with her doll across her lap.

Dr. Tyler moved back closer to the bed. He stared down at Matt, around him, then back at Nina. His face looked pale and strained. He came back to Nina.

Whispering, he said, "The voice is coming directly from Matt, Nina, don't you think?"

"It seems to. Maybe . . . just beyond him."

Dr. Tyler went to the other side of the bed, where no materialization had taken place after all. He stood there, looking around. The voice continued, laughing, giggling, cooing, talking now it seemed to her dolly.

Then suddenly her words came distinctly. "Daddy," she said, "Thank you for my dolly, Daddy."

The door opened. Halley crossed the room to stand at Matt's side, looking down at him. The little girl's voice went on and on, becoming indistinct again as if the child were talking very fast.

There came a brief pause, and the crying started, anguished sobs, soft, on and on, as if the child knew no one would hear and come to comfort her. As once before, they had the quality of being in a hollow space. The sound grew muffled, as if something closed off her cry. Suddenly it was gone and there was silence.

The room seemed to scream with its silence. Neither Halley nor Dr. Tyler moved. Nina stood against the wall, her hands behind her, her palms flat against the cool surface. She could feel herself trembling.

Dr. Tyler spun round and walked decisively toward the door. "Well that does it. I'm calling an ambulance."

"No! No!" Halley cried, and rushed to stop him. She clutched his arm. "You can't. Matt won't like it."

"Halley, there's something haywire with the man, and I don't know what it is. He needs some psychiatric care. An evaluation, something. I'm not qualified. I can't help him."

"No, please. Not tonight. At least not tonight." Tears ran down her cheeks.

"Halley—"

"Don't you see, Dr. Tyler, that's the voice of Coleen. My little girl. She's —she's been gone since she was ten years old. Thirty years ago. She's come back, Dr. Tyler. You can't take him away. If you take him away, you take her."

Dr. Tyler's eyes met Nina's. It seemed to her he looked as helpless as she felt.

TIME PASSED SLOWLY as Thomas and Glen waited. They had turned on every light in and around the club, had looked into every corner, every nook, and shined their flashlights into the trees on the hill rising within a few feet behind the club. Thomas had even stepped off that distance, and counted ten feet, from back of club to the trees on the hillside.

He avoided going back into the club where the body lay. He would have left, but didn't want to leave Glen alone to wait for the detectives.

The car with two detectives from the sheriff's department came at last, creeping slowly it seemed to Thomas.

Thomas watched it turn into the driveway leading up to the club. "Didn't you tell them we have a homicide here, Glen?"

"Sure did."

"Taking their time, aren't they?"

The car crunched into the gravel of the parking lot and stopped. Thomas looked at his watch. Only twenty minutes? He found it hard to believe. The sheriff's men had made fairly good time after all, but it seemed like a lifetime to Thomas. He had to tell what little he knew and hurry on. He knew of no way to tell Glen, or the homicide men, why he had to check on Megan Davis and Lois Trahem, and make them understand his anxiety.

Thomas and Glen had dealt with Richard Garnet and Kern Ward last year when they had been among the group that investigated the Moore murders. Richard Garnet was a jolly type who enjoyed his food. He looked easygoing, but Thomas had seen the opposite come out in him, when he could take control and everyone else paid attention.

Kern was second in command, a quiet, thoughtful man who had been in law enforcement at least ten years that Thomas knew of.

Richard Garnet asked lightly, "Is this becoming an annual event around your town, Tom?"

Thomas didn't answer. Just wait, Garnet, he thought to himself.

Garnet was so used to homicides that to him it might be a little funny that Spring Valley had only its second in its history. He was probably expecting a shooting victim, or maybe a stabbing, being here at a nightclub.

"Somewhat like the Fourth of July, eh?" Garnet chuckled.

He wore a smirk as he pushed the door of the car shut and ambled forward, adjusting his trousers. He wore a shoulder holster which would be covered by a coat if he hadn't left it hanging over the back of the car seat.

Thomas and Glen glanced at each other. Glen's face hadn't changed since he got his first glimpse of the body. His lips had pinched tight, his whole face tensed and shrunk into bones that protruded more than normally. His eyes met Thomas's briefly at Garnet's remarks, but held no amusement.

Both detectives went toward the front door of the club.

Thomas had locked all outside doors and put the three keys in his pocket. He pulled them out and handed them to Richard Garnet.

"It's all yours, Garnet," he said. "The body is right in there, on the dance floor. You can't miss it."

He hung around. Just one more minute, he told himself, just to see that smug look vanish from Garnet's face.

Detective Garnet unlocked the door, tossed the other two keys to his partner. "These, I gather, belong to doors of the club."

"Right," Thomas said. "The door to the apartment, in the back, and to the storage room. Also in the back."

Glen waited on the small porch. He had started to follow the detectives in, then faltered. He looked back at Thomas.

Thomas explained, "I'm going on, Glen, to check on a couple of places, a couple of people. I don't have any definite ideas about this. All I know is a small gang of kids did something of this nature to that dog. So we have to be on the lookout for them. You hang around here, see that everything is taken care of. I'll be back as soon—"

The door jerked open and the two men almost fell through the doorway. Kern stumbled past Glen, bent forward, his hand over his mouth. He ran to the corner of the building and out of sight. Thomas felt a twinge of pity.

Richard Garnet's face had turned as colorless as Glen's. Thomas couldn't see his own face, and didn't want to. But color leached from Garnet's skin had only deepened in his eyes. Anger, livid, at exactly whom Thomas wasn't sure.

Swallowing, as if he too were sick to his stomach, Richard demanded, "What the hell is this, anyway? You saw the body, Thomas, why didn't you say something?"

Seeing Richard Garnet lose his cool wasn't as satisfying as Thomas had thought it would be.

"How the hell is a person going to describe something like that and take the shock out of it, Garnet?" A little voice of conscience inside him chided, you could have tried, Tommy, you could have tried. It sounded a bit like his mother. It just wasn't right to get any satisfaction out of seeing Garnet sick to his stomach.

Richard Garnet went over to the unmarked car, leaned for a moment against the fender with his head down, then he looked toward the sky, and took a deep breath. He reached inside and picked up his radio receiver. Holding it, he said to Thomas, "Okay, do you have any idea of who could have done this, or why?"

"No. But while you're calling, tell them to send all the patrol cars they can, and keep on the lookout for a gang of kids, ages nine to thirteen or fourteen. Two girls, five or six boys. The youngest girl is carrying a large doll."

Richard stared at Thomas. "You've got to be kidding," he said, the anger in his eyes dissolving to disbelief.

Thomas shrugged. "No. Afraid not. Listen, I've got to do some checking around. I'll get back to you later."

"Anything else you can tell us?" Richard called after him.

Over his shoulder, as he got into his patrol car, Thomas answered, "Glen will fill you in. He'll stay here until I get back."

Thomas drove the two blocks to Megan Davis's small, white house, alert for any movement. The few houses he passed were closed and dark. The corner street light illuminated an area in which nothing but Thomas's own car moved.

He parked in the narrow driveway of Megan's house. There was a light on somewhere in the interior. He had a bad feeling about what he might find here, ever since he got the first shock of what had been done to Lane. He hoped he was wrong, and that he'd find her soundly asleep.

She lived in a small frame house that had been built shortly after the turn of the century. It was in good repair, kept up with fresh paint and an occasional new roof. The porches were small, not large enough to hold porch furniture. In her grassy, shady yard there was a lawn swing and a table with an umbrella. Moonlight spotted the yard, and total blackness beneath the trees seemed to hold eyes that watched his every move.

He went to the back door. If Megan had a dog or cat they made no sound. He knocked. The screen door was closed, but when he opened it he found the inner kitchen door standing half open.

He called out her name and received no answer. He felt for a light switch and turned them on. The kitchen suddenly was bright with light. It was clean and neat, in total contrast to the kitchen at Lane's place. Beyond the kitchen was a hall, and the light he had seen spilled out of a bedroom off the hall.

"Megan," he called again, hearing the hollowness of his voice in a skimpily furnished house.

He walked slowly and reluctantly along the short hall, passing one bedroom that was dark. He went on to the one with the light and stopped.

The thing on the floor could no longer be called Megan. The skinned body lay glistening beneath the light, red with blood, the muscles and layers of fat adding deeper and lighter shades.

Lying across the bed, obscenely deflated, like a plastic replica, was the skin. The head lay flat, curly blond hair the only part that seemed real.

On the floor at the side of the bed the telephone mewed persistently, electronically warning that it was off the hook.

The grisly work obviously had been done in the bedroom where the tormented body now lay. Blood smeared the carpet and spotted the walls.

With his .38 in his hand, Thomas backed out of the room. He turned on every light switch he could find along the hall and the one extra bedroom, then went out to his car to use the police radio to call back down to Lane's place.

Glen answered his call.

"I've got another one here," he told Glen, "Megan Davis. You know where she lives."

There was a loaded silence. Thomas understood Glen's inability to absorb more. Then he said, "Another one. Like Lane?"

"Yes." Thomas didn't want to say any more than he had to over the air. "Listen, Glen, have Garnet get some more help. You come here to Megan's as fast as you can and wait for a crime unit to arrive. Get the state police. I think I know where they may be headed next, and I have to get over there."

Glen didn't even ask where. "Okay," he said. Thomas checked the neighboring yards as he waited. He didn't disturb the sleeping owners. He hung around only because he had to leave an officer at the scene of the crime. He had reason to believe Lois Patison was in danger also, and felt a driving anxiety to go check on her. As soon as Glen's car turned into the driveway, Thomas was prepared to leave.

• • •

Lois stood in the darkened room looking out through the window from behind the curtain. She could almost laugh at herself. A paranoid old woman, peeking out from behind a curtain. Not old, yet. But paranoid, definitely. Especially tonight. She had heard footsteps across the front porch, soft, like a kid wearing sneakers, fast, like a kid running. By the time she had reached the front door and turned on the porch light, the footsteps had stopped.

Then, as she stood listening, the only light in her house coming from porch lights and moonlight through windows, it sounded like someone was fiddling with the screen somewhere in the back of the house.

With chills radiating up and down her backbone and her arms tingling with goosebumps, she hurried to the back bedroom. But there was no one at the window. She was looking out into the black shadows beneath a shade tree when the phone rang.

She almost screamed, the sound so startled her. She'd never realized before that her phone was so loud. She hurried to answer it before it could ring again. But by the time she had run to her bedroom down the hall it had rung three times.

She was half afraid to answer it. Who would be calling her this late at night? It must be midnight or after.

She snatched it up, and whispered into it. "Yes!"

"Lois?"

It was Dr. Tyler. It was an authentic call, not some ghostly haunting.

"Yes," she murmured, only slightly louder, so relieved she had begun to shake all over. She clutched the phone in both hands.

"Is that you, Lois?"

"Yes," she said aloud but still trying to keep her voice down. "Dr. Tyler?"

"Lois, I have a strange case going on over here at Matt Reed's. Could you come over for a while?"

"Sure. I'll be right there."

She hung up before he could say anything else. Normally she probably would have asked what on earth was happening, but tonight it was as if Dr. Tyler had thrown her a lifeline. She was only too glad to get out of her house.

She hadn't undressed. She paused only to grab her purse and car keys, and then hurried to her back door.

At the side of her house was a carport, covered by a roof, but unprotected at sides and end. She turned on the carport light and hesitated before opening the door. Through the glass on the door she looked out.

The child could be hiding on the other side of the car, beneath it, or even in it. But she had to take a chance.

She turned the lock button on her door after she opened it, then pulling it shut behind her, she ran to the car, feeling at every step that something mad was snapping at her heels.

She slid into the car and pulled the car door shut and pushed the lock button. Feeling safer than she'd felt in a long fear-filled hour, she started the car and turned on the headlights.

The driveway and street looked as peaceful and safe is it always did, and Lois began to breathe easier as she drove away.

The town had gone to bed. Only the street lights seemed alive and awake, humming on their poles at the end of each long block. The headlights of the car cut through each shaded, wide street, and found nothing moving. Not even a cat or dog crossed her path.

Lois pulled into the driveway at the Reed home. She parked behind Dr. Tyler's car. In front of the doctor's car was another, a small blue sedan. Nina's, Lois thought. She had brought Halley home from the revival after Halley fainted. Was Halley ill?

The front porch light was on, and the pathway to the porch lighted by a lantern yardlight, so soft and dim it hardly competed with the full light of the moon.

Nina stood on the porch, and as soon as Lois parked, came down the walk to meet her.

"Is Halley worse?" Lois said.

"No," Nina answered, "It's not Halley, it's Matt. After I brought Halley home I went on home myself, but not long afterwards, half an hour perhaps, Halley came running to my house. It seemed Matt had caught himself in one of his own traps and was lying in the backyard. Cory had stayed with him. Matt was bleeding and unconscious. Halley couldn't get him up."

They reached the house and went in. Lois walked with what she thought of as her business walk, a quick nurse's stride, beside Nina, climbing the stairs into a house Lois had never entered before.

"Why hasn't he been sent to a hospital?" Lois asked. "If he was so badly hurt that he was unconscious, I don't understand why Dr. Tyler hasn't sent him on. He usually never hesitates to pass a patient on. Especially in recent years."

"There are reasons. We just wanted you to come over and see what you think."

"Who, me?" Dr. Tyler wanted to know what she thought? At the clinic he often asked her opinion, but she had assumed it was something just between the two of them and never expressed to anyone else. "Everything I know I learned from him. I can't imagine why Dr. Tyler would need my opinion in this case."

Nina didn't answer. Lois thought it rather odd, but the thought was fleeting.

They had reached a second floor hall that led off the narrow balcony at the front. Lois paused, looking at Nina.

"What can I do?"

Then it occurred to her that perhaps the doctor just wanted someone to sit with a patient for the rest of the night, and Lois was happy to do that. Anything to get away from home at the moment, even though as she thought back she began to feel so foolish she knew she would say nothing about it. To even think she had seen her nephew was now taking the form of hysteria of some sort. Was it a case of mass hysteria they had at the revival meeting? In which they had seen Patrick? Then she, walking into the darkness of her own yard, had continued the hysteria and thought she saw Cliff?

But worse was the fact that it had scared her. She had been afraid of her own hallucination. That was it. Now that she was away from home, she could see it for what it was.

She entered the first room on the left. Dr. Tyler stood a few feet from the bed on which Matt lay, half dressed, his shirt and trousers unbuttoned but still on. A white sheet blanket lay partly over him. His right hand was bandaged in white from the tip of his fingers to his elbow. It lay across his stomach.

Halley sat in a chair near the corner.

Neither Halley nor Dr. Tyler spoke to her. Dr. Tyler nodded as she entered the room. Lois started to speak softly, as she would have in any room where someone was ill, but her words died in her throat. She stared at Matt.

The voice of a young boy was coming from him, or from somewhere close to him. Matt's lips were parted, but not moving.

The boy was speaking, laughing, but Lois could understand only a few of the words. Disjointed, they meant nothing to her. She felt a frown deepening on her forehead, and that same uneasy fear she thought she had left at home was returning, coiling over her like icy worms.

Dr. Tyler asked softly, "Is that Cliff's voice, Lois?

Cliff's voice? Lois's cheeks tightened. She felt them pulling the way they did when Janet at the beauty shop gave her an ice facial. She listened.

The boy seemed to be speaking a kind of street language, but it was only an impression. She couldn't separate word from word. But she had never heard the voice before.

She shook her head.

"Not Cliff," she said. "Why would it be—"

There was a brief moment of silence, as if her voice had surprised the other. Then, a few heartbeats later another child's voice began speaking. Instantly Lois recognized it.

Cliff.

"Please, please let me go home. My Aunt Lois will be worried. Let me go home."

Sobbing replaced the pleas, weeping, soft and forlorn, as if the child were alone and knew he would be alone forever.

CHAPTER NINETEEN

THOMAS FELT AS IF HE WERE WADING UP TO HIS NECK IN HOT THICK LAVA. What kind of answer would he have received if he had asked for a man to go over to Lois Trahem's house to check and see if she were still alive, and if she were, to warn her? Why would the murderer of two people who were connected to the town's only hot spot then go after the nurse of the town's only doctor?

Because, her child was one of the missing. Who seemed, for reasons that were as dark and mysterious as the children themselves, to have turned up tonight looking exactly as he had the day he disappeared three years ago. Turned up in the company of kids he probably hadn't even known. Who had in common with him only the fact that they too were missing town children.

He would have to talk to the detectives as soon as he could. He'd tell them the first death in town was a dog. He'd have to give them Dennis's name and address, so they could question the boy who had escaped. He wondered as he drove the few blocks on to Lois's house, why the murderous gang had attacked the children. Only because they were there? Outside playing long after dark? Probably. But he had a feeling there was a connection he hadn't seen yet.

He found Lois's place glaring out into the shadows and moonlight. The porch lights were on, and the carport light shone down on a bare concrete floor. Her car was gone.

The moment he saw her car was gone, he was profoundly relieved. The feeling was so strong his muscles felt affected by it, almost collapsing him onto the ground when he got out of the car. It was now past midnight. Where had she gone? It hardly mattered. The important thing was, she wasn't home.

To make sure, he went to the front door and rang the doorbell several times. A little dog barked shrilly, and another woofed. He remembered. Lois had gotten two puppies a few months after Cliff disappeared. Obviously they were all right.

He walked around the house. Unlike many of the houses in town, her backyard wasn't fenced. A hedge divided her large yard from the one on the west, and a row of trees separated her place from the neighbor in the other side. With his flashlight he looked into every shadow, and found nothing.

Dogs were still howling, but they were more distant, and the sound reached him as if in waves. The sound seemed to fit the eeriness of the night, of the terrible murder scenes he had so recently left.

His next stop was the small police station, a brick building with one cell and a couple of offices. He went in to find Noel Lyman on duty behind the desk in the front room.

Noel was in his forties, a volunteer both in the fire department and the police station. He was rarely needed. A man who wore a worried look all the time anyway, he now looked scared, his eyes rounded.

"What's going on tonight, Thomas?" He got up, as if he thought Thomas had come to relieve him and his duty done for the night.

Thomas waved him back down into his seat.

"If you don't mind, Noel, would you stay by the phone? We might need you." Thomas walked by without pausing. At the door to his office, he said, "Tell you later, okay? When I know more myself. I'll be in my office for a while."

With Noel standing in the office doorway, Thomas pulled out the file of missing children.

There were the pictures of Cliff Patison, Will Yardley and Karen Davis, young, smiling faces, most of them school pictures, clear and sharp. They were the children missing from town during his tenure as chief of police in Spring Valley. Three too many.

He began checking back, following a hunch.

He found her, quicker than he had hoped. A smiling little girl of ten. Her long blond ringlets lay over her shoulders in glossy tubes. She had a beautiful doll-like face.

The picture of the little girl who tonight carried this doll, was in a file of missing children that occurred thirty years earlier. Her face was lovely, just as he had seen it, her hair long and blond and hanging in carefully made ringlets over her shoulders, just the way it was tonight.

Coleen Reed.

There were also the pictures of two boys. One of them, Jeremy Arnold, age thirteen, had disappeared the same day as Coleen Reed. The other boy, thirteen year-old Daniel Hismet, had disappeared three months earlier. Both boys had been foster children of the Reed's.

A note on the boys' files indicated it was assumed they had gone to find their families. There was no similar note on the Coleen Reed.

There were no more children listed as missing from the town. Six children in all, over a thirty year period. But there had been at least seven or eight children in the group in the road in front of his car. He had no way of knowing who they were, but Coleen Reed was without a doubt the little girl with the doll.

Coleen at age ten.

Thomas sat down.

"What's wrong?" asked Noel. He still stood in the doorway. The police station was silent.

"I don't know." How could he even attempt to make someone else understand what he himself did not?

Noel came to the desk and looked down at the files open there, and the pictures of the children. Quizzically, he looked up at Thomas.

Thomas pointed at the pictures of Coleen Reed and the two foster children. "Did you know these kids, Noel? Did you live here when you were a kid?"

"Yes, I was born here. Lived here all my life except when I was in the army. I knew Coleen. She was a couple of years younger than I, but I remember her. Partly because of what happened to her, I guess."

"What happened?"

"She ran away, they said."

"Yes, but, was there anything else?"

He was silent a moment, looking from the picture of Coleen to the others.

"Nothing that I know of." He pointed at the picture of Daniel, the first child to disappear. "He was in my class at school. He was a skinny, scared kid who hung back, didn't make friends. I tried to make friends with him, and finally got him to play ball at recess. When I heard he ran away I wasn't surprised. He wasn't a happy kid. This other one, I never saw. He was only at the Reed's about a week before he and the little girl, ran away.

They said the only thing she took was her doll. Doesn't seem right, does it?"

"Sure doesn't." Thomas got up. He began to pace the floor behind the desk, unable to sit still, in a hurry to go, but wanting to hear anything that Noel remembered. "Was there anything else, Noel? Any rumor, no matter how vague? What police work was done on it? There's not much information here."

"Nothing. It happened in the summertime, but you can read that. I don't know what day."

"July fourteen. Well, say, if anything comes up, I'm headed for the Reed's. Matt had an accident tonight."

Noel followed him to the door. "Accident? What happened?"

"I'll tell you later," Thomas promised as he left Noel standing in the open front door as he had stood in the office door.

"There were some others," Noel said.

"What?"

Thomas stopped and looked back. Insects made running dives at the light beside the door. Noel walked out onto the steps.

"Other kids. Two, I remember. They were both my age. They ran away too, the year before."

"Two boys?"

"Yeah. I don't even remember their names now."

"Town children?"

"Well, they stayed with the Reeds."

Thomas stood staring hard at Noel, as if in his memory an answer lay.

"More foster children?"

"Yeah, I guess they were. They were there at the Reeds about two months apart, and only stayed a short time. One of them just a week or so, I think. There was a girl too. She graduated from high school here."

"What happened to her?"

"She went on back to her folks, as far as I know. I just remember that the boys kept running away. Then after Coleen ran away too, with the last one, they never kept any more kids. No one could blame them. They hadn't had very good luck."

"I wonder why there's no file on those two boys," Thomas said, thinking to himself that it explained the two vague figures who were described by the Niles boys as being a background part of the gang, and the shadowy figures he had seen in the street.

"I don't know. I guess whoever was in office then didn't think it was important. You say Matt had an accident?"

"Tell you later. Keep awake, Noel."

Thomas started the patrol car and moved it away from the curb.

What was going on? How could such a quiet little town cover so many secrets as it now seemed to? How could a group of kids, most of whom had not even known one another, now come together and be returned to the physical reality of what they were at the time of their disappearances?

Or had someone come across the file of missing children and in some way duplicated their appearances in other kids in order to commit the murders?

Crazily, the former seemed more likely.

Nothing about it made sense. How could a group of children so closely resemble children missing from town over a period of thirty years?

Never mind the how. The fact was, two people were brutally murdered. And they were the parents of two of the missing children. A bizarre pattern was unfolding. If the pattern held, everyone in the Reed house was in danger. Maybe even Nina.

And Lois Trahem, wherever she was, definitely was in danger.

He speeded, driving the distance to the northwest side of town in a few minutes. Along the way he passed houses dark and quiet, streetlights shining down on a buzz of insects and the silence of shrubs and grass.

When he pulled into the driveway at the Reed house he was surprised but relieved to see a grey sedan that looked like the one he'd seen parked in Lois's carport many times. He even remembered when she had bought it. As with any new car purchase everyone stopped to admire it. He had. If he remembered correctly, it was a Dodge, now four years old. In fact, hadn't she bought it the same year Cliff had come to live with her?

The porch light was still on, as was the light at the back. Lights from windows indicated that both hall and kitchen lights were burning.

Thomas found the front door unlocked. Yesterday he would have thought nothing about unlocked doors. Most of the people in town left their houses unlocked, at least during the day. Now, he entered, and pulled the door shut and locked it.

Too late, he thought. Whatever it was, had already invaded their lives.

CHAPTER TWENTY

Dr. Tyler stood with his arms folded. His patient seemed now to be asleep, but he had seemed to be asleep when the voices of the children had issued from somewhere around him. Tyler had stooped once, put his ear close to Matt's face, and could not tell for sure if the voices were coming from Matt's own lips. It really didn't seem as if they were. He only knew they were in the air close to Matt, as if a ventriloquist were at work in the room.

Halley, still sitting in the black recliner in the corner, looked more ill than Matt. She sat leaning forward, her bare feet flat on the floor.

Lois stood at the foot of the bed, as white as he had ever seen her.

Nina remained quietly by the door.

She jumped, trembling, when the door opened and Thomas stepped into the room. Dr. Tyler thought for a moment Nina was going to throw her arms around him. Relief put a touch of color back into her face. Tyler was as glad to see Thomas as Nina was.

"The front door was unlocked," Thomas said softly. "I thought you'd rather I just walked in than be disturbed by the doorbell."

Halley nodded.

Thomas continued, "I locked the door. I was wondering if there are any more doors in the house that are unlocked."

Halley looked up, but the dazed, stupefied expression on her face didn't change.

Nina said, "The kitchen door, Halley?"

"I don't know. Probably unlocked."

"I'll go down and lock it. Want to come with me, Thomas?"

They left the room. Neither Halley nor Lois took their eyes away from Matt.

Dr. Tyler stood a few minutes longer at Matt's side. He had no way of knowing for sure if the man were in a strange comatose state, but it seemed he was. His temperature was normal, as were his blood pressure and heartbeat. Tyler didn't know what the hell was wrong. There seemed to be no complications from the wounds on his hand and arm. Tyler had cleansed them thoroughly. There was no real threat of infection. What was coming from Matt, at intervals, had nothing to do with the wounds on his hand.

Halley didn't want Matt moved to a hospital. But if something weren't done, she was herself going to be ill beyond help.

Tyler moved over to stand by Lois where he could talk to her in a lowered voice.

"I wonder if you'd mind staying here with Matt and Halley for awhile? I'll be back as soon as I can."

She nodded. Her hands gripping the railing at the foot of the bed.

As he left the room he heard the eerie sound of children again. Like chicks, their voices chattered, coming from the area in the room where Matt lay.

He was glad to leave the sounds behind. Happy children's voices tonight were weird and horrible. Happy voices that he knew would change, become the voice of one child, then changing to tears.

He remembered to lock the front door behind him as he left. He crossed the porch, going out of the light to the black shadows beneath a tree. For the first time since he was a kid he felt nervous, and hurried to leave the darkness. He crossed the lawn to his car, going into the moonlight which seemed only a little less bright than it had earlier. Shadows slanted farther away from the trees and over the driveway as the moon, huge and fat and seeming about to burst on this strange night, made its way westward.

He was glad to reach his car. He pressed the lock button, and heard the click as the rear doors locked. Thank God for electric locks. Though he didn't know why he needed them tonight. He rarely used them.

He maneuvered his car out from among those parked in front and behind and turned right at the street. There were no more houses on his right, now, except the Moore place, sitting back in its field, dark and silent since the day the bodies had been removed a year ago.

As he neared the corner he heard more clearly through his half-open window the howling of the dogs at the shelter. Like the voices that came from Matt, the howls of the dogs rose and fell periodically, for some minutes leaving the world in silence only to rise again.

The street turned left, skirting the field in which the preacher's tent stood. In the moonlight he saw the tent, like an inflated mushroom. Behind it moonlight glinted on the roofs of vans, RVs, automobiles.

At the end of the street he turned right onto the road out of town, and saw several cars parked at Lane's place. Some of them, he noted with curiosity, were police cars from the county sheriff's department. The club was lit up like a wild Saturday night, but there was no music wafting out over the street.

A few men, a couple in uniform, wandered about in the parking lot as if looking for something. All of them looked carefully at him as he passed by.

He drove on, watching for the turn into the field. A culvert forded a ditch, which in rainy weather ran full of water. Over the culvert a narrow road led into the field between two fence posts.

Cars had made a trail through the weeds, which fanned out half way between the road and the tent. Weeds that had been mashed down earlier in the evening by cars were still trying to raise bruised heads. Dr. Tyler drove past the tent and parked a few yards from the group of automobiles and RVs.

He sat still, his fingers pinching his lower lip.

What was he doing here? Yesterday he would have snorted down any suggestion of what he was half thinking now. He was clearly out of his field with any psychiatric problem beyond the common things of depression, anxiety and some of the phobias. Those, in most cases, he believed, were caused by an imbalance of the chemicals that helped make up the brain. Not that he knew how to treat them. Who did? Not even the psychiatrists, who had studied the subject. Usually the matter took care of itself, and the chemical rebalanced. Patients didn't like to hear it, but he always told them, watch your lifestyle. You eat carefully, not too much, don't use drugs, don't smoke, don't burn the candle on both ends, don't pick fights with family members, and you'll feel good. Barring a serious disease.

He didn't believe too much in psychiatrists, but he would have been willing to send Matt on to one if Halley had allowed him to. He'd never run across anything like this before in his life. He'd never even heard of anything like this.

However, he felt sure a psychiatrist wouldn't know what to do either. Oh, they'd give him a spiel. This is wrong, or that. But then, maybe they wouldn't. Maybe they'd be as confounded as he, as willing to try the unorthodox.

In his thirty years of practice he had seen a couple of things that made him aware of the narrowness of human reality. He had seen it slip, leaving only madness behind. Something, tonight, had caused a terrible breach in Matt Reed. Medicine couldn't help.

He hadn't dared go to one of the ministers in town. They would laugh him out of the house. But this evangelist . . . cut of a slightly different cloth, maybe . . . a bit more unorthodox, maybe . . . At least Tyler wanted to talk to him.

But now that he was here, he had half a notion to leave again, go back to the Reed house, wait until morning, and see what happened. If Matt still was comatose, he'd insist on passing him on to the hospital. Wash his hands of it.

At that moment he noticed a figure standing at the corner of the big tent. He couldn't have said exactly when the person had stepped into view, but had a feeling he'd been watching for a moment. Then the figure separated from the shadows cast by the tent and walked out into the moonlight and toward the car.

It was a man, no taller than himself, but thinner and younger. As he drew near, Tyler saw a round, almost boyish face, thinning hair, a gentle expression.

Tyler got out of the car to meet him, and the man held out his hand. Tyler felt a strong handshake.

"I'm Dalton Walsh, of the Walsh Christian Alliance, traveling evangelist. What can I do for you, sir?"

"I'm Dr. Tyler. Were you already up enjoying the moonlight, Reverend?"

"Something like that. It has been one of those nights when sleep just didn't come for me. Do you ever have nights like that, Doctor?"

"Yes, occasionally." Tyler expected Walsh might suggest that in his case he'd probably take a pill, but he didn't.

Instead, Walsh said, "We had an unsettling situation tonight. The earthquake rather made us all nervous, and—"

"Earthquake!" What on earth was the man talking about?

They faced each other in the slanting moonlight, shadows of the tent consuming their feet and creeping slowly up their legs.

"Didn't you notice the tremor? About nine o'clock, I'd say. Not long after full dark had fallen. The earth definitely shook beneath our feet here on this bench of land."

"No, I didn't feel a thing. Hadn't even heard about any of that. At nine o'clock I was reading my Sunday paper. Sitting in my den with my dog at my feet and my cat on my lap."

Tyler thought of that cozy situation, which now seemed like it belonged to a different world. He had dozed off in the recliner, his head pillowed comfortably on a soft cushion that he left in the chair during the day. He had lived alone for many years now, since the death of his beloved Christine. He and his animals. Eventually he had gotten used to it and was comfortable with his life. Days were filled with work. On Saturdays and Sundays he worked in his garden, a small vegetable patch in his back yard. Right now his green onions were large enough their white little bulbs made a good bite, and the radishes were large and crisp. It was a life he felt was part of something he would never find again.

"In fact," Tyler added, "I guess I wouldn't know an earthquake if I felt one."

As if Tyler had been totally serious, Walsh said, "Yes, you'd know. Having the very earth rock beneath your feet is the ultimate in insecurity, Doctor. The one thing you've always taken for granted is deserting you. Even if only temporarily. To make the night even more unsettling, a young man appeared in the doorway who people said has been missing for a year. I think they said his name was Patrick, and he is wanted for questioning in the deaths of his parents and sister."

"Patrick! Patrick Moore was here tonight?"

"Yes, briefly. Less than a minute."

"I'll be damned. No one told me."

"He was here and then gone. Almost all the congregation saw him. My assistants saw him. I hurried out to talk to him, but he was gone."

Tyler thought of the police over at Lane's place, and wondered if they were looking for Patrick. But he didn't want to get into that with the preacher. He had a request to make, but didn't know how to put it. It was easier to just keep talking.

"Halley Reed and Nina Pole were here, so was my nurse, Lois, and none of them mentioned it to me.

"Miss Halley, who fainted? Is she all right now?"

"Halley fainted?" Tyler almost let out a string of swear words, and stopped himself. He hadn't felt so in the dark about everything in all his life. "She seems as well as can be expected, Reverend."

"Just Walsh, please. Or Dalton."

"Halley Reed's husband had an accident tonight. But that isn't why I'm here. We have a problem down at the Reed house that I'm at a loss to explain."

Dalton Walsh waited, full attention on Tyler. Tyler didn't know how to say this without making a fool of himself. Then he thought, what the hell. "Reverend, do you believe in spirit possession?"

CHAPTER TWENTY-ONE

WALSH DIDN'T KNOW WHAT TO SAY. HIS BRAIN BUZZED WITH POSSIBILITIES that splintered into a variety of answers. But the man in front of him was serious.

"Do you know, Doctor, in all my years as a minister of God's word, I have never been asked that question before?"

"I never thought I'd ever be asking it."

The doctor's eyes were steady, shadowed by the side of his face. If there was a twinkle in his eye, as if the man liked going around in the middle of the night making strange jokes, Walsh couldn't see it.

"You're serious," he said.

"I'm serious," Dr. Tyler answered. "I wonder if you would mind coming down to the Reed house and seeing Matt. Earlier tonight he had an accident. He likes to trap animals, and stuff them. He had given many of them to museums, so I've heard, and he keeps some of them in his house. Deer heads on the walls, that sort of thing. Anyway, he got his hand caught in his own trap. I wasn't very concerned about it. Frankly, I thought to myself, he deserved it. Let him know how it felt."

Walsh listened carefully. Dr. Tyler shifted his feet, made a half-turn eastward and looked back toward the darkened small town. His face was now completely shadowed, the moon edging westward behind him.

"I went over and cleaned the wounds, bandaged his hand and arm, did what I could. He seemed at that time to be dazed. We had to help him upstairs to his bed. He didn't want to be helped. He didn't want to be bothered. So I went home."

"An hour later, just as I was getting ready for bed, Nina called me. Nina is a young neighbor. She runs the local humane society. Has an animal shelter in the hills there, not far from the Reed place. If you've heard dogs howling tonight, that's where they are."

Walsh nodded. The intermittent, eerie howls was another reason he hadn't been able to go into his RV and settle down.

"Nina was with Halley and Matt. A problem had developed."

"Halley. Is she the lady who fainted tonight?"

Dr. Tyler looked at him straight and solemnly for a moment, but did not respond. Moonlight touched his features again, made his nose look oddly long, and his eyebrows shelf-like. Walsh motioned a dismissal. Dr. Tyler, obviously obsessed with his own problems, went on, facing east again. Walsh realized he must be looking toward the house of the man he was talking about. The dogs began barking again in the trees north of the tent. The barks soon turned into the unnerving howls Walsh had been hearing off and on since the service had ended and the congregation went home.

"Well, these voices come from him. Or from somewhere right next to him."

Walsh felt the cold brush of the hand against his cheek again. That ghostly brush of air he had felt when he looked up and saw the youth in his doorway. "Voices," he repeated. "What kind of voices?"

"Not the kind possessed people are supposed to have, like we occasionally hear about in a movie, or some such nonsense, like a deep, guttural voice. Not like that," Dr. Tyler said. "These are children's voices."

"From the man."

"Yes. But there's something else, Reverend. Those voices, a couple of them anyway, have been recognized as belonging to children who disappeared a number of years ago. In one case, thirty years ago. The man's own child, in fact."

"A voice, coming from the man, that sounds like his child who disappeared thirty years ago, Doctor?"

"Recognized by Halley, the mother. And the voice of my nurse's nephew. Who disappeared three years ago."

"Is the man aware of these voices?"

"No. At least, he appears to be sleeping. Maybe comatose."

Walsh blinked his eyes. They were beginning to feel strained from staring at Dr. Tyler, at trying to study the man's face. He still had a feeling of unreality. "You're very serious about this."

"Yes," the doctor said. "I can understand your reluctance to believe this. I found it hard to believe too. Then, I thought that maybe you'd had some experience with this sort of thing."

Walsh looked toward the road. "There seems to be a problem with children tonight. The chief of police was here earlier tonight asking me if I had seen a group of children. It seemed there was some kind of trouble concerning them."

"I don't know anything about that. But this, Reverend, is unlike anything I've ever heard before. I'm at a loss about what to do. I wondered if you'd mind coming down to the house with me."

"I'd be glad to. I'll drive my own car. It's right over here. Be with you in a minute."

On travels from one site to the next Walsh pulled a small Chevy attached by a strong, short cable behind his RV. He used the car for shopping and for sightseeing trips when he had time. He liked finding a quiet river or lake and just letting himself sit quietly with nature.

The keys were always in his pocket. His fingers toyed with them as he considered going to the door of one of his assistants and explaining that he'd be gone for awhile. But all of the other trailers and RVs were dark and quiet. Not even the dogs that traveled with the group had barked at the arrival of either the chief or the doctor. They were used to the sound of cars coming and leaving.

He decided against disturbing anyone. He couldn't read the face of his watch in the moonlight, but he knew it was now past midnight. He'd be back before any of them woke up.

He got into his car, started it and pulled it around to follow the doctor's sedan across the field and left onto the road into town. About an eighth of a mile down the empty road he saw a nightclub against the hillside, and in its yard a number of police cars. A few men milled about on the gravel parking lot in front of the club. A couple of them watched carefully as he and Tyler drove past.

Tyler turned left less than a block beyond the club onto an empty street that bordered the field. With the moonlight, a row of tall trees along the left threw shadows across the road. On the right a couple of houses almost hidden from the road in large, tree-filled yards seemed to be all that occupied the whole quarter-mile length of road.

The road curved to the right at the end of the field, passed by a field on the left and a darkened house far out in the middle of it, then pulled into the driveway of a large, two or three story house on the left. At least two other cars were parked in the driveway, and Walsh pulled in beside Tyler's sedan.

A porch light revealed a long porch, the kind that held a friendly collection of chairs, a few potted plants, railings and wide steps.

Walking beside Tyler, Walsh climbed the steps onto the porch. They waited in silence after Tyler pressed the doorbell.

Walsh heard no footsteps. Tyler evidently had chosen to say nothing more, and the only sound in the night were the howls of the dogs. Even the insects, whose sounds last night had filled the air, tonight seemed to have disappeared from the earth.

The door opened suddenly. The same young woman who had taken Miss Halley home smiled in surprise at Walsh. Beyond her, at the foot of the stairs, stood Thomas, the Chief of Police.

Dr. Tyler stepped into the foyer, and Walsh followed.

"This is Reverend Walsh," he said. "You've met him, I understand."

Walsh nodded a greeting at Nina and Thomas, and corrected Tyler, "Pastor Walsh. Or just plain Walsh, or Dalton."

Tyler now seemed slightly unsure of himself. He shoved his hands into his pockets in a boyish way that made Walsh want to pat him reassuringly on the back. He restrained himself.

Tyler asked, "How is Matt?"

"The same," Nina said.

Walsh looked at Thomas. There was a worried look on his face. He was a big man, with square shoulders. He wasn't bony, but had a look of leanness like a handsome racehorse. A Stetson would have looked right on him. But the look on his face was a contradiction. This man, accustomed to being in control of his world, was looking lost.

Nina seemed to know why Walsh was there, although Walsh himself didn't really know. What was expected of him? Suddenly it occurred to him he had forgotten his Bible. He had a feeling he was going to need it, as he had never needed it before.

"So glad you're here, Reverend," Nina said. "Matt's upstairs. Halley and Lois are with him."

He followed her up the stairs, with Tyler and Thomas coming behind him. As she climbed she kept glancing back, talking.

"Halley is the lady who fainted tonight, Reverend. You remember her. She's Matt's wife. Their grandson, Cory, is staying here while his daddy and mama take a trip. But he's asleep."

They reached the balcony above the foyer, went past a small area that contained a couple of chairs, a small table, and an open door to a room. They entered a hall that was dimly lighted, and seemed to reach back past several bedrooms. They stopped at the first door on the left.

It was a large bedroom, with large furniture. The carved walnut headboard of the bed stood against the inside wall to Walsh's right. There was a large chair in the corner, beside a table with a reading lamp.

Halley sat in the chair, slumping as if she had lost the will to hold herself upright. Her hair was loose, hanging over her shoulders, grey, coarse, straight. She was dressed now in a cotton robe.

On the other side of the bed was the other woman who had helped Halley. Lois. He remembered now that she was Dr. Tyler's nurse. She seemed restless, as if she had been pacing the floor. She smiled briefly at Walsh, but it was a sickly smile.

Walsh walked to the side of the bed and looked down. Several lights were on in the room, but the man on the bed seemed totally undisturbed by them. He was at least as tall as Thomas, but much heavier. Someone had unbuttoned his shirt and the top of his trousers. A few grey chest hairs rose and fell with his breathing. He had a beard that reached from the lobe of one ear around beneath his chin to the lobe of the other, but no mustache. His eyebrows were bushy and grey, his hair thick and dark, brushed with grey. He appeared to be sleeping, his lips slightly parted. They jerked and quivered occasionally, and behind his lids his eyeballs moved back and forth, then grew still. As if he were dreaming. Walsh was surprised that the presence of so many people in the room hadn't awakened him. Therefore, the sleep must not be a normal one. Nor the dreams, if they were dreams. People woke easily from a dream stage.

His right arm was neatly bandaged and lay across is stomach.

Walsh wondered what was expected of him. He felt awkward and embarrassed in these surroundings. He was lost without his Bible in his hands.

The others waited in silence.

Children's voices, Dr. Tyler had said. But Walsh heard nothing except soft breathings.

Walsh bowed his head and clasped his hands in front of him. "We will pray," he said.

With his thoughts wandering from the youth who had stood in his tent doorway, from the strange earth tremor that had preceded him, to the police at the nightclub on the road into town, to this odd, strained situation, he murmured a prayer. It came automatically to his lips.

"Oh God, we pray you bless this household, bless this good man and woman, and their friends, and heal these wounds that have penetrated the flesh, and heal the wounds that penetrate the souls of us all. Oh God, we pray in Jesus' name that—"

He stopped. Someone was screaming.

He glanced quickly at the others in the room, at the doctor, at the policeman. He saw in surprise none of them were reacting to the scream. No one was running out of the room toward the scream. Then he realized the sound was not from outside of the room, but here, there, somewhere very close.

The scream came softly, as if deeply buried. Like a scream on television that was turned low, Walsh heard it. Stunned, he listened, trying to find it in the room. Suddenly the scream became muffled, as if a hand had slapped against it. Then came the sobs, the weeping of a child.

Walsh stared at the man on the bed, aware vaguely that his own mouth hung open, the prayer dying. The man's lips weren't moving beyond the jerk and twitch of a sleeping, dreaming man, but the sound of the child appeared to come from him, the sound of crying abruptly stopped. The voice of a girl replaced it.

"Mama gave it to me," the voice said clearly. "She said when she was a girl she'd wanted a locket, so she got me one."

There came a brief pause, and then the girl continued. "No." She giggled. "I don't have a boyfriend. Mama says I'm too young. I have my mother's picture here, and my dad's, see?"

There was another pause, then the answer. "Well, my dad's . . . I don't know where he is. I barely remember seeing him. But I found this little picture in the album. Mama doesn't even know I have it. I put my own in behind my dad's."

"Yes, maybe," she giggled again, a soft, delighted sound of faint embarrassment. "If I ever get one."

Walsh turned his head. Nina was staring intently at the comatose man. But she had murmured something. A word. A name. The others also turned to look at her. She glanced briefly at Walsh and repeated, "Karen. That's the voice of Karen. A girl who—"

A sudden cry, in the voice of the young girl, came from the man. "No, no, please. I have to go now. Please let me go. No, don't—*don't*—" The child began weeping, softly, with growing desperation.

The man on the bed abruptly threw his head from one side to the other on the pillow as if he struggled under great distress. The voice dissolved into eerily indistinct cries and slurred words. Muffled screams and sobs, deep and hopeless. The man's body lay still on the bed, his shoulders pressed against the pillows. His head reared up, fell back and finally came to rest in its original position.

There followed a moment of silence, throbbing with the intensity of the sobs that had died away to nothing.

Then Walsh saw the man's eyes had opened. They stared at Walsh with the light of madness in them, and then came a sudden burst of laughter. It was thin and high, the laughter of a man mimicking a child. Or the shrill cry of a witch. It taunted them. It chilled Walsh, in a different way from the sound of the weeping child.

The man's lips hadn't moved. The muscles in his face lay lax. Only his eyes seemed truly alive. The laughter rose, then fell away to silence. The eyelids closed.

Walsh heard his own heartbeat. There was no movement in the room at all, no sound.

With his voice shaking, Walsh began to pray aloud. "Oh God, in Jesus' name we pray thee—"

As if his prayer had brought it about, a child's voice was suddenly speaking. This time it was a boy. Walsh kept his head down, his eyes closed. His trembling hands clasped against his stomach.

At first the voice spoke as if in a foreign language. Walsh felt he should be able to grasp the words, but they slipped past him, rapid, filled with delight, just as the girl's voice had been. Then abruptly they cleared and became intelligible. "His name is Frank."

Lois, standing at the foot of the bed, cried out softly, and her hands clamped against her mouth.

The little boy was saying, "Yeah." He giggled. "But he doesn't care what his name is. I named him after my grandpa. Did you know my grandpa? He used to take me fishing. Sometimes I take Frank, and we fish in the branch. It's not very deep, and there's not anything in it but minnows, but Frank has fun. We try to catch crawdads. He likes that even better than fishing. Once he got his nose pinched. And he yelped." The voice went on and on, a child telling of his experiences with his dog. At times the words grew unintelligible, and the timbre changed. From being a happy, carefree child, the boy became worried and tearful.

Dr. Tyler stepped forward and put his hand on Lois's shoulder.

"Please," the voice of the child said, "Please don't hurt my dog. Please. I got to go home." He started to cry, his words distorted by tears. "My

Aunt Lois will be worried. I have to be home before dark. Please, let me go. I have to go . . .

Then again came the weeping, soft and forlorn and continuing on and on, growing softer and softer and more indistinct until at last it was gone.

Dr. Tyler put his hands on Lois's shoulders and guided her toward the door. Nina went to Halley, took her hand and urged her up. Halley was weeping quietly, tears dampening her cheeks.

They were grouping in the hall outside the bedroom door, and after a hesitant moment in which Walsh stared at Matt Reed in puzzled horror, he turned and followed.

"You see, Reverend," Dr. Tyler said.

"Yes," Walsh answered, although he didn't. They were expecting answers from him, and he had none.

Lois said bitterly, angrily, "Do you think he's doing that on purpose? Do you think Matt knows we're here and . . ." She began shaking her head. "Oh God, no. He couldn't mimic Cliff's voice so perfectly. He couldn't."

Thomas said, "We ought to tell you, Reverend, those children, Cliff, Karen, Coleen, all those voices are of children who disappeared from town and were thought to have run away. Cliff, the little boy you just heard, the one with the dog, is—was Lois's nephew. He had been living with her for a couple of years. He disappeared three years ago. The girl, Karen, disappeared five years ago."

Nina said, "We've heard Coleen's voice too. Halley identified her voice."

Thomas explained to Walsh, "Coleen was Halley and Matt's older daughter. She was ten years old when she disappeared thirty years ago."

Dr. Tyler said, "I suppose it's logical that something in Matt's subconscious would remember her so vividly that he would be able to reproduce her voice."

"But what about the other children?" Nina asked. "We have heard at least four different voices. Coleen, Cliff, Karen Davis, and another child, a boy, whose voice sounded hoarse, as if he'd been crying a long time."

Dr. Tyler drew a deep breath that softly filled the interlude of silence. "I suppose it's also logical that . . . no, hell I don't know. I spent part of my internship working in the psychiatric ward of the state hospital, but never saw, or read, about anything like this."

Lois asked, "Did Matt know those children, Halley? Did he see them, maybe, up at the shelter?"

Halley straightened a bit. "Oh Lord no. He . . . " She glanced apologetically at Nina. "He hated having that shelter so close. He doesn't like dogs. He said they disturbed his sleep, they were always barking."

"But they're not," Nina cried defensively. "Well, tonight they're noisy, but when I'm home if they start barking or howling, I go right out. And anyway, I can assure you Mr. Reed was never once at the shelter. If he knew the children he met them somewhere else."

Lois said, "That was Cliff. I could never mistake his voice. Besides, he mentioned an Aunt Lois, and I'm the only one in town. I don't think it's Matt's subconscious, conscious, or anything else. I think it's something separate from him. Otherwise why would I have seen Cliff tonight before I even knew about the problem here?"

"You saw him?" Thomas asked Lois.

"Yes, I saw him. In my yard. He'd been on the porch. I heard the porch swing squeaking, and I heard his steps, clearly. Crossing the porch. I had walked home from the meeting, because the moon was so full and light, and it wasn't far, and when I came into my yard a boy was there waiting for me. He looked exactly like Cliff. He was even wearing a striped T-shirt, just like Cliff's. And jeans with the torn knees. The same clothes Cliff wore the day he disappeared."

Walsh was suddenly aware of a different kind of tension in the hall. The bedroom where Matt Reed lay was silent. But Thomas had tensed, and Walsh felt it.

Lois continued, "I started to go toward him. Then it dawned on me, this couldn't be Cliff. Cliff would be older now, larger. He wouldn't look exactly like he did three years ago."

"What time did this happen, Lois?" Thomas asked.

"I don't know. When the meeting ended."

"Shortly before ten," Walsh said. "We didn't carry on much longer after the—the incidents."

"And it took you about twenty minutes to walk home," Thomas said.

"Yes, probably."

"When you saw him, what did he do?"

"He just stood there looking at me. He didn't come closer, or anything. He just stood there. When I realized it couldn't be Cliff, I hurried on into the house and locked the door. But I kept hearing things. Scratches, footsteps on the porch, as if some kids were out there trying to scare me. I was glad when Dr. Tyler called."

"I think you were very fortunate," Thomas said. "I drove over to your house to see if you were okay, and found you'd gone already. I didn't see anyone around your house."

Lois asked, "Why? I mean, why were you checking on me?"

"I need to warn you all," Thomas said. "There's a gang of kids in town tonight that resemble those kids who are missing from town. Karen Davis, Willy Yardley, Cliff and Coleen. There were more boys I'd never seen. These kids fought with the Niles's kids over on Spring. Sandford Niles broke it up and the strange kids got away, but the dog was killed. And so were Lane Yardley and Megan Davis murdered tonight." The silence that followed had the quality of an invisible electricity that would snap to flames if anyone moved. Every pair of eyes stared at Thomas.

"I can't explain it," Thomas said. "I don't know what's happening, who the kids are, why they're committing such terrible crimes. I don't know where Patrick is. He's not at his house. I didn't check the barn, not yet. The state and county police have taken over the crime areas at Lane and Megan's places. And whatever it is with Matt, well, I don't pretend to know. That's out of my jurisdiction."

Walsh wished fervently for his old, soft Bible, the one his mother had given him when he entered his theology studies. It had always given him all his answers. He felt lost without it. Over the years it had conformed to his hands, bent when he needed it to bend, and held fast in times that were troubling.

Walsh said, "I'm sorry. But I have to tell you, I've never seen anything like this. I hardly know what to say. I have always believed that prayer and faith in Jesus Christ overcomes all. I don't know anything to do but pray."

Nina asked, "Do you believe in possession, Reverend Walsh?"

Walsh hesitated. His lips were so dry they felt sandy. "I believe it's an archaic explanation for medical problems, in most cases. Those I've read about I admit I discarded as the writer having been uninformed. Perhaps it's the man's condition, maybe he had fever—"

Dr. Tyler shook his head. "Temperature normal."

"—fever creates strange realities sometimes."

Dr. Tyler agreed with a nod. Then said, "But that's not the case tonight."

Walsh laid his hand on Halley's round shoulder. "Miss Halley, would you happen to have a Bible I can use? I forgot to bring mine."

"Yes."

She seemed glad to have something to do. She hurried down the hall and around the corner out of sight. In the room behind Walsh a faint murmur rose, and with it, the hairs on the back of Walsh's neck. He recognized a child's voice. There seemed to be no words at all as the voice grew louder. Only terrible sobs, as if the child had given up all hope.

Hope. Faith. It had been the foundation of his existence, Walsh thought as Halley returned with a Bible that was almost as softened by use as his own. Faith. Hope. Belief in God.

Belief in Jesus Christ.

Jesus would help them in their time of need.

CHAPTER TWENTY-TWO

THEY STOOD TOGETHER IN THE HALL IN A TIGHT LITTLE GROUP. BEYOND THE closed door the sounds of a young boy's hoarse weeping faded and rose and at last faded away. The silence that followed seemed to Walsh a blessing from God.

He had heard the boy's isolation, whoever he was, wherever he was. In his heart he had felt that isolation. A sudden and terrible fear coursed through him, and he realized that the horrors of this night, whatever they were, were nothing compared to the horror of facing another reality: the possibility there was no God after all. That they were as isolated and alone as the voice of that child.

Even as he stood there, with the Bible clutched against his breast, his hands crossed over it, those thoughts of there being no God were like a black pit beneath him. As the child beyond the door wept in terrible aloneness, Walsh prayed in silence, his desperation in a sense almost as deep as the boy's.

The silence, following, was God's blessing, filling him with relief, and a sense again of being within reach of the Great Altruistic Power, as he thought of God.

He turned. "I understand there's a child in this house?" he asked softly.

"Yes," Nina said. Halley turned with her, down the hall.

"I would like to check on him if I may."

They all went. Lois, Dr. Tyler, and Thomas following behind Nina,

Halley and Walsh. It was as if they were fearful of being apart, Walsh thought.

At the last door on the right near the end of the hall where a window looked out over a sloping roof on which the moon shined so brightly Walsh could see the shingles through the glass, Halley and Nina stopped. Nina stood back. Halley opened the door quietly. She whispered, "He's sleeping."

Through the slanting light, dim and pale, Walsh saw a bed on which a child sprawled, his face turned toward the window. The room looked rather small and safe with one window and one door. The child didn't move. "We won't wake him," Walsh whispered. "I just wanted to be sure he's all right."

Halley closed the door as softly as she had opened it and Walsh bent his head over the Bible and began a prayer.

"Oh God, in the name of Jesus Christ our Lord we pray you watch over this small child and bring him safely through this—this that hovers over the Reed home, over the little village of Spring River, over us all—this—"

He couldn't concentrate. He was aware of every movement of each of the people who were in the hall. Dr. Tyler stood slightly back, making no pretense at bowing his head. Only the ladies stood with bowed head, Nina the least attentive. Turning her face, she was watching Thomas.

Thomas had slipped quietly along the hall and was opening other doors. He went from room to room back toward the door to Matt Reed's room. He returned down the hall and opened a door that led into the back stairway, and Walsh, trying hard to find words of comfort for the women, for himself, and pleading for the safety of the child, heard Thomas's footsteps go down the stairs.

Walsh ended his prayer with, "Go with our law enforcement. Help them keep our world safe. Safe for children to grow up. Put your hand upon the faces of all who weep, and dry away the tears."

In his memory was the sound of the child weeping behind the closed door. It was a sound so pathetic it must have been heard only by the murderer of children.

"Let us understand, Lord," he began, and faltered. Let *us understand where the voice is coming from. How is it that a child has left the sound of its voice behind? What causes us to hear these voices?*

"Perhaps I should go back to—to the afflicted," he said.

Walsh went back down the hall. Behind him the doctor and the women followed. But Thomas had disappeared into the back stairs, and Walsh no longer heard his footsteps.

At the door to Matt's room he stopped and said to the small group. "I'll go in to stay with your husband, Miss Halley, and I'll see him through this. I'll stand beside him with God."

Beyond the closed door a young boy's voice suddenly said clearly, "Hey, a wolf! Neat! Where did you get it?"

Someone behind Walsh gasped.

They waited, frozen in their silences. Only their eyes met. Walsh saw in the eyes of the doctor and the women the same surge of surprise he felt within himself. No matter how many disembodied voices spoke from the haunted room, the haunted man, it continued to be a shock. The voice which had spoken about a wolf was without a doubt the voice of a young boy. It was a voice none of them seemed to have heard before.

The silence continued, and Walsh was aware of everyone taking a deep breath.

Dr. Tyler asked, "You have any ideas on this, Reverend?"

Walsh hesitated, then from somewhere deep within him, he brought forth a truth he had never admitted to himself, had never been forced to admit to himself. "I don't believe in evil possession. I don't believe the devil exists and can take over the spirit of human beings. Evil exists in man. It's born of the pleasure derived from cruelty, from doing injury to other living creature. And, perhaps, from trying to create a source of power, and thereby creating a power that seems to be supernatural. An entity of pure evil, for power."

Halley stood with her head down. Walsh couldn't see her eyes.

"Matt's a good man." Halley lifted her head. "We lost our ten year-old daughter, thirty years ago. One day she was gone. She and a foster child. Since then Matt has been . . . well, more to himself. But, he's not bad man."

"Of course tonight," Dr. Tyler said, "he's helpless. Not exactly what you'd call filled with power, evil or otherwise. Wouldn't you say?"

"But the children are totally powerless," Nina said. "And it sounds to me as if the voices and words we've heard are part of the last words those children ever uttered. How does it happen the voices are here apparently from or near Matt? How is it that children who answer their descriptions have been seen tonight on the streets of town?"

Walsh said, "I'm sure Chief Thomas will uncover the source of the voices. It's probably the children that were seen, somehow projecting their voices, from outside the window, from . . ." he trailed off. Knowing as he spoke that it was only an attempt to find an explanation they could understand and accept. The emotion he had heard in the voices was impossible to project, no matter how great the actor. It had held the sound of truth, a truth so deep that once it had been real.

He was supposed to know answers, but he didn't. He found himself turning the focus onto Miss Halley, who looked as if she were going to faint again. "Perhaps Miss Halley should go to her room and rest. Maybe take a sedative."

Halley shook her head. "I'm all right," she said. She looked ill and dazed with shock.

Walsh said, "All I can do is pray. Pray for our souls, or his, for the souls of the chil—"

As if his touch on the doorknob activated some distant mechanism, a scream rose abruptly on the other side of the door. It sounded as if it came from far away, but it was filled with horrors unspeakable. Walsh froze or a moment, his fingers gripping the cold, porcelain knob.

Then the voice began speaking through its anguished weeping. As Walsh opened the door, the words poured distinctly out at them, spoken through the liquid sound of tears.

"Please let me go home. I want to go home."

Lois cried out softly. Dr. Tyler put his arms around Lois's shoulders.

The child's crying sharpened.

"Frankie," he screamed. *"Give me back my dog. What are you doing to my dog? Don't hurt my dog, please. Don't hurt my dog."*

The screams were harsh and filled with pain, then settled into a constant weeping that went on and on.

Halley cried, "What's he doing? Oh my Lord, what's he doing?"

Walsh understood her torment. It was as if they were witnessing a death scene. They stood together, helpless to stop the destruction.

Suddenly the wretched weeping of the child was interspersed again with words muffled but understandable.

"Don't hurt me, please don't hurt me. I want my Aunt Lois. I want my mommy, my mommy Lois. Let me go home. I'll never tell. Just let me go home, please. *I want my mommy."*

The words ended, leaving only the agonizing weeping. It drifted away, softer and softer.

Walsh stared into the bedroom. The man still lay as he had lain when Walsh left the room earlier. But there was a dark, formless fog-like cloud moving over him. It roiled, like a storm cloud. It filled the corner of the room beyond Matt and the bed.

As the weeping gradually faded to silence, so too the dark cloud dissipated.

Walsh took a step forward, then threw his arm out against the door frame for support. The floor had tilted, an almost imperceptible movement. Behind him someone was sobbing.

He pulled the door shut behind him, closing himself alone into the room with the man and whatever it was that hovered over him.

HALLEY WANTED TO COMFORT LOIS, but her hands were shaking uncontrollably, her heart was racing, and a tightness that made her tremble was straining her chest. Lois wept, and Dr. Tyler held her. Halley felt the warmth of Nina beside her. But there was no comfort now, from anyone.

She could hear Reverend Walsh praying again beyond the closed door of Matt's room. The murmuring sound of the prayer went on and on.

"I can't stand it," Lois cried softly. "I can't stand it. That was Cliff. I would know his voice anywhere, anywhere. What's causing it? What's bringing it? He was killed. I know it now. Yet I saw him tonight. And heard him, crying. We all heard him. Is this some kind of terrible joke?"

Halley suddenly was shaking all over. She couldn't stop herself. "No, Cliff wasn't killed. He ran away. They all ran away."

As if Lois hadn't heard, she wept, "Someone killed Cliff. They killed his dog, killed Cliff. All those children are dead. Someone is playing a terrible joke."

Halley cried, "Matt wouldn't hurt anyone. He wouldn't. He loved Coleen more than anything or anyone in the world. After Coleen was born, there wasn't anything else for Matt."

Just the woods, the hunting, the hobby. That was all. He spent more time in the woods than he did at home, but that was all right. She got used to it.

"Someone killed Cliff," Lois wept, her face against Tyler's chest.

Halley cried, "Oh God, don't you understand? Matt couldn't hurt anyone!"

Dr. Tyler put his hand on Halley's shoulder. "Halley, no one said Matt hurt the child. Why don't you go rest now? I think both you and Lois should go rest. Come along, there's no reason to stand here in the hall. Reverend Walsh is with Matt. And the boy is sound sleep. Let's not disturb him."

Halley let the doctor take her to her room. She remembered Lois. Lois had come over to help out, and Thomas didn't want her to go home tonight. Something to do with the children.

"What is Lois going to do? Will she stay here?"

"Don't worry about Lois. I'll take care of her. Meantime, you go to bed, Halley. That's an order, take a couple of the tranquilizers I gave you, and try to rest."

She nodded. When the door closed behind him she went to the bathroom and opened the cabinet door where she kept her small supply of medicine. Aspirin, a potion for rubbing on aching muscles, even a little pink bottle of very old baby aspirin. And the bottle that still had a few sleeping pills in the bottom.

She drew a glass of water and steadied it against the sink. What if Matt woke up and needed her? She must be able to go to him. She should be with him now, by his side, on the bed beside him, holding his head in her arms, as she would have early in their marriage if he had been ill. But Matt had never been sick. He had never needed her.

She left the bathroom without taking anything and sat down on the bed. With her hands flat on the bed beside her she sat drooping forward. Her eyes closed and hot tears oozed out from under her lids. Even after Coleen's disappearance he hadn't needed her. Once she had put her arms around his shoulders as he sat, elbows on knees. And he had lifted an elbow and nudged her away. It was the last time she touched him.

What was wrong with her Matt, her king of the hills?

Where were those voices coming from?

Not Matt. They had nothing to do with Matt.

She knew he had never met those children.

THOMAS LEFT LIGHTS burning behind him as he searched through the house. Downstairs he found rooms that looked as if they hadn't been used in fifty years. There was an old parlor at the front furnished with hard, overstuffed pieces that probably dated from the nineteen thirties. He knew a little about the Reed family. One of the first settlers in the area, Matt's grandfather Jacob Reed had owned a feed mill and a general store, and had built the house. It had passed on, as property did in those days, to his eldest son, Simon Reed. Simon was Matt's father, and he and his wife had only one child, Matt.

Matt Reed's mother was still living when he married Halley, a girl from a nearby township. The daughter-in-law had lived for several years in the home of the mother-in-law. Then the elder Mrs. Reed had died. It was the kind of family history that was common in most rural areas. Nothing out of the ordinary had happened in their lives. Babies were born, elders died. Matt Reed inherited property and businesses which were sold or otherwise turned over to others to manage. There had never been a shortage of money in the Reed family, so far as Thomas knew. Matt Reed had been able to retire from running businesses he hadn't been interested in and devote more time to what he liked. Thomas had only rumors to go on, but it seemed Matt had a love for the woods, for hunting, trapping, and taxidermy. Maybe he stepped over the law and sometimes took animals that were supposed to be protected by the law, but Thomas had never tried to investigate him. The game wardens were responsible for that, but no one had ever bothered Matt, because Matt never bothered anything. You don't go around questioning a good citizen about his hobby.

But as Thomas came upon the locked door just off the little dark hall in the back of the house, the door into the addition Matt himself had built, he wondered why it was locked.

He stood with his hand on the doorknob, twisted it right and left. It was in that section of the house, Thomas knew, where Matt's taxidermy hobby was located. He went outside and looked at the addition. Moonlight glinted on the windows of the kitchen, on the old part of the house, but there were no windows in the new addition. It was a low, one-story, frame section that was larger than Thomas would have thought necessary. It jutted out on the northwest corner of the house, low-roofed, shaded by large trees on the west.

There appeared to be a window-less basement beneath it. Thomas found a cellar door, set flat in the ground, at the edge of the foundation. That door too as locked. He walked around the house, watching for movement in the black shadows of the trees. He saw and heard nothing. He went back into the house. He had to get the keys to the locked addition from Halley, and see what was in there.

CHAPTER TWENTY-THREE

THOMAS CLIMBED THE ENCLOSED BACK STAIRWAY AND CAME OUT INTO THE long bedroom hall where he had left the others. The hall was empty. He paused at Cory's bedroom, opened the door just wide enough to check and see that the boy was still in bed. He had changed positions and was now lying on his back. Thomas closed the door.

At Matt's room he heard a mixture of voices. There was the chattering of children, several, intermingling and the fervent monotony of Walsh's voice in an endless prayer.

Thomas opened the door.

He felt as if an invisible wall blocked his entry. An icy wind brushed his face. Walsh stood by the bed, a Bible clutched in his hands, his head bowed. His prayer went on and on, while somewhere in the room the children sounded as if they were playing. Thomas recognized the mulberry bush song. He heard the sounds of children's feet as they circled, laughing, singing.

Matt lay motionless on the bed, as if he slept peacefully. His face was relaxed, his eyes closed, his mouth open just slightly.

Thomas stood on the threshold, unable to enter. He had a sudden urge to pull the preacher out of the room. To close the door and leave it closed forever. Whatever was in that room was more dangerous, he suddenly knew, than he had ever imagined. Than he was capable of imagining now. He could feel its power, edging toward him, toward them all.

"Reverend," he called softly. The evangelist didn't look up. He was buried in his fervent prayer. Sweat had beaded on his forehead, and was beginning to make thin trails onto his collar.

Thomas waited a moment, cold to the bone with the realization that Walsh could be sucked into whatever power existed in the room. Whatever it was that had taken over Matt, now reached for Walsh.

Thomas crossed the room and examined the windows. Both were pushed up, and outside the screen green branches grew close enough to touch. He couldn't see beyond the thick leaves of the tree, but the voices of the children had faded the moment he entered the room, and now sounded far away. He could hear them laughing, as if they'd played a joke on him. But the sound was not out the windows. As he stood there, the giggles came softly from behind him, almost buried beneath Walsh's continuing prayer.

He began looking carefully at the floor, in the corners, beneath window draperies, and behind furniture, as well as he could without moving the large, heavy pieces out from the wall.

He found what he was looking for in two places in the room. Vents, connecting the room to an air conditioning system somewhere downstairs. Perhaps in the basement, or cellar, beneath the house. The voices could be coming through the pipes.

Thomas went around the bed and put his hand on Walsh's shoulder. "Excuse me, Reverend."

Walsh jerked as if he had been awakened. He opened his eyes, but didn't raise his hand to wipe the sweat away.

"Why don't you rest now, Reverend?"

Walsh shook his head. He brought the Bible closer to his chest.

"I hear them," he said. "They're all around. They are loudest near the poor man's head, but it isn't he who's making the sounds, the voices. It's . . . something else. Jesus, our Lord, will help us through this. I'll stay."

"Their voices may be rising in the heating vents, Reverend. I'm going downstairs to check it out."

"The heating vents? No. I wish it were so. But these voices, Chief, are—are *here,* in the room. I have seen the darkness of them."

Thomas said, "Are you sure you want to stay here?" There was no point in arguing about the strange voices seeming to come disembodied from somewhere in the room.

"Yes, I'll stay."

Thomas nodded, then left the room, closing the door quietly. The room behind him remained silent, the children gone. Walsh began to pray again.

The children were gone. When the children were gone, where were they? He saw Lane's body again, skinned like an animal, glistening with red, the muscles, sinews, the inner flesh of a human being, lying in its own blood. The skin discarded to the side, lying wrinkled and limp.

And Megan . . .

Her skin laid out on the bed as if in some kind of mockery.

He felt his stomach revolt and come sickeningly into his throat. He stood with his hand pressed hard against his neck as he leaned against the wall. When he was there, in her house, and earlier in Lane's place, he'd been able to observe without letting it knock him out. He didn't dare think of it now, let it make him sick now. He didn't know if he'd be able to stop them from further horrible carnage, but he had to try.

He had to get himself together and find the children. Find out who they were, and how to stop them. He had looked all around the house. He had even looked in the tree. Dr. Tyler, believing in some way the voices weren't real, had brought in Walsh to help, but Thomas didn't have much faith in prayer.

Thomas listened a few moments longer at the door. Only Walsh's voice continued. Thomas had a feeling the children were gone, for the moment, gone.

He turned and went out onto the balcony and to the room on the right. The door was closed. He knocked. "Halley?"

He looked over his shoulder, and down the stairway toward the foyer. He had no idea where the others were. They wouldn't be carrying on a normal conversation, not in this house, not tonight.

He was ready to turn away when he heard Halley say, "Come in."

He opened the door. She was sitting on the side of a bed in the corner, drooping forward as if the load on her shoulders was too heavy. The room was large, and contained two beds, each in an area of its own, with individual chests and reading chairs and tables. In another section of the room was furniture for children, a crib, a chest of drawers with cartoon decals decorating the white paint. It looked as if the room had served both as bedroom and nursery. There was also a child-sized desk and chair, and a blackboard on the wall at a child's reach. Stuffed animals crowded on shelves along with books.

"Thomas," Halley said, straightening, as if girding herself for an encounter.

"Are you alone?"

"Yes I wanted to be. I think Dr. Tyler and Nina are helping Lois. She was very upset. It was her child's voice, there at the last, I guess. He was crying over his pet dog, and then he was—he was—crying for himself, and wanting his mommy, who, I guess, was Lois that he meant. I don't know what's happening, Thomas. But I do know Matt would never hurt a child. He was always good to the children. He spoiled Coleen, in fact. And he even took in foster children, you know. We kept five foster children from the time Rachel was born until . . . three years later. Then after Coleen . . . was gone, he seemed to lose heart. We didn't take any more foster children."

"Halley," Thomas said gently, stopping her flow of words. "None of us know what's happening. No one's accusing Matt of anything."

"Coleen went away with the boy, you know. Somehow he persuaded her. Even Matt thought so. That was why he never wanted another foster child."

"Halley, I have to ask you some questions. There are vents in Matt's room that connect to a furnace somewhere. Is it in the basement?"

She looked up at him. She blinked as if she had just awakened. "Basement?"

"Yes."

"No, there's no basement."

"I saw a cellar door. Set into the ground outside the addition."

"Oh. That's Matt's shop. That's where he enters and leaves when he's working there."

"Where is the furnace?"

"It's in a room downstairs, off the hall by the kitchen. There used to be a furnace in the basement, the one that Matt uses, but he took it out. He had a modern system installed."

"The old furnace—are the pipes still there?"

"I don't know. Probably not. The heating men used the same pipes, but they were probably disconnected from the old furnace. I'd almost forgotten there was ever a basement. I never used it. I was never even in it. I don't think it's a full basement."

"Halley, Cory saw the children here tonight, and their voices are here. They sound as if they're in Matt's room, but I noticed the heating vents. The voices could be carrying from downstairs. I think I should search the house. Everything is all right, so far as I can see. But there was a section of the house I couldn't enter. The door was locked. Would you give me permission to search the locked rooms? I also need to get into the old basement where the furnace used to be."

She stared at him, her eyes round, her grey hair falling across the sides of her forehead from a center part and hanging down onto her breasts.

"Locked rooms?" She gazed at him blankly.

"Yes, the new addition. Matt's shop."

Something flickered in her eyes. Fear? "Oh. The children wouldn't be there. Those doors are always locked, even when Matt's working. I never bother those."

"Would you give me permission to check them out?"

She stared at him. "I don't have the key. I don't know where it is. Anyway, I couldn't do that. Matt never lets anyone go in there. They'd bother his things, he says."

She sat still. Her shoulders were beginning to droop again. Her lips pressed thin and small and unyielding.

"Halley, a couple of people have been viciously murdered tonight, and I think by those children. Their voices are heard in Matt's room. They must be downstairs."

He looked around. The heating vent was easy to see, one a few feet from the bed on which Halley sat, and another beneath windows. There were probably more in this large room.

"Have you heard anything in here?"

She shook her head.

Thomas touched her shoulder, hoping to comfort her, to ask in silence her forgiveness for disturbing her. "Be careful, Halley."

He stepped out of the room and closed the door.

He stood a moment, thinking. The doors to the basement and to Matt's shop were locked. They probably had been locked at the time of Matt's accident and what seemed the beginning of all this. With no windows in the addition, and the only doors locked, the children probably weren't there, unless they had a key. And that wasn't likely.

Yet as Thomas went down the front stairs he was as aware of the locked part of the house as he was of the cold presence of the strange children.

The front door stood open. Nina, Lois and Dr. Tyler were on the porch. Insects thumped against the ceiling lights and against the screen of the screen door, but the small group seemed unaware of them.

"I can't stay here," Lois said to Thomas as he joined them. "That was Cliff. He was killed by someone, Thomas. I heard him crying, and I can't stand it. I have to go home after all. There's no place else."

"Are you absolutely positive it was Cliff's voice, Lois, or did it just sound like it because your name was mentioned?"

She stared at him. Tears filled her eyes again. "What do you mean?"

"I think there must be a hoax of some kind. The voices you heard could be carried up from somewhere on the first floor of the house."

"I thought you searched," Dr. Tyler said.

"I did, as much as I could. There are areas I haven't been able to get into. But, don't go home alone, Lois. Don't stay alone until we find that gang and get them into custody."

"I won't leave her alone," Dr. Tyler said. "Not for a minute. But I think she needs to be away from here. Hoax or not, it's been very upsetting for her."

"Where will you go? I don't want to seem nosy, but I need to be able to have you checked on regularly, until we know you're safe."

"The clinic," Dr. Tyler said. "You can sleep tonight in the clinic, Lois. Or you can come to my house. You can't go back to your house tonight."

"Cliff is dead. How on earth can a dead child hurt me? If he needs me I'll be waiting."

Thomas said, "The kids that are out murdering are as alive as you and I, whoever they are. They're dangerous, Lois."

"It sounded like Cliff. It looked like Cliff."

"You said you realized something was different about him. Stay away from him, Lois. Megan is dead. Lane is dead. If you can't stay here, and I don't blame you, go with Dr. Tyler."

Nina said, "Yes, Lois. Stay with the doctor, or stay with us."

"I'll be all right.'' Lois went down the steps onto the grass. Thomas and Dr. Tyler followed.

Dr. Tyler said, "I'm going with her. If you need me you know my number; if I don't answer, I'll be at Lois's. Whether she wants me or not, I'm staying with her."

Thomas stood watching as Lois got into her car, started it, backed around and turned toward the road. Dr. Tyler's car followed. Thomas returned to the steps where Nina stood.

He looked at Nina, wondering if the helplessness he felt showed in his face.

"I want you to go back upstairs and stay with Halley while I do some more checking. Would you?"

"Why can't I go with you? Halley promised me she'd try to rest."

Thomas hesitated. "I think I'd feel better if you were safely inside. Locked in. But I need to get keys for the doors so I can lock them when I go out and get back in without disturbing you."

"I know where the keys are. I'll show you."

He followed her to the kitchen. In the brightly lighted room she reached to a hook above a kitchen desk and took down a ring of keys.

His heart quickened. Could it be possible that Matt's keys were on this ring? But as instantly he knew they weren't. If Matt had made Halley feel that neither she nor anyone was to go into his shop, he wouldn't be apt to leave a key to private quarters on a ring of household keys.

CHAPTER TWENTY-FOUR

Lois drove the wide, empty streets home slowly, her headlights on bright. The children had suddenly appeared in the street in front of him, Thomas had said, a group who looked at first to be strangers. They scattered when he stopped. But within an hour after that Lane and Megan had been murdered.

Within that same hour she herself had walked home through the calm moonlight and dark shadows and come face to face with someone . . . *something* . . . she thought was Cliff.

She trembled uncontrollably. The trembling had started back in the high-ceilinged, cavernous Reed house, where Matt lay on a massive, antique bed, in a room that was filled with dark antique furniture. It had started with the sound of Cliff's voice.

There was no mistaking that voice. It was ingrained in her as if he had been her birth child. She would never forget, in her waking thoughts, in her dreams, that at the end he had said, *"I want my mama."*

She could believe in her heart that he meant her.

Once, several months after he came to live with her, she was in the kitchen cooking his favorite dishes, macaroni and cheese, with lots of sharp cheddar, and apple pie. He had put his arms around her waist, leaned his head against her and murmured, "Mama."

"What?" she said, looking down at him, laughing. She hadn't been sure she'd understand what he said. She wanted so much to believe that he'd said *Mama,* because in her heart he'd been her little boy for a long time.

But he flushed, tossed his head, and ran out into the backyard and started shooting baskets.

She went to the window and stood watching him, wishing she could take back that laughing question. Wishing she could have known enough to have said nothing and just waited.

He didn't call her *Mama* again, but the tone of his voice when he called her Aunt Lois was so tender and gentle that it became almost as intimate as *Mama* would have been.

She loved him, he loved her. He would never have run away from her. She tried to convince the sheriff's officers who had come to talk to her, but they kept wanting to know about 'his parents', convinced that Cliff, as Willy had the year before, had gone to find one of them. But now she knew. Someone killed Cliff and his dog. Someone he must have known, or at least a stranger to whom he talked freely.

All she could think of now was his death. The killer remained faceless, formless, a dark shadow that she might begin to search for in time.

But tonight pain was sharp, and her vague hopes gone. She knew that somewhere in her heart she had gone with him, into his adventures out in the world, praying that he was well and had found happiness.

A baby. Eleven years old.

No, he hadn't run away.

Someone had killed him that day.

Where had they left his body? The town was surrounded by miles of hills and trees, with caves that were dark and dangerous, filled with caves within caves. The freeway was only a couple of miles west, leading to agricultural areas and a large city with an area of abandoned buildings and weedy vacant lots. There was the Illinois river less than ten miles away, with swift currents leading to the Mississippi and to the Gulf.

It would be so easy to lose that small body forever.

She almost missed her driveway and had to brake and swerve quickly. She had forgotten, during her drive, in the reveries of good times with Cliff, and in the fresh pain of knowing for certain he was dead, that Dr. Tyler was behind her. She heard his brakes squeal.

She pulled her car into the carport. Lights were still on, thank the Lord, in the carport, in the house, on the porches. The front porch light shined out on dewy grass and the curving walk. Dr. Tyler parked behind her.

He came to meet her, a round man with a kind face. His hair had thinned and turned grey since she'd started working for him seventeen years ago, but his face seemed hardly to have lined at all. He was one of those people whose face always remained rosy and firm, with only a touch of jowls.

She loved him, she realized as she watched him hurry toward her. The feelings of tenderness she'd always had for him had deepened tonight into love. She put out her arms, as naturally as if they had been meant to hold each other, and he came to her and gripped her in a surprising bear hug.

She began to cry. She put her face on his shoulder, against his neck, and sobbed.

He held her. He patted her, held her, and then led her gently toward the house.

"Your keys?" he asked.

She gave him her keys.

He opened the door. They entered the bright, clean kitchen. A door opened onto the hallway that branched toward bedrooms and to the opposite, the living and dining rooms. She had kept the original hardwood on the floor, using only accent rugs. The floors gleamed under the lights.

"You left all your lights on? Good idea."

"I usually don't. I was just feeling nervous tonight, and was very glad you called. I didn't want to be alone then."

"And I don't want you to be alone now."

Her animal family came rushing in to meet them, the little Chihuahua wriggling, the pug twisting her tail, the cat coming more sedately to rub against their legs. Dr. Tyler stooped to pet all three.

Dr. Tyler himself had bought the little pug, when she was small enough to lie on the palm of the hand, and given the puppy to Lois a few months after Cliff disappeared. He had said then, "Her name is Twiggy. I thought she might help."

A few months later Lois had gotten the other two. Tom had been a homeless kitten that Nina sort of pushed onto her. Chi-chi came from a pet shop, a lonely, scared little rat-like darling in a cage with a wire floor that was bound to hurt her tiny feet.

Dr. Tyler glanced around briefly, and Lois remembered he had never been in her house before. Nor had she been in his. Their communal gathering place was the clinic. The clinic, a small brick building with a waiting room, a couple of offices, two examination rooms, and one room which they used for emergencies, had been their workplace. They even had their lunches sent in.

On days when few patients showed up they sat and talked, usually with Dr. Tyler resting his feet on his desk, leaning back in the swivel chair that squeaked no matter how often she sprayed its coiled springs with WD-40.

Those were good times. She had always felt more complete, she realized now, when she was with him. Especially during the terrible times of the last three years.

He helped her to a chair in the living room, then went to the hall and out of sight, looking, she knew, to see if the house was empty. Empty of the specters of the children, the flesh and blood manifestations of a child who was dead.

"He's dead," she said with conviction when he came back. She looked up at Dr. Tyler's face, and saw his eyes filled with sadness.

"You don't know that he's dead, Lois." He took her hands in his and rubbed them, tugging at her to rise. "Come on, I'm going to put you to bed, and then I'm going to give you a shot of Valium."

She let him lead her to her bedroom. She sat on the side of the bed while he rummaged through a drawer looking for a nightgown.

The tears started again and wouldn't stop. She reached for a tissue on the stand. The window blind was up, the glass black, parts of it mirroring objects in the room. She could feel the black shadows beneath the trees on that side of the house. It was at that window that she had heard the fingers tapping, tapping, and then when she gathered the courage to go see, no one was there.

It was like the child she had seen. He was there, and then he was gone.

"What did I see, Dr. Tyler?"

"Tim," he said, "Call me Tim. It's easier."

"What did I see?"

"What did it look like, Lois?" He found a nightgown and came back with it. It was a long-sleeved gown in heavy satin, a winter gown, but she allowed him to slip it over her head.

She began undressing beneath the cover of the gown.

"It looked like Cliff. I thought it was Cliff. That little boy with the crew cut. His face was the same, only . . ."

"Only?"

She stared past him. Her memory of the child's face picked up on something she hadn't noticed at the time, and now her body grew cold, and her heart colder. She sat still, staring at nothing but the memory of the child's face.

"Lois?" Dr. Tyler asked softly. He sat down on the bed beside her.

"Dead," she said slowly. "It had a dead look in the eyes. They were like blue mirror glass. Cold. Hard. Nothing there. He didn't smile at me, or look glad to see me. And that was when I noticed that he was wearing the same clothes he had been wearing the last time I saw him. Three years ago. And he was no taller. His hair hadn't changed. It was still short. Crewcut. It was then I got scared. I left him standing there, and I came on into the house."

Tears that had stopped as she remembered his face and those strange, soulless eyes, started again. The pain was tearing her heart to pieces.

"I just left him standing there, Dr. Tyler. He needed me, and I was afraid of him."

"No, he didn't need you. Lois, that wasn't Cliff. Remember that."

"Then what was it?"

"I don't know. I don't know. It's far beyond me, Lois."

He hung her clothes over the foot of the bed, lifted her feet and helped her lie down. He pulled up a sheet to cover her.

"You stay right here, I'll be back."

She heard his footsteps, muffled on the occasional rugs along the hall, then more clearly in the kitchen. The dogs followed him partway, then came back, came to her to be petted, then got into their basket at the foot of her bed. The cat, Tom, leaped onto the bed and curled near her feet, which was unusual. Lois didn't disturb him. She heard the screen door close.

She lay looking at the reflecting glass of the window.

GLEN GALAWAY WANDERED the yard of the small white house that sat back in the trees. He had been inside, and had seen Megan Davis's bedroom. He had seen her, at first glance, lying on the bed, and thought there was something wrong with his eyes. Then with that awful sense of being somewhere else while your body and eyes were here, and seeing, *seeing,* he discerned the horror that had been done to another human being in his small town. He saw the long, glistening lumps of blood and muscles on the floor. The skinned body. While on the bed . . . *God . . . oh God.*

There was even a necklace draped across her neck. The skin of her neck.

After seeing Lane, and knowing what the killers—*killers*?—the word seemed weak, not telling the truth of the horror—even after he had seen Lane, he wasn't prepared for Megan.

You couldn't say it was because she was a woman that made it somehow worse. It was, he decided, the way they had laid her skin out on the bed, and had even placed a necklace across her neck. At first glance it looked as if her throat had been slit. But it wasn't that. It was only the damned red necklace. The slit was down the back, beneath the arms, inside the legs.

"As if," Detective Garnet said, "She was being prepared for a taxidermist, to be stuffed. Like an animal."

Orin Casper, an officer with the state police, said, "I hope to God these people were dead when the skinning took place."

There was a hushed silence. Horrible images of writhing pain entered Glen's vision against his will. He fidgeted, tried to escape the vision of hell. Garnet, for a change, had nothing to say.

Orin Casper said, as if he too needed a change of thought, "When in the hell is that medical examiner going to get here?"

Glen escaped outside. With his flashlight he joined three other officers in searching for clues. They had found one screen off at the front of the house, leaning neatly against the wall, and the window open. All the doors had been locked, Thomas had said. The entry had to be through the window. He searched through the grass within twenty feet of the window, again, as he had before, and found nothing. There wasn't even a suggestion of a footprint, even from the men who had walked there in the search.

"Hey, Galaway," a voice called through the spotted darkness. "You're wanted, Galaway."

As Glen ran through the shrubs and across the front yard, the young officer added with a grin, "You're a wanted man, Galaway." The officer hadn't been inside the house, or the nightclub. He hadn't seen the bodies. Glen felt as if he would never be able to appreciate a joke again.

The young officer, Glen didn't know his name, but saw by his uniform that he was part of the state police, was standing by Glen's car with the radio mike in his land.

"Call from your boss," he said.

Glen took the receiver, and discovered his hand was shaking. "Yeah, Tom?"

"Do they have any patrol out around town, Glen?"

"I don't know."

"Get somebody out there, as many as you can. Tell them they're looking for those kids. A boy with a crew-cut blond hair, about eleven years old, a dark-haired, good-looking boy just a little larger, eleven or twelve, a blond girl, long straight hair, about thirteen. A little girl, ten, with curly blond hair. She's carrying a big doll. And there are about three or four more boys, but I can't get a description on them except their ages seem to be around twelve and thirteen. These kids need to be carefully approached, never alone. Whoever spots them needs to get backup. That's important. And Glen . . ."

"Yeah?"

"I want Lois Trahem's place watched, especially, and also the area around the Reed place. Got it?"

"Yes sir." He wondered why those two places in particular, but he'd ask later.

"Glen?"

"You go down and relieve Noel at the office. Have the state police and the sheriff put out the patrol. Two men to a car, preferably."

Glen went back into the house, where it seemed a half dozen of the state police and sheriff's department had gathered. When he entered, Garnet called out "The medical examiner here yet?"

"No sir," Glen said, hanging back in the kitchen "Sir, we need some patrol cars. Thomas said we're looking for a gang of kids, girls and boys, ages ten to thirteen. About seven or eight of them. He wants a couple of places watched in particular. Do you have someone you can send?"

Garnet yelled an order at someone. The homicide detective had puffed up like a loaded bumble bee ever since he had stumbled out of the nightclub at Lane's place. Whiskers seemed to be sprouting visibly on his chin, black and prickly. Glen was aware Garnet had been called out of bed on a Sunday night, and had fallen into a mire of something worse than he'd ever experienced before.

Glen went back outside, glad he wasn't working for Garnet. Even through the walls he heard the orders and the complaints. No one for patrol, they'd have to wait for enforcement. Maybe one could go. No more. Not at this moment.

Glen waited restlessly a few minutes. After he saw that only one more patrol car was being dispatched, he got into his own car.

As he backed it out of the driveway he spoke through the open window to one of the men in the yard, "If anyone wants to know where I am, I'm patrolling, I'll be going over toward the Reed place."

He kept backing, swung around into the street, straightened and pulled away from the murder site.

He drew a long breath of relief. The night air was sweet and cool. The dark shadows beneath the trees a welcome sight. They weren't filled with flashlights and men searching for things that weren't there.

He wasn't going back to the office to relieve Noel just yet. He knew what Thomas was trying to do. Thomas knew Glen didn't have the experience or training that the men in the state police and sheriff's department had, and he was trying to put Glen in a safer place.

But Glen had an advantage over the guys with the experience. They didn't know the town, and he did.

He turned on Pine Street and crossed over to Reed Road.

Reed Road was a mile long, stretching from the northeast edge of town, across to the northwest. It was the northern border of town.

There were only a few houses on the north side of the street, situated in small farms. Or on land no longer farmed, such as the Reed house.

Glen drove the street slowly, letting the car idle along. He searched the moonlighted fields and the black shadows beneath trees. With his finger tight on the handle of the spotlight, he angled the strong beam into the darknesses. Sometimes he caught the reflecting eyes of an animal. Once, a cow gazed at him, her eyes glowing orbs that at first caused his heart to leap and race.

He managed a laugh at himself, and sprayed the light over her. A jersey cow, with a small, beautiful head and horns that curved inward. As pretty as a deer. And a welcome sight.

When he passed the grove of trees and came into the moonlight again, he turned off the spotlight.

The car eased on down the street.

The Reed house stood like a mansion back from the road. A row of trees lined the driveway. Tall, dark trees shaded the western side of the house. Lights appeared to be on in various places in the house.

Glen pulled to the side of the road and stopped. He turned the car lights off.

CHAPTER TWENTY-FIVE

"Come and play, Cory, come and play."

Cory tried to find them. They were somewhere beyond the black line of trees, the black brush that slapped his face and stung his skin. He had found a thin path through the tangle of brush, and lost it, though he knew it led to them. They danced and sang, weird songs. They played weird games. But he had to find them.

"Cory, Cory, Cory."

Cory woke, the dark chills of the dream easing away as he saw the moonlight in his bedroom window. In the dream there was no light, just a strange darkness, with a faintly illuminated path. It was as if for a while he had been in a different world.

"Cory, are you coming?"

It was one of the kids calling, still calling.

How did they know his name?

He lay still. Rachel wouldn't be happy with him if he got up in the middle of the night to go play with kids he didn't even know. Be careful of strangers, she had told him often. Once, he remembered, she had pulled him up onto her lap. It was the first time she ever held him. His dad's and her wedding had been only about a week before. Cory himself had been part of the wedding ceremony, in the little chapel in Las Vegas. He had held a tiny satin cushion with their wedding rings. There weren't very many people at the wedding. Grandma from back home had flown in, and a few other people Cory didn't know. Grandma Halley and Matt hadn't come. They sent blessings, and a surprise piece of paper that Dad and Rachel had said made them owners of a house in Spring Valley, where they'd be living.

But the day Rachel pulled Cory onto her lap was the first day Dad was gone to work, and he and Rachel were alone in their new house.

He had leaned against her, just a little. He liked the feel of her arms around him. It was like being enclosed in something filled with love and safety. It was feeling as if he would never be hurt, in all his life. It was like she had woven a spell around him.

"Cory, you're living in this little bitty town now, where you can ride your bicycle just about everywhere. You've been told never, never allow a stranger to entice you into his car—"

"What does entice mean?" His interruption was partly because the subject made him uncomfortable. Grandma, back home, had told him about strangers. Of course he'd never get into a stranger's car. Even if he offered candy. Or a puppy.

"Entice means talk you into it, as with a puppy," she said, as if she'd read his mind. He remembered the conversation as clearly as if it happened just now, rather than back when he was seven years old.

"What I want to tell you, Cory," Rachel said, "is, it's not only strangers. Don't even go into . . . places . . . with people you know, unless you've talked to your daddy and me first, okay? Kids disappear. Just . . . disappear. I had a sister once. When I was three years old, she disappeared. And there were no strangers, Cory, that we ever knew of. So when you play, don't leave the yard. And when you ride your bike, let me know where you're going, and don't leave the street, except to go exactly where you said you would."

The conversation drifted away, like foam on the shallow creek behind their house after a rain, and he didn't remember anymore.

He got out of bed again and went to the window. The shadows from the trees slanted way out over the back yard. The moonlight was still bright where the shadows hadn't covered the ground. The kids weren't there. He listened. The house creaked softly, somewhere, as if a foot stepped on a loose board. He felt movements he couldn't hear.

The kids were somewhere in the house.

NINA STOOD in the yard where the light from the porch grew pale and blended with the shadows thrown from the trees. She looked toward home. Yard lights blinked among the trees like distant stars, but the hillside, the bench of land on which her house and shelter were built, was lost in the darkness. The dogs howled sporadically—uneasy, wistful.

Nina had come outside in time to hear Thomas use his police radio to request patrols.

"I'm going home to check," she said, giving in to a fear that grew with the deepening night. "I'll be back soon, Thomas."

"No, wait. I don't want you to go alone. Let me go in and see if everyone is all right, then I'll take you. I need to look around up in that area anyway."

Nina watched him run up the steps to the porch and go out of sight into the house. She went to the patrol car and got in.

Brief minutes seemed to turn to eternities before Thomas came back, put his long legs in beneath the steering wheel and pulled the door shut. He started the car.

"Walsh was with Matt, and Halley's door was closed. Cory's was closed. We'll only be gone ten or fifteen minutes. I requested a patrol for the Reed place. It should be here soon."

He backed the car around and pulled out into the empty street. They could have gone with the lights out, Nina was thinking, the moonlight was still so bright. An immense white ball, the moon was lowering toward the western hills, though, and seeming to grow larger. It was beginning to take on a reddish cast, as it had when it was rising.

She looked toward Patrick's home. The house looked so isolated. Behind it a small barn had once housed a few animals. The pastures surrounding the house and barn had been safe grazing ground for those animals.

"Where do you think he's been this past year, Thomas?" Nina asked.

"Patrick? In the city, or in the hills. Or, who knows. He could have been living secretly near home, sleeping in the barn, maybe even in the house. There was probably enough canned goods in the house for him to live on all year if he handled it carefully. And he'd be safe if he came to the house at night. But, since he's a kid, I'd say the city." Thomas added, "I checked out the house, though, and there's no sign anyone has been in it since last year."

"Why do you think he came back tonight?" Nina asked. "Why do you think he came to the revival meeting? And then didn't come in."

Thomas drove in silence. They reached the driveway up into the trees, a narrow, graveled road that curved up behind her house and ended in a small parking lot between the house and shelter.

"Maybe," she said, when he hadn't answered, "All the confusion scared him away. The earthquake, Halley fainting. All that."

"I wonder if he really came back, Nina."

She jerked around to stare at his profile. He had an English nose and a strong jaw. His hair, pushed back often, fell across part of his forehead. The dash light exaggerated his features. He looked straight ahead.

"But I saw him. All of us saw him."

"Uh-huh. Karen, Willy and Cliff were seen tonight too. As well as Coleen Reed, still ten years old, still carrying a doll. Still dressed in the fancy blue dress she was wearing when she disappeared thirty years ago."

Nina searched her experiences for logical answers. "Mass hysteria, Thomas?"

He hesitated, then said, "Maybe."

"That sounds so metaphysical. I find it very hard to accept. If you had seen Patrick—"

"I saw the children, remember? I went back to the station and checked the pictures in the missing children files. The little girl was exactly like the picture of Coleen that is in her file at the station. I saw Willy, Karen, and Cliff also."

She had nothing to say. Boys don't choose to stop growing. A ten-year-old girl isn't small thirty years later.

He pulled the car up close to the shelter and stopped. "I can't figure it out. The voices are heard at Matt's, but the only place I didn't search was his shop. I'll have to get a search warrant to open that locked door. I'd knock it down tonight, but I don't really think they're in there. I've gone through every channel my mind will open, and that's damned few. I've considered it might be a hoax of some kind. But I saw the bodies of the people who were killed, saying nothing of the poor dog. How do I apply any kind of hoax to that? Thinking about it makes me feel like my brain is enclosed in a walnut shell. And it just keeps bouncing around in that small space."

Nina nodded in agreement. The description fit her own sense of limitation well enough.

A few of the dogs barked, but others were noticeably silent. Nina got out of the car before Thomas could reach her door. She hurried into the hallway of the shelter.

Mutter huddled back in her bed, whining. The puppies she was nursing were in a little pile, sleeping, twitching in dreams, perhaps nightmares older than time.

Nina went through the shelter, checking. Dogs and cats huddled as far back into their beds as they could get. Only two dogs paced restlessly from one end of their runs to the safety of their beds. Nina petted them, gently trying to calm them down. One little cocker spaniel whined and trembled.

Thomas called from outside.

"Something has torn the wire here, Nina."

She went out the door at the end of the central passageway. Thomas stood in the shadows at the outside corner of the fenced runs. Trees grew within feet of this area of the shelter, which was the most distant from the house. He shined his flashlight on the fence. The six-foot chain link wire had been ripped open as if it were made of gauze. Links sagged toward the tears.

"It wasn't cut with an instrument," Thomas said. "It was torn."

"But that's not possible. Nothing is strong enough to tear wire like that." Yet it had been done. She could see it.

"Were there dogs in here?"

"Yes. Two small ones. Harmless animals."

She entered the run through the tear, trying to hold back the growing sickness that was rising into her stomach. The yard light nearest to this corner of the shelter shone in patches on the floor. The two dogs that were housed here must be inside, she thought as she called softly to them. In the run next door a large, long-haired part shepherd whined and crouched, his tail tucked between his legs in fear and submission.

"Macy," she called softly, as she went down on her knees to crawl through the swinging wood door that separated inner beds from outer runs. "Butch."

They were two little dogs that had belonged to an elderly lady who'd had to go into a nursing home. Both dogs were elderly, too, and neither the dogs nor the lady should have been separated in these last few years, or perhaps even months, of their lives. But Nina was one of those people who didn't know how to remedy a sad situation other than promise the lady the dogs would be taken care of. So Nina had put them into their last permanent home, the end run of the shelter. At night they huddled together in their beds. During the day they stood looking through the wire at the path, waiting for footsteps of a loved one who would never appear.

"Macy, Butch."

She heard a stirring in the corner deep in the bed, and knelt toward it.

Her hands touched two warm, living bodies, sleek fur rippled over taut muscles. A couple of wet tongues licked her hands.

"Thank God," she murmured.

"Are they all right?"

"Yes," she answered. "But I'll have to move them to a different pen."

All of the beds and runs were occupied. She decided quickly on the bed that held three cats. The little dogs were used to cats, and didn't annoy them, and the cats wouldn't mind sharing with such small dogs.

Thomas joined her, helping her gather up dogs and straw.

"I'm going to bring them all inside, and lock the doors to the runs," she said.

"I'll see if I can tie that wire together enough for tonight. When daylight comes, maybe . . ."

He didn't finish, but she understood. They had the moment, and that was all, it seemed. She wondered if they dared take another few minutes for a cup of coffee once the dogs were settled again in another part of the shelter.

A STILLNESS, eerily different from anything Glen had ever seen or felt, hung over the empty field between him and the Reed house. He was parked half a block away, the car leaning a bit sideways with two wheels in the edge of a shallow ditch. Bear grass grew tall along the ditch, with brilliant blue flowers spiked at the top. Among those lily-like plants bloomed yellow flowers, white flowers, daisies.

But tonight something was wrong, even with the flowers.

Glen looked at them, just beyond the window. His mother had bear grass in her flower beds, because they were such a bright blue, and such pretty flowers, as she said. These outside his window were colorless in the moonlight. The moon changed and darkened colors, made them lifeless. Glen had never noticed that before.

He had looked at the face of his girlfriend in the moonlight, and thought her beautiful, mysterious. But he had never looked at what the moon did to colors.

It was more than just a change in wavelengths. The light this night seemed cold and distant, and even though the night was warm, still he began to shiver.

He thought he could see only one car parked in the driveway of the Reed house, beyond the row of trees that somebody had planted long ago between the driveway and the weedy field. It wasn't Thomas's car. It was a smaller sedan, and there were no beacons on the roof.

Lights were on in several places in the house, as well as the front and back porches. They were cold comfort. Glen rolled down the passenger window and listened. He caught just a suggestion of sound that didn't belong to the natural sounds of night. He couldn't be sure, but he thought it sounded like a child.

As if a sound wave undulated through the car, he all at once heard the voices clearly. A group of children were singing joyfully, a weirdly strange sound in this place, at this time of night.

"Here we go round the mulberry bush, the mulberry bush, the mulberry bush. Here we go—"

The sound moved away.

Glen jerked round. The group of children were in the field, not thirty feet away, their hands joined, dancing in a circle.

It was a strange scene, as if the moonlight had changed them as it changed the color of the flowers and grass. He could have been looking at a scene somehow captured from sixty or seventy years ago, or earlier, except for the way they were dressed.

He got out of the car. The light that came on when he opened the door was like a silent alarm.

The kids broke and ran, across the field toward the Reed house. Glen aimed his weapon at them, both hands required to hold the revolver steady. But he couldn't fire. They were children playing. How could he be sure they were the children Thomas was looking for? With his breath caught in his throat Glen ran after them. He fell over a barbed wire fence, got up and ran again. The kids slowed and appeared to scatter in the darkness under the edge of a shade tree in the yard.

Glen thought briefly of Thomas's warning. Don't tackle them alone. Make sure two guys are on patrol together.

Thomas had forgotten that getting even one guy out on patrol was usually a job and a half.

The kids stayed just in the edge of the shadows. It looked as if they had paused to enjoy his fall over the damned fence. Glen knew his jeans were torn. His leg burned where a barb had ripped it, and his hand was on fire.

The shadows moved, darkness fading into darkness. The kids could easily slip away, going into the trees on the other side of the Reed house, and on to the trees on the hills.

"Hey!" he tried to call, his voice breathless and hoarse.

As if they heard his call, they suddenly were visible again in the black shade of the trees. They were waiting for him.

He slowed when he reached the edge of the yard and let his arm hang limp, revolver aimed at the ground.

"Hey, I need to talk to you kids."

They didn't answer, but the figures beneath the tree shifted and moved and part of the children came toward him.

He walked slower and slower as he approached the group of children. He hadn't counted them when he had a chance, but his impression was there were seven or eight. Two boys and one older girl stood just in the edge of the moonlight. The others remained back in the shadows of the trees, and had become dark figures that seemed only black extensions of the darkness.

The palm of his hand grew sweaty and slippery on the butt of the gun. He walked slower, hesitating. A cold warning lifted the hair on his neck as if he were returned to a primitive state of being and stood in the wild facing life's worst enemy.

He stared at the kid with the crew cut. Stared. He saw the boyish face that still looked soft and round, though it had begun to lengthen at the chin. He stared, and recognized.

"Cliff Patison!" he said.

The boy didn't answer. The shadows of the tree appeared to move, and like fingers touched the boy's blond hair. His eyes were shadowed and made dark and colorless by the light of the moon.

Glen had just begun working as Thomas's assistant when Cliff Patison disappeared. He recalled vividly the search for Cliff, his bicycle, and his dog. Glen had talked to almost everyone in town. He had come here, to the Reed house, and knocked on the front door. No one answered, so he went to the back.

Halley Reed had come to the door and stepped out onto the porch. He asked the same question he had been asking at all the houses in this part of town, as he showed her pictures of Cliff.

"Have you seen this boy?"

She shook her head.

"He was riding a silver bicycle and had a little beagle dog with him."

Matt Reed came out of the kitchen and nodded hello at Glen. He was so big and husky that Glen felt like a pipsqueak in comparison. Thomas made him feel like an underdeveloped teenager, but this was worse.

Glen said, "He was wearing stone-washed jeans with rips at the knees, and a green and yellow striped T-shirt."

. . . faded jeans with rips at the knees, and a green and yellow striped T-shirt . . .

. . . his hair in a crew cut . . .

As if the past three years did not exist, Glen was face to face with the little boy he remembered seeing around town, the boy he had helped search for.

He stood, unable to move, staring at Cliff. Then his gaze moved to the taller boy, and recognition grew slowly. Someone, farther back, someone he had seen. And the girl . . .

She stepped forward on Glen's right, and his eyes followed her. To his left the third boy stepped out. They were coming at his right and left. He had seen them, but fear was pushing back recognition.

In front of him a beautiful little girl with a doll stepped out of the shadows. The smile on her face was as fixed and artificial as the smile on the face of her doll.

He lifted his revolver, then lowered it again. What good was it to him? He couldn't pull the trigger on that little girl, or those other children.

Glen rapidly began calculating distances. His car was halfway along the weedy field, probably forty yards away. The back door of the Reed house was beyond the trees at the edge of the driveway, twenty yards away.

His breath was like poison gas searing his lungs and throat. Thick and hard to breathe. He knew too late what he should have done. He should have stayed in his car and used his police radio to contact Thomas, or the state or county police.

He had a feeling he'd never be able to reach the back door of the Reed house. And even if he did, what would he find there? A locked door? The house would have looked vacated, if lights weren't burning. If people were there, they were buried somewhere in the silence of the large house.

He turned and ran.

He instantly felt the hard grip of their hands on his arms. He twisted. It no longer mattered that they were children. He felt the deadliness of their hands, like claws, tearing into his clothing and flesh.

He brought the revolver up and fired. The bullet whizzed harmlessly off toward the sky, and then he felt the gun ripped out of his hand.

They jerked him backward, throwing him hard to the ground. His head struck a half-buried rock. Blue and red lights flashed in the back of his head like jagged lightning. He saw round figures above him, outlined by that cold, silver moonlight. Heads, staring down at him, their faces as dark and blank as masks of black plastic.

They made no sound. No voice sang now, or giggled, or chanted.

He felt himself lifted. Several hands carried him, swiftly running. They were running through the shadows beneath the trees, out again into the moonlight. He tried to struggle, but his struggles reminded him, in a flash of light, of a beetle being carried along by ants. A helpless, doomed beetle.

They entered shadows again.

He felt them stop. Once more he tried to struggle free, but their hands tightened on him like steel clamps. He let out a scream, and small hands slapped over his mouth and cut it off. He gagged on fear and the smell of those hands. Musty, old, rotted.

He heard a door open. Hinges squeaked. Like a magic door it was lifted from the ground.

He was losing it. Magic doors don't exist. The door was a cellar door. Leading beneath the Reed house.

He struggled again, throwing his body in convulsive jerks, trying to loosen the holds on his arms, legs, head, body. But the fingers tightened, biting into his flesh with the strength of iron clamps.

As they carried him down the steps into a total cave like darkness words spoken by Detective Orin Casper returned to him broken and ominous.

"I hope to God—

—these people were dead—

—when skinning—

—took place."

CHAPTER TWENTY-SIX

"OH GOD, BRING US UNDERSTANDING . . .

The Bible in Walsh's hands slipped and almost fell, as if it had been tugged by unseen fingers. His hands tightened on it. His entire body sagged with fatigue, with a weakness both physical and spiritual that was new to him. His fingers felt numb.

For an uncounted time he had stood at the side of the bed, and the man stretched there seemed as always to be sleeping peacefully. But this man wasn't sleeping. This man was in some kind of coma or trance, because Walsh's continual prayers had not disturbed him or brought about any kind of change.

The voices of the children had drifted away to silence, as if they had moved to another place to play, to laugh and sing. The crying he had heard earlier had seemed to be from individual children, but the singing, the chattering, were many voices. He tried to remember a story in the Bible that might explain it, and found his memory lacking.

"Oh God . . . in Jesus's name . . ."

He stumbled backward and fell into the chair, his head bowed over the Bible in his hands. A great emptiness was in him, a hollowness as if God had pitched him forward to face that endless pit, the one he had never believed in. Fear made him breathe in hoarse, rasping sounds that his own ears found foreign, as the disembodied voices were.

He couldn't pray. The words of comfort had been drawn away from him, as his own security in his beliefs were being leached away.

He looked upon himself and saw a weak man, a child in spirit, parentless, who huddled in fear. When he tried to pray his tongue thickened and grew clumsy, and words failed him. He could not find them even in his mind. Like the dark shadow he had seen over Matt's bed, they drifted, beyond reach. All the hours of sermons, had they been mere empty words, as his prayers had come to seem tonight?

He was afraid. He lifted his head and looked at the sleeping man. It wasn't the voices that scared him. It was knowing, in the fevered rush of his prayers, that deep within himself he had never truly believed there was a living, altruistic God. In his ministries, in his preaching to others that all they had to do to find God was first to believe in Jesus Christ, he himself had been searching.

He hadn't believed in the devil. Is this man possessed, he had been asked. Possessed by what? If there is no devil, no spiritual negative, how could he then be possessed? What is there to possess if no entity beyond the human mind exists? And if no entity beyond the human mind exists, what of God? He had prayed for Jesus to comfort the man, the woman, comfort them all. And he had felt nothing but a growing fear.

Tonight, in the room with this poor man, he was forced to look into his own beliefs and accept them. He had been on a lifelong search for God, but didn't know it until now. While he preached his sermons, trying with everything within himself to convince his congregation there was a living God, who cared, who loved with a love greater than humans could know, who answered prayers, he himself had been trying to grasp that thread of belief. Because, without God, where were they? The black pit grew actual and ominous. They were souls cast upon the waters of the deep, the pits of the enormous dark. They were living flesh that tore upon living flesh for desperate survival on a world going madder by the moment.

And tonight he could cry, as Jesus had done, *O my God, where art thou?*

And there was no answer.

The sky was dark, pitted with the glowing lights of other worlds, and there was no voice from God. His soul was dark and lonely and crying, and there was no answer.

And the greatest of all horrors was knowing there was no God.

This world, without God, was an endless horror destined only to the unimaginable.

Walsh leaned his head into his hands and sought a release in tears, but none came. The pain within him seemed unbearable.

"Oh God," he whispered, "My God, where art thou?"

Silence answered him.

Then a child's voice began speaking, as clearly as if she stood in the room. Walsh lifted his head.

The dark aura hovered over Matt and eddied in the corner of the room where shadows fell most heavily.

A little girl was speaking, her voice like a jewel, like clear, sweet water trickling over clean stones in a creek, like the voices of birds, made of all lovely things on earth.

"Oh Daddy, she's beautiful. Thank you, thank you." She giggled softly, an innocent sound of happiness.

Walsh stared at the gently moving darkness, his gaze so intense the rest of the room blurred. He could almost see the child take form. He searched for the materialization of her with a need arising from the deepest corners of his soul. In silence he listened.

Her voice came again, weeping, that terrible, lost, empty sound of all the children. She was speaking, through her tears, her words muffled and at first unclear. Then Walsh began to understand.

"Why, Daddy, why? Why?"

Then the words were lost in the weeping, and, Walsh felt, as the weeping faded, lost forever.

No, not lost forever. Something preserved them. They were here, in the room with him.

Silence came. He wasn't sure when the voice had ended. But the silence replaced the sound, and then there was nothing at all in the night, not even the buzz of an insect in the trees outside the window.

The man was, Walsh realized with a surprising calmness within himself, indeed possessed. That which Walsh had never believed in, was before his eyes. The man was possessed of spiritual beings beyond himself. He was possessed of children who had been happy and who had been sad, and who at last had been filled with terror.

The voice returned, as from a hiatus that might have been filled with the unheard voice of the person to whom she spoke. The words were unintelligible. A child speaking.

Walsh stared at the man and listened to the voice of the child, and tried to understand. Tears eased silently from his eyes. He who once thought arrogantly that he could heal, that he could save souls, was reduced to helplessness.

"HERE WE GO ROUND the mulberry bush, the mulberry bush, the mulberry bush, faster and faster and *faster*. . . "

Coleen squealed, her long, golden ringlets flying out behind her as her daddy swung her around, her small hands caught fast in his large paws. Delight was as much on Matt's face as on Coleen's.

Matt had just driven up and parked his pickup on the grass near the garages, and Coleen had run to meet him. Rachel too had run, but she stopped several feel away, watching, as Matt caught Coleen up in a bear hug, and then swung her down for the game.

The new foster boy, Jeremy, stood looking on, his hands in his pockets. Halley didn't know him well enough yet to be able to read his face. Was the expression envy, or contempt? With these thirteen year olds it was hard to tell.

Matt swung back to his pickup and opened the door. "Three guesses," he said, smiling down at Coleen.

She followed closely behind him, as she always did during those few hours of the day when he was available. Only when he went into his taxidermy shop did he close the door against her. Halley thought it was because the sight of the animals in their various stages of being skinned and stuffed might upset Coleen.

"Daddy!"

He handed her a long box. It was so awkward for her to handle that she sat down on the ground, with the box across her lap. She lifted the lid. The lovely, long doll lay with its eyes closed.

On this strange, frightening night thirty years later Halley remembered that doll's dress as if it were yesterday. Pink and white dotted Swiss organdy, with pink velvet ribbons, it had a matching bonnet, with lots of ruffles and lace edgings. Matt hadn't purchased the doll in town. He must have gone to the city that day.

Halley was back again, standing on the grass, taking Rachel's little hand in hers as Rachel came in silence to stand beside her. Matt ignored everyone but Coleen. Halley knew from experience that Matt wouldn't have brought a gift for either Rachel or the foster boy. Even Coleen once had said, "Daddy, what do you have for Rachel?" Matt looked surprised, then shrugged and said, "Mama can take Rachel to the toy store and let her buy anything she wants."

So it wasn't that he didn't want Rachel to have things. It was just that he never brought her anything special, the way he did Coleen.

"Oh Daddy, a new doll," Coleen crooned. "She's so pretty. The prettiest, biggest doll I've ever had."

"Well I figured you're about to the age of getting your last doll, so she ought to be special, and big."

Coleen lifted the doll out of the box. It stood almost as tall as petite Rachel.

"I'll keep her with me always."

Matt walked past the other children as if they didn't exist, opened the cellar door into his taxidermy shop and ran down the steps. He pulled the door shut behind him.

They wouldn't see him again for hours, Halley knew and she was glad. It was difficult to contain her anger when Matt slighted the other children. Most of his spontaneous gifts to Coleen, always dolls, were brought when foster children were present. Halley didn't understand why. Nor did she understand why he slighted the other children. But to say something about it, in front of Rachel and the boy, would only point out the problem even more, she felt.

She tried to make up to Rachel for her father's negligence, the almost total disregard of Rachel, or any other child who happened to be living with them. If Matt wanted foster children, why didn't he spend some time with them?

In privacy she shed tears for Rachel.

THIRTY YEARS later Halley still felt the tears for Rachel, but the tears for Coleen were there too, both buried so deep they rarely reached expression. They had coalesced into a permanent lump of pain deep within her.

Halley lay on her bed, on her side, her knees drawn up. Her palms, together, cushioned her cheek. She tried to imagine that it was like any night, here in the nursery, in the bed that once had been used by a nurse, or nanny, and her husband in the room she once had shared with him. The night was so still. She lay awake, as she always did in the middle of the night. Always, since the first night she had slept in this room, where she could watch both the door and the bed in the far corner where Rachel slept, she had lain awake in the middle of the night. Her sleeping hours were near daybreak when at last she fell into an exhausted half-dead sleep.

She could imagine that only today she had asked Coleen if she wanted to go to the store with them.

"No," Coleen said. She sat in her favorite spot on the back porch, on one end of the long step, fixing her new doll. Coleen could always entertain herself with her latest doll, arranging its dress, straightening its stockings, retying its shoes.

Halley still felt hurt and angry as she looked at the latest addition of an already large collection of dolls. But the thing that hurt her most, made her most angry, was Matt's clear favoritism. Perhaps Rachel didn't notice. She was only three, and didn't lack for attention from her mother, at least.

The new boy, Jeremy, walked around in the backyard, his hands in his pockets. He was a freckled, skinny kid, as if he'd been underfed for a long time. Well, not now. Though he hadn't begun to eat well yet. He was still too bashful. He had been with them only a week, and he was very restless. Halley wondered if he would turn out to be like Daniel, and never really settle down. Daniel had stayed only a few weeks before he ran away.

"Jeremy," Halley asked, as she went toward the station wagon in the driveway, Rachel running along behind, "Do you want to go to the store with us?"

Jeremy shrugged skinny shoulders that already showed width and strength.

"Naw," he said. "I'll just hang around here."

"All right. Both of you, stay right here. We'll be back before time to cook supper."

She didn't like to go off and leave the children, but in times past when Matt had heard her frets he had assured her they'd be all right. "What on earth could happen to them here?" he chided, as if she were being a silly woman.

Actually, what could happen to them there at home? Now that Coleen was ten, what was wrong with her staying home alone, or with another child, for an hour or so while Halley went shopping? Coleen hated to go shopping. It had always been a chore to get her to look for new clothes, even. She loved the dresses, once they got to her, but she hated going after them.

Rachel was just the opposite. Halley's driving was the kind that could take her to local stores, but never out onto the freeways or into the city. So she and Rachel, almost daily now, ran down to the grocery store for something interesting for supper, and they usually stopped at the Dairy Queen for a cone, or at the drugstore for a soda or a coke. They rarely took time to walk in the shaded and grassy town square or sit on the benches. They had their own park, acres and acres, in the hills behind their house. And when the meadow flowers were in bloom, as they were now, lots of afternoons they picked wild meadow bouquets and then climbed the hillside to sit for awhile on a cool bluff where they could see through the trees and watch the squirrels and chipmunks.

They bought one bag of groceries that day. Halley had no premonition, no sense of something happening that would forever change their lives.

She drove home cautiously. She'd had her driver's license since she was sixteen, but had seldom driven. Only last year Matt had turned over the keys to the station wagon to her and told her she could drive herself around. He had other things to do, especially since he was like Coleen, and hated going shopping.

Halley pulled awkwardly into the driveway. There were no deep ditches, but she drove as if there were. She carefully avoided the row of trees along the edge of the driveway.

Rachel stood in the back with her arms on the back of the seat beside Halley's head, as trusting as if she rode with an expert.

Halley parked near the kitchen door. Coleen was not sitting on the step where Halley had left her. Jeremy was not in sight.

"They must be watching cartoons," Halley said to Rachel.

Halley got out and opened the door for Rachel. As Rachel went running toward the steps up onto the kitchen porch, Halley got the sack of groceries.

Rachel opened the kitchen door. Halley walked into a house so quiet it seemed somehow totally vacated. There was no television sound, no voices, no footsteps, other than hers and Rachel's.

She put the groceries on the kitchen counter and began unloading milk, eggs, ice cream. Rachel ran into the central hall, toward the front of the house. Her steps were light and quick. She was always running, or skipping, or jumping. "Can't you keep that kid still?" Matt had said irritably more than once. It was true, Rachel was a more active child than Coleen ever had been. Coleen was the kind to sit quietly, for hours, her fingers busy with dolls, or games, or some artwork.

For a while there was silence. Halley listened as she finished putting away the groceries and then folded the sack and stuffed it into the basket of sacks she kept in the utility room. She lined the wastebaskets with grocery sacks, instead of bags made for that purpose. She had never been denied money, but it was second nature for her to spend as little as possible.

Rachel came running back. She stopped in the middle of the kitchen floor and looked up at Halley, her round blue eyes innocent and questioning.

"Mama, where's Coleen?"

A huge hollow spot opened somewhere within Halley at that moment, with that question. It was a question that Rachel would ask often, for months to come. Halley had finally told her to stop asking. She could no longer bear to hear it.

With Rachel behind her, Halley went upstairs to the bedrooms.

Coleen's was neatly arranged, the bed made. The spread had not even been sat on. Her dolls lined the walls, shelf after shelf. The new large doll was not among them.

"Coleen!" she shouted, and the house threw back an echo from somewhere. It felt as if it came from the awful hollowness in Halley. A hollow filled with blackness and depth and endlessness.

"Coleen! Jeremy!"

She hurried into Jeremy's room, remembering that it was only a few months ago that she had gone into the same room to find that Daniel was not there.

If Jeremy had taken any of his clothes, which at the best would not have filled a small suitcase, Halley couldn't say. He had a few pairs of jeans, a few shirts and underwear. She had gone shopping for him once. His clothes were still in the closet and dresser drawers.

She looked through the house, with Rachel behind her. She looked everywhere except the rooms where the door was kept locked.

Matt was not home. She didn't know where he was.

She searched the grounds around the house, calling, calling. She went to the neighbors and asked if they had seen Coleen. Sometimes Coleen played with the neighbor children, but the houses sat on their own acreages, not close as they were over toward the center of town, and the neighbors had not seen Coleen, or Jeremy.

Matt drove in at suppertime. Halley by then was trying hard to keep from crying.

"Matt, Coleen and Jeremy are gone. Shouldn't we call the police?"

She remembered how he stared at her. His expression didn't change. He made no effort to retrace her steps in a search of his own.

"Of course call the police," he said.

No trace of Coleen, or the boy, was ever found. Matt met the chief of police in the driveway, and Halley heard him tell the chief that the house had been searched and the children were gone. She heard him tell about Daniel, who had run away.

Matt said, his voice carrying clearly to Halley, "I guess that's what we get for taking in older foster boys and trying to give them a chance."

THE PAIN WAS raw within her tonight. It was as if the past thirty years didn't exist. She had heard Coleen's voice again, tonight, in this house. The voice of Coleen lingered in her mind, with the sound of her crying a terrible, continuous background accompaniment to her sorrow.

Her child was listed as missing. For years, Coleen Reed was missing. Was her file still at the police station? A little girl with long, golden ringlets. Halley remembered sitting in a chair with Coleen on the floor between her feet. She'd brush that lovely, silky hair and coil it around her fingers.

Rachel's hair was straight, and no amount of coiling ever created a curl for her.

After Coleen's disappearance, Halley could not rest if Rachel were in a room away from her. Halley took her to school each morning, and it was all right. She didn't worry. Not until school was out and it was time for Rachel to come home. What was she protecting Rachel from? In her own home?

Probably it had been a form of self-protection. Halley was scared. She was so afraid something would take Rachel from her.

As if there were something in the house that had taken Coleen, and would take Rachel too if Halley weren't constantly by her side.

All marital relations with her husband ended with the disappearance of Coleen.

Matt, perhaps, had also wanted it that way, because he never approached her. He never asked why she moved out of his room. It was as if he hardly realized she wasn't there anymore.

Everything went out of Matt with the loss of Coleen.

He spent more and more of his time in the woods, hunting, trapping. And more and more time in his taxidermy shop. Halley didn't bother him, or ask to go into his shop, even to help clean. She didn't want to see the animals.

She remembered suddenly Rachel's own attempt to explain what had happened to Coleen.

"Mama, I know where Coleen is."

She was almost four then. Coleen had been gone several months. Halley would have thought Rachel had almost forgotten by now.

Halley couldn't answer. She could only look at Rachel, the raw hurt bleeding inside her.

Rachel sat in the middle of the nursery floor, where they spend most of their time now, playing with an arrangement of miniature farm animals.

"The giant got her," Rachel said.

"The giant?"

"Yes."

"What giant, Rachel?"

Rachel looked up at the wall. "There's a giant that lives in our house. And it eats children."

"Where did you ever get that idea, Rachel?"

"Coleen told me."

Halley encouraged Rachel to turn her attention back to her play, and began to ask her about the animals. She had no doubt that Rachel had dreamed something. Or perhaps, Coleen had teased her earlier.

Halley got up now, easing her aching muscles into other positions, and walked over to the window. She pulled the curtain aside and fastened it back, and pushed up the window.

The night was still. Bright moonlight contrasted with the black shadows cast by trees and buildings.

A giant living in their house? That ate children?

Another scene came suddenly to her mind. The day of Coleen's disappearance, when the day was dying and twilight created darknesses almost as black as those tonight, she had heard Matt's pickup truck pull to a stop outside the kitchen. She had heard the door slam. She assumed he had come from one of his businesses in town, but now suddenly she saw the truck again.

It was turned wrong.

Instead of driving in from the street, he had driven from somewhere on the property, and the pickup was facing the street.

He had lied to the police when he said he had been gone all afternoon.

CHAPTER TWENTY-SEVEN

Rachel drove. Dark outlines of trees undulated at the distant roadside, beyond the wide shoulders of the interstate. David slept at her side, his seat leaned back into a recliner.

Out of the heavier traffic now, she eased the speed to eighty-five and held it.

Yawning before he tipped his seat back and fell solidly asleep, David said, "I don't understand this. I thought you wanted a honeymoon. A real one."

"Go to sleep," she answered, and patted him tenderly.

She couldn't say, "I know—I know what happened to my sister, Coleen. I know it as surely as I know who I am, where I am now. I know. . ."

Car lights on the lanes across the median occasionally blinked over the next rise. Truck lights gleamed. She watched for the lights of patrol cars. And as she drove through the night her memory brought back the children one by one. Her mother had written her about them, and talked to her on the phone about them.

Karen . . . Willy . . . Cliff . . . Then, Patrick.

She knew what happened to them.

As if a curtain had been yanked from in front of her eyes as she yearned back toward Cory, her child, she knew.

She had left him in a house of unspeakable horror.

• • •

Cory scooted down into bed, pulled the sheet over his head and tried to sleep.

There were things he didn't understand. He knew that Matt was sick now, since he had hurt his hand. But there were sounds in the house sometimes that puzzled and scared him. He could hear someone crying sometimes, it seemed, and it sounded like a little kid.

Sometimes he heard them playing. Once he heard a firecracker. Or maybe it was a gunshot.

He got out of bed and slipped down the hall, because there was light there, and he went looking for Halley, or Nina, or someone. Matt's door was closed, and the crying was inside Matt's room.

Matt wouldn't be crying, he knew. Maybe it was Gram, and just sounded like a little kid. But then the crying stopped and a man's voice like the preacher's at the tent began to pray.

Cory then heard Gram talking to someone at the front of the house. She was coming closer, and Cory had run back to his room and climbed into bed.

Footsteps came down the hall. Someone opened the door and looked in, but Cory kept his eyes shut.

He thought it was Chief Thomas. He heard a man's deep voice, trying to be quiet, and Chief Thomas was the only man who sounded like that. Dr. Tyler wouldn't have tried to be quiet. He always talked as if everyone were awake, or if they weren't, they should be.

Even with his head under the sheet, the children's voices reached him.

They were in the backyard singing and playing.

"Go in and out the window," the voices sang, a lively, interesting tune. "Go in and out the window, go in and out the window, and . . ."

The children began laughing as they sang, and the last words of the song became all mixed up. But Cory found a smile coming to his face, and a growing eagerness to join them.

He got up again, felt about in the darkness for his jeans, found them and pulled them on.

Were the kids crawling in and out a window? What would Gram think? Or was it just a game like '*Here we go round the mulberry bush*'? If there was a mulberry bush in the yard, Cory didn't know about it. There were spirea and japonica and lilac and mock orange, and many others Gram had shown him when they were in bloom a few weeks ago, but she hadn't mentioned a mulberry bush.

Suddenly a memory surfaced. One of those spot check things that came after something is learned and forgotten. In one of his classes at school they had studied old English living standards, and in it had been some games. They were old English games, for children, and they were played a lot back before kids had television and Nintendo and things like that.

Cory went to the window again and looked out. He couldn't see them. They had gone again, slipping away as quickly and silently as they had been doing since they came to help Matt.

Cory didn't want to stay in his room any longer. He had slept some, but now felt as if he would never sleep again.

There were kids somewhere in the house, and he had to find them. He could hear them calling, again. A girl, calling, "Cory, Cory," in her musical voice, as if she were teasing him.

"Come and play, Cory."

The voice was so soft, as if meant only for him, yet he wondered if other people in the house could hear her. He'd have to be very careful or they'd send him back to bed again.

Then, even as he opened his door and stepped into the hall, the girl stopped calling.

In the hall there was no sound. Just a few steps away the door to the back stairs stood open. Someone had turned on lights there.

Cory waited, listening. He had left the voices back in his room. He retraced his steps, his bare feet almost soundless on the floor.

Inside the room he could hear them again. They were murmuring together, as if they had huddled into a group. Maybe they were looking at something. Maybe they were planning something.

They were below him. As he put his ear to the floor, their voices grew more clear, although he still couldn't hear what they were saying.

Cory went out into the hall again. He hesitated, looking toward the distant end of the hall, where Matt's room was, where Chief Thomas might be. Would he go with Cory to find the kids? To see what they were doing in Gram and Matt's house?

He hesitated, and then, hearing no one, no sounds of the adults, he turned toward the stairway.

Downstairs he found that lights were on in almost all the rooms. The kitchen light was on, it shone into the utility room so Cory was able to see the washing machine and dryer, the sinks and cabinets. The children's voices sounded close, but they weren't in the utility room, or the small alcove with the locked door.

In the kitchen he barely heard the children. As he searched for them toward the front of the house their voices faded to silence. He returned to the kitchen, and then to the utility room.

The voices were close again. The closer he came to the locked door in the dark hallway off the utility room, the more distinct the voices became.

He stood in the hall, strange feelings of anxiety making his skin cold. Those were Matt's rooms beyond that locked door. He knew that. But it was there the children were playing.

How had they gotten in? The door was always locked.

He started to put his hand on the doorknob, then jerked it back to hold it tightly at his side. He wanted to see the children, again, but he was afraid.

His eyes had adjusted to the darkness in the narrow hall, and he saw the edge of the door frame looked funny. And something was wrong with the door too.

Cory tried to figure it out. The door seemed to be a little ways open, and hanging crooked. The black stripe was really a crack in the wall, between the door frame and the corner of the hall. It looked as if a giant hand had wrenched the door from the wall, and then set it back.

He began to see in the half-dark that the entire hall looked ripped, with wide cracks in the dark corners. Had the kids torn the door out of the wall because they didn't have a key to open it?

Cory touched the knob. The door fell toward him suddenly as if pushed from the other side. He flattened himself against the wall as the door scraped by and settled in an awkward lean wide enough for him to crawl through. The noise thundered in Cory's ears, and he stood still, his hands gripping the edge of the tilted door, waiting, listening. There was no other sound. Only the fierce thudding of his heart. No one had heard, not even the kids.

They suddenly sounded much closer now, their voices somewhere beyond the door that was now partly open, somewhere in the solid blackness beyond the hole in the wall.

If the children had heard the door fall, they still had not responded to it. Cory tested the door and found that it was leaning solidly against the wall. He stepped through the opening.

He stood in a long, dark hallway. Walls were within reach of both hands when he put his arms straight out. But he couldn't see. The children sounded as though they were beyond the wall.

Cory went back to the utility room and turned on the ceiling light. When he crept back into the dark hallway the light behind him cast a dwindling illumination along the hall. In the shadowy dark at the other end Cory saw the frame of another door.

The children were there, beyond that door.

He slipped down the hall, slow step by step, his hand sliding along a wall of rough, splintered, and cracked wood. His bare feet felt rough wood on the floor. He walked carefully to avoid getting a splinter.

He came to the door and saw that it wasn't quite closed.

He stood now in almost no light. The glow from the utility room was like a moonbeam far down at the other end of the hall.

The children's voices had hushed suddenly.

Had they heard him coming?

His fingers gripped the edge of the door and pulled it farther open, toward him. He peeked around the edge. Darkness.

Cory had a feeling of hugeness, as if the room took in all of the addition. A strange, unpleasant odor assaulted him. He cringed away from it. It was like coming alongside a ditch to find someone had hit an animal with his car and it had gone into the ditch to die. He didn't like this place.

He was going to go back to his own room, and stay there till the sun came up. But even then, with the sun shining outside, this room would be totally dark. He thought of it, always dark. Black, like the inside of a place that light never entered.

The kids weren't here after all. Why would they be playing in the dark?

His right hand gripped the door edge, and his left touched the wall and inadvertently slid into a light switch. It clicked on. Cory jumped in surprise and almost screamed.

The light came from his right. Ahead of him a dwindling glow filled the huge space beyond with a twilight almost as frightening as the darkness.

Animal eyes looked at him from the edge of what looked like woods.

Cory's heart thudded in his head, filling it with sound and pressure.

Straight in front of him stood a large grey wolf, its eyes reflecting the dim light with a reddish fire, its muzzle open and its fangs long and sharp.

Cory was incapable of moving. He returned the stare of the animal.

With the part of his mind that wasn't paralyzed with fear, Cory saw that the wolf stood permanently on a board and was held up by a stake through its stomach. The small corner of woodland behind the wolf was only a setting.

Cory swallowed the knot in his throat, and eased the door a few inches farther open. He leaned forward to look into the room. To his right he saw two oblong metal tables. There were shelves on the right wall, and lots of bottles and cans. Something furry lay on one of the tables.

He almost drew back, but stopped, staring. It was a dead animal on the table. It looked like a raccoon, oddly flat, as if there were nothing inside its skin.

He turned his head slowly, still standing in the hallway safely out of the awful room. His stomach felt as if it were turning over and over inside of him. His throat was full of something that he kept trying to swallow.

On the other side of the room he saw a forest of animals. A forked tree limb had been planted in a large pot, and on the limb were several squirrels and even a bluejay and a cardinal. They looked as real as if they were outside, except for their eyes. There was something terrible about their eyes.

On the floor behind the limb were a collection of animals. Both small and large animals many of which Cory had never seen. Some of them were dogs. There was one little spotted dog, who stood on short legs, with the stake embedded in its stomach to hold it up. It had tilted sideways, and its half-open muzzle pointed toward the floor.

Farther away, toward the corner to Cory's left, stood a black bear. It wasn't much larger than the wolf, and it stood on its hind legs, its paws out, as if begging for help.

Then Cory saw the little girl.

She stood in the shadows behind the bear, a little girl only about two years old. She smiled and smiled at him. She wore a blue and white bonnet with white trim.

His first blink of surprise changed to curiosity. It wasn't a little girl, it was a doll. A pretty doll with pink cheeks and a smile that was painted on her round face.

The room was entirely silent. As if it were a world alone, with nothing beyond, it was removed even from sound. These animals didn't move, or whine, or growl or bark. The doll had been left among them. It added a human quality that somehow soothed Cory.

He crossed the threshold into the room. He thought briefly of what had brought him here. But the children weren't here, and probably never had been. They would not play here.

Cory tiptoed along the rough boards of the floor. Shadows filled the corners of the room, and lay heavily behind the groups of stuffed animals. In the corners behind those on stakes others were piled together as if waiting to be buried.

He peered behind the bear at the doll, and stopped still in surprise.

Behind the doll, as if hiding behind dead branches and crisp leaves, was a girl as tall as himself. Her face looked at him from the shadows of the bear. But she looked strange and still. Her lips were pulled into a grimace, twisted to one side, with her teeth showing and her tongue, or something, protruding like a black lump out of her mouth.

Cory stared at her fixedly, not certain of what he saw. Was she real, or. . . ?

Her skin was dark and wrinkled, her hair in long coils over her bony shoulders, dead and lifeless.

There was nothing visible holding her up. She leaned between piles of animals, the wall, and the doll.

Cory blinked at her, words of greeting dying before they were uttered. He was no longer sure it was a real girl. It looked more like the wax figures he had seen in museums, except it was like a mummy, its skin all wrinkled, and its face all wrong, mouth twisted in a weird way.

Yet at first glance he had known it was a real girl.

A little girl wearing a ruffly blue dress, that was all covered now in dust.

CHAPTER TWENTY-EIGHT

WALSH SLUMPED IN THE CHAIR, HIS HEAD LOWERED, HIS EYES CLOSED. HE HAD stopped trying to pray. The house held the silence of ages. They might have been alone in a strange world, he and the comatose man on the bed. The night was long and terrible and was going to continue forever, and only he and Matt had been left within it.

He was being morbid, he knew it, but felt unable to lift himself out of the mire into which he had sunk. It was more than depression. It was something darker and far more terrible.

Walsh became aware that he no longer heard the man breathing.

He lifted his head. His heart leaped in surprise.

Matt sat leaning on his left elbow, staring at Walsh. The dark, slitted expression in his eyes was wild and cruel and inhuman. Walsh was trapped by that look, so fierce, as if it could penetrate and kill with only the thoughts driving it.

Walsh moved, straightening in the chair, and the totally mad, cruel expression in the man's eyes cleared, like a reptile eyelid lifting away.

Walsh cleared his throat, trembling from having seen something in a man's eyes he had never dreamed existed. He wasn't sure what it meant.

"Who the hell are you?" Matt asked.

His voice was deep and gruff. There was nothing in it to suggest the voices of the children Walsh had been listening to during the past hours. Walsh tried to speak, heard his own voice rasp hoarsely from the hours of praying. He coughed to clear it and sat straighter. He was aware of aches in his bones and tightness in his muscles. His heart continued to race, and a strange new sense of horror that came with the waking of Matt Reed couldn't be put aside.

"You had an accident," Walsh began, knowing there would be no way to explain his presence to this man whose eyes had at first held such cold, inhuman darkness. It was far beyond hostility. Beyond surprise at finding a stranger in your bedroom. It was something else, and Walsh knew he wouldn't forget it as long as he lived. He stood up.

Matt changed his position, swinging his legs to the floor. He appeared to be taking note of his unbuttoned shirt and trousers, and the bandage on his arm.

"The doctor was concerned," Walsh said. "Your family and friends were concerned. I'm Dalton Walsh evangelist, with the traveling revival—"

"Oh, yeah. The preacher. So somebody brought you down, umm? What for? To pray for my soul?" Matt laughed briefly.

Walsh stood still. He wanted to leave. His heart was heavy with what he had learned about himself, and he longed for his own bedroom, his own Bible, and the privacy of his thoughts. He couldn't equate what he had heard here tonight with anything in his experiences or beliefs, but he could continue to pray, to try to reach God again. To feel at least that God existed. Even the reality of Jesus Christ had taken on an entirely different aspect. Jesus Christ, the world's great leader had died like a man on a cross. Jesus Christ had spent his whole life searching for God, only to lose his faith at the last. Walsh couldn't handle it. He had to somehow revive his faith.

"I'm sorry to have intruded, sir. But you were having some problems the doctor didn't quite understand. And he thought I might be able to help." It occurred to him that Matt Reed was now sitting up, talking to him as might be expected of a man who had awakened in the middle of the night to find a strange preacher in his bedroom. The thought came to Walsh with a flush of his face, almost like a blush. Perhaps he had done some good after all.

"At any rate," Walsh added, "I can see you no longer need me."

Matt slowly raised his head. With his left hand he buttoned his shirt. Walsh recoiled inwardly from the look in Matt's eyes in that first upward glance, then as if an inner curtain had closed, blocking it from human view, it was gone.

"What problems?" Matt asked. "I had a stupid accident. Lost my balance and fell. Came home. Might have been a little feverish or something. First thing I knew they were helping me upstairs. Wanted to take me to some goddamned hospital, for Christ's sake. I've never been in a hospital in my life, and don't intend to start now. Would you, Preacher?"

"Uh . . . well, if I needed to be. I think they're quite humane places."

Walsh had tried to put a smile in his voice. He had tried to be a bit facetious, but it failed. Matt didn't appear to notice. Looking down, the man zipped and buttoned his trousers, leaning back to straighten his body enough to accomplish the job.

"They left me here, and I went to sleep. So, what problems?"

"It was a matter of children's voices."

Matt's stare snapped back to Walsh. His eyes were hooded and dark. His eyebrows drooped over his deep-set eyes, heavy and shading, the light behind him casting shadows over the features of his face. This man, Walsh felt suddenly, was not a kind man. Halley had probably seemed to be a cowed, obedient woman because her husband would have tolerated nothing else.

"Children's voices," Matt said in a toneless lack of expression. But the statement was also a question.

"Yes," Walsh said, unsure of himself. "Maybe it would be better if the doctor explained it to you. I'll go now and leave you to rest properly." His hand nervously clasped and unclasped the Bible he held. "Your good wife lent me her Bible. I wouldn't want to disturb her now. Perhaps I should leave it here."

He glanced at the clock on the dresser and saw it was almost two o'clock. The night that surrounded the house, the town, had grown very quiet.

"What do you mean, children's voices?" Matt demanded.

He sat on the side of his bed looking up at Walsh, still fumbling left-handed with buttons on his shirt. With his white hair and oddly white and dark striped beard, the heavy eyebrows and narrowed eyes, he didn't look as if he had ever lain helpless with the sound of a child's voice emanating from him.

"Children talking to someone," Walsh said carefully, watching Matt Reed, seeing his eyes narrow as he talked. "Children laughing, and then crying. Children begging to be allowed to go home. It seems some children disappeared over a number of years, and their voices were heard tonight. They seemed to be coming from you, or from somewhere near you."

Matt Reed licked his lips. Color had leached from his face as Walsh talked. Walsh met Matt Reed's stare without wavering, and he knew as well as if Matt had told him, that this man knew more about the children than he had ever told.

Matt whirled suddenly, as if someone behind him had spoken. The light in the room began to change, to dim. Then Walsh saw the darkness was forming again behind Matt. Walsh stared into the darkening room. He felt he could see the forming of a shape in the dark swirl that reached from Matt to the corner of the room to the ceiling above it.

A child began crying, a forlorn, hopeless cry that rose in volume to a scream.

Matt hunched, his left arm coming up as if to ward off the sound and the darkness. A low cry came from him. The scream of the child cut off, ending abruptly with the sound of Matt's voice.

The room gradually lightened.

It had lasted only seconds, but it seemed endless.

Walsh heard a long sigh. It was Matt. He leaned back, lying again on the bed, pulling his feet up, his head on the pillow. He was shaking.

"They've finally come," he said.

Walsh stood staring at Matt Reed. He lay with his left arm over his face. His voice had sounded weakened.

"Sit down, Preacher," he said.

Walsh continued to stand, the Bible clutched against him.

Matt lay still, his arm over his eyes. Then he began to laugh. A deep, sporadic chuckle that frightened Walsh, where the sound of the child's weeping had only cast him deeper into sadness.

Walsh didn't move. The laughter came in spurts, yet there was no movement of Matt's chest. His lips were closed, and he seemed to be breathing deeply, as if he had gone to sleep again. Walsh felt a primitive and instinctive urge to run. But he stood still, waiting.

"Preacher," Matt said suddenly. "Do you believe in demons?"

Walsh tried to answer. The hideous laughter had faded now along with the swirling shadows and the crying of the child. Walsh's throat seemed thick with mucous. He tried to clear it.

"No, I never really—"

"Well, you've just had the privilege of meeting one, face to face, so to speak. I always called it the giant."

"The giant," Walsh repeated. "The voice of a child in pain—"

"That's what it wants you to think. But beware, Preacher, they're not children."

Walsh waited.

After several long moments Matt continued, "Do you think a demon can eat away at a man until there's so little of the man left that he only looks like a man? Do you think there is a hell with a door right in front of us, all the time, that we can't see, but that we can suddenly walk right through?" He paused, and urged again, "Preacher?'

"I—uh—I always preached hell and the devil and—but truthfully, sir, I don't—I didn't believe there was anything beyond the natural worlds. And even that, sir, is horrible enough."

"But that's not all there is, Preacher."

Walsh stood still, staring down at the man on the bed. It seemed he had gone to sleep, then abruptly he was talking again.

"Sit down, Preacher."

Walsh backed up until his legs touched the soft edge of the chair. He lowered himself.

"Something happened tonight, Preacher," Matt said. "It was like there was some upheaval of this thing you call nature. It was the demons, Preacher. They're here. They're gathering. I saw them myself. Saw them in the woods. You don't know fear until you've seen the demons, Preacher. They can drive a sane man insane. In a flash, in a thought. That's because we never thought they existed, isn't it so, Preacher?"

Walsh didn't know what to say. When he was stumped, he always got by with asking a question. His voice rasped hoarsely, even after he cleared it again. "You saw demons?"

"You're supposed to be able to pray demons away, aren't you, Preacher?"

Two hours ago Walsh would have assured Matt that the power of prayer could handle any problem. But now he said nothing.

The man said, "I'm going to tell you something I've never told anyone before. The children's voices have always been here, Preacher. I heard them when I was no older than Cory. At first I was scared. I thought it was my brother, Lew, back from the dead. It sounded like his voice. He disappeared one day and was never heard from again."

He sighed deeply, his eyes covered with his left arm.

"Would you mind turning out all the lights but the one on the table by you, Preacher? I don't like much light."

Walsh obeyed quietly, and returned to his chair. The light, now pale in the large room, was a small source of comfort in this increasingly uncomfortable situation.

Matt continued, "Lew told me he saw a giant come out of the cellar. After I grew up I added a shop room and built it over the old cellar, and extended the cellar to join the old basement. But when I was a boy, the cellar was just a wooden door set in the grass. Lew told me a giant that eats kids lived there. I thought he was only teasing me. He used to chase me and tell me the giant was going to get me when the moon was full. I knew it wasn't true, but I was scared shitless, anyway."

"Then one night the moon was full, the way it is now. I saw the giant, for the first time. I saw the shadow in the moonlight. Lew disappeared that night and was never seen again. Now I knew the giant had gotten him. The next full moon the giant came for me, I heard it in the hall. It filled the doorway. I made a bargain. I would do its bidding, if it would leave me alone and let me live."

Walsh sat in silence, listening to the words of a madman, or a jokester who was making fun of religion and of the beliefs he attributed to Walsh.

"He was the only brother I had. After that I could hear him. Sometimes he'd call me. Sometimes I could hear him crying as the giant carried him away."

There was a long pause and Walsh felt obligated to fill it. "The psychological trauma of losing someone close to you—"

"Bullshit. Save your breath, Preacher. I thought maybe you, of all people, would understand. You're not listening to me. I never told anyone else, because I knew what their attitude would be. All that psychological babble. Something in the subconscious causing me to hear voices. Well, Preacher Walsh, you heard the voice."

"Uh—yes."

"A child. Playing. Crying. Screaming."

"Yes."

"When I was still small I learned it wasn't really Lew's voice I heard. But it wasn't out of my own mind, either. It was the demons, pretending to be children, calling me to join them. It was the giant, testing me, to see if I'd fail to do his bidding."

Walsh stared in horror at the man on the bed. He felt compelled to ask this madman, "And what was its bidding, Mr. Reed?"

The hairs on Walsh's arms raised as stiffly as the hairs on an animal's spine when it sensed danger. He was keeping his voice normal with effort.

Matt shook his head. He was not going to give Walsh an answer.

Walsh let a moment pass, then he asked, "You told no one?"

"Not until now."

Walsh said, "I can understand how a child would be so frightened, after his brother disappeared. Was there ever any trace of him?"

He could understand a young boy's fear, after the disappearance of a brother. He could understand the child thinking of supernatural reasons for the disappearance. But he didn't understand his own fear now, nor did he understand the voices he, and others, had heard.

"No," Matt said. "I knew where he was, but no one else did. How could they, when the giant had gotten him?"

Walsh was trembling. His cheeks had grown icy and numb. But he had a feeling now that somewhere within Matt Reed lay the answer to the voices. Because, maybe, of the horror of his own early experience. "What about the other children?" he asked.

"What others?"

"The boy with the dog. The nephew of the lady who is a nurse. Lois. I believe they said the boy's name was Cliff. He seems to have disappeared three years ago."

Matt eased his arm over and peered out beneath it at Walsh. He said nothing.

"And the others. They seem to come from you, Mr. Reed."

Still Matt didn't answer. His eyes were in deep shadow, but Walsh saw they stared at him steadily.

"And there were other voices. The voices of several different children. Some of the folks that were concerned about you even wondered if you might be possessed. That's why they came after me. There are ministers in town, but I'm sure they thought they were too orthodox and would never believe in possession by the devil. They thought I might."

"But you don't," Matt said.

Walsh started to answer what he had always thought was the truth, but couldn't, because he no longer knew a truth. Instead he said, "The children sounded happy part of the time. They sang an old song, '*Here we go round the mulberry bush.*'"

Matt said, "Lew and I used to play that. Our grandmother taught us. Sixty-five years ago."

"One child, they said, was Coleen." Walsh had seen Halley's reaction. "Your wife was extremely upset. It was as if she were being tortured. She never knew what happened to the child, she said, but she knew it wasn't true that Coleen had run away with the boy, Jeremy."

"No. All those children, even Coleen, my adored Coleen. It was the giant, don't you see? Just as it was with my brother." Matt moved his arm just enough to allow the light to touch his eyes as he stared at Walsh. "And of course the voices would come now. I should have known. All those voices. Gathering strength. I should have known it wouldn't go away, no matter how I've worked to appease it. You know what that means, don't you, Preacher?"

"No, I'm afraid I don't."

"It means the demon is more real than life, and it's playing its final hand. It will keep on, till it gets what it wants."

"What it wants? Do you mean it wants you?"

"I thought so, but now, maybe everyone. Everyone in town, in the country, in the world. All the children, first. Then the parents of the children. You, Preacher." He covered his eyes again, and his voice was muffled and slow, as if he were losing contact with the world. "Can't you feel it coming? Something happened tonight, didn't it, Preacher? At your revival."

Walsh was aware of a small, inward shock as he was reminded of an earlier time. So close, but so distant.

"Yes. There was a minor earthquake, so it seemed. Then a young boy, Patrick, whom they say murdered his family last year, appeared in the doorway."

"You woke the dead, Preacher. Why did you come here? Take your revival and go away. You woke the dead and disturbed the sleeping demons."

Walsh felt his face flush. A strange sensation of heat warmed his neck and moved into the hair at the back of his head. The man's accusation had made him feel responsible, and guilty.

"I don't believe in demons, Matt," he said, but got no response.

Walsh waited, but Matt said nothing more. His arm covered his eyes, and he breathed evenly and deeply in what appeared to be a natural sleep.

The silence seemed to go on and on, then suddenly it was broken by a little girl's voice. It was soft and very clear, yet seemed distant, as if Walsh were listening to it over a telephone, or as if it were beyond a wall. "Daddy, where's Daniel?"

Matt didn't move or change the even rate of breathing. Walsh watched and listened intently and knew with certainty the voice was not generated by the man. It seemed instead only to be drawn by him.

There was a pause, then the child asked, "But why would he run away? Didn't he like living here?"

There came the pause, as if the words of the person to whom she spoke now answered somewhere beyond Walsh's hearing.

"Why would the giant want him?"

Then, after a long pause, the child began to weep. Through her tears she murmured, "I love you, I love—you—love—Daddy—please—Daddy—let me go—Daddy—I promise I won't tell—about the giant—I won't tell."

Walsh bowed his head over the Bible and prayed in a murmuring voice the Lord's Prayer. He became aware of a hushed and listening silence in the room beyond his own voice.

He ended the prayer softly and leaned his head back on the chair and closed his eyes.

Soft footsteps in the hall alerted him and he stood up. Matt still appeared to be sleeping. If it hadn't been for the children's voices, heard by so many people, Walsh would see Matt as someone who enjoyed spinning long yarns, getting a kick out of who might believe him. He could see him holding a child on his knee and telling stories that thrilled, even scared the child, and then hearing Matt laugh it away as a joke. He felt as if he had been treated as a child. And yet . . .

The footsteps moved just outside the door with an uncertainty that added to the unreality of the night. Walsh slipped quietly to the door, to avoid waking Matt, and opened it.

Halley stood there, her hair hanging loose. She was wearing a faded cotton robe and terry cloth slippers that seemed barely to hang on her feet. Walsh stepped into the hall and closed the door softly.

"He's sleeping," he said. "I'm sure he'll be fine tomorrow. He woke once and lay talking, for quite a while."

"Talking?"

It seemed to Walsh she looked hopeful, and he was encouraged to add, "Yes, quite normally." He glanced back toward the closed door, but all was silent beyond it.

He said, "I have no way of understanding the voices, but a psychiatrist might be able to."

Halley only stared at him, her eyes slightly narrowed. Walsh felt compelled to explain.

"That is, it must have something to do with the loss of his brother when he was so young."

Halley's eyes rounded. *"Brother?"*

"Yes," Walsh said, "Lew. The brother who disappeared when they were children."

Halley shook her head. "He was an only child, Reverend. Lew is his middle name. Matt never had a brother."

Walsh stood with her, looking into her eyes.

She walked past him and opened the door. He watched her go to the side of the bed. She stood looking down at Matt, then she turned and left the room.

CHAPTER TWENTY-NINE

HALLEY'S HAIR SWUNG FORWARD OVER HER SHOULDERS AND ACROSS THE SIDES of her face as she bent over the desk in Matt's private office. She had rarely entered this room, except to vacuum the floor a few times a year and do a small amount of dusting, or to make an even more rare phone call. She felt as if his hand would fall on her shoulder any moment and his voice would demand to know what she was doing.

Her hands trembled as she opened drawers, shuffling through papers for that key. That one key that would open Matt's taxidermy shop.

In the days after Coleen's disappearance, and Jeremy's—she mustn't forget Jeremy—that freckle-faced boy who was as helpless and vulnerable as her own little girls—in the days after she had come home with Rachel to find the house so empty, she had not once thought of going into Matt's locked taxidermy shop.

The police hadn't asked about it. They hadn't even asked to search the house, or the garage or sheds. They had come from the sheriff's department, a couple of men appropriately solemn, and asked what clothing the children had been wearing. They hadn't even asked to see the rooms where the children had slept.

Why should they? The Reed's were one of the most respected and stable families in the community. She and Matt had kept foster children before, without incident. A teenage girl, Gloria, had stayed with them six months. She had graduated from the local high school, and taken a job and eventually made friends with her family again. Two more boys had stayed a few weeks, then Matt took them back to their homes.

The first boy from the child welfare agency, though, had stayed two months and then ran away. His name was Daniel.

Then Jeremy, just weeks later, was also gone, and gone too was Coleen, ten years old.

"She would never run away," Halley remembered crying to the police, to Matt, to Rachel. "Coleen would never run away."

A search crew was organized and the woods for miles around walked through by teenagers and adults. There was no sign of Coleen, or Jeremy.

Matt had grown so silent. It had seemed to Halley he was holding in emotion. He did not seem to want to talk to her after Coleen disappeared. But, now, in her memory, she realized they hadn't talked together much since the birth of Coleen.

On her knees by the desk Halley searched through the bottom drawers, removing papers, envelopes, working fast, feeling through papers, at last dumping contents on the floor and looking beneath the drawers for the key.

She sat back and suddenly she knew where the key was. Of course. He would be carrying it with him. In his pocket.

She stood up.

She could see him, in her mind, stretched on the bed upstairs, his bandaged arm across his stomach, and his left arm across his eyes. Even in the helplessness of his strange sleep, he was formidable. She was afraid to approach him, to try to take from him the key he would never allow another hand to touch.

For the first time in her life she sat down in Matt's desk chair. It was large and comfortable, soft, black leather with a high back and padded arms. It swiveled, with a faint squeak as she turned. She looked at the room. Two walls were lined with bookshelves, and so many books that some of them were stacked in front of others. He had always haunted city bookstores, and brought home volumes of books, but she had never looked at them. Many were on taxidermy. Even from the chair, she could see the only novels were very old, purchased as a leather-bound set before Matt became owner of the house.

Another wall had a fireplace, and on each side long, narrow windows, covered with the heavy velvet draperies that were there when she came to the house as a bride, forty-four years ago. Even then she had seldom come into this room. At his father's death, the room became Matt's, and he did not invite her in.

On the long mantel of the cavernous fireplace were framed pictures. Grandparents, parents, people of the family Halley had never known. There was also a picture of a little boy. Matt. Mathew Lew.

The picture seemed highlighted now by the lights in the room. She left the chair and went to the mantel to look at the face in the photograph. He was smiling, sitting in a photographer's studio with a background of rippled velvet. The colors were gone. Behind him was a strange darkness, as if the picture had become discolored.

Or as if something threatening hovered there.

Halley could almost find a shape in it, she could almost see something like large wings, or arms holding out a wide cape. She could almost see a face forming above little Matt's head, an evil face, a pointed chin, and upward slanted eyes.

She turned away.

In all spare places on the walls were animal heads. Deer, wild boar, a couple of wolves, a moose. Matt's hunting trips had taken up portions of each autumn until just a few years ago when he had begun confining his hunting to the local hills.

SUDDENLY A SCENE RETURNED TO HER, and she stood with one hand gripping the walnut edge of the fireplace mantel as the scene grew sharply clear and replaced her present surroundings.

She was in the kitchen cooking supper one year ago when a man pounded angrily on the kitchen door.

She went to the door and out onto the porch. Clyde Moore stood there, a trap in his hand. He was livid with fury. Halley didn't know him well. She had seen him drive by as she worked in her flower gardens, and had returned his wave. He had always seemed friendly, but she didn't socialize with her neighbors. She tended her flowers, and stayed at home.

"I want to speak to your husband, Miss Halley."

Halley nodded and stepped back. Matt came out onto the porch, the daily newspaper in his hand. It was turning dusk. They had just finished supper and Matt had gone into his room to read.

She stepped back into the kitchen and continued cleaning. But she couldn't help hearing Clyde's angry voice.

"I've asked you, Reed, to not trap on my land. I've been as tolerant as I could be. But this is the last straw. This goddamned trap of yours was on my property and it killed my dog. And you're going to court, sir!"

Halley heard the clatter of metal as the trap was thrown onto the floor.

Matt didn't utter a word. Halley stood still, the dripping dishrag in her hand, her heart thundering. She heard a car start and roar backward out of the driveway. It turned west. She heard it slow for the turn into the Moore driveway.

Matt came back through the kitchen. Halley slipped a glance at him, and saw his face was set in cold fury.

He said nothing to her. He went through the kitchen carrying his newspaper.

As soon as she could she slipped into the back hall and went upstairs.

She couldn't sleep.

She thought she'd heard firecrackers. Even though they were illegal in the city limits, sometimes kids played with them anyway. The explosions she heard, so muffled, were firecrackers, she told herself. Or perhaps it was Matt, back in the hills, checking his traps. Perhaps he had shot an animal.

She sat tense on the side of her bed, in the dark. She thought she heard a sound, somewhere outside, and she went to her window, pulled her curtain back and looked out. The moon was shining brightly that night, illuminating the field that lay between their yard and the Moore house.

At first she saw nothing. There were no lights on at the Moore place.

She went out into the hall, and walked through the dark to the window that faced the backyard. She saw Matt coming through the moonlight with something thrown over his shoulder. Another dead animal. This one large. Matt carried it easily. As he drew nearer she saw the animal was wrapped in something.

She drew back from the window wondering why he would wrap an animal before he brought it home.

She heard the cellar door close.

She hurried to her bedroom and huddled in the dark.

The next day when police came asking if she had seen Patrick Moore, or heard anything, she learned that Clyde Moore, his wife and daughter had been shot to death by their son, Patrick.

Now she knew what it was that Matt had carried home that night, wrapped in something dark.

She knew now, suddenly, as if her memory had opened on a closed door, why she had fainted when she saw Patrick. She knew he was dead. Matt had carried him home that night of the murders. It wasn't Patrick who had killed his family, it was Matt. And Matt had killed Patrick, and his body was hidden somewhere in the cellar.

Halley released her tight hold on the mantel and started across the room. How could she have forgotten that one evening and night a year ago? How much more in her memory had she pushed aside and refused to acknowledge?

For one year Patrick Moore's body had been in the cellar beneath Matt's taxidermy shop.

As if she were lost in time, jerking from one year ago to twenty or more, she heard the footsteps of a child running. As if Rachel were small again, and running barefoot along the hall. Or as if in the silence of the children's voices they now had materialized and become real and one of them had entered the house. Halley heard the running steps.

Then in a blink she knew it was more real than any of those. *Cory.* Where was Cory? She hadn't checked his room to make sure he was asleep, not for a long time.

She stepped into the hall.

Cory came running from the back of the house, his eyes round and expressing fear, or perhaps awe.

"Cory!"

He slid to a stop and stared at her a moment as if he were still lost in whatever nightmare he had awakened from. Then he hurried toward her.

"Gram," he cried breathlessly, "Gram, come with me."

He took her hand and pulled. She resisted. She was living in the house of a murderer, and she had to go find Thomas. How could she have forgotten so completely that night almost precisely a year ago? Police had come to her house for days after the murder asking questions. Have you seen anyone, heard anything? Did you hear shots? Did you see Patrick? When was the last time you saw any of the Moores?

"Gram, the earthquake knocked the door down, and there's a big crack, and I went in and I saw animals and a big doll and—"

"Doll?"

"A big doll. It's been there a long time, and there's a—"

The doll. Coleen had taken her doll when she ran away. Coleen, her baby.

Halley began to listen to Cory.

"Where did you see the doll?" The only dolls left in the house were in the nursery. Rachel's dolls. Years ago Halley had emptied Coleen's room. She had gathered all the dolls and given them to the Child Welfare people to give away to children who had no dolls. She had even given away Coleen's dresses, frilly, lacy dresses she had made herself. There was no big doll in the house that she knew of.

"It's—it's—it's in those rooms, Gram. Matt's private rooms."

A determination came over Halley. She felt oddly calm. The perpetual trembling within her body, that constant trembling that had been part of her for thirty years, suddenly ceased.

"Show me, Cory."

He nodded. "Ok-k-kay, Gram."

She had never known him to stutter. She clasped his small, cold hand inside her own large hand. "It's all right, Cory. Calm down. Show Gram."

He led her into the small dark hall where Matt's private locked door was, but the door was no longer locked. It looked as if it had been ripped out of the wall. It leaned askew. Cory started to slip through, pulling her.

She stared at the splintered wood. The entire door frame, she saw, had slipped sideways. It hadn't been done by a human hand. The earthquake, perhaps, had done more damage than she would have imagined. Especially to this addition.

A light was on in the hall beyond the door. For the first time in her life, since Matt had built the rooms he called his shop, she saw the hall. It was at least twenty feet long, and narrow. One small bulb in the ceiling lighted it.

Cory clung to her hand although they were positioned awkwardly in the narrow passageway. He walked ahead of her. Her arm brushed against the wall, and it rasped her skin like coarse sandpaper.

At the door Cory stopped.

Over his head Halley saw into a large, dim room. A light came from somewhere to the right of the open door. At first it looked as if the farther side of the room was filled with dark shadows, then suddenly a form took shape. An animal stood in the dim light staring their way.

"It's only a wolf, Gram," Cory said in a subdued half whisper meant to comfort her, but which instead made her want to turn and hurry away. "He won't hurt you. He's dead. All the animals are dead."

Halley entered the shop.

The room was larger than she had expected. It seemed like a jungle of animals. Matt had even brought tree limbs and set them into naturalistic settings, and perched upon their stark limbs squirrels, birds, even small things that looked like butterflies.

To Halley's right was a wall of shelves, holding bottles and jars of solutions. Some of the jars also held things that looked as if they once had been part of an animal. She saw a heart in one that had been bleached pale by its long years in its solution. There were narrow tables, almost like operating tables in a hospital surgery suite. A tube of fluorescent lighting glowed down on the table beneath with a bluish white light that left the rest of the large room in shadows.

Halley became aware that Cory was silently tugging at her to turn the other way.

Halley turned reluctantly, slowly, as if she had suddenly become a very old woman.

The area to her left was deep in shadow, but she saw the small, shining round face of the doll.

Coleen's doll.

Its cheeks caught the light behind them in a reflecting way that made the dust settled in the creases of the face look like black lines. Black lines around the mouth, the small, snub nose, the eyes.

Halley's gasp of surprise hung in her throat. She stood unbreathing as her eyes searched deeper into the shadows.

The figure of a girl . . .

A little girl's blue dotted Swiss dress, blue with white dots, dusty and greyed now . . .

The figure of a little girl, half fallen, half hidden behind the doll, her face dark and mummified, her lovely golden hair lifeless and dead, a horrible grimace on her lips, drawn back so her teeth were revealed, as the teeth of the wolf had been more successfully preserved.

Halley went closer. What she saw didn't penetrate her mind, her long-held beliefs. Coleen, grown now, living in some far away land. Coleen, with children of her own. Coleen, who, maybe, would come home someday.

Halley went closer, with Cory forgotten behind her. She walked on dusty forest leaves that shattered like old glass into bits beneath her feet.

The doll stood on a pedestal, but behind it the little girl had fallen from her pedestal sideways as if to make her bed in the leaves. Her skin was dark and wrinkled, her eyes oddly bright and shining. They looked up at Halley without seeing her.

Then Halley realized the eyes were made of glass.

Halley began to scream. All the breath in her, all the life, pushed out scream after scream.

She couldn't move. She stood with her hands to her cheeks, staring down at the thing that once had been her lovely child.

She screamed.

CHAPTER THIRTY

MATT REED LAY STILL AGAIN, BREATHING AS IF HE SLEPT NORMALLY. THE VOICE of a child came from somewhere, and drifted off to a faraway place and then to silence.

The shadow in the corner beyond the bed darkened and lightened, in a slow pulsing, and Walsh began to notice that its changes came with the waning of the child's voice.

The voices changed. A little girl spoke, her words unintelligible but sounding very alone and lost, then after a pause and a pulsing of the shadow a different voice spoke. A boy. Weeping drifted in and out like an eerie background music.

He had to walk into the shadow. He knew he had to. It was as if a telepathic message flashed into his mind. *Go,* it said. *Go into the darkness.*

Nearly paralyzed with fear, Walsh went around the bed to the other side, the Bible in his hand. He began to murmur the Lord's Prayer. He was incapable of spontaneous prayer now. Hesitant and unsteady, he approached the fog that thickened and darkened as he went forward.

Walsh stopped at the edge of the roiling darkness. Someone, somewhere, was screaming.

The screams reached Walsh at first like the voices of the children. For a moment he could not separate the sound from the room, the darkness that waited for him. He stood immobile.

Then the power of the scream penetrated his consciousness, and he knew it was different. He heard within it absolute terror.

It came from somewhere in the house. It was real.

The Bible slipped from Walsh's hands, and he let it fall. He hurried to the door and flung it open.

The scream was more distinct, coming from a lower room. He turned back toward Matt, but the man lay without moving, undisturbed, held in his own demon-possessed world.

Walsh hurried out, pulled in a dozen directions. He turned toward the wide front stairs, and the screams receded, so he reversed his plunge toward the unknown and ran toward the back stairway down which Thomas had gone earlier. He didn't know where it led, but it was taking him closer to the desperate cry.

THOMAS DROVE down the narrow driveway from the shelter to Reed Road. The Moore house was shadowed by the shade trees that surrounded it, as if buried. Farther down, across a two acre field that hadn't been mowed this season, the peaked roof of the large Reed house rose through the shade trees.

Nina sat in the passenger seat looking straight down the street with the headlights. The dash light revealed the worry on her face. He reached over and took her hand in his. It felt thin and cold.

"The night will end, Nina. Sun will shine again."

She nodded. "Maybe we shouldn't have left Cory and Halley, Thomas."

The large house, half a block farther on down the street, looked as if every room in the house were lighted. Thomas had done that when he searched the rooms, turning on lights and leaving them on.

"Tom, isn't that a car?"

Half a block beyond the Reed driveway, in a slanting park at the side of the road, sat a car. Light-colored, it was almost invisible in the moonlight.

"Glen has a tan-colored car. I'll bet that's him. I told him to go back to the station and relieve Noel."

Thomas drove on past the Reed driveway and pulled up beside the parked car. The moment he came near he could see through the windows that no one was in the car unless they were lying down. Leaving his car door open, the dash light shining out onto the pavement, Thomas took his flashlight and went to check out the parked car.

A glance inside told him it belonged to Glen. On the seat was the beacon that Glen popped onto the top of the car when he needed it. A black notebook lay beside it, with a pen attached.

Thomas walked to the ditch, turned off the flashlight and looked out over the field. Moonlight played tricks of illumination. Fireflies flickered in the grass and in the air. Trees cast black shadows. But Glen was nowhere in sight.

Thomas suddenly was gripped with concern. Where the hell had Glen gone, and why? Why would he have left his car? Why hadn't he followed instructions?

"Tom!"

He turned. Nina ran toward him from the car.

"Tom, someone's screaming. At the house."

He heard it then, as if it came on air waves that rose and fell. His first instinct was to run, back down the driveway and to the house. But he turned instead, gripped Nina's arm, and pushed her into the patrol car.

He put it in reverse and roared backward down the street and sharply around into the driveway, past Nina's car and close to the kitchen. Even before he turned off the motor he could hear the scream. It sounded as if it came from underground.

He threw the door open and ran to the back porch and across it to the kitchen door. Light splayed down on him from the porch light, and from the brighter light through the glass on the kitchen door. He had only one key that he knew for sure would fit, and that was for the front door. The scream continued, so close now he could hear its breathlessness, as if whoever it was had been screaming for a long time.

He looked for something to break the glass, when suddenly Walsh, with round, wild eyes and a pale face, appeared on the other side of the door.

Thomas shouted at him to open the door. It seemed as if Walsh were moving in slow motion, as if he were about to turn away without letting Thomas in. He kept looking toward the door beyond, pulled by the sound of the scream.

Thomas shouted, *"Unlock the door!"*

Walsh jerked forward, turned the door knob, and then whirled away. He ran a few feet toward a door leading out of the kitchen, and stopped.

Thomas entered the kitchen. The scream stopped. Suddenly there was only an echo of the scream, and nothing to guide them.

"Halley!" Nina cried, close behind Thomas.

The kitchen door stood open, and a large beetle whirred in and began a battle with the light in the ceiling. Nina ran past Walsh and Thomas.

"That was Halley's voice!"

She ran directly to an inner door and passed through it, and Thomas remembered it was the door to the hallway and the utility room. He followed, with Walsh closely behind him.

Nina had paused at the door that Thomas had found locked earlier. Now it was broken from the wall, the frame looking as if it had been ripped out by the hand of a giant.

"Halley?" Nina shouted into the ripped wall. She slid through. Splinters pulled her shirt. She went on into the narrow passageway beyond.

Thomas grasped the door on one side, and Walsh grasped the other. It tore away with a loud ripping sound. Working in silence, they placed it in the corner, out of the way. The door that had been locked less than an hour ago was now a hole in the wall. Thomas didn't have time to wonder what had happened.

Their footsteps pounded on the wide boards of the floor. Nina had already gone out of sight through a door near the end of the hall. There continued an ominous silence. Then as he ran Thomas heard a woman's anguished sobs.

Nina appeared suddenly in the doorway with her arms around Halley. Halley's face was covered by her hands and by long strands of her grey hair. She stumbled along at Nina's side.

Nina's face was drawn with horror, and so pale Thomas was afraid she was going to faint. But she looked up at him with no sign of helplessness.

"I'm getting Halley out of here. I'll take her to her room." She jerked her head toward the room beyond the door. "Take a look in there, Thomas."

Thomas crossed the threshold. Cory stood facing him, his face set as if in a mask, mouth small and pinched, eyes large and wide. He stepped out of their way, and stood with his back against the wall.

Thomas started to tell him to go with Nina, but then he saw the wolf. It stared at him from reflecting brown glass eyes, its fangs yellow beneath updrawn lips. It had been mounted in a natural posture, and looked pitifully real. Beyond it a brown bear, hardly larger than the wolf, stood on its hind legs.

"My God," Walsh said.

Thomas turned toward the light. He saw the surgical tables. Lights hung over them, but they had not been turned on. The only light burning in the room was a fluorescent tube over a table against the wall.

Shelves of solution lined the wall by the table and the wall on the left. Skins of animals lay piled beneath the shelves. Jars held organs, from brains to hearts and kidneys. As Thomas stepped closer, staring at a brain in a jar, he began to see it was too large for an animal brain.

Scarcely believing what he saw, he turned.

Walsh stood in a shadowed area of the large room on the other side of the door staring at something with a human face. Thomas saw him stoop and put his hand out.

"A doll," Walsh's voice carried back to Thomas in a dreamlike softness. "A child's—"

His voice cut off. He remained in a stoop, staring.

Walsh turned, stared a moment at Thomas. Thomas approached him and stopped.

The dusty doll stood in crisp, old leaves, held by a pedestal similar to the ones that supported the animals. Behind her, lying half fallen, her arm half around the doll, was the mummified body of a little girl, her dusty curls hanging into the leaves, her face frozen in a dark, wrinkled grimace of horror.

Behind Thomas was a sound almost like gagging. Then Walsh murmured something Thomas didn't hear. He stared at the doll, and what was left of the little girl.

It was the doll Thomas had seen tonight, being carried by a child with a pretty face and long, blond curls. The dress was the same blue and white dotted Swiss, trimmed in lace, her belt in a large bow at the back. Child and doll both dressed in dotted Swiss, except the doll's dress had once been pink.

It was the child he had determined from old photographs was Coleen Reed, age ten, disappeared thirty years ago, and never heard from again.

All that was human within him refused to accept what he saw. His brain felt as if it closed against all response, all emotions. He was blocked from thoughts, from feelings. He knew if they came now they would crush him. His psyche had closed off to protect him.

Halley had not had such protection.

He turned, and saw that Walsh was still stooping slightly, holding his stomach. He was colorless. Thomas touched Walsh's shoulder, and Walsh jumped, then apologized.

"I've never seen anything like this," he said. "I'll go back upstairs. I'll be with . . . Mr. Reed."

Thomas hesitated. "Be careful, will you? My assistant's around here someplace. I'll send him up at soon as I find him."

Walsh nodded, and went out through the door. Thomas heard his footsteps in the hall. They faded away to silence.

Thomas stood still. This room, filled with so many presences, so many bodies, was the most silent room he had ever entered in his life. Standing there, unwilling to turn, to search further, he could imagine a state of nonexistence, of nonbeing, and the horrors it raised. Yet he couldn't allow himself to feel, not yet.

His footsteps sounded loud and intrusive as he walked back to the work table against the wall, behind the light, and looked for more light switches. He found them, a row of switches beside a row of receptacles.

He brushed his hand down over all the switches. Lights came on all through the room. He turned to see that lights over each table were burning, and in the far corners of the rooms lights illuminated the wildwood settings, the animals mounted and arranged. It illuminated more clearly the little girl who had fallen sideways.

Thomas stood, turning, looking. He saw another door, set back in the wall beyond the shelves. It stood open a crack, just enough for him to see that lights were on there.

He walked to the door, his footsteps loud. He pushed the door open, and saw steps going down into an underground room.

After a hesitation, in which the utter silence of the area seemed to emphasize the contrasting lack of silence within his head, he began to descend.

The steps were of crude boards, just as the floor and the walls were, without any attempt to finish of any kind. They creaked when he stepped on them, but they were thick, heavy boards, secured with large nails. They had held the weight of Matt Reed, they would hold him.

He came down onto a dirt floor. To his right was another row of steps leading up to a flat overhead door. The cellar door, leading out. A padlock hung beneath it, woven in webs. Matt had not used it in several weeks, perhaps longer. He had not removed anything from his taxidermy workplace in recent years. He had only added.

Thomas saw the entire area was lighted dimly with one naked bulb hanging from a floor joist. Spiders had woven webs beneath the joists, the only living creatures ever to enter this area safely.

The bicycles were stacked in a pile beneath the stairway.

Toward the back of the room what had once been five boys had been tossed like so much refuse. Some stood leaning as if hanging out somewhere. Some sat, and leaned, in a mournful droop. The taxidermy efforts had been only partially successful. Their skin had wrinkled and hardened and turned dark, their lips drawn back from their teeth.

Thomas recognized the short crewcut of Cliff's hair, the boy he had seen so clearly in the lights of his car. Spiders had woven old webs in the spiky hair, and dust had settled, putting a layer of dark over the blond.

Willy was there, sitting frozen forever against the wall in the pale light from the spider-woven bulb, his face twisted, mouth open in an expression of horror.

A third boy was so mummified that Thomas knew it had to be the body of one of the boys who had disappeared thirty or thirty-one years ago.

Thomas forced himself to walk past them. They had not been placed in a setting, they had merely been thrown there together, out of the way, against the wall. Experiments of human taxidermy that had failed, perhaps, or had not turned out as Matt had wished, just as the work on his own child upstairs had not turned out well.

Thomas pushed back the rise of emotion that felt as if it would strike him down, and walked past the children's remains and toward the darker areas.

A more recent limp skin of what had once been a little spotted dog lay on a pile of other animal skins. And behind them Thomas saw the dark hair of a human.

He went closer. His toe nudged something. It moved, the long black barrel for a moment like a living snake. Then Thomas recognized a shotgun. Its barrel had rusted only in a few spots. It was the gun that had killed the Moore family, Thomas had no doubt. It hadn't been there long enough to rust, a year at the most. Thomas stooped to pick it up, then stopped.

The body of a tall young boy lay in the darkness behind the animal pelts, facing the wall. As Thomas eased the gun away, the body moved, rolling partway onto its back.

Patrick Moore stared up at him; his eyes had been replaced with brown glass.

He had fallen. He had been mounted on a wooden stand, and it had tipped, taking the stuffed skin of Patrick with it.

Without thinking, Thomas bent and stood the boy upright.

The young boy had been only a few inches shorter than Thomas, and for a moment it was almost like looking into Patrick's eyes. In silence they pleaded for mercy.

Emotion rushed into Thomas. The odor of death and decay, of rodents and insects and moist earth, became too much. He turned blindly and hurried toward the stairs.

Then the smell of blood reached him, and he paused. Once the fresh blood of a murdered victim touched his nostrils it had lingered, never forgotten. He smelled it now.

He didn't want to look.

In the darkness of a corner beyond the steps he saw the glistening body, thrown in a heap with its own skin.

Thomas approached it reluctantly.

He stooped.

The skin of the face lay across the bloody body, flattened, the eyelids half-closed.

Glen.

Thomas wasn't sure if he had cried out his fury and anguish. His head thundered with silent screams of refusal to believe. Images of children who weren't even alive, had come back to carry on Matt's work? Children he had killed, skinned and stuffed, now returned to continue that terrible carnage? While Matt lay as if comatose, in a half-trance, something created by him now hovered in the darkness.

Thomas had never known the power of a real evil before, something that built over the years to a point of its own creation. How did he fight something that was there on a different level from one's daily experiences?

He turned and reached for the steps that would take him out of this cellar of horrors.

He climbed, and closed behind him the heavy plank door that led to the cellar. He found a metal bolt on the wall, and slid it shut on the door, locking it.

He rushed out of the horror of the taxidermy shop, the site of so many murders, leaving behind questions he knew would never be answered.

CHAPTER THIRTY-ONE

THE GHASTLY SCENE OF THE DOLL AND THE CHILD WERE WITH WALSH AS HE climbed the back stairs and walked down the long, silent hall to the room where Matt lay. He looked upon the man on the bed with different eyes.

He had seen the enormity of a man's work, more evil than he had ever imagined possible. The man had not only wantonly destroyed animals, but he had destroyed his own child. Walsh saw the shadows that appeared to hover more and more darkly beyond Matt Reed. For Walsh the depths of hell were opening, revealing to him things he had doubted. Somewhere in the man who lay presently helpless was evil incarnate. It was an evil worse than he ever suspected. It was as if this night had been forced upon Walsh, so that he was able to sink into this madman's world and believe the demons of which the man had spoken actually existed.

If demons existed, so did the devil.

So too the angels and . . .

. . . and every negative has its positive and . . .

Walsh sat down on the chair, his eyes on Matt. He still slept with his left arm over his eyes.

At times he could hear cries, or perhaps only the echoes of cries of other times. Then silence predominated. A door closed somewhere. The world seemed to sleep, in the darkest part of the night, with the moon hovering over the western ridge of hills, soon to go out of sight and leave them in a moonless dark.

• • •

THOMAS FELT a little better with the cellar door firmly locked. The odors of death, of long years of being closed into a trap of death, clung to his clothes. The odor of the blood of a friend drew a sense of horror worse than the smell of his own blood.

Oh Christ, guy, why did you choose this one time to disobey orders?

He stood in the main room, staring at the jars on the shelves. They had new meaning for him now. Human hearts, he was sure, not animal. Though either seemed an abomination of all that was good and right, an abomination against nature herself.

He turned away. He was losing his hold on his emotions. The shock was beginning to wear off, as if he were being peeled of his own skin, leaving him raw and hurting.

He couldn't believe, even yet, what he had found. What kind of mind did it take to kill so repeatedly, so without evident conscience, and then to preserve the victims like this? This was not a taxidermist's desire to preserve, this was cruelty at its most extreme.

But the death of Glen was not Matt's work. And yet whose work was it? The children who had been seen were children whose bodies had died long ago.

He didn't want to see the little girl again, but his eyes were drawn against his will to her doll, and then to her. The grimace on her darkened, wrinkled face seemed to be one caused by pain and torture. She stared at him with blank, artificial eyes of glass, dulled by years. Dust had gathered in the creases of her face and her clothing is it had on the doll. The silence in the room stifled, like the dust that hung in the air, disturbed by the footsteps that were so alien to this horrible world Matt Reed had created.

Thomas hurried to the door, and into the hall. He leaned a moment against the wall, to let pass the weakness, the illness. Shaking, he hurried on, to leave behind this which he would dream of for the rest of his life.

He had to call for assistance.

He had been chief of police in town for ten years. During that time three children had disappeared. Each of them had been riding bicycles, which disappeared with them. Each of them had been working at Nina's and had left to go home.

He remembered clearly asking everyone within miles of Nina's if they had seen the child they were looking for. Karen, Willy, Cliff. He had talked to Matt and Halley Reed. The sheriff's men had talked to the Reed's, just as they talked to the neighbors across the street and down east, and, in those days, the neighbors to the west, the Moore's.

Why was it none of them ever suspected Matt Reed?

It hadn't occurred to Thomas to get a search warrant for Matt's shop. There was no evidence to tie Matt with the murder of the Moore family, or the disappearance of local children. No reason to harass someone who was considered a stable member of the community. He had an unusual hobby, but lots of men, and women too, were hunters, trappers, fishermen. And some of them came to Matt to have an especially large fish mounted, and the heads of deer, moose, or whatever they considered a kill to be proud of. Only Nina had harbored dislike for Matt Reed, but even she hadn't accused him in the disappearances of the children.

For several months after Cliff's disappearance Nina had stopped allowing children to work at the shelter unless they were brought and then picked up by their parents, or some other grownup. Then, she had relented to the children coming in pairs.

If that rule had been in existence from the beginning of the shelter, would Karen, Willy and Cliff still be alive?

No, he couldn't get into the endless world of what ifs. Matt would have found, somewhere, the children he needed, as he needed them.

Thomas went out the back door and stood with one hand on a post of the porch and took a deep breath of fresh air. He walked out onto the grass. Moonlight slanted across the fields behind the house. Shadows beneath the trees grew longer, reaching across the yard and the driveway. He crossed through the darkness quickly, aware of the murderous children blending into the darknesses and appearing at will. He opened his car door, and picked up the radio mike.

"Noel," he said when the deputy picked up the receiver, "We need the homicide crew at the Matt Reed house, as fast as they can get here. Glen has been murdered, and we've uncovered a horror chamber in Matt Reed's taxidermy shop. Stay where you are, and be careful. Make sure you know who you're letting in. Don't open the door for anything that looks like a child just yet. Send me all the help you can call in, from anywhere in the state."

Just before he broke the connection he heard Noel mutter, "Good God." But nothing in Noel's imagination would prepare him for the truth.

Thomas stood by the car, the door open to block the darkness. The dome light glowed softly, and a moth flew through the open door and began a worshipful pressing of the warm light.

As soon as help arrived they would try to get Matt admitted to the psychiatric ward in the prison hospital. Detectives would take control of Matt's private rooms and all they contained.

But somewhere here in the night lurked the murderous beings that looked like children. They had somehow taken Glen into a locked cellar. They sought darkness.

He took his flashlight from the car and turned it on. Its beam swept the black world of shrubs against the house and beyond. The moonlight was dimming. Thomas didn't know how to fight them. He faced the darkness frozen with fear.

A thought struck him. Patrick, seen only at the revival, had not been among the other children. The children who killed.

CORY STARED AT THE BICYCLES. The one on top was silver. A three speed. It had a name painted on the crossbar, like a kid would do. The letters were a little crooked. Cliff. Cory didn't know a kid named Cliff. There was something sad about the bicycle. It was dusty, with spider webs woven around the spokes of the wheels. Cory thought to himself Cliff wouldn't have allowed such a pretty bike to get dusty.

There was a whole stack of bicycles, it seemed. Piled on top of one another there were at least three, maybe four. They had been shoved back under the stair, making little ditches in the dirt floor. Cory squatted peering into the shadows beneath the steps. The one on the bottom was a girl's bike, Cory thought. He went down on his hands and knees, his head in the striped dark created by the steps above him, and crept closer to the bike. Yes, a girl's bike. It didn't belong to the poor little girl he had seen upstairs, the one with the doll. She wouldn't have been large enough to ride it very well.

He crept back out and sat back on his heel remembering the children who had gathered when Matt was in the yard. There had been a girl with a doll. She was pretty, with long curls that hung like tubes over her shoulders. The doll upstairs was the one she had carried. The same doll.

And the girl up there, the poor dead girl with the darkened, wrinkled skin, had the same hair.

The dead girl was the same girl he had seen.

He hadn't thought of it before. When he had seen the girl among all the animals he hadn't really thought of anything. Even when Gram saw the girl and it scared her so, he still hadn't thought of the girl he had seen in the yard. The girl who had been calling to him to come and play.

How could it be possible that a girl who was dead, was also the girl . . . ?

He twisted on his heel and called in a voice that echoed from somewhere in the depths of the cellar, "Chief Thomas?" Maybe the chief would know.

The echo bounced off the dusty, spidery rafters. It came back at him from the parts of the cellar he hadn't seen yet, and from out of something that sounded like a long, hollow tunnel.

But Chief Thomas didn't answer.

The fear built rapidly to a crescendo that pounded in the depths of his being. Cory stood up, rushed out from beneath the stairway and looked toward the distant and shadowy end of the long cellar. Chief Thomas had been less than ten steps in front of him when he followed him down into the cellar. Cory had vowed he'd be quiet. He wouldn't bother the chief. But there was the question about the dead girl. And there was something about the bicycles that the chief might want to know. There was a big girl's bike. It was too big for the little girl with the doll to ride. Then there was the one that had belonged to someone named Cliff. Wouldn't the chief want to know?

Cory walked out toward the center of the cellar.

One bulb in the ceiling not far from the foot of the crude wooden steps left a pool of light on the lumpy dirt floor at Cory's feet. Beyond, toward the distant end, stood a figure.

"Chief?" Cory inquired, his voice breaking.

The figure didn't turn, but Cory could see it was a tall person. His shadow was long and thin, falling across the rough stones of the wall.

The figure didn't move or answer. Cory knew he should go the other way, climb the board steps into the upper room and find his way to the kitchen, to people. But he stood still, looking at the person at the end of the cellar.

The face of the figure began to take on features in the shadowy dimness and look familiar to Cory. A tall boy with dark hair falling across one side of his forehead. He had high strong bones in his face. The skin looked stretched tight. Too tight. The mouth was pulled unnaturally wide, the lips thinned, teeth showing.

Recognition slowly reached Cory.

"Patrick!"

What was wrong with Patrick? He looked so strange.

Patrick didn't answer. He stood still, staring at Cory across the dim cellar, the hideous grin pulled across his face.

A wave of a sickening odor reached Cory and made him feel as if he were going to throw up. That smell of something rotting, and other things left locked up so long they had grown rancid and moldy, seemed to fog around Cory like an invisible cloak.

Cory took a step forward. The angle of the dim light changed with his movement and he saw that Patrick was being held up with a post at his back. He had been strapped to it like someone from colonial days being tied in public for punishment. Patrick was not alive. He had been stuffed, like the animals, like the little girl upstairs. Only his skin hadn't grown dry and brown and wrinkled.

Cory's mouth worked in silence, in horror. He tried again to call the chief. The chief was somewhere here it the cellar. Cory knew he was. He had been, Cory knew, just ahead of him. Cory had followed the chief. *He was here.*

Cory's lips moved, opened, his mouth widened, but nothing escaped. His attempt to cry out became a soft moan, a high-pitched mew.

Then he saw there were other figures in the room, standing together against the wall, like a bunch of kids hanging out on a street corner. Only these were leaning in peculiar positions, against one another, against the wall. Webs, pale in the darkness, had been woven around them like thin nets.

One girl sat, bent over, as if she were studying. She had long blond hair that hung straight over her shoulders and down onto the desk. It was the girl he had seen help take the trap off Matt's arm. But now she stared downward with her head permanently turned sideways.

On the floor beyond her, sitting with his knees up, was the boy who had helped her. Something small and dark, like a mouse or small rat, climbed the boy's leg, stopped for a moment on the bent, bony knee, and then when it saw Cory rushed away out of sight behind the boy.

Cory was deathly sick to his stomach, but nothing came out. He turned for the stairway, and saw it was a long way off. As if it had slowly and silently moved away from him, to leave him among the children who were like mummies in a weird museum, it was gradually fading away. Everything was gradually fading away, as if night were falling in his life, to snuff it out into darkness.

He tried to run, he reached for the railing on the steps, but then he stumbled over something slippery and fell. His hands came down onto a wet, red body that had no skin. A flattened face, dark hair like a brush, stared at him.

Crying, Cory crawled backward. His hands touched dirt, and the dirt clung, like mud. He clambered to his feet and searched blindly for the stairway.

The way seemed endless, but then he felt splinters in his hand and knew he had reached the stairs. He climbed, searching for escape. The chief was gone from this world, and Cory had been left alone with the bloody, skinless person who lay on the dirt floor. He was left alone with dead children who in a way were still there, unmoving, so different now from the children he had seen in the moonlight when they were alive, strangely, children who moved, for a while, freed from their deaths.

Cory struggled toward freedom. The steps seemed to move slowly beneath him, his feet touching one, then the other.

Then he came to the top and there were no more steps. But he faced a solid wall. Where once there had been an opening, a door, it now was closed. He pushed but the door was locked.

Cory screamed, but his voice was as silent as the voices of the others who occupied the cellar.

CHAPTER THIRTY-TWO

"I'm going to call the doctor, Halley."

"No. No."

Halley clutched Nina's sleeve and held it. Nina had brought her to her room, the old nursery. Halley couldn't remember how they had gotten here, but she felt that she had walked through the fires of hell, the image of her child's ruined face in front of her, then found she was sitting on the side of the bed, and Nina was persuading her to lie down. Nina just couldn't understand that Halley couldn't bear to lie down. She couldn't bear to sit, or stand, or live.

"How could I have lived all these years in this house, with my child there? Like that? How could I have had no inkling of what *he—that monster* —was doing? He killed her. He murdered our own child. I thought he loved her so much." Halley wept, needing to express those words, those questions, but not expecting an answer from Nina or anyone else. "How could I not have known?"

Or had she known, somewhere deep in that part of her which did not come to the surface, ever, except in twisted nightmares, in tortured dreams? Things she had pushed down.

"When she disappeared I said to him, out loud": 'Coleen wouldn't have run away. She wouldn't have gone away with a boy. Coleen wasn't old enough to want to go away with a boy.'

Nina stood beside her in silence, her sleeve caught in Halley's fingers. Her other arm lay gently over Halley's bent shoulders.

"Then, I just stopped talking. I kept Rachel close and wouldn't let her out of my sight. And when he wanted to take in more foster children, I asked him not to. I didn't have a reason, I just didn't want another child in the house that I couldn't watch night and day.

"Halley, do you have a tranquilizer you can take? Didn't the doctor leave you something? Why don't you let me call him again?"

"I think he must have been afraid I would finally realize what he was doing, otherwise he would have taken in more foster children. He never would have listened to me if he hadn't had his own reasons."

Nina stayed quietly at Halley's side, letting her talk.

It occurred to Halley that Nina had mentioned calling someone. "He never allowed me to have my own phone. And he didn't like me to use his. I never understood why, but then it never mattered. I didn't have friends anyway."

Now she knew. If she made friends, if she talked to people, if she said too much, someone might get suspicious.

He had said to her, "There's no point in you women gabbing, gabbing." Even when at church if she had stopped to visit awhile, Matt would get impatient. Even before the children began disappearing.

Now she understood. Now she had to do what she should have done long, long ago. She needed to be alone. Nina would not leave her, she knew, unless she had a mission elsewhere in the house.

Halley released her hold on Nina.

"Maybe you should go make the call, Nina. Thank you."

"Will you lie down, Halley, and try to relax?"

"Yes."

"Can I get you something first? A glass of water?"

"No, I'll be all right."

Halley allowed Nina to help her lie down. She closed her eyes and felt Nina pull a corner of the spread over her legs. With her eyes closed she listened to Nina's footsteps cross to the door, pause, then go out. The door closed softly.

Halley opened her eyes and listened hard. Boards somewhere within the lower part of the house moved with faint creaks and splinterings, as if the damage the earthquake had done to the flimsy extension had been sustained throughout. But Halley listened for footsteps, for the intrusion of a human presence. She heard Nina's footsteps on the stairs as she stepped on the old riser that had always creaked. Then the sounds of her departure stopped. Nina was gone. Everyone was gone.

Halley and Matt were alone in the world that Matt had made.

Halley got up, stooped and felt between the mattress and springs. Her fingers touched the cool, sharp edge of the long butcher knife she had put there long ago, when a deep instinct told her she had to protect Rachel from something within her own house.

She slipped the knife out from its hiding place of thirty years.

Her hand gripped the handle, as it would have a lifeline, the blade pointed downward.

With the blade hidden in the folds of her gown, she left her room.

Dr. Tyler lay on the covers of Lois's bed, his head supported by his arms. He had stifled the instinct to slip one arm under Lois's head. She slept deeply, thanks to Valium and the comfort it sometimes afforded.

Sleep was not in Tyler's plans for the night. He was waiting for daylight, but when he looked at the clock, he found that only minutes had passed.

There was one small light on in the bedroom. A round blue lamp with a pleated blue shade sat on the dresser, a seven-watt bulb creating a glow that only gave him the outlines of Lois's cheek, and made her dark hair look black. The few strands of grey that had begun to highlight her hair was blended in the dim light back to the solid dark it had been last year, or the year before.

He had let too much time slide by. Years piling up when they might have been together.

For years after his wife's death from a cancer no mortal man could cure, he had seen Lois only as the girl who had come to work for him. He tried to comfort her through her husband's death. And he was happy for her when the little boy, Cliff, came to live with her.

He and Jennie never had children. Jennie had wanted babies, and so had he, but he learned later that whatever it was that had caused her to be unable to conceive had probably also caused the ovarian cancer. He hadn't had her with him many years, and his grief for her lasted over half a lifetime.

Then he had begun to drift away from the grief. It was as if over the years he changed from the young doctor who had settled in this small, peaceful town with the pretty nurse who he had married. Over the years he had become Dr. Tyler, not Timmy, as Jennie had called him.

Sometime in those years he began to fall in love with the mature woman who worked with him every day five days a week. But he had let time slide. What would she want with an overweight, bald-headed creature who was probably set in his ways? Who went home, fed his pets and himself, then spent the evening in front of the TV with the cat on his lap and newspapers or journals or books in front of his nose?

What would she want with him?

When she woke up, when life was right again, he might ask her.

A light flashed through the trees outside the window and for just a blink brightened the room.

Tyler jerked up and hurried to the window. A spotlight pierced through the undergrowth that separated yard from yard, turning the black leaves and grass green for a moment, then moved on.

Tyler pulled the blind against the intrusive light, and hurried out of the room, closing the door behind him. He didn't want Lois disturbed.

He went through the living room to the front door. There was a glass on the door through which he could see part of the front porch, the steps down, and the front lawn. The light moved across the porch like a round glaring eye.

Tyler unlocked the door and went out.

A police car with the beacon lights darkened but the spot light moving was parked in the driveway. The light flashed past Tyler, then moved back and stopped on him briefly before easing off to one side.

Tyler went down the steps and across the lawn to the car. He saw as he approached that it was a sheriff's department vehicle.

A young man in uniform leaned over toward the passenger window. He was alone.

"Good evening, sir. I didn't mean to disturb you. But I was told to check this house often. If I understand, it's Mrs. Trahem's house?"

"Yes. I'm Dr. Tyler. Mrs. Trahem is asleep."

"You haven't had any disturbances?"

"No, not since we've been here."

The young man nodded, and put the car in reverse. Tyler stood in the yard and watched him back out of the driveway and drift slowly down the street, the spotlight crossing every driveway, every yard, every darkened house. Tyler remained in the yard after the patrol car turned the corner at the end of the street. Long after the quiet movement of the car was gone, the light still flashed through the trees, across the grass, finding small openings, reaching through in faint, thin rays.

Tyler felt a strange anxiety. He wanted the night to end, but he had a feeling it would never end. Even though the hours might pass and the sun rise, the night would linger forever.

• • •

"PLEASE LEAVE your name and number and I will call you back as soon as I can," Dr. Tyler's voice claimed from the answering machine at his house. At the clinic Lois's softly modulated voice said, "The clinic is closed. If you have an emergency please call 911. The clinic will be open at nine in the morning."

At Lois's house her voice claimed, "Please leave your name and number, and I'll return the call as soon as possible." The phone had rung only twice before the answering machine clicked on. No one had picked up the phone. Also, Nina had begun to wonder what Dr. Tyler, or anyone, could do for Halley now. Halley had grieved for Coleen for thirty years, and now only God understood the hell she was going through. Numbing medicine could help only so much.

Nina had to get out of the house. The high ceilings seemed to collect a darkness the lights couldn't dispel. And the odor of the horror room seemed now to have permeated every pore in the house. She felt as if she would never escape that smell, or those sights, or that knowledge of what had been done. She wondered how people live with horrible memories, and then realized those memories are often buried, forgotten superficially.

The office in which she stood, where severed, stuffed animal heads stared down from the walls, seemed only an extension of the horrible taxidermy shop beyond the long hallway. She had to get out of the house and try to find pure air to breathe again.

Where was Thomas? Was he still in that awful place? She looked around. Matt's office showed its distant library past, with rows of books, dark brown leather sofas and chairs and a large desk with that same dark brown leather top. The telephone, the only one in the house, was an old black dial phone. The animal heads on the walls looked down at her, making her feel helpless in her inability to save them from the horror of having their heads removed from their bodies and mounted on the walls as if they were nothing more than ornaments for some people to enjoy.

Far overshadowing them was the vision of the distorted and ruined face of the child she had seen, in her woodland setting, dusty and old, with her animal companions. She could only imagine Halley's horror at what Matt had done to Coleen. Nina's own sense of horror was so saturated by disbelief that her feelings seemed suspended, to crash down upon her at another time.

She wondered at the mind of a man who would let his curiosity about death and the preservation of a body lead to experimentation on his own child. Was it an attempt to play God and keep her a child forever, only for himself? Could it be mere curiosity that had led him, as curiosity led so many atrocities?

Or was it something far more sinister, far beyond anyone's ability to understand?

Why hadn't someone answered the phones at Dr. Tyler's or Lois's? She couldn't allow herself to think beyond that.

She left the office and went into the long, dim hallway that led to both back and front of the house. She started toward the back. Would Thomas still be there, taking note of the hideous room, or would he have gone to his patrol car to call for help?

She turned and went toward the front of the house, into the wider, lighter foyer and out onto the porch. For a moment she stood, taking in a deep breath of fresh night air. She noted almost subconsciously that the dogs at the shelter were quiet. Over toward the center of town one dog barked a couple of times and stopped. All night sounds seemed to have ceased. The slant of the moonlight was more extreme, and had lost some of the brightness of earlier hours. She had no idea what time it was. This night seemed to exist on its own, isolated from other nights, other days, a separate creation that had no end.

She went down the steps and across the walk to the driveway. To her almost tearful relief, Thomas stood by the car. The driver's door was open, and he stood in the light from the dome. In his hand he held the radio mike, but he wasn't speaking into it.

Nina hurried toward him. Her shoes rattled the gravel in the driveway and Thomas turned.

They spoke each other's names simultaneously.

Then with a sense of awakening shock Nina saw that Thomas was alone. Cory had been with him, hadn't he? Had Thomas taken Cory back to his room? She couldn't imagine that he would have left the little boy alone in his room, not now, not after what they had seen in the taxidermy shop.

"Where's Cory?" she cried.

Thomas hesitated, the mike lowered. "Didn't he go with you?"

"No. I thought he was with you."

Nina turned toward the house. It loomed over them, its shadow heavy and dark. Lights shone on the front porch, and again on the back, but the rooms between were now dark.

Somewhere deep within the house boards moved against boards, and the sound was like the moaning of a monster.

CHAPTER THIRTY-THREE

Driven by icy, voiceless fear Cory ran. He turned, arms out to protect himself, and ran. He fell, bumping down stair steps. No, he was falling down rough stone steps into a place like a cave, or a cellar. He was coated in the thin ice of this freezing place. The air was so cold it hurt when he sucked in a breath. He got to his feet and ran again, his arms out. Figures formed of shadows chased behind him. He tried to scream for help. Chief Thomas wouldn't have gone off and left him.

The light was growing very dim, and he couldn't see. Odors of death hung like fog. He gagged on the smell of empty skins lying across metal tables, with the knife still glistening, with now-rotting fat that had been scraped off. He was sick with the smell of blood of a man's skinless body on the floor of the cold cellar, his skin flat and empty beside him. And jars of things that had come out of them . . .

He stumbled on something in the dark, and fell. His hands felt the curve of stone steps leading up. He climbed, in the dark, and came to a ceiling. No, a door, overhead. His fingers traced a crack in the wood and came to a padlock. Crying within, his blood rushing like a train through his head, he struggled with the lock. But even as he tried to open it, he knew he would need a key. He was trapped. Everywhere he turned he came up against walls, and locked doors.

He huddled on the stone steps with his eyes closed and made himself not be so scared. He had been like in a terrible nightmare, running, running, and all the time he was in the cellar.

The dead man wouldn't hurt him. The kids who were like mummies wouldn't hurt him. The mice and the spiders, they wouldn't hurt him either. Chief Thomas would come back. When he remembered, he would come back.

He heard a sound. A real sound, not just something rising from his fears. A movement. *Someone . . .*

The sound of the childrens' voices was like music. As if they were down a road and coming nearer, as they had come when Matt lay wounded in the moonlight, Cory heard them.

Warmth returned to him. The children!

Hey guys, he tried to call, as he also tried to stand. But his voice croaked deep in his throat, and his arms and legs felt as if they had shrunk into his hunched body. He had tried so hard to become part of the stone steps, he felt like stone.

Where were they? *Where were they?*

They were coming closer. Boys' and girls' voice chattered excitedly. And now he could hear their footsteps. It was as if they had been to a game, and they were talking about it as they walked home. He could hear their voices through the cellar walls. They were coming near to the cellar door, walking through the grass outside.

He tried again to call. *Help me, please help me.*

Then he saw they weren't outside at all, they were in the distant, shadowed end of the cellar. They were coming toward him. At last, he wasn't alone.

But . . . how had they gotten into the cellar?

Was there an opening at the other end? Somewhere in that cold darkness where there was no wall, but an endless darkness that went on and on. It was from that darkness the children came, and the cold that paralyzed Cory. In wave after invisible wave the cold washed into Cory, freezing him into a terrible fear of the children.

They came to the center of the cellar and stopped. Cory sat still, huddling against the stone steps and wall, with the locked cellar door above his head. They hadn't seen him. He was in the shadows on the step and they hadn't seen him!

The biggest blond girl chanted, "Fee fi, fo, fum, I smell the blood of Rachel's son!"

They all began to laugh, and started circling, their feet in rhythm, dancing little steps. They went round and round, this time without joining hands. The girl's long, straight hair bounced on her shoulders.

With her danced the boy with the dark hair, and the boy with the real short hair that stood on end. Three other boys who seemed always to be in the shadows, no matter where they stood, went round in the dance.

The girl with the doll moved to the middle, and Cory watched her laughing and chanting with the others and saw her eyes cut his way.

He stared at her.

It was the girl he had seen behind the bear. The same girl, whose face had been wrinkled and drawn like a mummy's. He looked again at the other kids. The dark boy—he wore a T-shirt with a lion on the front, just like one of the boys that even now sat against the wall, like the animals upstairs, fixed forever in his dried skin.

They turned toward Cory, laughing, chanting, *fee, fi, fo, fum, I smell the blood of Rachel's son.*

They knew where he was after all. They had always known.

Walsh tried again to pray, but his lips moved without words, and his brain felt heavy with shock. The man on the bed appeared to be sleeping. The voices of the children were stilled.

He picked up Halley's Bible and went down on his knees at the side of Matt's bed. The man stretched like a giant, his feet touching the walnut posts at the foot of the bed. His beard rose and fell with his breathing. The heavy eyebrows shadowed his eyes, making them look sunken.

It was not Walsh's place to judge, he told himself again, and again. With effort he had re-entered the man's room. With different eyes he looked upon this man, and everything within him cringed at the sight of the man. He who had spoken of demons had committed the act of murdering his own child, then preserving her as he would an animal?

Walsh wanted to turn away, return to his innocent world where he had thought so naively that he was helping to save the souls of sinners. That world now seemed made of dreams. There was nothing for him to return to. A tent. A tiny house on wheels. A work beyond his window. A world of innocence.

"Oh God, let us not put ourselves . . ."

He swallowed. With his eyes closed, he tried again—his hands tight on the old, rough leather cover of the Bible.

"It is not my place to judge, God, but I am human and I—God, please forgive this man for what he has done. As Jesus said, forgive them God, they know not what they do—"

He heard a step. Soft, very close. He had not heard the door open.

He looked up.

Halley, her grey hair streaming forward over her shoulders, was walking past the foot of the bed. Her eyes were fastened on her husband.

Walsh stood up and stepped back.

He started to speak, then paused. Halley edged around the corner of the bed and went up the other side and stood. Her eyes hadn't moved from the face of her husband. There was something about that steady stare and the silence and almost deer-like motions of her movements, that made Walsh stand silently, watching.

Then suddenly her right arm flashed upward, above her head, and the long blade of a knife glittered briefly in the light.

Walsh opened his mouth, but nothing came out. Whether he had intended to cry out for her to stop, or to cry out to God to stop her, he didn't know. His voice was as silenced as the voices of the children.

Halley's own voice suddenly filled the room, a half-cry, half-growl, animal-like in its intensity, its emotion so strong there were no words. Both her hands grasped the curved wooden handle of the butcher knife when it was raised above her head, and both her hands brought it down with all her strength, and with strength added from somewhere, from her grief, her fury.

Her cry became a scream as the knife penetrated the man's flesh. Walsh heard the crunch of bone, of muscle. He saw blood spray upward, a fine, red mesh of droplets.

The man's voice blended with the woman's. The man curled upwards, like a worm curling around its tormentor. His left hand tried to grip the blade of the knife as it was ripped from him, and the flesh of his palm was laid open.

Walsh dropped the Bible and tried to run, around the foot of the bed, to stop her. He saw the knife plunging again and again, and the cries of both man and woman rang in his ears and crashed through his brain.

He was within inches of reaching her, of grasping her arms and struggling to wrench the knife from her when the world tilted.

Furniture began sliding across the floor, the room moved upward on one side, and then abruptly dropped back and downward.

Walsh fell to his knees. He grabbed for support, and his flailing hands clutched the carved wooden posts at the foot of the bed. As the floor swayed back and forth, faster and faster, he held to the bed.

The door to the hall swung wildly open and shut, the sound of its banging like gunshots amid the crashing world of sound that filled Walsh's ears. The lights blinked off, back on, then began a mad fluttering. As they went out it seemed the moonlight entered from somewhere above, as a thin, silver light shone into the room. Then that too was closed off.

Darkness surrounded him. He blinked, and thought himself blinded. Then a firey light appeared like a pinpoint in the distance, and he saw they were in a long passageway, or tunnel. It was whirling, lighted by the fire that rapidly grew larger and closer. He saw the bodies falling ahead of him, round and round. He could still see the blood spewing from the opening in the man's chest, and he saw the woman's hair flying, as if the speed of her fall swept it backwards. His ears were bursting with the sound of cries, and the sound of splitting timbers as the house swirled, sucked into the maelstrom of this terrible world.

Then he knew, he was looking into the depths of hell.

He came to an abrupt halt, and found himself looking into a cellar. Through the swirling darkness he saw rough, stone walls, and the dirt floor. In the center of the cellar a group of six or seven children tore at something among them. Their faces held a strange, terrible glee. Faces that were born beautiful were turning ugly with their cruel delight. They whirled, their hands tight on the object on which they pulled.

Had they caught an animal?

Walsh saw the face of the smallest girl, her mouth wide with silent laughter. He stared at her. Recognition dawned. Though now her skin was porcelain, the perfect skin of a lovely child, it was the same little girl with the dried, wrinkled skin he had seen in the taxidermy shop. He cringed inwardly from her, from all the children, even as he struggled to reach them to try to stop them from what they were doing.

Beware of the children, the madman had said, they are not what they seem.

The children danced in a circle, their hands pulling in all directions at the thing around which they danced.

As if Walsh had lost all senses but sight, he saw but did not hear. He couldn't see what they held. He tried to scream at them to stop. But as if he were no longer physical, he was totally powerless, his voice gone, his ability to move gone. Helpless, he watched.

No, no, God, make them stop. Stop them. Stop them.

The children stopped laughing and turned, as one, their faces looking at something from the distant, dark end of the cellar. The thing they had been tugging dropped to the ground, and to Walsh's horror he saw it was another child. A small boy, smaller than the youngest girl in the group. He lay limp and unmoving on the ground, his clothes torn to rags.

Someone was coming from the darkness at the end of the cellar. Walsh saw first a pale, silver light, as if the moonlight had entered through an opening made in the walls of the falling house.

Then a figure bathed with the silver light came forward, making a path out of the darkness, and Walsh saw the light came from the figure.

It was a youth, with a handsome, narrow face, dark hair, dark eyes, the same youth who had stood in the doorway of the tent.

He came forward, toward the child crumpled on the ground.

The tormenting children ran, scattering into the darknesses that hung in curtains among the rocks of the walls and the endlessness that opened beyond.

The youth stooped and lifted the little boy from the ground. Walsh glimpsed the child's pale, still face. His arms swung limply, his clothes hung ripped and shredded.

Cory.

Walsh tried to make himself known to the youth, but the youth turned and walked away, carrying Cory toward the stone wall.

"THOMAS!" Nina screamed.

The ground heaved upwards, as if bulging over a bubble soon to burst. As if the world had gone mad, as if the ground had become an ocean of waves, it rolled one way and then the other. The car door swung almost shut then swung open again. Nina fell, her hands clutching for a hold on something solid. Lights in the house and on the porches went out, and the yard light swayed, dimmed and brightened. The house crumbled, sinking upon itself, its wood crashing in the night. The yard light swayed wildly and darkened.

Thomas was a figure in the shadows. He had started toward the rear of the house to look for Cory, and Nina had gone toward the front. But she had taken only a couple of steps away from the car when the earthquake struck.

On her knees beside the patrol car, her hands clutching the rear bumper, she watched the collapse of the house. As if a great cavern had been dug beneath all of its foundations, it settled within it. The roof collapsed in the center, and the porches lifted.

Nina was aware of sounds, of the rocking earth, then of the sudden stillness.

Thomas was still halfway between the car and the great heap of splintered wood that had once been a house. The light pole in the yard leaned against a tree. All the trees stood upright, and the moonlight slanted through them just as before.

Nina sat on the ground, unable to move, her fingers painfully tight on the bumper of the car.

In the sudden stillness of the night Thomas shouted, "Oh my God! They're all in there! Cory's in there!"

He started running, toward the rear of the huge pile of timbers that once had been the house.

Nina was aware of a car's lights on the street. She was vaguely aware that the house across the street had not been touched, that the town's lights still glowed softly through their screen of trees.

As Thomas ran out of sight around the tilted back porch, the car pulled into the driveway behind Nina.

Nina heard someone screaming. A woman came running from the car.

Nina turned.

Rachel.

CHAPTER THIRTY-FOUR

THE WORLD HAD STOPPED MOVING, THE HOUSE WAS NO LONGER IN ITS VIOLENT fall. Walsh lay in a muted darkness. Above him a streak of pale light shone steadily down through a dark jungle of boards. Around him the house still moved bits at a time, with the scraping sounds of boards settling against boards.

He was beneath the house in part of a basement. He could see above him the edge of a wall built into the ground, made of crude stones. Had he dreamed he was in a cellar?

Where was he? His head ached. Noises filled his brain. Timber still moved, somewhere in the solid mass above him.

He stood up, his head touching the sagging floor above.

His fingers clutched the stones set in the wall, and something cool and slick crawled quickly over his hand and was gone. There was not so much as a shudder left in Walsh. A board fell across the only opening he saw, and the moonlight was cut off. He grasped the fallen board with all his strength and pushed, and the board moved. Moonlight rushed in upon him again. Ahead of him a thin pathway led toward the steps reaching up into moonlight. It was the cellar steps Patrick had climbed in his dream, carrying Cory.

Or was it a dream? Was his vision of hell real, after all? Where were Halley and Matt, Patrick and Cory? And the children, who, as Matt had warned, were not what they seemed.

Where were Nina and Thomas?

The world seemed oddly quiet. Were they all buried in the rubble that once had been a house?

Stooping to avoid the heavy joist above, Walsh entered the stone stairway.

He was trapped. The floor had sunk, the boards, broken and jagged, covering the top of the steps. No one could have climbed these steps.

He twisted, the boards above slipping downward another inch, another foot. He looked back into darkness. The cellar was filling, bit by bit, as the house above settled.

If he shouted for help, would anyone hear him? Or was everyone gone, crushed into the debris of the fallen house? He seemed now to exist in a world of silence, except for the creaking and scrape of boards that eased into any opening they could find.

The prayer came naturally to his heart, spoken in silence. "Our Father who art in heaven . . . thy will be done . . ."

Walsh felt a touch on his shoulder. He twisted in his tightening burial bed, and found a hand extended to him.

Thomas!

Walsh grasped the hand with both of his, but shouted, "There's no way out. I'm trapped."

Thomas didn't answer.

The hand began a steady pull, and Walsh found that if he wriggled from one opening to the next, he could manage to squeeze through. The hand drew away, and Walsh concentrated on lifting himself through the broken cellar door.

He stood up. Cool night air struck his face. He looked for Thomas, but he was alone. He turned, looking. There was no one there.

He was on the western side, between the ruined house and a large oak shade tree. The roof of the house had collapsed, doubling in the center like a bridge over a river. Porches at each end of the house had lifted a few feet off the ground.

He heard voices, but his first heart-leap of happiness turned cold with that sense of horror and fear that seemed part of a terrible dream.

The children.

Their voices came from somewhere at the northwest corner of the house. They chattered excitedly, like a group of small chickens over a tidbit they had discovered. Walsh understood nothing they said.

A figure materialized suddenly to his right. A tall man came around the end of what had been the porch, and into the shadows by the cellar door. It was Thomas.

"Walsh! Is that you? Are you all right?" Thomas cried. "Thank God. The others—do you know where the others are?"

Walsh stared at him, knowing then whose hand it was that had helped him from the cellar of death. Not Thomas, but Patrick. The youth.

Thomas's hand clasped Walsh's shoulder. It was warm and human, and Walsh put his own hand briefly over the hand of Thomas. The man's features were dimly visible in the dark, and Walsh saw he was looking toward the sound of the children voices.

Thomas moved toward the voices, and Walsh followed. At the edge of the tree's shadow, Thomas put out his arm in silent warning. Walsh stopped.

The group of children appeared at the edge of the fallen house. They rose out of the rubble of plaster and boards into the yard. The six larger children carried something among them. Like pallbearers with a casket, they carried their burden into the bright moonlight of the backyard. Following them was the younger girl, with a doll. She danced and skipped, the doll dangling from her arm.

Walsh stood staring, Thomas's arm still protectively in front of him. The scene, played out in moonlight as if the children were alone in the world with their burden, chilled Walsh to the depths of his soul. He couldn't have moved if he had tried. He could only stand and watch, and slowly shrivel with the cold terror that shrouded him.

The world stood still. The small group passed by, so closely Walsh could see the faces of the children. Lovely faces, and yet . . . everything was wrong.

He saw suddenly they were carrying the body of a large man. Effortlessly they carried Matt, supporting his arms, his legs, his head.

In wordless shock Walsh stood with Thomas and watched them go by. They danced and skipped blithely through the moonlight, their chatters almost like laughter, or like music, a horrible kind of dirge.

Then, a hundred feet beyond the shadows in which Thomas and Walsh stood, they began descending. As if they were going down steps, they disappeared, one by one, the little girl with the doll the last to go.

Their voices closed off. The night was silent.

For a moment Walsh stood stunned, the cold terror that had seemed as deep as space gone with the children.

As if released from the same fear that had held Walsh, Thomas ran. Into the backyard, toward the place where the children had disappeared.

Walsh ran behind him.

In the center of the backyard they stopped. Thomas walked in circles.

There was no opening in the ground. The grass looked undisturbed. Moonlight lay peacefully on the grass.

"The others," Thomas said suddenly, and whirled back toward the ruins of the house. "The little kid. Cory. Halley. Where are they?"

He ran around the house toward the cars, and Walsh followed partway, then paused. A car had stopped behind the patrol car, its headlights bright.

Suddenly the night seemed filled with human confusion. Thomas ran to his patrol car and spoke into a police radio mike. Nina ran back to meet the young woman and the man who came from the car.

"What happened?" the young woman cried, her body outlined in the headlights of the car. "Where's Cory? Where are Mom and Dad? Oh my God, where's Cory?"

Nina had met her, and seemed to be trying to calm her. The small group stopped at the open door of the patrol car.

Thomas left them and hurried back toward Walsh.

The headlights of the car did not reach the backyard where Walsh stood. Moonlight slanted through the branches of a pine tree. Thomas stopped, staring beyond Walsh.

Walsh turned.

The youth walked through the deep shadows created by the oak tree and the fallen roof of the house and paused in the edge of the moonlight. He kneeled, and laid the child he carried on the ground.

He lifted his head and looked directly at Walsh. For the second time this night, Walsh met the gaze of the youth. But the expression on his face was different this time. It seemed to Walsh there was the suggestion of a smile on his lips.

Patrick rose, stepped back and became part of the dark shadows beneath the tree.

The child lay alone, as if sleeping, in the soft light of the moon.

Thomas started to bend, to pick him up. Footsteps pounded on the ground, a bright beam of light found the child and steadied. The young woman ran to him, and fell to her knees at his side, gathering him up into her arms.

Cory moved, and began to whimper. His arms went around the neck of the young woman.

The woman rose with him in her arms, with Nina and Thomas surrounding her.

Walsh looked for the youth who had rescued the child and carried him to safety, but knew in his heart he would never see him again.

Automobiles began arriving and pulling into the yard. Walsh saw the flashing lights of a fire truck and police units.

In the east pink light suddenly made a streak across the sky, and in the west the large, round moon moved visibly below the horizon.

The night had ended.

EPILOGUE

THOMAS SLOWLY PATROLLED THE TOWN. HE TURNED AROUND IN THE LANE'S place parking lot. The old tavern was dark now, all the neons out. The town was arguing over what should be done with it. Some suggested turning it into a recreation center, both for youths and for seniors.

The field where Reverend Walsh's tent had stood had been empty now for a month. Thomas wondered at times where the preacher was now. Had he gone on with his ministry? Thomas recalled Walsh saying, "Tom, I didn't realize how little I believed."

Thomas wasn't sure exactly what he meant, but the look on Walsh's face mirrored his own feelings that day as they stood watching rescuers working through the rubble of the house to find Halley Reed.

They found her, hours into the afternoon. She was dead. Thomas felt in his heart that perhaps God had stepped in and taken her, to protect her from having to live with their ghastly discovery.

Cory was safe with his parents. Thomas drove by their vacated house. They had left town, and gone away to live somewhere else.

Lights in most of the houses were out, or dimmed, all over town. Street lights shone down on empty streets.

The moon was full again, but didn't seem to hold that brightness of one month ago.

The tremor that had caused the Reed house to collapse into the large cellar Matt had dug was felt nowhere else in town. Neither was the tremor that had shaken the preacher's tent earlier in the night. Experts appeared to doubt there was a tremor of any kind. Not in this part of the country. The reason the house fell was one of stability. Matt had undermined it, digging his hideous cellar foot by foot beneath the house and not properly installing supports for the house above.

Thomas allowed the experts to form their own opinions. The gang of kids who had fought with the boys on Spring Street and killed their dog was considered by the investigating officers to be strange kids in town, probably drawn by the revival.

The vicious murders of Lane and Megan were to remain unsolved, possibly connected with drugs. Glen, they theorized, had cornered the killers, or had known too much. The location of his body was just another of the strange facts about the case.

The atrocities uncovered in the cellar and taxidermy shop in Matt Reed's house closed all of the town's missing children files. Discovered were the four foster children who had stayed with the Reeds beginning thirty-one years ago, Ralph Aimes, age twelve, Daryl Web, Daniel Hismet, and Jeremy Arnold, all thirteen.

Also Matt and Halley's daughter, age ten. It was speculated that Matt had experimented with the bodies of the boys, in preparation for permanently sealing his daughter into her ten-year-old form. But none of the taxidermy experiments were successful. The skin of the victims had aged, like old leather not properly tanned.

Matt had improved his art over the years. His stuffed animals began to look as if they were frozen in the wild.

The later children again were less successful than the animals. Among them was Karen Davis, Willy Yardley, Cliff Patison.

The missing children had been found, and given proper burial. The town struggled to keep the media from discovering their hidden horror. Every citizen in town felt responsible. How could they live so close to a man, grow up with him in some cases, grow old with him, and never know what he had done?

Thomas's guilt was more intense than any. Why had he not ordered a search of Matt's taxidermy shop? No one had even known the cellar existed. Not even Halley, Thomas thought. She knew only at the end that her little girl had been stuffed like one of Matt's trapped animals.

Walsh had told Thomas about the stabbing. The state's criminal investigators had found the knife in Halley's hand, and the front of her robe spewed with blood that was not her own.

But Matt's body was never found. Ironically, Matt himself was now listed as missing.

Neither Thomas nor Walsh had mentioned what they saw. As far as the state police were concerned, Matt disappeared somewhere within the house, or he had gone into the woods to die the death of a wounded animal.

Thomas would never forget the children, the sounds of their voices, and what he and Walsh had watched at the last. Because they both saw it, Thomas knew he hadn't lost his mind in that strange, horrible night of discoveries. He had seen things he made no attempt to understand. It was better to go on, and try not to think about it.

There were happier things to think about. The whole town, what there was of it, was invited to the wedding of Dr. Tyler and Lois. It was going to be held in the town square.

He drove past the place where the Reed house had stood. The cleaning up had started. The investigation had ended.

The Moore place was up for sale now. Patrick was cleared of the murder of his family, and his body laid to rest beside them in the cemetery east of town.

Thomas figured Clyde Moore had gone to Matt Reed and asked him to stop trapping on the Moore land, which included a couple of hundred acres in the hills behind the house, and it had angered Matt. He had gone to the Moore house, and killed the family. For a reason only Matt knew, he had carried only Patrick's body home.

"Also, Tom," Nina said, "I think Halley must have seen Matt carry Patrick into the cellar. Maybe she blocked it out, or maybe she hadn't accepted what she saw. But I think she knew Patrick was dead, and that's why she fainted when she saw him in the doorway of the tent."

"Could be. Sounds possible."

"He was so real-looking, Tom. How can that be? He had been dead a year."

Thomas had no answer for her.

It was better not to think about those things.

The human mind wasn't meant to see so much, and understand it.

He drove up the driveway toward Nina's, and his feelings grew warm and soft and eager. Their wedding wouldn't be in the town square, they had decided. At least, they didn't think so. Maybe at the city hall, such as it was.

Walsh stood behind the portable pulpit with his arms raised. The lights of a large city arced through the sky above the tent, and every chair in his tent was taken.

"God lives!" he shouted. "If in the logical part of your mind you cannot see the God you have been taught to believe in, look deep, my friends. Look deep into your souls and—"

A sudden feeling of dizziness swept over Walsh. The ground swayed beneath his feet, and he clutched the pulpit to steady himself. The congregation murmured, and half-rose. They were in earthquake country now, and Walsh saw the fear on their faces.

Suddenly he noticed a youth had stepped in from out of the darkness and stood in the doorway of the tent. The young face held his gaze steadily toward him, the dark eyes intense with their silent message.

Walsh stared at the youth, into eyes he had never seen before, and a feeling of great dread filled him. He remembered another youth, in another doorway, on a night of full moon in a village hundreds of miles away. Tonight again the moon was full, and a youth stood in his doorway.

OTHER NOVELS BY RUBY JEAN

1974 The House that Samael Built
1974 Seventh All Hallows' Eve
1974 House at River's Bend
1975 The Girl Who Didn't Die
1978 Child of Satan's House
1978 Satan's Sister
1978 Dark Angel
1982 Hear the Children Cry
1982 Such a Good Baby
1983 The Lake
1983 MaMa
1985 Home Sweet Home
1985 Best Friends
1986 Wait and See
1987 Annabelle
1987 Chain Letter
1988 Smoke
1988 House of Illusions
1988 Jump Rope
1989 Pendulum
1989 Death Stone
1990 Vampire Child

OTHER NOVELS BY RUBY JEAN

1990 Lost and Found
1990 Victoria
1991 Celia
1991 Baby Dolly
1992 The Reckoning
1993 The Living Evil
1994 The Haunting
1995 Night Thunder
Pending Bear Hollow Charlie
Pending Cry of the Soul
Pending Pride of Bella Terra
Pending Animal Backtalk

www.ingramcontent.com/pod-product-compliance
Lightning Source LLC
Chambersburg PA
CBHW020609310726
48979CB00008B/1398/J

* 9 7 8 1 9 5 1 5 8 0 5 3 7 *